Mills & Boo
a wonderful sel
her trademark Mediterranean males from
international bestselling author

JACQUELINE BAIRD

Each volume has three terrific, powerful
and passionate stories written by
a queen of the genre.
We know you'll love them…

September 2014

October 2014

November 2014

December 2014

January 2015

February 2015

Mediterranean Tycoons

MASTERFUL & MARRIED

JACQUELINE BAIRD

MILLS & BOON

Published in Great Britain 2014
by Mills & Boon, an imprint of Harlequin (UK) Limited,
Eton House, 18-24 Paradise Road, Richmond, Surrey, TW9 1SR

MEDITERRANEAN TYCOONS: MASTERFUL & MARRIED
© 2014 Harlequin Books S.A.

Marriage at His Convenience © 2001 Jacqueline Baird
Aristides' Convenient Wife © 2007 Jacqueline Baird
The Billionaire's Blackmailed Bride © 2008 Jacqueline Baird

ISBN: 978-0-263-25021-3

010-0115

Harlequin (UK) Limited's policy is to use papers that are natural, renewable and recyclable products and made from wood grown in sustainable forests.The logging and manufacturing processes conform to the legalenvironmental regulations of the country of origin.

Printed and bound in Spain
by Blackprint CPI, Barcelona

Jacqueline Baird was born and brought up in Northumbria. She met her husband when she was eighteen. Eight years later, after many adventures around the world, she came home and married him. They still live in Northumbria and now have two grown sons.

Jacqueline's number one passion is writing. She has always been an avid reader and she had her first success as a writer at the age of eleven, when she won first prize in the Nature Diary of the Year competition at school. But she felt a little guilty because her diary was more fiction than fact.

She always loved romance novels and, when her sons went to school all day, she thought she would try writing one. She's been writing for Mills & Boon ever since and she still gets a thrill every time a new book is published.

When Jacqueline is not busy writing, she likes to spend her time travelling, reading and playing cards. She was a keen sailor until a knee injury ended her sailing days, but she still enjoys swimming in the sea when the weather allows.

With a more sedentary lifestyle, she does visit a gym three times a week and has made the surprising discovery that she gets some good ideas while doing the mind-numbingly boring exercises on the cycling and weight machines.

MARRIAGE AT HIS CONVENIENCE

JACQUELINE BAIRD

CHAPTER ONE

LUCAS KARADINES stood before the plate-glass window of his New York office, his dark eyes staring out over the Manhattan skyline without really registering the landscape. He ran a long-fingered hand through his night-black hair, a predatory smile curving his sensuous mouth, and a hint of triumph glittered in his eyes. Lunch had been a resounding success; he had done it! Tomorrow afternoon at Karadines London hotel, he and his father Theo, and the head of the Aristides Corporation, Alex Aristides, would sign the deal that would make Karadines one of the largest international hotel chains, and shipping lines in the world.

Like his own father, Alex Aristides was not in the best of health, but unlike his father he had no son to carry on the family business, one of the oldest firms in Greece, hence the sale to Karadines at a discounted price. Tomorrow night a party would be held for the families, the lawyers, and a few friends to celebrate the deal.

Lucas turned back to his desk, his glance falling on the telephone; as for the rest, a brief frown marred the perfect symmetry of his strikingly handsome face. It was time he made the call. He glanced at the gold Rolex on his wrist— at a pinch he could make it back to London tonight. Amber would not mind him arriving in the middle of the night… Amber was a born sensualist—he had never known a sexier woman. Amber with the long golden brown hair, and the long legs; legs that entwined with his as though they were made to match. He felt the familiar stirring in his loins and for a moment felt a flicker of regret.

5

No, he ruthlessly squashed the wayward thought. There was more to life than wild, white-hot sex. And he hadn't forgotten he'd had to wait a long time for even that the last time he had returned to London a day early. Amber had been at work and when she'd finally returned to the apartment, had only been able to spare half an hour as she'd had a business dinner to attend. They had made up for it later, but Lucas Karadines was not the kind of man to wait around for any woman, or play second fiddle to a woman's career. Several times he had suggested she resign from her job and allow him to keep her, but she had refused.

No, his mind was made up. In fact his decision had been made weeks ago. Lucas had been in the first stages of delicate negotiations to try and buy out the Aristides Corporation when he'd been introduced to the daughter of the owner, and fate had played a hand. Christina, sweet, innocent Christina, was everything he wanted in a wife. She was the opposite of Amber. She had absolutely no desire for a career other than marriage and children. She was Greek with the same cultural background and traditions as himself. And Christina adored him and hung onto his every word. They were totally compatible, and she would make a brilliant wife and mother.

The timing was perfect. After his father's last Angina attack he had confided in Lucas his ambition to see him happily married with a family of his own before he died. Lucas needed no urging to propose to Christina; he was ready to settle down and raise a family. His father was delighted at the deal and the prospect of Lucas marrying was icing on the cake.

Lucas knew he owed everything to his father. He had rescued him at the age of thirteen from the streets of Athens. His mother had left a letter with the Karadineses' lawyers before she died, giving proof that Lucas was the illegitimate son of Theo Karadines. His father had searched for him, found him and taken him into his home, paid for his education, given him his name and moulded him in his own image, for which Lucas was eternally grateful. Lucas's much older half-brother had been killed with his wife in a plane crash when Lucas was twenty-six. Without hesitation his father had made Lucas head of the company and he had repaid him by expanding and increasing their holdings and profits a hundredfold.

He turned, strode to his desk, and picked up the telephone, one long finger jabbing out the number he knew by heart. He straightened his broad shoulders beneath the exquisitely tailored dark blue silk jacket, and shoved his free hand in the pocket of his trousers, and with a look of grim determination on his face he listened to the ringing tone.

Amber Jackson walked back into her office with a dazed look in her lovely eyes and a broad grin on her face. She'd just had lunch with Sir David Janson, the chairman of the merchant bank by the same name, and she was still in a state of shock at what he had revealed to her. The ringing of the telephone brought her back to reality with a jolt. It might be Lucas, and, dashing across to her desk, she picked up the receiver.

'Amber, good I caught you. I'm sorry, but I won't be able to see you tomorrow. It will be Saturday before we can meet, pressure of business, you understand.'

The happy expression that had illuminated Amber's face when she'd picked up the receiver and heard the deep rich tones of her boyfriend's voice turned into a disappointed frown.

'Yes, I understand.' What else could she say? Lucas was

the managing director of his family firm, a large hotel and leisure company, and he spent much of his time travelling between the main offices in Athens and New York, and the various holdings around the world. In the year she had known him, she had accepted the fact he could not be with her all the time. She had a high-powered job herself as a dealer with Brentford's, a large stockbroking firm, and she knew all too well the pressure of work. 'But I'm not very happy,' she added huskily. The sound of his voice alone was enough to make her pulse race, and she was missing him quite madly. 'It is almost two months since I saw you. I was really looking forward to tomorrow—it is the anniversary of our first date and I have some marvellous news for you. You won't believe it.'

'I have some news for you as well,' he drawled, and the trace of sarcasm in his tone wasn't very reassuring. 'But it will keep until Saturday.'

It was not the response she would have liked, but then for the past few weeks Lucas's telephone calls had been few and brief, and her confidence in his love had begun to waver a little. She told herself she was being stupid. He loved her, she knew he did. But she knew the last time he had come back unexpectedly early hoping to surprise her he had been chillingly angry because she had refused to leave her office the moment he'd called and she'd insisted on keeping her work commitments. Later that night he had suggested yet again she give up her job, declaring a man of his wealth did not need a girlfriend who worked. Amber had tried to make a joke out of it, by answering with, 'I will when I am married and pregnant, but not before,' hoping he would take the hint and ask her to marry him. He hadn't. But when Amber had had to go back to work on the Monday he had casually informed her he had to go to New York for a while. The while had stretched into two long months.

Amber was desperate to see him again. She had taken tomorrow, Friday, off work especially to be able to meet him. Now he was saying Saturday, and she could have wept with frustration. But she wanted nothing to upset their reunion, and so she responded with determined good humour.

'Okay, but I miss you. It has been so long and I'm suffering from terrible withdrawal symptoms. I expect you to cure me on sight,' she said throatily.

'Sorry, darling, but it is only one more day—but it might be more if I don't get off this line and back to work.'

The prospect of their reunion being delayed even further was enough for Amber to end the conversation within a minute. She replaced the receiver, her smile somewhat restored at his use of the endearment and his apology for the delay. She had waited so long, she could easily wait another day.

But on leaving the classic old building that housed the prestigious offices of the Brentford brokerage firm, she could not help a pensive sigh escaping. She thought her surprise was special, but would Lucas? Lucas had come into her life like a whirlwind and she'd changed from a serious young woman of twenty-two, who had never worn a designer dress in her life, into the sophisticated, elegant creature she was today. But sometimes when she looked in the mirror she did not recognise herself...

Securing the gaily wrapped parcel she was carrying more firmly under one arm, Amber waved down a passing cab by swinging her briefcase in her other hand. She was completely oblivious to the admiring glances of the dozens of men pouring out of the city office. At five-feet-seven, with a slender but curvaceous body clad in a smart navy suit, the short skirt ending inches above her knees, and the snug-fitting jacket enhancing her tiny waist and the soft swell of her breasts, she was an enchanting picture. She moved with a natural, sensuous grace. Her long light brown hair, gleaming like the colour of polished chestnuts, fell from a centre parting, and was loosely tied at her nape with a pearl clasp, before falling like a silken banner almost to her waist. Her face was a classic oval with high cheekbones, a small straight nose and a wide, full-lipped mouth, but it was her huge eyes, hazel in colour and tinged with gold, shining beneath extravagantly long lashes, that animated her whole face.

'Where to, miss?' The cab stopped at her feet, and with a bright smile she slid into the back seat and gave the driver the address of her friends Tim and Spiro.

She alighted from the taxi outside the door of a small terraced house in Pimlico, and, after paying the fare, she glanced up at the white-painted house. It was hard to believe it was five years ago since she had moved into the house with Tim, a lifelong friend from the small Northumbrian village of Thropton where they'd both been born and brought up. Tim had comforted her when her mother had died when she was seventeen, and he had been in his first year at art college when Amber had been about to start at the London School of Economics. It had been Tim's suggestion she move into the spare room where he stayed. The house actually belonged to Spiro Karadines, a Greek student who was studying English at a language school before going to work at the deluxe London hotel which his family owned to learn the business from the bottom up. He reckoned he needed to let the rooms to students to pay for the upkeep of the house, because his closest relative was an uncle, Lucas Karadines, who controlled his trust fund, and was as mean as sin.

Lucas would not be pleased if he knew Amber was visiting his nephew Spiro, but he had been a good friend to her whatever Lucas thought about him. She rang the bell and waited, a reminiscent smile on her face. It was exactly a year ago tonight, Spiro's twenty-second birthday, when she had first set eyes on Lucas. He had arrived unannounced at the party, and, after a furious argument with Spiro, Lucas had calmed down and accepted a drink.

For Amber it had been love at first sight. She had taken one look at the tall, dark-haired man, incongruously dressed in a house full of motley-clad students in an immaculate grey business suit, and at least a decade older than anyone else, and her heart had turned over. She'd been unable to take her eyes off him; her fascinated gaze had followed him around the room.

Well over six feet tall, broad-shouldered, and long-legged, with thick black hair slightly longer than the present fashion, he'd been *the* most handsome man she had ever seen. Even when it had been obvious he'd been hopelessly out of place in a room where quite a few of the men had been openly gay, he'd exuded a powerful sexuality that had been totally, tauntingly masculine. When his dark eyes had finally rested on her, he'd smiled and she'd blushed scarlet, and when he had casually asked her to have dinner with him the next night she had agreed with alacrity.

Spiro had tried to put her off. He had told her his uncle was a predator of the first order, a shark, who would gobble up a little girl like her for breakfast. He was thirty-five, far too old for her. He liked his women smart and sophisticated—women who knew the score. Amber had replied she was smart, and Spiro had laughed.

'In the brains department, yes, but you dress like—a blue stocking, I believe is your peculiar English term.'

Amber had thumped him, but had ignored Spiro's warning and gone out to dinner with Lucas anyway.

It had been a magical evening. Lucas had asked her all about herself, and she'd responded by telling him her ambition to be a successful investment analyst. How she had just completed her first year at work and was delighted to have earned a huge bonus. She'd even told him she was the only child of an unmarried mother, but he had not been shocked. Finally, when Lucas had seen her to her door he had asked her if she would like to accompany Spiro and Tim to the family villa on the Karadineses' private island of the same name in the Aegean Sea for Easter. Amber had again accepted his invitation. The kiss-on-the-cheek goodnight had been a bit of a let-down. But after questioning Spiro the next day about Lucas, she had blown a few thousand pounds of her first year's bonus in buying a wardrobe full of designer clothes, visiting a beautician, and transforming herself into the sophisticated kind of woman she thought Lucas liked.

By the end of the island holiday, she had met the senior Mr Karadines, and Lucas had no longer been seeing her as a student friend of Spiro, but had been looking at her with blatant male sexual speculation in his dark eyes. On returning to London he had called her and wined and dined her half a dozen times, but the relationship had not developed past a goodnight kiss, admittedly each one more passionate and lingering than the last, but nothing more. Then he had gone to New York on business and she had thought he had forgotten her. Two weeks later he'd been back, and the next dinner date they'd shared she'd ended up in his hotel suite and they'd become lovers.

He was her first and only lover so she had no one to

compare him with, but she did not need to. She knew she had found her soul mate. He only had to look at her and her stomach curled, and when he touched her he ignited a fire, a passion she had never known existed. She had a vivid mental image of his magnificent naked body looming over her, his powerful shoulders and hair-roughened chest, the long, tanned length of him, all straining muscle and sinew as he kissed and caressed her, and taught her the exquisite delight only two people who loved could share. Within a week, at Lucas's insistence, she had moved into the loft apartment he had bought overlooking the Thames, and their relationship had gone from strength to strength. Just thinking about him made her heart pound, and brought a dreamy smile to her face.

'What are you looking so happy about?' Tim's demand brought her out of her reverie.

She looked into the sparkling blue eyes of the blond-haired man holding open the door. 'Happy memories,' she said, and, walking past him, she brushed her lips against his smooth cheek. 'Where is the birthday boy? I have a present for him.'

With the ease of long familiarity Amber strolled into the small living room. 'Happy birthday, Spiro.' She grinned at the slender dark-haired man elegantly reclining on a deep blue satin brocade sofa, and, gently dropping the parcel she was carrying onto his lap, she kicked off her shoes and sat down on the matching sofa opposite.

'My, I am honoured. My esteemed uncle has actually allowed you to visit us. It must be over six months since we saw you,' and, lifting an enquiring eyebrow to his partner, he added, 'or is it more, Tim?'

'Cut the sarcasm, Spiro. Amber is our friend, even if we do abhor her taste in men. Open your gift.'

'Yes, Spiro, where Lucas is concerned we've agreed to

differ. So open the present—I'll have you know I went to great trouble to find just the right gift,' Amber declared with a grin.

'So-rry, Amber,' he drawled dramatically. 'You've caught me in a bad mood; I am finally beginning to feel my age.'

'At twenty-three!' she exclaimed. 'Don't make me laugh.'

'You deserve to laugh, Amber. You deserve to be happy,' Spiro suddenly said seriously.

'I am happy.' She grinned back. 'Now open the parcel.'

Two minutes later Spiro was on his feet and pressing a swift kiss on Amber's cheek. 'I love it, Amber,' he said, his gaze straying back to the small sketch of two young men, clad in loincloths, facing up as if to wrestle. 'But it must have cost you a fortune—it is an original from the nineteenth century, isn't it?'

'Of course, I would not dare give you a fake,' she replied, and all three laughed. Amber knew Spiro hated working for the family firm and his burning ambition was to set up his own art gallery.

Unfortunately she also knew Lucas controlled the purse strings, and Spiro could not inherit his late father's share of the firm until he was twenty-five, or married. Spiro had a very generous monthly allowance, but he spent every penny.

The week after she'd moved in with Lucas, she had tried to put Spiro's point of view to Lucas but he had withdrawn behind a cold, impenetrable mask and told her curtly to keep out of their family business, and also suggested she keep away from his nephew.

The ease with which he had turned into a hard, remote stranger as though her thoughts and opinions were nothing had scared her. Amber had wanted to argue, she'd tried, but Lucas had simply blanked her. Unfortunately it had put a strain on Amber's friendship with her former flatmates. She did keep in touch with Tim on a regular basis—they talked on the phone every week or so—but Spiro was right. It was months since she had seen them both.

'I bet my uncle does not know you spent a fortune on this for me?' Spiro said, propping the framed sketch on the cast-iron mantelpiece, before turning back to look down on Amber.

'It has nothing to do with Lucas. I found out two weeks ago my bonus at the end of this financial year, on the fifth of April, is—wait for it, boys,' and with a wide grin, she said, 'almost a quarter of a million.'

'Well done, Amber, love,' Tim exclaimed. 'I always knew you were a genius.'

'This calls for a double celebration! Break out the bubbly, Tim, and let the party start,' Spiro added his congratulations. 'The three musketeers are back in action.'

Moisture glazed Amber's eyes at Spiro's reminder of what the three of them used to be nicknamed by their friends when they had all lived together. She'd changed and moved on, and the carefree days were long gone, but not forgotten.

The champagne was produced and toasts drank to Spiro, to Amber, to Tim, to life, and anything else they could think of. It was like old times.

Two hours later, her jacket long since removed and the clip taken from her hair, Amber was curled up on the sofa with a glass of champagne in her hand when Spiro dropped a bomb on the proceedings.

'So, Amber, what do you think of this idea of Lucas's to get married? I saw Grandfather yesterday—he is staying at the hotel while having a check-up at his Harley Street doctor, and he is delighted at the news.'

Suddenly the world seemed a wonderful place to Amber, even in her half-inebriated state. 'He told you that? Lucas is thinking of getting married! I can't believe it!' she cried happily. Lucas had actually told his father they were getting married; she couldn't wait for him to get home to ask her. Of course, she would have to pretend she didn't know. 'I spoke to Lucas this afternoon and I was disappointed because he can't make it back from New York until Saturday.' Her golden eyes sparkled like jewels in her flushed face. 'But he did say he had some news for me, and I never guessed.' Her not-so-subtle hint about giving up work when she was married and pregnant had obviously worked after all, she thought ecstatically.

'According to Grandfather, Lucas has news for you, all right, but—' Spiro started to speak but was cut off in mid-flow by Tim.

'Shut up, Spiro. Amber does not need to know second hand.'

'Please, Spiro, tell me what your grandfather said. I have only met him the one time we were all in Greece but I thought he liked me.'

A harsh laugh escaped Spiro. 'Oh, he likes you, all right, but not for what you think.'

'Spiro, no. It is none of your business,' Tim interjected again. 'We are having a good time—leave it.'

'Why? Amber has been our friend for years—she deserves to know the truth. Do you really want her to find out cold?'

Lost in her dream of wedded bliss, she was only half listening but it slowly began to dawn on Amber that the two men were arguing. 'What's the matter?' She glanced from one to the other. They looked serious. Straightening up in the seat, she drained her glass and placed it on the floor at her feet. 'Come on, guys, find *what* out cold?' she demanded cheerfully.

The two men looked at each other, and then Tim nodded. 'You're right, she deserves better.'

'Better than what?' Amber queried.

Spiro jumped to his feet. 'Better than my bastard of an uncle.'

'Oh, please, Spiro, not that again. Why can't you just be happy that Lucas and I love each other? We accept you and Tim are partners, why can't you return the favour and accept Lucas and I are partners just the same, instead of bleating on about him being a bastard?'

When she'd first told Tim and Spiro she was moving out to set up home with Lucas, Spiro had tried all ways to get her to change her mind. Finally, in a rage, he'd told her Lucas was the illegitimate child of his grandfather, and his mother was little better than a prostitute, notorious in Athens for her string of lovers, and Lucas was no better. Amber had refused to listen then and she refused to listen now. 'In case you've forgotten, I never knew my father. So what does that make me?'

Spiro, his anger subsiding, looked at her with glistening brown eyes full of compassion. 'I didn't mean it literally, though that is true. I meant it figuratively, Amber. Lucas does not consider you his partner. He considers you his mistress, nothing more, and easily dispensable.'

'Only married men have mistresses, Spiro,' Amber snapped back. 'You know nothing about my relationship with Lucas.' Her face paled at Spiro's hurtful comments. 'And I think it's time I left.' Rising unsteadily to her feet, she glanced down at her old friends. Tim was watching her with compassion, and that hurt more than anything else did. Tim had known her since infant school, surely she should be able to count on his support? But apparently not.

'Listen to Spiro, Amber. It's for your own good,' Tim said quietly.

'Lucas is good for me and to me, and that is all I need to know.' Picking up her purse, she slipped her shoes back on her feet.

'Wait, Amber.' Spiro stood up and caught her arm as she would have moved towards the door. 'You are a lovely, highly intelligent girl, with a genius for picking winners in the money markets, but you're hopelessly naive where men are concerned. Lucas is the only man you have ever known.'

'He is the only man I want to know. Now, let go of my arm.'

Reluctantly Spiro let her go. 'Just one more thing, Amber. I know who Lucas intends marrying, and it is not—'

Amber cut in angrily. 'I am not listening to any more of this,' an inexplicable fear made her yell. Spiro was half drunk and he was lying, he had to be. 'You're lying, and I know why—you can't bear to see Lucas and I happy together. You want to hurt Lucas by trying to break us up, just because he won't give you your inheritance ahead of time. I can read you like a book, Spiro, you have to dominate everyone around you. Tim might be happy to let you get away with it, but Lucas won't and that is what sticks in your craw. Grow up, why don't you?'

Spiro shook his dark head. 'You're blind, Amber, plain blind.' His dark eyes sought Tim's, his exasperation showing. 'Now what?'

Tim grimaced. 'Give it up, Spiro, she will never believe you.'

'All right, Amber, think what you like.' Spiro held his hands up in front of him. 'But do me one favour—I am dining with my grandfather at the hotel tomorrow night. He is having a bit of a party to celebrate a business deal and hopefully his return to good health. He has asked me to bring you along, and, as you say Lucas will not be back until Saturday, there is nothing to stop you. Will you come?'

Amber was torn. She didn't want to go anywhere with Spiro, but on the other hand… 'Your grandfather actually asked you to invite me?' she queried.

'Yes, in fact he was insistent.'

'In that case, yes.' How kind of him, Amber thought, the old man must know Lucas was not in London, and so had asked Spiro to bring her to his party.

'Good, I'll pick you up at your place at eight.' She never saw the gleam of determination in Spiro's eyes, that made him look uncannily like his uncle for a fleeting instant, as she said her goodbyes and left.

Later that night as she slipped a satin nightgown over her head she walked restlessly around the large bedroom she shared with Lucas. Spiro's bitchy words had upset her more than she wanted to admit. She slid open one of the wardrobe doors that lined two walls, and let her hand trail across the fine fabric of a couple of Lucas's tailored suits. The faintest lingering trace of his cologne teased her nostrils, and somehow she was reassured. Lucas loved her, she knew he did, and on that thought she climbed into the king-sized bed and sleep claimed her.

Amber glanced at her reflection for the last time in the large mirrored doors of the wardrobes that formed one wall of the bedroom. She looked good, better than good. Great, she told herself. Her hair was washed and brushed until it shone dark gold, and she had clipped the sides up into a coronet on top of her head, while the rest fell down her back like a swathe of silk. She had opted for a classic black DKNY dress—the fine black silk jersey clung to her body like a second skin, the sleeves long and fitted, the skirt ending inches above her knees. The low-cut square neckline exposed the gentle curve of her firm breasts, setting off to perfection the emerald and diamond necklace she had clasped around her throat. The matching drop earrings glinted against the swan-like elegance of her neck. Both had been presents from Lucas. On her feet she wore three-inch-heeled black sandals, adding to her already tall stature.

Picking up her purse and a jade-green pashmina shawl, she walked down the spiral staircase to the vast floor area of the apartment. She loved the polished hardwood floor, and the carefully arranged sofas that picked out the colour in the cashmere rug. In fact she loved her home. But where was Spiro? He was ten minutes late.

She crossed the room to a large desk, her hand reaching out for the telephone. She would try one last time to ring Lucas in New York. Picking up the instrument, she dialled the number. Two minutes later she replaced the receiver, the same reply as she had got earlier echoing in her head. 'I'm sorry but Mr Karadines is not in the office today, if you would like to leave a message...' She had also tried his suite at the Karadines Hotel in New York, and got no reply.

The bell rang and she had no time to worry where Lucas was. Spiro had arrived.

Two minutes later she was seated in the back of a taxi-cab with Spiro looking very elegant in a conservative black dinner suit and white shirt; the only hint at his rebellious personality was a vibrantly striped bow-tie in red, green and blue.

'You look rather nice,' Amber said with a grin. 'Though I don't know about the bow-tie.'

'And you, dear girl, look as stunning as ever.' But there was no smile in his eyes as he reached out and caught both of Amber's hands in his.

'Where to now, Gov?' the taxi driver asked.

'Hold it a minute or two,' Spiro responded, then, glancing back at Amber, he added, 'You must listen to me and believe me. Tim made me promise that I would tell you before we arrive at the hotel so if you want to cancel you can do so. I am sorry, truly sorry, Amber, but Lucas will be at the party.'

Her hands jerked in his hold but he did not set her free. His brown eyes held hers, and there was no doubting the sincerity and sadness in their depths.

'How...?' All the blood drained from her face. 'How do you know?' she asked quietly.

'Because, a rare occurrence for me, I admit, I actually went to work for a few hours this afternoon in my capacity of Assistant Manager at the hotel. I saw Lucas arriving with two guests, Alex Aristides and his young daughter Christina. They went to Grandfather's suite. Ten minutes later I escorted the two family lawyers to the same suite. Karadines have bought out the Aristides Corporation. The deal was signed this afternoon. Needless to say they didn't need my signature, although I own half the company. My trustees did it for me. I was given the task of amusing the teenage daughter for an hour. An hour spent standing around in the boutiques in the hotel lobby. The girl could shop for the world.'

'So it was business—Lucas said he was tied up with business, he would not lie to me,' she declared adamantly. Though he had lied by omission—he had led her to believe he was staying in New York...

'Stop, Amber.' Spiro squeezed her hands in his. 'Please don't do this to yourself. Christina Aristides is eighteen years of age and obviously part of the deal.'

'No, no, Spiro, you're wrong. Lucas would never do that to me,' Amber said firmly, but deep down inside a tiny voice of dissent was telling her he might.

'He is a chip off the old block, as you English say. How do you think Grandfather made his money? As a young man he went to sea on a cruise liner as a waiter. Twelve months later he married the owner's daughter, a woman ten years older than him, but for a waiter that was some step up. To give him his due, under his control the firm went from strength to strength. But my grandmother was no fool—she knew he had several mistresses and Lucas's mother was one of them. So she kept the stock in her name, and on her death half went to Grandfather and half to her son, my father. Do you really think Grandfather would have risked his whole business on taking Lucas in, and giving him his name, if my grandmother had still been alive? My parents did not object because they already had half the business.'

'But that does not mean Lucas would marry for money. He does not need to,' she defended him staunchly.

'Amber, Grandfather wants this deal, and Lucas is exactly like him. They are both very Greek, very traditional. Everything is business to them. Lucas will marry the girl. You have no chance, Amber. Believe me, you never did.'

'You don't know Lucas as I do. He might just be stringing the girl along until the deal was signed...' She stopped, realising how desperate she sounded, as if she would rather think of Lucas as a ruthless, manipulative businessman than face the fact he might leave her.

'Well, I suppose it is a possibility and if that is what

you want to believe...' Spiro shrugged his broad shoulders... 'we might as well go.'

'You say Tim told you to tell me this.' She looked at Spiro with icy eyes. 'I don't believe you. Tim would never be so cruel.'

'You're right, of course—Tim has not a cruel bone in his body. I, on the other hand, wanted to walk you straight into the party and let you come face to face with Lucas. In fact I was hoping you would cause a scene in front of my grandfather. Then my precious uncle would be seen for the devil he is, but Tim would not let me.'

'You actually believe all you are telling me,' Amber whispered, the full horror of Spiro's revelation finally sinking into her troubled mind.

'You don't have to take my word. You can go back into your apartment and bury your head in the sand like an ostrich for one more night. Or you can come with me and see for yourself.' A challenging smile curved his full lips. 'If you have the nerve.'

Amber had never refused a challenge in her life and she was not going to start now. Besides which, she did not believe Spiro. Her heart would not let her...

CHAPTER TWO

AMBER, tall and sophisticated in the black silk dress with jewels gleaming at her throat, handed her shawl in to the cloakroom attendant, and turned back to Spiro.

'Ready.' She smiled. Spiro had to be mistaken, she told herself yet again, her golden eyes straying to the wide open doors of the private function room where the party was being held.

'Take my arm, Amber.' Spiro picked up her nerveless hand and slipped it through his arm as they walked into the elegant room.

Lucas Karadines saw Amber before she had even got through the door. She looked sensational. Shock held him rigid for a second, then he looked away hastily but not before seeing her companion, Spiro! Lucas's black eyes closed briefly. Oh, hell! He almost groaned out loud. For the first time in his adult life he felt about two inches tall. He knew deep down he should have made the effort to see Amber some time today and finish their relationship, but he had been reluctant to do so. But what the hell was she doing here? He did not need to ask. Spiro, of course. Spiro would find it amusing.

He felt a tug on his sleeve, and looked down into the round open face of Christina. Thank God his betrothal to Christina was not to be announced until next week—at least that would give him time to explain to Amber. He would not wish to hurt her for the world. His dark eyes were fixed on Christina, but more worrying was that in his mind's eye he was seeing the stunningly sensual naked

24

figure of Amber, the night he had given her the necklace as a birthday present, the emeralds blazing around her neck her only adornment. Brutally he squashed the image, much the way he would like to squash Spiro for putting him in this position. Determinedly he smiled down at Christina, and, slipping an arm around her shoulder, continued the conversation with their respective fathers.

Amber's golden gaze urgently scanned the crowded room, hoping against hope she would not find the man she was looking for. Then she spotted Lucas. It was two long months since she had seen him, and she could not help it as her eyes drank in the sight of him. Why he was here instead of New York didn't matter, he was here...now...

He was the tallest, sexiest man in the room. His superbly muscled frame was clad in a black dinner suit, the exquisitely tailored jacket fitted perfectly across his broad shoulders, the pure white of the dress shirt he wore contrasted starkly with his bronzed skin. Her heart squeezed in her chest, her gaze slanting down over the long, elegant length of him with loving, hungry eyes. She knew every inch of his magnificent body as intimately as she knew her own. She would have gambled her last penny that neither one of them could have walked into a room without the other being instantly aware of it. She waited for his head to turn, for those incredible dark eyes to meet hers, for his smile of delighted recognition. But she was wrong... Lucas wasn't aware of her at all...

She blindly allowed Spiro to lead her slowly through the crowd of guests; she had eyes for no one but Lucas. He was standing at the far end of the room with a group of three other people: his father, another elderly gentleman, and a young girl. He was smiling down at the girl with a look of such tenderness in his eyes that an inexplicable fear made Amber's blood run cold. His head was slightly bowed, his shoulders curved in a protective attitude towards the girl, and Amber's heart froze in her breast. She was vaguely aware of the long table they were standing beside; for a second her eyes flickered to the centre point, a magnificent ice sculpture of a sailing ship. Wildly whimsical, she wished she could get in it and sail away, but inevitably her gaze was drawn back to the small group. It was just a business deal, it had to be, she told herself. She dimly felt Spiro squeeze her hand, and heard through the roaring in her ears.

'I hate to say it, Amber, but I told you so...'

'Thanks.' She cast a furious sidelong glance at Spiro; he was enjoying this. 'But it still does not mean you are right. Lucas might not have had time to call me if, as you say, he had a business meeting this afternoon.' She had to hope; she could not face the alternative or it would destroy her.

'If you believe that, you will believe anything. Where's your pride, girl?' Spiro queried, raising one elegant brow, but, sensing her distress, he added, 'Chin up, Amber. Don't let the devil get you down.'

'He is not a devil,' she defended Lucas, but without her usual conviction, and, glancing back at the group, she finally looked at the young girl at Lucas's side.

She was short and very Greek with an olive-skinned complexion and long black hair tied back in a ponytail. Pretty if a little plump. The dress she was wearing was a concoction in pink satin with a gathered skirt, probably ruinously expensive, but it did nothing for the girl's figure. The girl was gazing up at Lucas, with a dreamy smile on her face. One of her hands rested on his arm, and the other was on his chest—there was no mistaking the intimacy of the gesture.

'Is that child Christina Aristides?' Amber asked. 'The daughter you mentioned.'

'Yes.'

'Then you're wrong, Spiro. Lucas is no cradle-snatcher and that girl is young enough to be *his* daughter.' Her gaze strayed helplessly back to the dark head of her lover, and at that moment his head lifted, and his dark eyes clashed with Amber's.

She stared at the man she loved with all her heart, and she saw the coldness in his hard gaze as their glances locked. He did not even look surprised to see her. But she noticed his pupils dilate slightly, and the flare of desire in his eyes before he lowered his gaze, to sweep down over the shapely length of her and return blandly to her face.

Lucas Karadines shifted uncomfortably and shoved his hand in his trouser pocket. He had thought he had got himself under control enough to look at her again, but his body thought otherwise, much to his disgust. What the hell was she doing here with Spiro, anyway? He had told her to keep away from Spiro and she had deliberately defied him. But then that was Amber—she took a delight in challenging him on every level. A trait he could put up with in a girlfriend but not a trait a man wanted in a wife.

She looked stunning as always, her waist-length chestnut hair gleaming gold in the artificial light, the sleek black dress lovingly clinging to every curve of her magnificent body. Every man in the place was secretly eyeing her, he knew. She was sex personified, and his body had reacted instantly. He cursed under his breath. No man in his right mind would marry a girl like Amber, a girl who would have to be guarded every minute of every day from other predatory males. He smiled down at the young girl by his side. He had made the right decision; Christina would never cause him a moment's worry. Then he eyed Spiro again, and any guilt he was feeling at his own behaviour he transferred to Spiro. He might have guessed it was his damn nephew's entire fault. He had done it deliberately to embarrass him.

Amber watched Lucas shove his hand in his trouser pocket and knew he still wanted her. The beginnings of a smile curved her full lips as she waited for him to acknowledge her. But his desire was quickly replaced by anger as his dark eyes moved to narrow on her companion. The smile died from her lips before it was born as Lucas, with a dismissive arch of one dark brow, turned slightly and said something to his father, and then, smiling at his young companion, he took her hand in his and moved through the crowd, stopping as various people spoke to them.

Amber took the drink Spiro handed her and immediately took a long swallow; she needed something, anything. She was shaken to the core; she had never felt so utterly humiliated in her life. It was like being trapped in a nightmare, unable to move, or breathe. A frantic glance around the room, and she was amazed no one seemed to be aware of the enormity of what had just happened. Lucas had looked at her as if she was of no more interest to him than the dirt beneath his feet. It had to be a mistake, and for a wild moment she thought of flying over to him, and snatching his hand from the young girl.

'Any minute now, Amber, be cool,' Spiro murmured, his dark head bending towards her, shielding her face from view. 'Take a deep breath, don't let him see he has hurt you, don't give him the satisfaction.'

Hurt didn't begin to cover how she felt, and a slow-burning anger ignited in the pit of her stomach. She took a few deep, calming breaths, schooling her face into calm immobility.

'That's it,' Spiro said, and moved to her side just as Lucas and Christina stopped in front of them.

'Glad you could make it, Spiro, and you too, Amber,' Lucas said smoothly, and proceeded to introduce his companion. 'Allow me to introduce Christina Aristides. I have just acquired her father's business, and this evening is to celebrate the deal.'

Amber wanted to smash her fist in his face, scream and yell, demand to know why he had lied to her, but this was neither the time or the place. Instead she straightened her shoulders and pinned a smile on her face as she shook the young girl's hand. It wasn't the poor girl's fault, it was Lucas who was the swine.

Christina smiled demurely, and then, turning to Spiro, she punched him playfully on the arm. 'My, you are a dark horse, Spiro, you never mentioned that you were bringing your girlfriend with you tonight.' And then she added for Amber's benefit, 'I hope you did not mind me stealing your boyfriend for the afternoon, but Lucas was too tied up with business to go shopping with me.' The inference being Lucas was her boyfriend.

The tension between the other three was electric. Amber's eyes flew to Lucas's face—surely he would say something, deny it. She saw the cold anger in the depths of his eyes. He was furious she was here. Her presence had obviously upset his glittering celebration, or maybe for the first time in his life he actually felt embarrassed. But in a second Amber knew she was wrong. He stared back at her, his gaze chillingly remote. Amber had seen that look only once before when she'd tried to argue with him about Spiro—it had scared her then, but now it confirmed what she had probably known for the past twenty-four hours but refused to admit.

Shattered by his duplicity, she let her gaze trail over his

tall, muscular body. He was the sexiest man alive, but also heartless. She finally saw him as the hard, ruthless Greek tycoon that he had always been, but love had blinded her to his real character. She tilted back her head, her golden eyes challenging him, but he avoided her gaze, his whole attention fixed on the young girl.

'Don't worry, Christina. I'm sure Amber didn't mind,' Lucas said softly, and, turning to Spiro, he added, 'Though I did not know you and Amber were still seeing each other.'

'Oh, yes, Amber is not the sort to desert her friends, are you, Amber, darling?' Spiro drawled pointedly, and, clasping an arm around her slender waist, he pulled her into his side and pressed a swift kiss on her brow.

Amber let him—in fact she was glad of his support. Her stomach churned and she wanted to be sick as the full extent of Lucas's betrayal hit her. Her beautiful face lost what little colour she had. How dared he introduce her to Christina as though she were merely an acquaintance, a friend of his nephew, instead of the woman who had shared his bed for the best part of a year?

'So I see,' Lucas drawled mockingly. He knew Spiro was gay.

His mockery was the last straw for Amber. Her wild golden eyes clashed with Lucas's. 'I wonder, can anyone say the same about you, Lucas? But, no, I seem to remember you telling me once you had no real friends. Perhaps because you only use people.' She saw his jaw clench, a dark tide of colour surging up under his skin, and a leap of fury in his eyes. Serves him right, Amber thought.

'My, Lucas, a woman who does not admire you unreservedly, that must be a first,' Christina piped up.

'Amber is an old friend, and she and Spiro delight in

trying to needle me, it's just a joke.' Lucas smiled down at Christina, his voice softening. 'Nothing for you to worry about.'

Fury such as she had never known sent all the blood rushing back to Amber's head. Old friend! He had a nerve. The hand holding her glass of wine began to rise. Spiro, guessing her intentions, grasped her wrist.

'I am starving and I think you need a top up, Amber. Excuse us.' With his arm at her waist, he urged her away from the other couple. 'It would have been a futile gesture, Amber, throwing your drink over him—your glass is virtually empty,' he murmured, turning her back to the crowd to face the buffet table.

Amber was shaking, visibly shaking. She'd never felt such overwhelming rage in her life. 'I wasn't going to throw it over him,' she denied, turning blazing eyes up to Spiro's. 'I was going to screw the glass in his arrogant, lying face,' she confessed fiercely.

She was not a violent person, she had never harmed a living thing in her life, but for a second she had completely lost control. Suddenly she was appalled at her own actions, and her anger subsided. 'Thank you for stopping me, Spiro.' She tried to smile. 'Your better nature got the better of you—you said earlier you wanted me to cause a scene, and I thought you were joking. But the joke is on me and I've never felt less like laughing. I want to cry.'

'No, Amber. Tim was right and I was wrong.' His arm dropped from her waist and he lifted a hand to her chin and tilted her head up to face him. 'I should never have brought you here. I have to speak to my grandfather but then I am taking you straight home. Ten minutes at most, can you do it?'

A film of moisture hazed her glorious eyes, and she blinked furiously. 'I have to, I have no choice.' Imperceptibly she straightened her shoulders, her back ramrod straight as she fought for control, and won.

Spiro's hand fell from her chin, his dark eyes admiring her elegant form. 'You are the most beautiful, elegant lady in this room. You have more class in your little finger than the whole of this lot put together, and don't you forget it.'

Before Amber could respond old Mr Karadines interrupted them. He gave Spiro a hug and spoke to him in Greek, before turning to Amber.

'Amber, isn't it? Good to meet you again, and I'm glad to see you are still keeping this grandson of mine in order.'

'Hello, and I'm trying,' was as much as she could manage to say. A blessed numbness had enveloped her. She felt as if she were viewing the proceedings from outside her body—the pain was waiting for her, she knew, but her heart had not broken, it had simply solidified into a hard black stone in her breast.

'Good, good. I have been hearing great things about you from Clive here. Allow me to introduce you. Clive Thompson, my grandson's friend, Amber Jackson.'

Amber didn't have time to wonder why the old man had referred to her as Spiro's friend as the name of the tall, elegant blond-haired man registered, and she was holding out her hand to him. He was a top manager with Janson's merchant bank. He was only forty but already his reputation was legendary in the City.

She sensed rather than saw Lucas and Christina walk up and join the group, but she did not dare look. If she did she knew she would break down. Her hand was still held by Clive and she was grateful because it enabled her to find the strength not to tremble at Lucas's towering presence beside her.

'I have been longing to meet you as soon as Theo told me your name. Allow me to say you are as beautiful as you are brilliant, if not more so; a truly stunning combination.' His bright blue eyes smiled down into hers, and, lifting her fingers to his lips, he kissed the back of her hand before letting go.

'Oh, how gallant, Mr Thompson!' Christina's accented voice interrupted.

Amber glanced sideways and saw Lucas had moved closer to her with Christina clinging onto his other arm. Quickly she returned her attention to Clive, and saw his slightly raised eyebrows and brief polite smile at the young girl, before he returned his attention to Amber again and continued as if the other girl had not spoken.

'Brentford's are very lucky to have you, is the word in the City. Apparently you got your clients out of...' and he mentioned a high-tech company whose shares were on the way down and out '...even better than I did,' and he gave her an appreciative smile that Amber returned. They discussed the company in question in some detail. They were like-minded people.

'I was lucky,' she finally finished. Anything to do with business and she was not in the least intimidated. It was only in the love stakes she was a total idiot, it seemed.

'People make their own luck, Amber—I may call you Amber?' Clive grinned.

'Of course.' She heard what sounded like a grunt from Lucas, and felt the slight brush of his trouser-clad thigh against her hip.

Lucas did it deliberately. Inexplicably it angered him to hear Amber discussing business with the elegant Englishman, and he wanted to disconcert her, but she simply moved away. In that moment Lucas recognised the truth and his arm tightened around Christina. Amber did not need a man for anything other than sex and even that, as he knew to his cost, could be delayed because of her work. He had never been in love but his idea of it was to protect and care for his wife and family. Christina needed his protection and in return he knew that as she was a well-brought-up young Greek girl, her husband and children would always come first.

Amber felt as if she could feel Lucas breathing down her neck and carefully moved closer to Spiro as Clive slid one hand into the inside pocket of his jacket to withdraw a gold-edged card. 'Here is my card—if you ever feel like changing firms, I promise we will offer you a much better package.'

A wry smile curved her full lips; she could not help it. The ultimate irony. From her surprising lunch on Thursday it had been like a roller-coaster ride of highs and lows, finally to this, the worst night of her life, when it was taking all her strength to simply keep standing, she was being head-hunted by Janson's of all firms...

'And would your chairman, Sir David Janson, agree to your proposition?' she prompted with an enviable touch of cynicism, considering the tall, dark presence of Lucas was within touching distance; the familiar scent of him that filled her nostrils had her nerves at screaming-point.

'It would depend on the proposition, would it not, Clive?' Lucas's deep voice queried sardonically.

'Oh, I'm sure Amber and I could work out a mutually satisfactory arrangement.' Clive's blue eyes, gleaming with very male appreciation, didn't leave Amber's as he tagged on, 'And Sir Janson, of course.'

'I'm sure Amber does not want to talk business all night with you men,' Christina inserted, smiling across at Amber. 'I thought this was supposed to be a party.' Then she added, 'Let's go find the rest room, and we can have a gossip. I love your dress, and your necklace and earrings are gorgeous; you must tell me where you got them.'

The bluntness with which Christina changed the subject stopped the conversation dead. Lucas's black eyes clashed with Amber's over the top of Christina's head, and she saw the warning glint in their depths, but she ignored it. Boldly she held his gaze, contempt blazing from her hazel eyes. For the first time that evening she felt in control.

'They were a birthday and Christmas present.' Amber smiled down at Christina. 'And, yes, I'll come with you,' she said, taking the young girl's arm. Let the swine sweat, let him wonder if she would tell his innocent *girlfriend* exactly who had given Amber the jewellery, she thought bitterly. Her rage was the only thing that kept her going as she walked out of the party and along the quiet hall to the powder room.

'Thank God we've escaped,' Christina groaned as they entered the powder room together, and, walking across to the row of vanity basins and dropping her purse on the marble top, she admired herself in the mirror above. 'An hour of my father and his friends and I feel like climbing the walls.' Turning to Amber, she added, 'You're lucky Spiro is young and doesn't take himself seriously. Lucas can be mind-bendingly boring, you've no idea.'

Shocked into silence, Amber watched the younger girl pull at the pink satin bodice of her dress. 'I ask you, Amber, would you be caught dead in a dress like this?'

'Well…' How to be diplomatic? Amber pondered. 'You must like it.' A high-pitched laugh greeted her comment.

'You're joking. I hate it, but then you are not Greek so you would not understand.'

Slowly Amber crossed to stand beside Christina. Her eyes met the other girl's in the mirror, and suddenly Christina seemed so much older and harder. 'Understand why you wear a dress you hate?' Amber prompted.

'Because my father expects me to look like his innocent

young daughter, and of course Lucas expects his fiancée to look like a shy young virgin, otherwise I would not be caught dead in pink satin.'

'Your fiancé!' Amber exclaimed, unable to disguise her horror.

'Yes, didn't Spiro tell you?' And, not waiting for an answer, Christina continued, 'Next weekend at our home in Athens my father is holding a huge party for my betrothal to Lucas and three weeks later we are getting married. He would have announced it tonight except it looks a bit too blatant even for a Greek to sign the business deal and sell your daughter in one afternoon.'

So it was all true. Amber's brain reeled under the shock. Spiro had not been exaggerating. She looked into the face of her rival and asked the question uppermost on her mind. 'Do you love Lucas?'

Christina laughed. 'No, but he loves me, or so he says, and it does not really matter anyway. I want to get married, the quicker the better.' Christina fiddled nervously with the clip of the small satin purse on the marble bench. 'Once I am married, I'm free. I get the money my mother left me, and, to give Lucas his due, he is renowned as a shrewd operator, so I have no doubt he will greatly increase the wealth of the family company. Therefore mine,' she said with some glee, and, finally noticing the look of shock and horror Amber could not hide, Christina laughed out loud. 'Don't look so shocked; it is a typical Greek arrangement.'

'But...but...' Amber spluttered '...you are so young.'

'I have just spent a year in a Swiss finishing-school, and those ski instructors are something else again. I'm not that young,' she offered with a very adult smile. 'Though I know what you mean—Lucas is a bit old. But Spiro did me a favour this afternoon. I think he was trying to warn me, but actually I was delighted when he told me Lucas apparently keeps a mistress, so I don't think he is going to be bothering me much in bed even when we are married.'

'You really don't mind?' Amber said slowly, the callousness of Christina's statement ringing in her ears. 'You don't care if your husband is unfaithful to you?'

'Not in the least, why should I with a fortune at my disposal?' And, picking up her purse, she opened it and withdrew some rolling tobacco. 'Do you want a smoke?'

Amber looked at the girl and the tobacco. 'No, I don't smoke.' Amber wondered why with her wealth she rolled her own.

'Pity.' Placing a hand on Amber's arm, Christina said, 'Don't look so surprised, and do me a favour, go out and tell Lucas I will be another five minutes. He does not know of my little vice.' She chuckled as she urged Amber towards the door.

Amber found herself out in the corridor without realising how she had got there.

'Where is Christina?' Lucas's deep voice demanded. Amber lifted her head, her stunned gaze meeting his dark brooding eyes. He was standing in the middle of the hall, his large body tense, waiting... But not for Amber...

'She said give her five minutes,' Amber stated bluntly. 'She also said you are her fiancé. How can that be, Lucas?' she hissed furiously. 'You live with me, it has to be a horrible mistake.'

'It is not a mistake.' The dark-lashed brilliance of his eyes clashed with hers; she was too upset to try and hide the hurt and anger in her own gaze. His expression hardened. 'I regret you had to find out this way. But then I had no knowledge of your continued association with my nephew or that he would bring you here tonight...'

Amber's mouth opened but no sound came out. The colossal arrogance of the man! Lucas was as good as saying it was Spiro's fault, that she had discovered his wicked betrayal.

'Look, Amber—' he laid a large hand on her arm, and furiously she brushed him off '—we have to talk.'

'A bit late for talk,' she snapped.

He straightened, squaring his broad shoulders. 'Keep your voice down,' he commanded, his dark eyes narrowing on her flushed, furious face. 'I will call tomorrow morning as arranged and explain.'

'My surprise,' she whispered, realising the full horrific extent of his betrayal. 'Christina was going to be my surprise!' Her voice rose an octave.

'Someone talking about me?' Christina came sauntering out of the cloakroom, her dark eyes almost feverishly bright, her smile brilliant.

Immediately Lucas curved a protective arm around Christina's shoulder, making it very clear where his loyalty lay. 'We were just discussing the engagement party next weekend. It was supposed to be a secret, you're very naughty.' He chided the young girl with such indulgence Amber felt sick.

Spiro sauntered up and slipped an arm around Amber's waist. 'What's all this? Plotting in corridors now.' He chuckled, and Amber clung to him like a life raft in a storm-tossed sea. Her knees were buckling and she thought she would faint; there was only so much hurt one body could stand and she was at the limit. Spiro, sensing her desperation, tightened his grip on her waist and listened as Christina, seemingly inexhaustible, went on at great length about the following weekend and extended an invitation to the party.

Finally when the young girl paused for breath Spiro

leapt in. 'Well, on behalf of both Amber and I, our heart-
iest congratulations to you, and we hope you both get the
happiness you deserve!' he drawled sarcastically. 'Now,
you will have to excuse us, but we have a prior engagement.' And within minutes Amber found herself out in the
foyer of the hotel.

'I'm sorry, I am truly, truly sorry, Amber, I should never
have brought you here.' But Amber wasn't listening.
She'd been functioning on shock and adrenalin for the past
hour, and now she was as spent as a burst balloon—she
wanted to curl up and die.

'Take me home, Spiro.' And he did.

Sitting in the back seat of the cab, with Spiro's protective arm around her, Amber asked bleakly, 'Why, Spiro?
You said your grandfather invited me. Why would he do
that knowing Lucas and I...?' She broke off, to swallow
the lump rising in her throat, her lashes wet with tears.
'How could he be so cruel?'

'You still don't see it,' Spiro said ruefully. 'I've avoided
the subject for too long. I should have told you at the time,
Amber, but it seemed a harmless enough deceit.' He
glanced apologetically down at her tear-stained face. 'Remember the first time you saw Lucas, when he arrived at
my party madder than hell? Well, it was because he had
just discovered I was taking Tim to our villa in Greece for
the Easter holiday and I was about to confess to
Grandfather that I was gay. Lucas tried to talk me out of
it, saying it would kill the old man if he thought his only
grandson was gay. Which is why he asked you out to
dinner, and asked you to accompany Tim and I on holiday.
Lucas is not above using anybody to protect the old man.
Consequently, he subtly let Grandfather know you and
Tim were like brother and sister. But you and I had a much
closer relationship; after all, you had been living in my

house for four years. Lucas can be very convincing, as you know.'

'You mean all this time your grandfather has thought you and I are a couple? But that's impossible...' But was it? she asked herself. Lucas had made no approach to her until they had returned to England, and she had never met his father again until tonight.

Then she remembered their very first dinner date. When Lucas had invited her to the villa, he had also asked her to do him a favour. He knew she was close to Tim and Spiro, and he had asked her to use her influence on the pair to tone down their behaviour in front of his father when they were all at the villa. The old man was rather old-fashioned that way. Of course, Amber had said yes.

Now it all made a horrible kind of sense. Lucas would do anything for his father, including marrying a suitable rich little Greek girl. Spiro was right...

'Think about it, Amber. Has Lucas ever taken you any-where in public where Grandfather was likely to hear about it? No. While you thought you were building a re-lationship, a home, with a thoroughly modern man, Lucas had no such intentions.'

Amber's face was bleak, her mouth bitter and twisted as the full import of Spiro's revelation sank in. She tried to speak and found herself shivering compulsively. She could not believe she had been so blind, so stupid...

CHAPTER THREE

AMBER knew once she let the first tear fall that she would never be able to stop. Kicking off her shoes, she locked the door and padded across the polished wood floor to the spiral staircase. Grasping the rail, she ascended to the galleried sleeping area like an old woman. Spiro had asked her to go back to his place, but she'd refused. He had done enough for her for one night, she thought bitterly.

Stripping off her clothes, she walked into the huge bathroom. She glanced at the circular white marble Jacuzzi sunk into the floor, and quickly away as too many memories flooded back. Skirting the bath, she stepped into the double shower. She turned the tap on full, and stood under the power jets and let the water pound her slender body. She closed her eyes, but she could not block out the image of Lucas naked on his knees in the shower with her. Soaping every inch of her tender flesh from the tips of her toes to her head in what she had thought was complete adoration.

Why? Why had Lucas done this to her? her mind screamed, and the iron control she had exerted over her emotions all evening finally broke. The tears slowly squeezed from her eyes to slide down her cheeks. The trickle became a flood as she wept out her pain and grief, the tears mingling with the powerful spray until Amber fell to her knees, her arms wrapped around her middle, her head bowed, completely broken, defeated...

Her body shivering, Amber slowly opened her eyes. She was huddled on the floor of the shower. When had the hot water run out and turned to icy cold? She had no idea. She was freezing, her limbs numb. Slowly she staggered to her feet, turned off the tap and stepped out of the shower. Pulling a large bath towel from the rail, she wrapped it toga-style around her shaking body. She caught sight of her reflection in the mirror above the vanity basin—her eyes were red-rimmed and puffy, her skin pale and cold as death.

She was still wearing the emerald necklace and earrings. Carefully she removed both, and, walking out of the bathroom, she dropped them on the dressing table, then pulled out the seat and sat down. Picking up the hair-dryer, she switched it on and methodically began drying her long hair.

Lucas had loved to see her naked with her hair smoothed silkily over her breasts. Her eyes filled with moisture at the memory, and, leaping to her feet, she staggered across the room and flung herself down on the bed. She turned her face into the pillow, shaken by another violent storm of weeping.

When it was over she felt curiously calm, and as it was just dawn she got to her feet and began to dress. She did not bother with a bra, she had no need for one, but slipped into skimpy white lace briefs. She withdrew grey- and blue-checked trousers from the wardrobe and a V-neck button-through matching blue cashmere cardigan, and put them on. She slipped her feet into soft leather loafers and descended the spiral staircase. She crossed the vast expanse of the living area to the kitchen, and opened the door just as the first rays of sun shone though the window.

Amber switched on the kettle, made herself a cup of instant coffee, and, taking it back with her into the living room, she sat down on one of the soft-cushioned sofas. She picked up the remote control for the television and switched it on. It was the twenty-four-hour news channel. She watched and waited...

Amber heard the key turn in the lock, and, switching off the television, she stood up and slowly turned to face the door.

To the man entering the room, she looked cool, calm and collected, and beautiful. 'Amber, I am glad you are here. I thought you might have gone back with Spiro after last night,' Lucas said smoothly, closing the door behind him and striding towards her.

Amber watched him approach. He was casually dressed in faded denim jeans, a cream-coloured roll-neck sweater and tan leather jacket. His black hair was windswept; he had never looked more attractive to her, or more out of her reach.

Her heart hardened against his masculine appeal. 'Why would I do that, Lucas? This is my home,' she queried coolly. A bone-numbing anger had replaced her earlier grief.

'Good, I hoped you would be sensible.' His long legs slightly splayed, he stopped about a foot away from her, his dark eyes sweeping over her long hair falling loose to her waist, and back up, lingering for a second too long on the proud thrust of her breasts against the soft cashmere sweater.

Amber saw his pupils darken, and the sudden tension in his broad frame. He was not immune to her, that much was obvious, and it simply fuelled her anger. 'Sensible is not the word I would have chosen,' she declared bitterly. 'I don't feel in the least sensible after last night, I feel madder than hell, and demand an explanation. I thought you were my boyfriend, my partner. We live together, for

God's sake!' she cried, aware of the consuming bile rising in her throat as she studied his hard features.

Abruptly Lucas stepped back a pace, and she had the satisfaction of seeing his face darken with suppressed anger, or was it embarrassment? He didn't appreciate being called to account for his behaviour. 'I agree,' he said curtly. 'And I apologise—last night should never have happened. Christina should not have told you we were getting engaged next weekend. But then you should not have been at the party. You have Spiro to thank for last night's fiasco, not I.'

'Oh, no, you can't blame this on Spiro, you lying swine,' she shot back furiously. 'You told me you could not get back from New York until Saturday—pressure of work, you said. What a joke!' Blazing golden eyes clashed with his and what she saw in their obsidian depths sent an icy shiver down her spine.

'I did not lie. I said I could not *meet* you until Saturday, which was perfectly true. I had a prior engagement for Friday evening,' he drawled cynically.

'An engagement for the rest of your life, if Christina is to be believed. I have never been so embarrassed or humiliated in all my life, and I want to know *why*? You owe me that much,' Amber demanded, her voice rising stridently.

Lucas stepped forward and closed a powerful hand over both of hers. 'Calm down and listen to me,' he snapped back, his black eyes hard on her lovely face. 'I had no desire to embarrass or hurt you in any way. I had every intention of telling you our affair was over before announcing my betrothal. I have never in my life begun a sexual relationship with a woman without first divesting myself of her predecessor. It is a rule of mine.'

'Bully for you!' she snorted inelegantly, but just the

touch of his hand on hers made her pulse race and she despised herself for it. 'You are so moral,' she managed to drawl sarcastically. 'Is that supposed to make me feel better that you are dumping me?'

'Dumping...' a grimace of distaste tightened his hard mouth '...is not how I would have put it. Our affair has reached its conclusion, and I hope we can part friends.'

This is not happening to me, this cannot be happening to me, Amber told herself over and over again. The blind, arrogant conceit of the man was unbelievable. *Friends*— he wanted them to be *friends*... Didn't he know he had broken her heart, destroyed her dreams, her life? She looked up and saw the flicker of impatience in his dark eyes, the aloof expression on his handsome face, and she had her answer. It was obvious he was wondering how to extricate himself as quickly as possible.

'And what about me?' Amber asked quietly, amazed that her voice didn't break.

'Amber, we have had some great times together, but now it is over, it has to be. I have reached the age—' he walked away from her, pacing the length of the room '—when it is time for me to settle down. I want a wife, a family, a home, and Christina is going to give me all that.' Then, spinning on his heel, he walked slowly back towards her.

'You're bright and ambitious, I know you have a brilliant future ahead of you. But, for me, Christina is the answer. You understand.'

The numbness that had protected her for the past few hours vanished. He was ripping her heart to shreds with every word he spoke. 'No, no, I don't.' She raised her eyes to meet his. 'I thought we were a couple, and that this was our home.' Even as she said the words, she saw the gleam of cynical amusement in his dark eyes as he glanced around the room and back at Amber.

'Oh, come on, Amber, don't play the innocent, it does not suit you. This was never meant to be a home, a living area with an open-galleried bedroom and a sybaritic bathroom. Could you see me entertaining my family and friends in this place?' One dark brow arched sardonically. 'I think not…'

Amber exploded; her hand swung in a wide arc and smashed across his face. 'I should have done that last night,' she yelled. 'You arrogant, conceited, two-timing bastard.'

Lucas raised a hand to his cheek, and rubbed where she had hit him. 'Perhaps I deserved that, so I'll let you get away with it, Amber, but only once,' he declared grimly. 'Accept it is over between us and move on. I have.'

She watched the dark stain appear on his cheek where she had hit him, and immediately regretted her action. Involuntarily she raised her hand, intending to stroke the side of his face, but her wrist was caught in an iron grip. 'No.'

She moved forward and lifted her other hand to rest on the soft wool sweater covering his broad chest. 'I'm sorry,' she murmured. But the familiar feel of his hard muscles beneath her fingers sent shivers of delight arcing though her body. She loved this man with all her heart, and helplessly she tilted back her head and looked up into his darkly attractive face. 'Please, Lucas.' She felt him stiffen, and she moved even closer, and slid her hand up over his chest and around the nape of his neck.

'We are so good together, Lucas, you know we are.' It had been two long months since she had felt the warmth of his caress and she ached for him. Suddenly she was fighting for her man, and using every skill at her disposal. She saw his pupils dilate as her breasts brushed against his hard chest, and involuntarily her fingers trailed with tactile delight up through the hair at the back of his neck. 'Kiss me, Lucas, you know you want to.' Gently she urged his head down towards her eager lips.

'No, Amber.' His large hands gripped her shoulders to push her away just as she brushed her lips against his, the tip of her tongue darting out to gain access to his mouth. She heard the intake of his breath as his arms jerked her to him and their bodies met in searing contact, and she was lost in the dark, heady hunger of the kiss for an instant, before his hands caught her shoulders and he forced her back at arm's length.

Lucas Karadines didn't like the way she affected him. His dark eyes glittered dangerously. His own mother had been addicted to sex, one lover after another until she'd died. Her last lover had kicked a young boy of thirteen out on the street. So he fought the temptation and won. 'You are a very sexy lady, Amber, but I am not such a bastard as to take what you're offering. It's over.'

'But if you want a wife, why not me? I love you, Lucas, and I thought you loved me,' Amber pleaded, raising an unsteady hand and tenderly brushing a few black silky strands of his hair from his brow. 'I could give you children, anything you want.' She was laying her heart, her life, on the line, begging him. She had lost all pride, all anger, and she didn't care. She looked deep into his dark eyes, her own beseeching his. She thought she saw a flicker of uncertainty in the depths of his, but she was mistaken.

'No, Amber.' A grim smile twisted the corners of his sensual mouth. 'I never lied to you—I never once mentioned love.'

His words lashed her like a whip flailing her alive; she closed her eyes for an instant, searching her mind. He was

right, he had never said he loved her. How had she made
such an enormous mistake? His hands fell from her shoulders and she opened her eyes. She could actually see him
mentally withdrawing from her as he physically moved
back a step.

'You are a lovely girl, but you are not the wife and
mother type.' His breathing was heavy but his dark eyes
held unmistakable, unyielding will-power. 'You're a career woman—you compete in a male-dominated industry,
and you are as good as, if not better than, most of the men,
by all accounts. You wouldn't last six months as a stay-
at-home wife. You would be bored out of your skull. So
don't fool yourself, Amber. You're strictly lover material.'

She listened with growing horror. 'Is that really what
you think?' she muttered sickly. 'All this time you saw
me as your lover, a sex object, nothing else.'

He shrugged his broad shoulders. 'The term is not important. What we shared was a mutually agreeable relationship.' His dark eyes skimmed over her shapely figure
and he made no effort to hide his masculine appreciation.
'And great sex.'

His deliberate sensual scrutiny made her breasts swell
in instant awareness, and hot colour flooded her cheeks
and he noticed. 'Be honest, Amber, you're no shy young
maid, never were. You're a born hedonist, you thrive on
sensual pleasure, the pleasure I gave you. But you're a
sophisticated lady—admit it, if we have spent six months
together since we met it would be a miracle, and that
mostly in bed. Ours was a sexual relationship, nothing
more.'

For him maybe, but for Amber it had been everything.
She only had to look at him to remember the powerful
strength of his all-male body when he possessed her, ca-

ressed her. 'Nothing more,' she parroted his words with horror.

'Exactly.' He sounded relieved, actually believing she had agreed with him. And blithely carried on adding insult to injury. 'But Christina is different. She is sweet and innocent and has no desire to do anything other than be my wife, and bear my children.'

Her teeth had bitten into her bottom lip as she listened to him praise his Christina, and the salty tang of blood coated her tongue. 'I was innocent until you seduced me,' she reminded him, the hurt almost too much to bear. He knew she'd been a virgin when he'd first made love to her. She had given him the greatest gift a woman could give a man, her heart, body and soul, and he had the gall to label her a hedonist...

'Ah, Amber...' He shook his dark head in a mocking gesture. 'You know as well as I do that it was no great moral conviction that kept you a virgin. It was probably the fact you had spent the last four years living with a couple of gay men and their friends and hadn't much opportunity. You would have jumped into bed with me the first day you arrived at the villa.' Lucas shot her a cynical smile. 'With your minuscule bikinis, and designer clothes, you were no retiring violet. You were desperate for a man, and it was my restraint, my strict rule not to take on a new lover without first leaving the old that meant we waited until I had got back from New York. Seduction did not come into it.'

'I see.' And she did... She closed her eyes for a brief moment, blocking out the picture of his hard, cynical face, her hands clenching into fists at her sides. He thought of her as a sexy woman who had been easy to take, who could respond to any man's caress with equal fervour, not just his. Eagerly she had followed where he'd led, plunging the erotic depths with a hunger that had known no bounds, confident that he'd loved her, and everything had been permissible between two lovers. Her own innate honesty forced her to admit it was not all his fault. She had deliberately set out to appear to be the sort of woman she'd imagined he wanted. 'Hoist by her own petard' was the phrase that sprang to mind... Lucas did not know her at all, never had, and, worse, did not want to.

'Tell me, Lucas, if I had held out for a ring, would you have married me?' Amber demanded, black anger filling her heart at his chauvinistic attitude, never mind his betrayal.

He stared at her, his hard mouth suddenly cruel. 'With you the question would never arise. If you remember, I did ask you to give up work so we could spend more time together, and you could not even do that. So the answer is no. You're a thoroughly modern woman, equal to a man, you work hard and play hard.'

'And your Christina is not?' She arched one delicate brow in a gesture of mocking disbelief. 'A year in Switzerland, all those hunky ski instructors,' she taunted him, the memory of the young girl's conversation last night still clear in her mind.

That appeared to catch him on the raw, and for a moment he looked almost savage. 'Leave Christina out of this,' he ordered curtly. ' You disappoint me, Amber, I did not think you could sink so low as to maliciously malign a young girl's reputation, a girl you hardly know,' he drawled contemptuously.

Amber stared at his hard, cold face, willing herself not to feel hurt by his immediate defence of the girl. Then it hit her. 'You've never slept with Christina, and you think you love her. I'm right, aren't I?' she demanded, not sure whether to laugh or cry. Lucas Karadines, a powerful, dynamic businessman viewed with fear and awe by his competitors, was fooled by a pseudo-innocent eighteen-year-old going on eighty.

'Yes, I love Christina, and I am going to marry her.' He gave the only answer he could. He wasn't sure he believed in love. His mother had fallen in *love* with depressing regularity, when basically it had been sex. He had no intention of making the same mistake. He had chosen carefully and made the commitment to Christina and both of their families in traditional Greek fashion, and he was determined to honour it and make his marriage a success.

Amber stared at him. Oh, heavens, she silently screamed. It was true. She saw the absolute sincerity in his dark eyes, heard it in the tone of his voice, and was convinced. Never mind business, Lucas honestly thought he loved the girl. Her shoulders drooping, she closed her eyes for a second, all the fight draining out of her, and a dull acceptance taking its place. 'I suppose I'd better go and pack.'

'No.' Lucas caught her shoulder and turned her back to face him. 'Sit down, Amber. I am not so unfeeling I would see you deprived of your home.'

It never was a home, he had made that abundantly clear, but her traitorous limbs gave way beneath her and she sank thankfully down onto the soft cushions. 'No.' Amber looked at him towering over her, with all the bitterness of her feelings in her eyes. 'Then what now, Lucas? If you're waiting for my blessing, you're wasting your time.' He was sliding something from the inside pocket of his jacket—a long manila envelope.

'You have no need to leave—I am going. I'll send someone round this afternoon to collect the few things I have here, and you'd better keep these—you will need them.'

The last half-hour had been the hardest of Lucas Karadines's life. It had taken all his monumental control not to take what Amber had been offering. He would not dare come back himself, because deep down he knew he would not be able to resist making love to her one more time. He dropped the envelope and his set of keys to the apartment down onto the sofa beside her. 'Goodbye, Amber.' He hesitated for a second, his night-black eyes lingering on her pale face. 'I'm...'

'Just go.' Her lips twisted; if he said sorry she would kill him. His dark head bent towards her and she felt the brush of his lips against her hair and flinched. She didn't need his pity. And, flinging her head back, she sat rigidly on the edge of the sofa, her golden eyes hating him.

Lucas straightened up. 'Look after yourself.' And, brushing past her, he headed for the door. He opened the door and paused, finally turning to add, 'By the way, if you're thinking of taking up the offer Clive Thompson made you, don't. The man is not to be trusted.'

A harsh laugh escaped her. 'It takes one to know one. Get out.' And, picking up a scatter cushion, she flung it at him. It bounced harmlessly off the closed door and fell to the floor.

Amber looked around her at the apartment that she had mistakenly thought was a home with new eyes, and groaned out loud. Lucas was right. How could she have been so stupid, so gullible? She had tried to add a few touches, the scatter cushions, a couple of framed photographs of her mother, and Tim. A painting she had bought on a trip around a gallery with Spiro. The rug was the only thing in the place that she and Lucas had chosen together. It was exactly as Lucas had said: a bachelor pad, or a love-nest.

She had to get out, she thought brutally. It didn't matter

where as long it was somewhere that did not remind her of Lucas. But first she had to pack up his clothes—hadn't he said he was sending someone over to collect them?

She jumped to her feet and the manila envelope fell from her knee to the floor; she bent down and picked it up. Slitting open the envelope, she withdrew a folded document. She read it, her eyes widening in amazement that quickly turned to fury. Her first thought was to rip it up, but she hesitated... The paper dropped from her hand to flutter back to the floor.

It was the deeds for the apartment in her name, and it was dated two weeks ago. She felt sick and defiled; he had paid her off like some cheap whore. Perhaps not cheap, she amended, but her fury knew no bounds. She marched into the kitchen and took the scissors from the kitchen drawer, and then headed straight upstairs. With grim determination she slid back the wardrobe door. Earlier she had run her hands over Lucas's clothes, in need of reassurance. Now she touched them for a completely different reason.

Working quickly, Amber emptied the wardrobe and drawers of every item that belonged to Lucas, and packed them in one suitcase. That told her something. Her mouth tightened in a rare grimace of cynicism. If she had needed any further convincing that Lucas had considered her nothing more than a convenient bed partner, the fact that he had left so few clothes in the place she had thought was his home said it all.

When a little man called a few hours later and asked for Mr Karadines's luggage she handed over the suitcase without a word, and closed the door in the man's face. She only wished she could close the door to her heart as firmly on the memory of Lucas Karadines.

*   *   *

A few hours later on the other side of London, Lucas Karadines stood in the middle of his hotel bedroom and stared in fury at the pair of trousers his father's valet was holding out to him.

'I'm afraid, sir, I've checked, and all three suits in the luggage I collected from the lady's apartment are the same.' The little wizened man was having the greatest difficulty keeping the smile from his face. 'The fly panel has been rather roughly cut out of all of them.'

A torrent of Greek curses turned the air blue as Lucas stormed across the room and picked up the telephone and began pressing out the number he knew by heart. Then suddenly he stopped halfway through, and replaced the receiver. No, there was no point—Amber was out of his life and he wanted it to stay that way. But a reluctant smile quirked the corners of his firm mouth. He should have expected some such thing. Amber was a passionate character in every way; it was what had drawn him to her in the first place. A shadow darkened his tanned features as he instructed the valet to press another suit. With brutal honesty he recognised Amber had some justification. She should never have discovered by a third party their relationship was over, and certainly not in so public a manner.

CHAPTER FOUR

CARRYING her mug of coffee, Amber made her way to the kitchen. Draining the last dregs, she rinsed the cup in the sink, and dried it with the tea towel.

It was little more than a week since Lucas had told her he was marrying Christina and walked out of her life. She had gone to work as usual, and she had waited. Waited and hoped for a miracle—for Lucas to change his mind. But by Wednesday she had bowed to the inevitable and set the wheels in motion to move out of the apartment. And if in the deepest corner of her heart hope lingered, she ignored it.

When Spiro had called her Sunday afternoon from Athens, confirming that the engagement party of Lucas Karadines and Christina Aristides the previous evening had been a great success, it was simply the final nail in the coffin that held all her dreams.

If she needed any more confirmation, she only had to look at this morning's newspaper lying on the kitchen bench open at the gossip page. A picture of the couple was prominently displayed. She crushed up the paper and wrapped the coffee mug in it. Then she carefully placed it on the top of the rest of the kitchen implements already packed in the large tea chest that sat in the middle of the kitchen floor. Finished...

She had applied on Friday to have today, Monday, off work, because realistically she'd known she would be moving out. Everything was packed, the For Sale sign had been erected an hour earlier by the carpenter employed by the estate agent she had consulted to dispose of the apartment. She could not live in it, and the proceeds would help some charity. She did not care any more.

Since the night at the London hotel, and the sleepless nights since, she had gone beyond feeling pain into a state of complete detachment. It was not completely Lucas's fault. She should have remembered 'To thine own self be true.' She had transformed herself virtually overnight into a sophisticated lady in her determination to win Lucas, and that was how he had seen her. She had never let him see the naive young country girl she had been, who just happened to have a gift for figures. Now it was too late. He had fallen in love with someone else, and she would never be that girl again anyway.

On Saturday she'd made a start on getting her life back. She had rented a small cottage with a garden in the village of Flamstead, within manageable commuting distance of the City. Amber recognised she had loved unwisely and too much, but she had silently vowed no man would ever be able to hurt her like that again.

Amber walked back into the living room, and glanced at the gold watch on her wrist. The removal firm was due to arrive at three. Another two hours to kill.

The telephone was still connected: she could call Tim, but she had no desire to talk to him or Spiro for that matter. She was still mad at Spiro's revelation yesterday that, at the engagement party, for a joke he had hinted to his grandfather and Lucas that his engagement to Amber might be next. Spiro was a wickedly mischievous devil— he could not help himself.

She heard the knock on the front door and sighed with relief. Good, the removal men were early, almost unheard of in London. Walking over to the door, she opened it, the beginnings of a smile curving her generous mouth. At last something was going her way. Her smile vanished, her mouth falling open in shock as she found herself staring into the hard black eyes of Lucas Karadines.

Her first instinct was to slam the door in his face but he anticipated her action by brushing past her and into the centre of the room.

Mechanically, she closed the door behind him. 'What do you want?' she demanded, her mind spinning, fighting to control the tremor in her voice and the swift surge of hope his appearance aroused in her. On a completely feminine note Amber wished she were wearing something better than a battered old cotton shirt and a pair of scruffy black leggings from her student days.

Spinning around to face her, Lucas regarded her silently for what seemed an interminable length of time, but Amber quickly gathered from the harsh expression on his dark, slightly saturnine features that he had certainly not sought her out for reconciliation.

'I said, what do you want?' she repeated coolly. He looked dynamic and infinitely masculine, his casual jeans and heavy wool sweater barely detracting from the raw vitality of the man. His eyes didn't leave hers for a second, and she began to feel a rising tide of bitter resentment as the blood raced through her veins in the old familiar way.

'I want to study what a woman scorned really looks like,' Lucas stated with studied indolence, his eyes raking over her from the top of her head, over her face, her hair hanging loose about her shoulders, down over the firm thrust of her breasts clearly outlined against the fine cotton, then lower to her slim hips and long legs perfectly moulded by the black leggings. His narrowed gaze rested on her bare feet, then back to her face.

'I ignored the destruction of a few suits,' he drawled silkily, taking a step towards her.

She swallowed painfully, colour flooding her cheeks. She'd forgotten about her futile attempt at revenge: the mangled suits, and all the gifts he had ever given her flung on top. But it was as nothing to what he had done to her. Her head lifted fractionally. Pride uppermost. 'You can afford it,' she snapped.

One eyebrow lifted slightly. 'A bagatelle, I grant you, compared to the price of this apartment. I see you have wasted no time in trying to sell it,' he opined silkily and moved closer. 'I ignored the insult intended by the return of the presents I gave you.' And, catching hold of her hand, he drew her towards him, despite the struggle she made to break free. His glance spearing her ruthlessly, he added, 'But I will never allow you to marry Spiro simply so he can get his hands on his inheritance before he is of age. I'll see you in hell first.'

The statement was quiet and deadly, and Amber suddenly realised his temper was held in check by a tenuous thread. 'Let go of me,' she demanded, her own anger rising. as she tried to escape his steel-like grasp.

'I will when I have your promise you will stay away from Spiro.'

She almost laughed out loud. Lucas actually thought Spiro had been serious when he had voiced the prospect of marrying her to his grandfather. But she saw no reason to make it easy for Lucas. How dared he come here and threaten her?

'I can live with who I like and I can marry who I like, and it has damn all to do with you. In case you have forgotten, you are engaged to be married. In fact, I am amazed you could tear yourself away from the arms of your fiancée so quickly after your betrothal. Not as passionate as you hoped, hmm?' she prompted. 'Now, let go of my arm and get lost.' And with a fierce tug she freed her wrist from his grasp and swiftly stepped around him, heading for the stairs.

With an angry oath he spun around and caught the back of her shirt, bringing her to an abrupt halt. She strained forwards and he tugged harder so she fell back against him, the buttons popping off her shirt at the rough treatment. She tried to elbow him in the stomach. But he quickly turned her around and held her hard against the long length of his impressive frame. She began to struggle in earnest, striking out at him with her fists, making little impression on the broad, muscular wall of his chest.

'Let go of me, you great brute.' Her temper finally exploded. 'I know your game. Not content with marrying a poor kid half your age for her father's business, you're so bloody greedy that you're terrified Spiro will manage to get his hands on his half of the business. God, you make me sick!' she told him furiously.

Her wrists were caught and held together with effortless ease behind her in one large hand, his dark eyes leaping with rage as they burned into hers. 'You foul-mouthed little bitch! You would marry a man you know is gay simply to get back at me.'

'Don't flatter yourself,' she jeered. 'I don't give a toss about you.'

'But you enjoyed what I could give you,' he said harshly as though he wasn't really making a statement but remembering. 'Something Spiro is not capable of.'

If Amber had not known better, she might have thought he was jealous on a personal level, but she knew he was only worried about retaining complete control of the company. Once Spiro came of age, heaven knew what he would do with his share. He was a loose cannon in the business sense, her own intelligence told her that. But it was still no reason for Lucas to try and bully her.

'How would you know what Spiro is capable of?' she taunted him. 'He could be bisexual. But it does not really matter because Spiro is a friend, and with you for an uncle he needs all the friends he can get,' she opined scathingly.

'And of course you have no ulterior motive in befriending Spiro,' Lucas drawled cynically. 'What did my nephew promise you for marrying him—a percentage of his inheritance, or is it pure, old-fashioned revenge you're after?'

He towered over her, dwarfing her not inconsiderable height. Suddenly she became aware of the hard heat of his body. His aroused body! Her eyes clashed with his, and his darkened as the chemistry between them renewed itself with frightening force.

'Certainly not his body, we both know that is not his scene,' Lucas drawled huskily, his dark gaze moving down to the luscious outline of her lips.

Amber could not help it. She regarded him hungrily, his harshly etched features as familiar to her as her own. She lowered her eyes in case he might see the need, the hunger flooding through her, and suddenly she became aware that in the struggle her shirt had come open almost to her waist. One firm breast was completely exposed, the other only partially covered. But she was not alone in her discovery; Lucas's sharply indrawn breath and something in his eyes that had always warned her in the past of his stirring hunger for sex made her tremble. His free hand slid cool fingers down her flushed cheeks, circling the outline of her full mouth.

Amber realised she should be fighting him, but could only gaze at him mesmerised as his hand captured the gentle curve of her nape, and electric tension filled the air.

'*Christos!* But you probably could turn Spiro!' He laughed harshly. 'You are sinfully sexy.' His gaze swept down to her bare breasts, and her nipples peaked in telling arousal; she was incapable of hiding her response to him. In that second Lucas knew he should never have come back here—she was utterly irresistible.

Speechless, Amber remained pinned against him, her pulse racing wildly out of control, and suddenly she realised with blinding clarity she did not want to hide her response. The musky scent of masculine arousal teased her nostrils, and, as she felt the muscles of his powerful thighs pressing against her, she tilted back her head and saw his eyes were all black pupil, his desire a primitive need as great as her own. Involuntarily her back arched ever so slightly, lifting her breasts to greater prominence.

She heard his guttural curse a moment before his mouth found hers, kissing her with a bruising, demanding hunger, grinding her lips back against her teeth. A wild, basic recklessness filled her, and she responded with a fiery fervour, her mouth opening to his. She forgot he was engaged to another. She forgot he had betrayed her. There was only the moment…

He kissed her with a searing passion, and she shuddered, responding to his passion, matching it with her own. The kiss they exchanged was primitive and out of control. Every bit of Amber burned with a need, a hunger that was almost pain, and when he trailed sharp, biting kisses down her throat and finally closed his teeth over one pouting nipple she whimpered, but not with pain.

Her hands were set free, and instead of pushing him away she gloried in her freedom to touch him. Her hands worked frenziedly beneath his sweater. Lucas helped her by lifting his head and tearing his sweater off, before hauling her back against him. Her fingers traced over the breadth of his chest, finding the hard male nipples in the silky mat of hair and doing some tantalising of her own.

It had been months and she hadn't realised how needy she had been.

Lucas lifted her high in his arms and laid her down on the hardwood floor in one smooth motion. 'Damn you, Amber,' he growled, following her down, his chiselled features dark with passion.

His words hurt and angered her, but nothing could stop the storm of desire sweeping through her. He removed her leggings and briefs with enviable ease, while Amber fumbled with the belt of his trousers; quickly he guided her hands and in a second he was almost naked.

She heard the sharp intake of his breath as her fingers slid along his thigh and his mouth ground down on hers with furious greed. Their bodies met with a searing impact that made her shudder with pleasure.

Lucas lifted his head, his black eyes sweeping almost violently over her naked body. His head bent and he suckled the hard, aching peak of her breast as swiftly he parted her legs. Every other time he had enjoyed making love to her long and slow, teasing and tantalizing, drawing out the experience for ages. But this time it was like a dam bursting, sweeping everything before it, as without hesitating he positioned himself between her slender thighs and joined them fiercely together.

Amber gasped and writhed, half mad with wanting him, the hardness of the floor, the anger not love that fuelled the joining—none of it mattered. It was enough he was here with her—in her—and if it was to be the last time, she didn't care. He wanted her.

Hot and breathless bodies wet with sweat, they moved together in a mind-blowing, consuming passion. The climax when it came was a shuddering ecstatic release that lifted Amber to another universe, where her mind closed down, and the body was everything. The ecstatic shivers went on and on long after Lucas lay heavily on top of her, the rasping sound of his breathing the most wonderful music to Amber's ears.

She refused to believe he could behave like this with her and yet love someone else, and when he moved to roll off her she followed him around. Sprawled across his wide chest, still joined, she looked into his darkly flushed handsome face, but his eyes were closed.

'Lucas,' she tenderly murmured his name, and, reaching up, she brushed the sweat-slicked hair from his brow. Slowly his eyes opened and he looked at her with such contempt she almost cried out.

'Amber,' he grated, mockingly brushing her off him as if he were swatting a fly and jumping to his feet, as though he could not get away from her quickly enough.

She lay where he had left her and watched him. He had not removed his shoes, and he should have looked stupid with his trousers around his ankles, but he didn't. She let her eyes stray over every perfect inch of his bronzed body, committing every curve and muscle, pore and hair to memory, because she instinctively knew this was the very last time she would ever see him this way.

His dark eyes wandered insolently over her as he pulled up his trousers. The taut line of his mouth gave way to a thin, cruel smile. '*Christos.*' He laughed harshly, and slipped his sweater over his head. Adjusting the sleeves, he added, 'I was right about you—as sexy as sin and far too seductive to wed.'

Lucas knew he was being cruel, but it was a pure defence mechanism. He could not believe what he had just done! He had lost control completely, and he hated himself for it. He was strongly puritanical when it came to women, totally monogamous for as long as the relationship lasted, and he had every intention of being totally faithful to his wife. Hell! He almost groaned out loud. Betrothed three days to Christina, and already…

'You're no saint,' Amber's voice cut into his tortured thoughts.

His black eyes roamed over her lovely face, her cheeks burning with angry colour. She was exquisite, and briefly he closed his eyes, a deep black pit opening up before him, his supreme self-confidence shaken to its core as for a moment he doubted his decision to marry Christina. He opened his eyes. It was too late now. He was Greek, first and foremost, he was engaged to a Greek girl, his father was delighted, Christina's father was ecstatic. He had made the right decision. It was simply he had been celibate for too long, he told himself, and *almost* believed it…

'So much for your moral code, off with the old before the new,' Amber declared fiercely, breaking the tension-filled silence, and, sitting up, she pulled the shirt that was hanging off her back around her chest.

He smiled down at her mockingly, forcing himself not to weaken. 'Oh, for heaven's sake, get dressed.' If she didn't he was in grave danger of falling down on top of her again, eyeing her flustered attempt to pull her shirt around the luscious curve of her breasts. Shame and guilt made him add, 'You disgust me. I disgust myself.'

Amber bowed her head for a moment, the long curtain of her hair hiding her face from his glittering gaze. She squeezed her eyes tightly shut to hold back the tears. She disgusted him, he had said, and yet she was only what he had made her, and in that instant the new Amber was born.

Swiping back the mass of hair from her face, she rose to her feet. Ignoring Lucas's looming presence, she picked up her briefs and leggings and, turning her back on him, took her time about putting them on. Then, straightening her shoulders, she turned to face him.

She lifted hard golden eyes to his. 'What are you waiting for?' she demanded bluntly. She was furiously angry at the undisguised contempt in his expression. But she refused to show it. 'I thought a man of your high moral values would be long gone,' she mocked him. She had learnt her lesson well. Never again in this life, she vowed, would she show any man how she really felt.

'The floor show is over,' she said facetiously. 'If you're hoping for a repeat performance, forget it—go back to Christina and I wish you both joy. Though I have a suspicion you will not find her quite the pure, malleable little bed partner and wife you imagine. After all, she already knows you have a mistress—' she wanted to hurt him, dent his arrogant pride '—and she doesn't care, which must tell you something.'

She had gone too far. He stepped towards her, his hand lifted as if to hit her. Involuntarily she flinched and stepped back.

'No.' His hand fell to his side, his fingers curling into a fist, his knuckles white with strain. 'You are a lying little bitch.' Amber knew he would never believe her or forgive her for her comments. 'And you will never speak to my fiancée or mention her name again.'

Amber stared at him, her anger dying fast as his glance roamed contemptuously over her. There was sheer hatred in his eyes, and a clear message he would not touch her again if his life depended on it. But then she already knew that, she thought sadly. The last half-hour had been nothing more than animal attraction fuelled by rage on his part. He didn't want her love, never had… The realisation was the end of everything for Amber. 'Just go,' she said wearily, brushing past him towards the door. Good manners decreed she see him out, she thought, and had to choke back hysterical laughter.

She opened the door and held it. Lucas reached out to grasp her arm, but she pulled away. 'Goodbye, Lucas.' The finality in her tone was unmistakable.

He went rigid. 'Not so fast, you still have not given me the promise I asked for. I...I want your word you will not marry Spiro.'

She was sick at heart and halfway to being physically sick. 'Okay.'

'I mean it, Amber,' Lucas said with deadly emphasis. 'If you marry him your life will not be worth living, and you will find no solace in your work, that I promise.' The taut line of his mouth gave way to a thin cruel smile as he paused. 'I will personally make sure no one in the financial world will ever employ you again.' He had to convince her for his own sanity to break all ties with Spiro. If the last hour had taught him anything it was that there was no way on God's earth Lucas trusted himself to be in the company of Amber ever again. Not even a simple social occasion, or he was in danger of succumbing to the same sickening addiction to sex his mother had suffered from. The realisation of his own weakness shocked and horrified him, and he reacted with the same icy determination that made him a ruthlessly successful businessman. 'I will totally destroy the career you love, and, believe me, I can and will do it.'

It was no idle threat, and the really scary part was that Amber had no doubt he could destroy her career with a few chosen words to her most influential clients. 'Your threat is unnecessary. I have no intention of marrying Spiro.'

Amber's golden gaze roamed over Lucas as though she were seeing him for the first time. He stood in the entrance door, tall and broad and as still as a statue carved in stone. She registered the soft wool sweater moulding the muscles of his broad chest, the hip-hugging jeans. Raising her gaze, she noted the thick black hair, the broad forehead, the perfectly chiselled features—he was incredibly handsome, but his face was hard, cold, the inner man hidden. One thumb casually hooked his leather jacket over a shoulder, but there was nothing casual about the man. Spiro had called him a shark and Amber finally realised it was true.

It was a revelation to Amber's bruised heart. Lucas thought he loved Christina, but it was not what Amber considered love to be. It was no great consuming passion on Lucas's part, he was incapable of the emotion. He had simply planned to fall in love with Christina with the same ruthless efficiency he planned a takeover bid. Christina simply met his criteria for a wife. Amber's golden eyes met his, black and not a glimmer of human warmth in their depths, just a ruthless determination to succeed be it business or private, family or friend. He was incapable of differentiating between them. How had she ever thought she loved this cold, frighteningly austere man?

'If you knew your nephew a little better, or at all,' Amber said softly, one perfectly arched brow lifting eloquently, 'you would have realised he was only winding you up when he said it. Now please go.'

With the door closed behind him, Amber silently added, If Lucas allowed anyone to know him, he might possibly develop into a halfway decent human being. But she had a suspicion he never had, and he was too old to change now.

Three weeks later in the same Monday morning paper Amber viewed the wedding photo of Lucas and Christina with a cynical smile. She read the gossip that went with it, the gist of it being that there were great celebrations at the high society wedding in Athens and the joining together of two great Greek families, not to mention the amalgamation of two international corporations to make one of the top leisure companies in the world.

Amber settled into her small house, bought a neat Ford car to drive into work, and as the days and weeks went past tried to put her disastrous love affair out of her mind. During the day she could block Lucas out of her thoughts with work. But at night she was haunted by memories of the sheer magic of his lovemaking—only it hadn't been love, she had to keep reminding herself, and then the tears would fall. The only thing that kept Amber from a nervous breakdown over the next year was her growing relationship with her father. The news she had wanted to tell Lucas so eagerly, after lunching with Sir David Janson.

Two weeks after Lucas Karadines had left her, Amber had met Sir David again for lunch at a restaurant in Covent Garden. Much to Amber's surprise his wife Mildred had accompanied him. It could have been embarrassing, but Mildred quickly explained she did not blame her husband or Amber's mother. At the time Mildred had left her husband and two children and had lived with another man for over a year. Sir David had found solace with his secretary and Amber was the result.

Sir David quite happily acknowledged Amber as his daughter, saying a certain notorious Member of Parliament had recognised an illegitimate daughter without any ill effect, so why shouldn't he? It was a one-day wonder in the papers, and his family—a married daughter and a much older son—were equally welcoming.

But Amber refused to take a job with her father's company. Her feminine intuition told her she shouldn't. Sir David's son, Mark Janson, accepted her in the family, but as heir apparent to the business he was nowhere near so happy about having her in his father's firm. Especially as Sir David told all and sundry Amber had obviously inherited her skill in the money markets from him.

CHAPTER FIVE

FIVE years later...

As Monday mornings went, this had to be one of the worst, Amber thought sadly. She'd just returned from two weeks' holiday in Tuscany at her father's villa feeling relaxed, and revitalised. June in Italy was beautiful; unfortunately June in London was rain, the stock market had dropped three per cent, and now this...

Her long fingers tapped restlessly on the document lying on the desk. She'd read the letter countless times, but she still could not quite believe it. The letter was from a firm of lawyers in New York, the lawyers dealing with the estate of the late Spiro Karadines. It was dated eleven days ago. Spiro had died the day before, apparently, and it was informing her of the time and place of his funeral in Greece, and a legal document in the usual lawyer speak that 'Amber Jackson may learn something to her advantage'. Amber didn't think so... Spiro was trouble...

A sad, reminiscent smile curved her wide mouth. It was four years since she'd last seen him, and they had not parted on the best of terms.

She had gone to New York for the grand opening of his art gallery. Spiro had been so excited as he had shown Amber around the exhibition. It had been incredible, or perhaps unbelievable was a better word, Amber had thought privately. Spiro had told her the artists whose work was on display were all up and coming in the modern art world. To Amber's untrained eyes it looked more as if they had been and gone... Gone crazy...

'Are you sure about this stuff?' she had asked Spiro, recoiling from a massive red and green painting that appeared to be bits of body parts.

'Yes, don't worry, in half an hour people will be fighting over these paintings. Trust me!'

Her smooth brow pleated in a frown as she fiddled with the letter on her desk. She'd trusted Spiro when he had assured her that if she gave him the money from the sale of the loft apartment to start his art gallery, he would never tell Lucas, and return it with interest when he came into his inheritance a year later. He had persuaded her that charity could wait, and, being honest, Amber admitted she had thought it was poetic justice, letting Spiro have the money as it was Karadines money after all. He had also told her Lucas would not be at the opening. Spiro had lied on both counts...

Although it had been over a year since she'd last seen Lucas, the gut-wrenching pain she had felt when she'd turned around from viewing the 'Body Parts' painting to find him, and Christina his wife, his *pregnant* wife, standing behind her had been almost unbearable.

She'd glanced at Spiro, and seen the devilment in his eyes, and known he had done it deliberately. Shifting her gaze to the couple, she'd made the obligatory greeting portraying a sophistication she had not felt. She'd even managed to congratulate the pair on their forthcoming happy event. But she'd been shaken so badly she'd had to clasp her hands behind her back to hide their trembling.

But Lucas had had no such problem. His eyes had slid over her with cool insolence, stripping away the stylish green silk sheath dress she'd worn to the flesh beneath, but Amber had forced herself to withstand his scrutiny, and done some scrutinising of her own. Thick dark hair had curled down over the collar of his impeccably tailored light linen suit, he'd been leaner than he had been the last time she had seen him, his features slightly more fine drawn, but as devastatingly attractive as ever, until he'd spoken.

'It seems congratulations are in order for you too, Amber. Spiro tells me you are his partner and put up most of the money for this little venture,' Lucas said smoothly. 'A remarkable achievement for a young woman. Your passion...' his hesitation was deliberate '...for finance must be truly exceptional,' he opined with mocking cynicism.

Amber felt the colour burn up under her skin. Lucas wasn't referring only to her passion for business. He obviously knew where the money had come from and for a moment she felt like strangling Spiro. But instead she forced herself to look at Lucas. 'Luckily I seem to have a gift for it.' Amber stared at him, deliberately holding his eyes. 'But I'll never be in your league. Men have a certain ruthlessness...' and it was her turn to pause '...in business, women find hard to emulate.'

'Not all women,' Lucas said flatly, and Amber surprised what looked very much like a flicker of regret in his dark eyes before he turned his attention to his wife, and began a conversation in Greek, ignoring Amber completely.

Instead of being insulted Amber was glad to escape the attention of Lucas; breathing an inward sigh of relief, she turned away. It hurt her more than she wanted to admit to see the two of them so close, and she was going to have a very serious talk to her so-called partner. Spiro was talking animatedly to a guest in the now crowded gallery. He could wait!

Spying Tim, she'd begun to walk towards him when suddenly someone grabbed her bare arm. The tingling sensation of the long fingers on her bare flesh was electric. Lucas...

'What?' Amber snapped.

'Will you follow Christina to the rest room, make sure she is all right?' he asked, his expression one of deep concern, the worry in his dark eyes there for all to see as they tracked his wife heading for the powder room.

Amber did see. His request reinforced what she had tried to deny. Amazing for such a predatory male, Lucas, a man who was ruthless in the business world, a man whom she'd thought incapable of love, was actually madly in love with his wife.

'She is pregnant, not sick.' Amber shrugged off his hand and stalked away without looking back. Listening to Christina rhapsodising about Lucas and the soon-to-be family was the last thing she needed. Lucas was a fantastic lover, and, once Christina had discovered the wonder to be found in her husband's arms, she had to have fallen in love with him, even if she had not been at the beginning.

After a furious row with Spiro, Amber left New York the next day, and she had not seen or spoken to Spiro since. As for the money she had given him, she had written that off long ago.

With the benefit of hindsight Amber had come to realise that Lucas had been right about Spiro. She should never have given him the money, because within a week of the gallery opening Tim and Spiro had split up. Spiro had been having an affair with the artist of 'Body Parts'.

Tim had returned to England, and back to his home in Northumbria. Six months later he had received a brief note, not from Spiro, but from a New York clinic telling him to get himself tested. Spiro had been HIV positive, as had been the artist lover who had somehow forgotten to mention the fact!

Restlessly Amber swivelled around in her chair, and stared out of the plate-glass window of her office, not really seeing what was beyond. She felt guilty and half blamed herself for Spiro's illness. If she hadn't given him the money, he would not have gone to New York, and it might never have happened.

Tim was a successful wildlife artist living and working from his home in the north and perfectly healthy. He had told her over and over again, it was not her fault Spiro had done what he had. Tim firmly believed Amber and himself had both fallen victims to the charm of the Karadines men; it was that simple, and they had both had a lucky escape.

Swivelling back to face her desk, Amber picked up the telephone and dialled Tim's number in Thropton. He had a right to know Spiro was dead.

The conversation was not as difficult as she had expected. Tim was quite philosophical about it: the past was past—so they had lost a good friend, but in reality they had lost him years ago.

'You're right, Tim...' Suddenly her office door swung open and someone walked in unannounced. Amber lifted her head. Recognition was instant, her golden eyes widening in shock. 'I'll see you soon, love,' she finished her conversation, and replaced the receiver.

She was thankful she was sitting down because she doubted her legs would support her. Lucas Karadines... She didn't dare meet his cold black eyes, and, carefully taking deep breaths, she sought to calm her suddenly erratic pulse. She should have expected this as soon as she had read the line 'something to her advantage' she realised too late.

He was standing in the middle of her office as though he owned the place. Amber's first thought was that Lucas at forty-one looked little different than he had done when they had first met. His body beneath the conservatively tailored charcoal-grey suit was still lithe and firm, his face was still handsome, but the harsh symmetry of bones and flesh mirrored a cold bitterness that she had never noticed before. He looked lean and as predatory as ever, but he looked older, harder than she would have expected for a happily married man, was her second thought. The lines bracketing his mouth were deeper, the hair at his temples liberally streaked with silver. But nothing could detract from the aura of dynamic, vibrant male he wore like a powerful cloak, masking his ruthlessly chauvinistic nature. He would be a handsome devil to his dying day, Amber acknowledged wryly.

Amber felt colour creeping under her skin as he made no immediate attempt to either move or speak. His hands were slanted casually into his trouser pockets, accentuating the musculature of his long legs. His eyes were hooded so she could not tell what he was thinking as they slid slowly over her head and shoulders to where the collar of her blue silk blouse revealed a glimpse of cleavage. She fought the impulse to slip her suit jacket off the back of the chair and put it on. This was her office, and Lucas was the intruder, and as he made no attempt to break the tense silence between them she finally found her voice.

'What do you want?' she asked abruptly.

Lucas Karadines for the first time in his life was struck dumb. The instant tightening in his groin shocked him into silence. His body had not reacted this way in years. His memory of Amber had not done her justice. She'd matured into the most exquisitely beautiful woman he had ever seen. His dark eyes drank in the sight of her. The hair scraped back from her face only accentuated the perfection of her features, the elegant line of her throat, the shadowed cleft between her luscious breasts her conservative blouse could not quite hide.

'Not a great welcome for an old friend,' Lucas finally murmured, his dark eyes gleaming with mockery, before scanning the elegant office. 'So this is your domain.'

A corner suite with windows on two sides, it was light and airy, and in keeping with her present position in the firm as the youngest partner, and Amber was justifiably proud of her achievements. 'Obviously,' she said dryly.

'You have done well for yourself, but then I always said you would.' Lucas's glance skimmed lightly over her desk as he moved towards it, noting her hand still on the phone. 'Sorry if I interrupted your conversation with your lover, but you and I have some pressing business to discuss.'

Her hand gripping the telephone was white-knuckled, and, realising she was betraying her shock, she smoothly slipped her hands to her lap and managed to smile coolly back at him. She was fiercely glad that the sophisticate she had pretended to be when they had first met was now a reality. She refused to be intimidated by Lucas—or any man, for that matter.

'I can't imagine we have anything to discuss, Mr Karadines. As far as I am aware you are a client of Janson's and I am not in the habit of poaching my father's clients.' It gave her great satisfaction to say it. Whether Lucas was aware Sir David was her father, she did not know. But she was making it abundantly clear he was not about to treat her like some inferior being to be discarded like yesterday's newspaper as he had before.

'Yes, I heard. I'm surprised you didn't choose to join Sir David's firm,' he opined smoothly. 'I seem to remember Clive Thompson was rather keen on the idea.'

'He still is,' Amber shot back, angry that Lucas had the nerve to remind her of that horrible party. 'But I like it at Brentford's and I don't believe in nepotism,' she said with a shrug. 'Nor mixing business with pleasure.' Let him make of that what he liked. She'd been dating Clive for the past year and part of the reason she had spent the last couple of weeks on holiday was to decide if she should accept Clive's proposal of marriage.

'Very wise of you. I dispensed with their services myself some months ago.'

That did surprise her. Neither Clive nor Mark, her half-brother, who had been the head of the firm since their father had retired two years ago, had mentioned the fact.

'I didn't know,' she said blandly, implying that she didn't really care.

'Now, if there is nothing further, I am rather busy.' Tilting back her head, she stared up at him, deliberately holding his eyes. 'And it is usual to make an appointment.' The sarcasm in her tone was very evident. 'I am a busy lady.'

Lucas was not the slightest bit fazed. 'I'm sure you are, Amber—a little too busy, it would seem.'

Amber raised her eyebrows. 'Too busy, says a man who was the most driven, competitive workaholic!' she mocked lightly. 'Marriage has changed you. How is the family? Well, I hope.' She was proud of her ability to ask the conventional question, and was surprised to realise it actually did not hurt at all.

Lucas stilled, his handsome face as expressionless as stone. 'I have no family. Spiro was the last—that is why I am here.'

Amber's face went white. Oh, God! In her shock at seeing Lucas again, she had forgotten all about Spiro's death. How could she have been so callous? 'I'm sorry, Lucas, truly sorry,' she hastened into an explanation. 'I only found out this morning. I've been on holiday, and the news hasn't really sunk in yet. I'm sorry I missed the funeral. Please sit down.' She indicated a chair at the opposite side of the desk with the wave of her hand. 'I'll order some coffee.' She was babbling, she knew, and, pressing for her secretary, she quickly asked Sandy to bring in two coffees.

He lowered his long length into the chair she had indicated. 'Cut out the phoney sympathy, Amber,' he commanded bluntly. 'We both know Spiro hated my guts, and the fact he left everything he possessed to you simply underlined the fact.'

'He what?' she exclaimed, her golden eyes widening in astonishment on Lucas's hard face, and what she saw in his night-black eyes sent a shiver of something very like fear quivering down her spine. 'No, I don't believe you,' she amended quickly. 'Spiro wouldn't.' Then she remembered the 'something to her advantage'.

'Yes, Spiro would, and did, and your innocent act does not impress me,' he said harshly. 'You knew damn fine you stood to inherit Spiro's share of the business.'

'Now wait just a minute—' Amber began, but at that moment Sandy walked in with the coffee.

Amber sat bristling with frustration as she watched her secretary, the girl's eyes awestruck as she asked Lucas breathlessly how he took his coffee.

'Black, please.' He favoured her with a broad smile and just sat looking dark and strikingly attractive until the flustered girl handed him a cup of coffee. 'Thank you.'

Amber thought Sandy was going to swoon. No wonder she had let Lucas in without an appointment. Even her secretary, who had only been married a few months, was not immune to Lucas's lethal male charm.

When Amber had first seen Lucas walk into her office she had been in shock, but now the shock had worn off, and another much more dangerous emotion was threatening her hard-won equilibrium. Lucas was a handsome devil and he still had the power to stir her feminine hormones.

Amber hastily picked up her cup of coffee and took a long drink of the reviving brew. The days were long gone when she was a slave to the sexual excitement Lucas could arouse with a mere look or touch. He had killed them dead when he had accused her of being an oversexed female, excellent lover material, but never a wife, and then had gone off and married Christina.

For months after his desertion her self-esteem had hit rock-bottom. She'd questioned her own worth; perhaps Lucas had been right about her. She was sex mad, the hedonist he had called her. She certainly had been when she'd been with him. In consequence she had, without really being aware of doing it, adjusted her style of dress to elegant but conservative—no short skirts, or revealing necklines. She wore little make-up and kept her long hair ruthlessly scraped back in a tight chignon, and she had no idea she looked even more desirable.

The door closing as Sandy left brought Amber back to the present with a start, and, straightening her shoulders, she was once again in command. She looked at Lucas with narrowed hostile eyes. 'I don't need you to tell me what I do or don't know,' she said curtly, and, picking up the letter from the desk, she held it out to him.

'Read that. I saw it for the first time this morning, and as yet I have not had time to respond, basically because I have an unscheduled guest. You.' His fingers brushed hers as he took the document from her outstretched hand, igniting a tingling sensation on her soft skin. Her golden eyes narrowed warily to his face, sure he had done it deliberately, but he was unfolding the document.

She waited as he read the letter, and then with slow deliberation folded the document back up again. 'This proves nothing,' Lucas said bluntly, dropping the letter back on her desk.

'I don't have to prove anything to you, Mr Karadines.' She shrugged dismissively. 'Now finish your coffee and leave. I have work to do.' Yes, Amber congratulated herself, she was back on track; the cool businesswoman. 'And when I get around to contacting the lawyers, and discover the true state of affairs, then if I need to get in touch with you, I will.' When hell freezes over, she thought silently. Standing up, she drained her coffee-cup and replaced it on the desk, before walking around heading for the door, her intention to show Lucas out as swiftly as possible.

'Well, well. The hard-bitten businesswoman act,' Lucas drawled sardonically, rising to his feet, and when she moved to pass him he reached out for her.

Amber felt every hair on her skin leaping to attention as his long fingers encircled her forearm. 'It is no act. Believe me!' she retaliated sharply. If he thought he was going to walk all over her again, he was in for a rude awakening.

'You don't fool me, Amber.' His voice dropped throatily, his fingers tightening ever so slightly on her arm. His eyes wandered over her in blatant masculine appraisal, taking in the prim neckline of her blue blouse, the tailored navy blue trousers that skimmed her slender hips and concealed her long legs to the classic low-heeled navy shoes, and then ever so slowly back to her face until she thought she would scream with the effort to remain cool and in control. 'You may dress like a conservative businesswoman, but it doesn't change what you are. I always knew you had a passion for sex, but it was only after we parted that I realised you had an equal passion for money,' he drawled cynically.

She wrenched her arm free from his hold, her whole

body rigid with anger. Just who the hell did he think he was? So now she was a gold-digger, as well as a sex maniac in his eyes... With the greatest effort of will, Amber managed to control her fury and say calmly, 'What exactly do you want, Lucas, barging into my office unannounced? I have neither the time nor the inclination for playing games. You obviously know something about Spiro's will, which concerns me. So just spit it out and then go.'

His eyes darkened, and for a moment Amber saw a flash of violent anger in their glittering depths, and she knew she had been right to feel threatened. Then he was smiling mockingly down at her. 'You used to like playing games,' he reminded her, his eyes cruel. 'Sexual games.' His finger lifted and stroked down the curve of her cheek.

'Cut that out,' she snapped, taking a deep, shuddering breath. 'You're a married man, remember.' Her golden eyes clashed with his, and as she watched it was like a shutter falling down over his face.

Lucas's hand fell from her face, his black eyes cold and blank. 'No, I am not. I told you before, I have no family.'

Confusion flickered in Amber's eyes. Had he? Then she remembered, but she had thought he'd meant Spiro. 'But what about Christina and your child?'

'The child was stillborn. My father died three years ago, and Christina was gone the next,' he informed her in clipped tones.

Her soft heart flooded with compassion, and unthinkingly she laid a hand on his arm in a tender gesture... Such tragedy must be heartbreaking even for a man as hard as Lucas. 'I am so sorry, Lucas, I had no idea.'

'These things happen...' he brushed her hand away '...and, as you never cared much for any of them, I can do without your hypocritical sympathy. I would ask you not to mention the subject again. Except for *Spiro*, of course,' he demanded with chilling emphasis.

Why was she wasting her sympathy on this man? Lucas meant nothing to her. He was simply another irritant in an already bad day, she told herself. So why did her cheek still burn where he had touched her, her pulse still race? It wasn't fair that one man could have such a terrible effect on her senses. She glanced up at him, and briefly his towering presence was a threat to her hard-won sophistication, then she casually took a step back.

'You want to talk about Spiro, fire away,' she said flatly, retreating behind her usual hard shell of astute businesswoman, and deliberately she lifted her wrist and scanned the elegant gold watch she wore. 'But make it quick, I have a lunch appointment.'

'You have changed, Amber.' His lips quirked in the semblance of a smile that did not quite reach his eyes. 'I can remember a time when you begged for my company, you couldn't get enough of me and pleaded with me to stay with you,' he said silkily.

The unexpected personal attack made her go white, a terrible coldness invading her very being that he could be so utterly callous as to mention the last time they had been alone together. 'I can't,' she denied flatly. He might even now make her heart race, but no way was she foolish enough to get personal with Lucas Karadines ever again.

'Liar.' He smiled sardonically. 'But I'll let it go for now, as you say you are busy, and we have a much more pressing item to discuss, *partner*.'

'Partner.' She bristled. What on earth was the man talking about? She'd rather partner a rattlesnake.

'All right, pretend you're innocent, I don't really care. But, put simply, the will Spiro made when you invested

in his art gallery made you his heir if anything happened
to him.'

'Oh, no!' Amber exclaimed, a horrible suspicion making her face pale. It couldn't be. But one look at Lucas's
dark countenance confirmed her worst fear. When she had
given Spiro the money he had insisted on making a will
naming her his heir as collateral for the loan, until he could
pay her back.

'Oh, ye-es,' Lucas drawled derisively. 'Spiro never
changed his will. You are now, or very soon will be, the
proud owner of a substantial part of Karadines.'

He was watching her with eyes that glittered with undisguised contempt and something else she could not put
a name to.

Amber simply stared at him like a paralysed porpoise,
her mouth hanging open in shocked horror. How typical
of Spiro. He would get a bee in his bonnet about something, do it and then forget all about it. His business sense
had always been negligible, but Amber hadn't seen it until
it was too late.

Lucas laughed, but there was no humour in it. 'Struck
dumb; how very typical of you. The silent treatment might
have worked for you in the past with Spiro,' Lucas
drawled, a smile creasing his firm mouth, 'but not this
time. I am a totally different male animal to my late
nephew.'

He'd got that right! Amber had a hysterical desire to
laugh—a more ruggedly aggressive macho male than
Lucas would be impossible to find. Her lips quirked, while
she damned Spiro for landing her in this mess.

'You find something amusing in this situation?' he challenged icily.

The ring of the telephone saved her from answering.
'Yes, Sandy, what is it?' she asked briskly. 'Clive.' She

glanced sideways at Lucas and caught a thunderous frown on his dark face.

'Tell him two minutes, my client is just leaving,' she informed Sandy before turning towards Lucas. 'My lunch date has arrived, I'm afraid I must ask you to leave.'

'Clive Thompson, I might have guessed—he was lusting after you the first time he met you,' Lucas opined bluntly. His dark eyes swept over her cynically. Her wide, oddly coloured gold eyes, and the full sensual lips that begged to be kissed. Her startling beauty combined with a slender yet curvaceous body was enough to make a grown man ache. Lucas was aching and he bitterly resented it. 'Obviously he has succeeded, but by your ringless fingers I see you have had no success getting him to the altar yet,' he taunted.

The arrogant bastard, Amber thought angrily. He was still of the opinion she was good enough to bed, but not to wed. Well, he was in for a big surprise.

'Ah, Lucas, that is where you are wrong.' Amber smiled a deliberately slow, sexy curve of her full lips. 'Clive appreciates my talents.' Let the swine make of that whatever his lecherous mind concluded. 'He has asked me to marry him, but I have yet to give him my answer—perhaps over lunch,' she said. 'So, if you will excuse me.'

He moved so fast Amber didn't have time to avoid him. One minute there were six feet of space between them, and the next she was hauled against the hard-muscled wall of his chest. Before she could struggle, one large hand slipped down over her buttocks, pressing hard against his thighs, and she felt the heat of him searing into her even through her clothes. 'No, I won't excuse you,' he rasped.

Amber's throat closed in panic. The years since they had last met might never have been. It was as if Lucas had rolled back time, his sexuality so potent that it fired her blood, making her once again the young girl who had been a slave to her senses. Then his dark head descended and he kissed her.

'Lucas, no,' she managed to croak as his mouth plundered hers, as he ground the tender flesh of her lips back against her teeth in a brutal travesty of a loving kiss. But even as she hated him, her body flooded with a feverish excitement and she fought the compulsion to surrender with every ounce of will-power she possessed, but it was not enough. The sexual chemistry between them had always been explosive. The years had not dulled the effect, and with a hoarse moan she responded. Lucas's hold relaxed as he sensed her surrender, and, realising how completely she had betrayed herself, she swiftly twisted out of his arms.

'Get out,' she ordered in a voice that shook, her arms folded protectively across her breasts as she put as much space between them as her office allowed.

'*Christo!* It was only a kiss—since when have you ever objected to a kiss?' he derided savagely. 'I was wrong, you haven't changed. You can't help responding. It is to be hoped Clive knows what he is taking on.'

The cruelty of his attack drove every last vestige of colour from her face.

His narrowed eyes studied her pale face for a long moment before a self-satisfied smile tilted the corners of his mouth. 'Well, well, you haven't told Clive about you and I.' He was far too astute; he had seen the answer in her lowered gaze.

Lifting her head, she looked straight at him. 'There is no you and I,' she declared angrily. 'There never was, as you were at great pains to point out when you married Christina.' Her eyes sparkled with cold defiance.

His temper rose as swiftly as her own. 'Leave Christina

out of this,' he commanded. 'And if you want Clive to stay in ignorance...' he paused, his narrowed gaze cold on her lovely face '...you will have dinner with me tonight. I will pick you up here at six and we will continue our talk. We have a lot to discuss.'

Panicked by his kiss, her lips tingling with the taste of him, Amber had forgotten Lucas's real reason for seeking her out. There was still the will to discuss...

'All right,' she said curtly. 'I'll check with New York this afternoon. The sooner this matter is settled, the better.' The thought of Lucas back in her life filled her with horror and fear.

'Amber, darling.' Clive strolled into the office, saw Lucas and stopped. 'Lucas Karadines.' And he held out his hand for Lucas to shake. 'Thinking of changing bankers yet again?' Clive asked conversationally.

'No, nothing like that. A private matter concerning my late nephew Spiro. Now, if you will excuse me...' Lucas glanced at Amber, his dark eyes holding a definite threat '...until later.' And he left.

Clive quickly crossed to Amber's side, and put a comforting arm around her shoulder. 'I forgot to tell you when I spoke to you yesterday. I heard about Spiro a week ago. I know he used to be a good friend of yours; it must have been a shock.'

A tragedy. A calamity that Amber had a sinking feeling was only going to get worse.

Lunch was a disaster. Amber toyed with the food on her plate, her mind in turmoil. One kiss from Lucas Karadines, and her carefully considered decision taken after two weeks in Italy to accept Clive's proposal of marriage was shot to hell...

Clive was very understanding when she told him she needed more time. But she saw the hurt in his blue eyes when they said goodbye outside her office building, and she hated herself for it. He was a true friend.

CHAPTER SIX

RETURNING from lunch, Amber stopped at her secretary's desk. 'Sandy...' she looked hard at the pretty brunette '...what possessed you to let Mr Karadines walk straight into my office? You know the rules. No one gets in unless they have an appointment, especially not Mr Karadines, you must inform me first. Do I make myself clear?'

'Sorry.' Sandy apologised and then grinned. 'But he said he was an old friend and he wanted to surprise you, and I couldn't resist. I thought you would be pleased. I know *I* would. Smart, charming and sexy as hell; what more could a girl want?'

'He is also a domineering, chauvinistic pig, with the mind-set of a medieval monarch,' Amber declared with a wry grin. Sandy was an excellent secretary but a hopeless romantic. 'Now get back to work,' Amber commanded and walked into her office, closing the door behind her. She couldn't blame Sandy. Lucas had a lethal charm that few women, if any, could resist...

A fax to New York was her first priority and then Amber spent all afternoon trying to work, but without accomplishing much. It was five in the afternoon when she finally received a reply to her fax. She read it, and groaned; her worst fear was confirmed. Lucas, damn him, was right! She was Spiro's sole heir, and clarification of what that entailed would follow by mail.

Amber did not need to know. She'd made up her mind that whatever Spiro had left her she would give to Lucas. She wanted nothing to do with Karadines ever again...

She'd been badly burnt once and only a fool put their hand in the flame a second time. Ruthlessly she squashed the wayward thought that Lucas was a single man once more. He probably wasn't, she thought dryly. Lucas had a powerful sex drive, he was not the sort to do without a woman for very long, and there were millions of women out there only too ready to fall into bed with the man.

She was walking out of her personal washroom when the telephone rang. Crossing to her desk, she pressed the button on the intercom to hear Sandy at her most formal announcing the arrival of Mr Karadines.

'Send him in,' Amber responded briskly.

A moment later with an exaggerated flourish Sandy flung the door wide open. 'Lucas Karadines.' Strolling past Sandy, Lucas gave the girl a smile and a thank-you.

Even though Amber was ready for him, her heart still missed a beat, and anger with herself made her tone sharp. 'Thanks, Sandy, you can leave now. I will see Mr Karadines out myself.'

'As I have no intention of leaving without you, your last statement was rather superfluous, wouldn't you say?' Lucas queried sardonically.

Amber forced herself to meet the mockery she knew would be in his eyes. 'Not at all. I think when you hear what I have to say, this meeting will be over in a few minutes.' She was slightly reassured when she realised he was still wearing the same charcoal suit as before. Like her, he had not bothered to change; with a bit of luck, she could avoid having dinner with him.

'Really?' he drawled silkily. 'You intrigue me.'

'Yes, well. I have checked with New York, you were right about Spiro's will. I don't have the details yet, but it does not matter, because I have decided to sign everything over to you.'

'Such generosity, Amber.' He was laughing at her, she could see it in the sparkle in his black eyes. 'But then you were always very generous, at least in one department,' Lucas drawled softly, a flick of his lashes sending his gaze skimming over her with deliberate sensual provocation.

She shivered, with what must be cold, she told herself as she stared at him in silence for a second, then lowered her gaze to the desk and picked up her briefcase. She was over Lucas. She had been for years. He had humiliated her, and caused her more pain than any woman should have to bear. So why? Why did the sight of him, the sound of him, still have the power to disturb her? With no answer, she continued as though he had never spoken.

'That being the case, I don't think there is anything for us to discuss at this time. When I am in possession of the full facts of Spiro's legacy, I'll have my lawyer contact yours as soon as possible.' Clutching her briefcase, she stepped forward, about to stalk past him, but his hand reached out and his fingers bit into her shoulder. Instinctively she froze.

'It is not that simple, Amber, and you promised to join me for dinner,' he reminded her pointedly. 'I'm holding you to that.'

She wanted to deny him, but his closeness, his hand on her shoulder were a brittle reminder of her own susceptibility to the man. She was not indifferent to Lucas, no matter how much she tried to deny it. Whenever he came near her she was rigid with tension. Her heart pounded and her mouth went dry, a throwback to the time they'd spent together, and something she'd thought she'd got over long ago.

'If you insist,' Amber managed to say coolly, and, shrugging her shoulder, she slipped from under his restraining hand. 'But it is totally unnecessary. I've told you, you can have the lot.'

'If only it were that easy. You're a businesswoman, Amber, you should know better,' Lucas opined sarcastically. 'But now is not the time to discuss it. Unlike you, I missed lunch and I'm starving. Let's go.'

She didn't really want to go anywhere with Lucas, but one glance at his granite-like profile and she knew it would be futile to argue. Much better to go along with him now, than put off the discussion to another day. 'Okay,' she agreed, and preceded him out of the office. Entering the lift, she tried to ignore Lucas's brooding presence lounging against one wall, apparently content to remain silent now he had got his own way.

Her mother had always told her it was better to take bad medicine in one go, and Lucas was certainly that where she was concerned. How bad could it be? A couple of hours in his company and then she never need see him again. Amber consoled herself with the thought as the lift hummed silently to the ground floor, and she stepped out into the foyer, her chin up, her expression one of cool control.

'There is quite a nice little Italian restaurant just around the corner from here,' she offered with a brief glance at Lucas, tall and indomitable at her side.

'No, I have already made arrangements.'

Amber shot him a sharp glance. She didn't like the sound of that, but as they were exiting the building the early rain had given way to brilliant sun and dazzled her eyes for a moment. When she did focus, Lucas was opening the door of a black BMW parked illegally at the kerb.

She stopped. 'I have my own car, tell me where we are going and I'll follow you.'

'Not necessary. Get in, I can see a traffic warden coming.' His large hand grasped hers, urging her forward. 'Don't worry, I'll bring you back.'

Amber didn't want to get in his car, but a brief glance along the road told her he was telling the truth, at least about the traffic warden, so she did as she was told. It was only as he deftly manoeuvred the car through the rush-hour traffic that she realised to a man of his wealth a traffic ticket was nothing. When he stopped the car outside the impressive entrance to the Karadines Hotel, Amber's face paled. Lucas had to be the most insensitive man alive, or else he had brought her here deliberately and was just plain cruel.

'Why here?' Amber queried as Lucas helped her out of the car. She didn't want to put her hand in his, but she did, refusing to let him see how much he still affected her. 'Not very discreet of you.'

'It is too late for discretion, you own part of the place.' Lucas's hard, intent gaze held hers. 'So follow my lead and behave.'

She stared at him, their eyes warring for a second, and she was the first to look away. 'All right.'

The foyer was relatively empty, but even so the hotel manager appeared and greeted Lucas effusively. Amber, to her consternation, was urged forward and Lucas insisted on introducing her to the man as a partner in the business.

'What did you do that for?' she snapped as soon as the man took his leave of them. 'I have not the least intention of—'

'Keep it till we get to the suite.'

'Wait a minute. I am not going to any suite with you.' She stopped dead and looked up into his cold dark eyes. 'The restaurant will do perfectly well.'

'And run the risk of some employee tuning into our

business discussion?' he drawled sardonically. 'I think not, Amber.'

'Then you should not have brought me here in the first place,' she snapped.

Lucas's dark head bent towards her. 'I thought you would appreciate somewhere you knew,' he suggested softly, his breath feathering across her cheek as his hand settled in the middle of her back and he urged her across to the bank of lifts and into a conveniently empty one.

'You thought wrong,' she declared angrily, twisting away from his hand, her body taut with tension. She stared at his broad back as he pressed the required button and the doors closed, entombing them in the small space.

Slowly Lucas turned and lounged back against the carpeted wall, his dark eyes narrowing speculatively on her furious face. 'It can't be the place, because you are familiar with the hotel. So why the anger, Amber? I could almost believe you are afraid of me.'

He hadn't moved, but all at once the atmosphere had become charged with sexual tension. Amber's mouth was dry, the blood moving rapidly through her veins. 'I'm not afraid of any man.' She raised her eyebrows, her air of sophistication firmly back in place. 'And I am not familiar with the hotel,' she said sweetly. 'I have only been here twice, and *both* times were a disaster. The first you dragged me into bed, and the second you drove me out.' She managed to say it all with a light, even tone of voice, and she watched with interest as a red tide of colour ran up under his skin. 'Or had you forgotten in the old days you had a preference for discreet little restaurants, as I suggested earlier?'

The lift came to a halt, and Amber had the distinct impression Lucas was relieved he did not have to respond. Stroke one up for her, she thought irreverently as she followed him down a short corridor, and brushed past the door he held open for her without a glance.

The elegant sitting room was exactly the same with its luxury fitted carpet and period furniture. The large patio doors leading out onto the terrace were wide open and she had a glimpse of a table set for two. Some of her hard-won sophistication evaporated as she recalled the only other time she had been in this suite. The first time they had made love.

She stared at the floor with unseeing eyes. She had been a virgin, and totally ignorant of the power of love. She had been shy at first but so desperately eager. She felt the colour rise in her cheeks at the memory. A few passionate kisses and he had carried her into the bedroom and she had let him strip her naked—helped him, in fact. Then he had told her to undress him, and she had fumblingly complied. With breathtaking expertise he had taken her to the heights of ecstasy over and over again, and from that night on she had been completely addicted to the man. She had been madly in love, and willingly she had followed where he'd led. With hindsight she realised she should have guessed then for Lucas it had only been sex. She felt a deep ache in the region of her heart, and gritted her teeth. She hadn't expected the memory to hurt so much...

Lucas walked past her, discarding his jacket and tie on a low velvet-covered sofa, and headed straight for the drinks trolley. 'What will you have?' he asked, and only then did she lift her head and glance at him.

'Nothing,' she croaked. With his shirt half open and a tantalising glimpse of silky black chest hair exposed and his pleated trousers resting snugly on his slim hips, he looked exactly as he had all those years ago.

One ebony brow rose enquiringly. 'You must, I insist.'

'No, I'm driving later.' She swallowed hard and looked away. 'A fruit juice, maybe,' she amended.

A moment later Lucas was handing her a glass of orange juice. She took it with a steady hand but made sure her fingers did not come into contact with his.

'You look hot,' he opined, his dark eyes searching on her flushed face. 'Let me take your jacket.'

'No, no.' With a glass of juice in one hand and her briefcase in the other, there was no way she could remove it, and he certainly wasn't going to. She had no faith in the fine silk of her blouse hiding her body's reaction to his intimidating male presence.

'Please yourself, but at least let me take this.' And before she could react, his large hand prised her fingers from the death-like grip she had on her briefcase. 'We are eating on the terrace. Are you sure I can't persuade you out of your jacket? It is a warm night.'

Warm did not begin to describe how Amber was suddenly feeling and she almost fell over her feet to rush out onto the terrace, and take a great gulp of air.

A moment later Lucas followed her out with a glass of whisky in one hand, and, casting a sardonic glance at her stiff body standing by the balustrade, he pulled out a chair at the perfectly set table.

'For heaven's sake! Sit down and relax, Amber. I'm not about to jump you.'

'I never thought you were,' she responded with admirable poise and took the seat he offered.

Surprisingly Amber enjoyed the meal, probably because she had hardly eaten any lunch, but also because Lucas was at his charming best. Not a hint of innuendo, or mention of the past. The conversation was topical; some politics, the latest show to open in the West End, which Amber had seen, Lucas had not.

'I didn't know you liked the theatre,' Lucas remarked. 'I never thought to take you when we were together.'

Sitting back in her chair, sipping at a cup of black coffee, Amber almost choked. He was back to personal and she did not like it. 'You never took me anywhere,' she said flatly, draining her cup.

'You're right. Except to bed, of course, as I recall we had the greatest difficulty leaving the bedroom.'

Hot colour flooded her face but Amber wasn't touching that one with a bargepole. 'Shall we stick to business? I meant what I said earlier—whatever Spiro has left me, you can have. I know the will must have been an oversight on his part, or laziness. Either way you are the rightful heir. I don't see any problem.'

'Even if I believed your offer, there are several huge obstacles,' Lucas intoned cynically. 'Never mind the death duty, which will be quite substantial, his medical bills are enormous.'

'Did he die of Aids?' Amber asked, but she'd already guessed the answer.

'Of course, after a protracted illness,' Lucas stated flatly. 'I gather you have not had much contact with Spiro.'

'I hadn't spoken to him in four years,' she said, nervously fingering the waist button on her jacket and slipping it open. She felt terribly guilty, though she knew deep down it wasn't rational. Spiro had been a law unto himself.

'Okay. In that case I'd better fill you in.'

For a brief second she imagined his long body, naked, literally doing just that, and to her horror her own body betrayed her, a wave of heat washing over the surface of her skin, her breasts swelling against the constraint of her bra. Thankfully Lucas did not seem to be aware of the effect his simple statement had aroused.

'Well, you know Spiro,' Lucas prompted, exasperation lacing his tone. 'From taking control of his inheritance, he spent money like a madman. He bought most of the pictures in his art gallery from the artists himself. ''Friends'', he called them. For the last few years he has hired a house on Fire Island every summer, apparently a very popular place with the gay community, and he always took a crowd of pals along to share it with him. He sold off twenty per cent of his share of Karadines without my knowledge. I don't think he did it deliberately to harm the company, but it didn't help. He needed money fast and a friend fixed it for him.'

'How so Spiro,' Amber groaned with feeling. 'Even in death he caused chaos.'

'You knew him well,' Lucas commented dryly. 'But settling up after my father and Christina has left me with a bit of a cash-flow problem. I haven't got the capital to buy Spiro's shares at the moment—but if I don't own them, the company will be very vulnerable to predators.'

And he should know, Amber silently concluded. Lucas was the biggest predator she knew. She glanced across at him, her golden eyes narrowing shrewdly on his darkly attractive face. That was it! Amber saw the flaw in his argument. Lucas *should* know the solution. He had a brilliant brain and was a sharp operator of worldwide renown. He was also wickedly sexy with his shirt unbuttoned, came the unbidden thought. Stop it, Amber. Concentrate, she told herself firmly. Lucas was up to something, but what?

'But why can't I just give you Spiro's share?' she asked, feeling her way.

'I have never taken money off a woman in my life and I am not going to start now. I will buy your shares, eventually.'

'When you're over your cash-flow problems.'

He nodded. His eyes were hooded, masking his expression. Hers were hopefully blandly business-like. The treacherous thought did flicker through her mind that she was in the perfect position to exact a devastating revenge on the man who had thought of her as little better than a slut, a sex object to be used and discarded when he felt like it. For a fleeting moment she let her mind dwell on the idea of selling to another party. It was no more than Lucas Karadines deserved; her lips curved in a wry smile. But she knew she couldn't do it…

Rising abruptly from the table, Lucas said, 'It is getting distinctly chilly out here, we can carry on our discussion inside.'

Amber's mouth opened to deny him, but, catching the cynical expression on his handsome face, she thought better of it. She had the distinct impression he had read her mind and was not talking about the weather at all.

Rising, she followed him back into the sitting room, and, carefully positioning herself on the edge of an armchair, she refused his offer of a brandy. She simply watched and waited.

'My solution…' having poured himself a generous helping of brandy into a crystal goblet, Lucas turned and walked towards her…'is as I said earlier today… You and I, Amber, are now the major partners in Karadines. As you have probably worked out, you can make life very difficult for me, and I could hardly blame you, after the way I treated you.'

His answer floored her. He actually sounded contrite. Her golden eyes widened to their fullest extent on his, and he smiled down at her, a small smile, but a smile nevertheless.

'Don't look so surprised.' His gaze narrowed and swept over her tensely held body perched on the end of the chair, lingering at where her breasts were outlined beneath the fine silk of her blouse. She had forgotten she had undone her jacket. 'The past four years have taught me that love is an illusion and what we shared was a lot more honest emotion.'

Amber gulped, and jumped to her feet. No way was she going there! And, fastening the button of her jacket, 'This is all very interesting but I really must be going. And if you want my advice…' she said briskly, spying her brief-case leaning against the end of the sofa and she headed towards it. Picking it up, she turned and finally glanced up at Lucas. 'I'm a stockbroker—if you need to raise money, float the company on the stock market.'

'Come now, Amber,' he drawled mockingly. 'Do you really think that I, Lucas Karadines, would ever give up control of Karadines?'

His impregnable confidence made her suddenly angry; her golden eyes flashed. 'You might have to.'

'Not if you agree to my plan, Amber,' he murmured, his glance intent on her lovely face as he towered over her. 'If you are as honest as you say, you know Spiro would never have intended the family firm to fall into other hands or even collapse.'

Lucas was right. Spiro used to rant and rave about his family, but deep down he had cared for them. Amber's golden gaze studied Lucas, and her pulses raced. She'd been struggling to keep her eyes off him all evening, the tempting view of his near-naked chest, and with only inches separating them she knew she had to get away.

'What exactly is your plan?' she asked abruptly. She would listen to him, agree and get out fast.

'It's quite simple,' he murmured. His black eyes lingered on her high cheekbones, the thick, curling lashes framing her wide-set golden eyes, and then lower to the full curve of her lips, and lower still to the soft swell of her breast.

'Get on with it,' Amber prompted, terrified by the latent sensual gleam in his dark eyes.

He was too close. Far, far too close. 'Just—just *tell* me,' she stammered, somewhat breathlessly. *Turn, run,* her mind screamed. But she had waited too long.

Lucas hauled her hard against him, his dark head swooped down and his mouth closed over hers. Amber gasped, and his tongue gained instant access to the moist, dark interior of her mouth. Her briefcase fell from her hand and clattered to the floor. But Amber was unconscious of the fact. She was only aware of the hard heat of Lucas, the rock-like strength of his arousal pressed against her lower body, the greedy hunger of his mouth as he ravished hers, and her own instant fierce response.

His hands slid down from her shoulders, and she lifted her own to clasp them around his neck. She clung to him, as one large hand delved down the front of her blouse to cup the soft curve of her breast, long fingers slipping under the strip of lace that was her bra. Amber shuddered as he flicked a nail over a nipple, bringing it to a rigid, pulsing peak. With his other hand closed over her bottom, she instinctively rotated her hips sensually against his hard thighs, wanting more.

Lucas lifted his head, his breath hot against her cheek, and watched her with night-black eyes. 'You haven't changed,' he said huskily with an edge of triumph in his tone. 'Still the sexiest girl alive.' His lips caressed hers softly.

Amber stiffened, her hands fell from his neck, and she turned her head away from his searching mouth. He was right, damn him... Nothing had changed in the intervening years, she realized. She was still helplessly enslaved to the potent sexuality of this one man… But she was older and wiser…and, fighting for every bit of will-power, she flattened both hands on his chest and pushed.

'Let me go,' she demanded bitterly. She could feel the heavy pounding of his heart beneath her hand, the angry tension in his body. She lifted her eyes to his, and caught a flash of something violent that quickly vanished.

'As you wish, Amber.' He threw his arms wide and stepped back. 'I have discovered all I needed to know.' His dark eyes had a glitter in them, and more than a hint of triumph.

Amber gazed at him, her eyes clouded with puzzlement and the lingering traces of passion. To hide her confusion, she bent down and retrieved her briefcase, and, straightening up, she smoothed her jacket down over the curve of her hips with a trembling hand. 'If you want my co-operation over Spiro's legacy, you can cut that out for a start,' she said icily. 'Otherwise you can sort Karadines' problems out yourself. I'm sure you're more than capable.' She headed for the door.

'I am.' Lucas smiled, catching her wrist and spinning her back to face him. 'The solution is simple: I marry you,' he declared, a hint of satisfaction in his voice. 'You did ask me once before, remember?' He taunted softly.

Amber would have given everything she owned not to. Her face went ashen, the passion and the pain inextricably linked in her mind. She had swallowed her pride and begged him to love her. Until finally he had told her the truth—that she disgusted him.

'Over my dead body.' Wrenching her wrist from his grasp, she looked at him with loathing in her eyes. 'My God! Your arrogance is only exceeded by your colossal conceit in daring to ask the question.'

'I did not ask a question.' His black eyes glinted mockingly. 'I made a statement of intent.'

CHAPTER SEVEN

AS AMBER tried to find her voice through the anger that consumed her she told herself, He has to be joking! But Lucas did not look particularly amused. In fact, the cold determination in his black eyes sent an icy shiver of fear slithering down her spine. 'I don't have to listen to this,' she declared forcibly. 'I'm leaving.'

'No, you are not,' Lucas countered coolly, and slipped an arm around her waist, drawing her ruthlessly closer. She felt the heat of him searing her even through her clothes. Amber's lips went dry, her throat closing in panic. Lucas was holding her tightly. She tried to struggle free, but he simply increased the pressure, crushing her to the hardness of his body. 'I have no intention of letting you go,' he muttered, 'ever again.' He grasped her chin with one large hand and tilted her head back. 'Look at me!' he commanded.

She wanted to escape, and planted her hands firmly on his chest intending to push him away, but the old familiar sexual chemistry held her in thrall, and had he actually said 'ever again'? The notion was beguiling and the best she could do was stare up at him with puzzled, angry eyes.

Her anger seemed to amuse him, and as his dark gaze bored into her she felt the surge of blood in her cheeks, and began to tremble, her legs suddenly weak as with a faint, mocking smile he told her exactly what he wanted.

'You and I will marry a week on Saturday in Greece.' His fingers traced up over her lips in intentional provocation. 'I can take you to bed now, and remind you how it was with us, or we can wait for the wedding. But that is the only choice I'm giving you.'

Amber knew she should be fighting him, but could only gaze at him in shock, with increasing need and desire scorching through her. 'No,' she denied. But his mouth found hers, deriding her negative with a demanding hunger that had her weakening helplessly against him. With sensual expertise he deepened the kiss until a drugging passion had emptied her mind of everything but a growing physical need, an ache she had to have assuaged.

He was using the potent force of his sexuality to get his own way, and even as she recognised the fact Amber suddenly did not care! A wild recklessness filled her, sweeping away the years since Lucas had held her like this, kissed her like this, and, slipping her hands over his chest, she clasped them behind his neck, pressing her slender body to his mighty frame. It was only when he broke the kiss and held her slightly away from him, his breathing ragged, she realised the full extent of her capitulation.

'Come to bed with me, you know you want to.' His dark eyes blazed with triumph; he had sensed her complete surrender and taken it as a yes, now he was simply discussing the terms. 'Now or next week, what does it matter?'

Amber would have denied him, even as her body was on fire for him. His assumption he only had to kiss her and she would give in was an insult to her pride, her self-esteem. But then he groaned.

'*Christo!* I certainly need you.' The hand at her chin was suddenly gentle, and he stared deep into her golden eyes. 'Say yes.' She gulped at the unguarded hunger, the desire she saw in expressive eyes. 'I'll wait for the wedding night if you insist,' he said, his smile almost tender.

It was the tenderness that did it. She wanted him. Oh!

How she wanted him, and why not? her sex-starved body demanded. She was not going to marry him, she was no longer a lovesick girl, or a fool, but with every nerve in her body screaming with frustration she murmured, 'All right.' At least she could have this one night.

Lucas smiled, a slow, sensual twist, then raised his hands to her head and deftly unpinned the severe chignon, and trailed his fingers through the long length of her hair, spreading it over her shoulders. Eyes closed, Amber trembled as his arm slid down around her waist and he rested his head in the curve of her neck, breathing in the fragrant scent of the tumbling mass of hair.

'I have been longing to do this,' he murmured. 'From the second I walked into your office today and saw your magnificent hair scraped back, my fingers ached to set it free. It should always be free.' His lips moving over her burning cheek finally found her mouth.

The years since they had last met might never have been. Her pulse leapt as Lucas kissed her with a wild, yet tender, passion she was helpless to deny. She didn't want to. She felt the sudden rush of damp heat flooding her lower body, and feverishly she clung to him, silently abandoning herself to the sheer ecstasy of his kiss, his touch.

Swiftly Lucas swept her up in his arms. She put her arms around his neck and she kissed him very slowly and long. Amber wasn't really conscious of him lowering her to her feet and removing their clothing as desire mounted fiercely inside her. She touched a slender finger to his lips, remembering, tracing the firm outline—he had such a sensual mouth. Lucas drew a ragged breath, and urged her down onto the bed. She felt the mattress at her back, and stared up at him with passion-glazed eyes. He was magnificent in his nudity; his shoulders were broad, his hips were narrow and his belly flat and hard, and the awesome sight of his aroused manhood made her shudder in almost fearful anticipation.

For a long, tense moment Lucas looked down at her, drinking in her naked beauty with black hungry eyes, then, leaning over, he kissed her, his mouth possessive and urgent on her own.

Then, rearing back, he touched her and she quivered like a leaf in the breeze. His hands swept slowly down her body in a long, sinuous, almost worshipful motion, then up again, his palms flat on her stomach until they reached her breasts. He teased her gently, the fingers of one hand grazing slowly over the tips of her breasts, first one and then the other, bringing them to rigid, aching peaks, while his other hand smoothed back down between her legs that parted involuntarily at his caress. She was moist, ready, aching for him, and with a delicate, erotic touch he caressed her until desire mounted crazily inside her and everything else was blotted from her mind.

He caught her to him, and their mouths met and fused, and she arched herself blindly against him. With tactile delight she slipped her hands down across his shoulders, and along under his arms, across his taut abdomen, and then they swept around the outside of his thighs and finally to his inner thigh, her slender fingers curving around the hard, pulsing strength of him. She wanted him now...

She heard the sharp intake of his breath as his head tilted back. 'No, Amber.' And he closed his hand over hers, pulling it from his body. For a horrible second she thought he meant to deny her. 'Not yet. I was a brute the last time,' he rasped. 'I vowed...'

She could see the muscles of his thighs bunch with tension in the effort of control. But after five years of celibacy Amber didn't want to talk. So she wrapped her arms around his neck, and pulled him back down over her.

He kissed her with a wild hunger, his tongue exploring deep in her mouth, his hands caressing every inch of her burning flesh with sensual delight, and she responded with equal passion and helpless moans of pleasure.

She sank back under his hard, hot body, whimpering with need. But Lucas was not to be hurried. He kissed her mouth, her breasts, her thighs, until she jerked helplessly beneath him, her senses swimming with desire. 'Please, Lucas, don't make me wait,' she begged.

And as though he'd been waiting for her plea Lucas moved between her parted thighs. Amber tensed for a second. It had been a long time for her. The hard length of him moved slowly, easing himself deeper and deeper inside her, sometimes to his full length and sometimes with shallow strokes that teased and enhanced the pleasure almost to pain. Amber had never felt such need, such fiery tension, until her inner muscles convulsed around him in a shattering completion. But still he moved, their bodies locked together.

Lucas rolled onto his back and brought her up above him. His hands clasping her hips, he held her against him, but now he could kiss her breasts. Amber cried out at the feel of his mouth on her taut nipples, and shockingly felt the excitement building all over again.

'Yes, yes,' Lucas cried, and as he held her fiercely down on him his great body bucked violently beneath her as he reached his climax. At the same time Amber cried his name, and tumbled over into her own headlong fulfilment yet again.

She collapsed on top of him, breathless and mindless, feeling the sweat of passion cooling on her skin. She buried her head on his shoulder. She did not want him to see her, not yet. Not until she had recovered some of her shattered control. She felt his large, warm hand stroke her back gently, and she could almost fool herself it was love… But not quite…

Rolling off him, she lay flat on her back, and swallowed a despairing sigh—from the heights of ecstasy to the depths of despair in a few moments. Amber knew herself well—no way would she allow any man the intimate liberties she had gloried in with Lucas unless she loved him. The enormity of the realisation made her heartsick.

She loved him, she always had and probably always would. But she had been too badly hurt before to believe he wanted to marry her for any other reason than Spiro's legacy. Tonight would have to be enough. It was ironic in a way, she thought as a wry smile curved her love-swollen lips. Lucas had called her a gold-digger, but in fact it was Lucas who was now in that position.

'What are you thinking?' Lucas propped himself on one elbow, his dark, slumberous eyes boring into hers, his breathing still unsteady. 'That smile looks decidedly smug.'

It was a question she did not want to answer, not truthfully. The night was young and she intended to make full use of it. She lifted her hands and trailed her fingers through the silky mat of chest hair, caressing his body. As her finger grazed a hard male nipple she felt his magnificent body tremble, and she smiled again. 'I was wondering how long it takes you to recover these days,' she murmured throatily, her eyes gleaming with invitation.

Surreptitiously Amber glanced at her wrist-watch—it was the only thing she was wearing. It was close to one o'clock in the morning. She looked down into the face of Lucas Karadines. Somehow he seemed much younger in sleep. His eyes were closed, his long dark lashes brushing his cheeks. He was deeply asleep, not surprising after their second encounter, Amber thought, remembering his seemingly insatiable desire. But she could not sleep—she had to leave. Even now, with her passion for him momentarily quenched, she felt no lessening of desire, but she knew on Lucas's part it was only lust... He had told her so quite truthfully years ago. Dear heaven! What was it going to take for her to get over him? Death?

On that morbid thought she stifled a sigh and slid out of bed, and by moonlight she managed to find her clothes and get dressed. Slipping her shoes on, she crept quietly towards the door. She turned for one last look at his bronzed body spread out on the bed, and almost went back to join him. Instead she closed the door on the temptation he provided.

She didn't get far! Finding her jacket on the arm of the sofa, she slipped it on, and, picking up her briefcase, she stepped towards the exit and escape, just when the bedroom door was flung open.

'Amber.' Lucas walked into the sitting room, totally unconscious of his nudity. 'What are you doing?'

'I am leaving.'

Lucas glared at her for a startled second. 'What the hell is wrong with you? Are you out of your mind? We have just shared mind-blowing sex and now you are sneaking out of my bed in the middle of the night!'

Pushing the tangled mass of her hair behind her ears in a futile attempt to tame it, she glanced up at Lucas. He had the angry, puzzled look of a child who had had his favourite toy snatched from his grasp, and his crude comment on sex simply angered her further. 'Why, was I supposed to wait until you left first?' she asked cynically.

If tonight had taught her anything at all, it was that she had to stay away from Lucas. Because, loving him as she did, she had no resistance against him; she was his for the

taking. Even now the temptation to close the distance between them and run her hands over his hard, tanned body,
to feel once more the wonder of his possession, was almost
irresistible. But one thought stopped her. The memory of
his leaving her naked on the floor in the apartment they
had once shared was something she would not let herself
forget. She moved to walk past him, but his hand shot out
and he captured her arm in a steely grip.

'I have no intention of leaving you—' he glared down
at her pale face and bruised, swollen mouth '—or of letting
you go. You belong to me!'

'Spiro's money belongs to you is what you really
mean.'

He frowned at her acid comment. 'If that is what you
want to think, so be it. But it does not alter the fact you
are marrying me. I had hoped willingly.' His black eyes
raked appreciatively over her. 'You're a very beautiful,
intelligent woman; any man would be proud to make you
his wife.'

A harsh laugh escaped her. 'Oh, please, Lucas,' she
drawled scathingly, tugging her arm free and stepping
back. 'It's a bit late for compliments.' Five years too late,
she thought bitterly.

His dark eyes blazed angrily for a second before adopting his more usual expression, coldly remote. 'If you say
so.' He shrugged his broad shoulders. 'But if not willingly,
I am quite prepared to use coercion. The end result will
be the same.'

He sounded so uncompromising that Amber flinched.
'But why?' she demanded in exasperation, trying not to
look at his naked body. 'I have told you to contact my
lawyer. I will put it in writing here and now, if you like.
You can have the lot.' Her temper was frayed, she was
tired and beginning to be afraid. There was something

about his insistence on marriage that was finally getting through to her. He was deadly serious.

'Because of the time-scale, Amber, even if I believe your assurance that you don't want Spiro's legacy, I don't want you to give it to me,' he insisted for the second time, much to Amber's puzzlement. 'I will pay you the going rate for your holding. But first there is the small question of probate. It usually takes months for a will to get through, and in the meantime the company will become vulnerable to rumour as to how you intend to disperse Spiro's shares,' Lucas answered grimly. 'You will be inundated with offers, and, much as I want to believe in your altruistic nature, I prefer to make sure. As my wife it will be apparent to any predator the company is being kept firmly in the family.'

Amber had enough business sense to realise there was a flaw in his argument. 'In that case the answer is simple. I will give you first option to buy the shares at a knockdown price when I finally inherit. Problem solved,' she said jauntily.

'I prefer my solution. We both know there is the possibility of you marrying Clive Thompson—' he almost spat the name out '—and there is no way he is getting anywhere near my business.' Lucas's glittering glance was full of macho rage. He knew Amber would not be easy to fool, she was too damn smart. But after the great sex they had shared there was no way on God's earth he was letting her get away again. He had spent far too many long, lonely nights frustrated as hell. He looked grimly down at her. 'And if you have any fondness for your new-found father and family, you will do as I say.'

To Amber's ears that sounded suspiciously like a threat. A terrible coldness invaded her and, cautiously lifting her head, she looked into his jet-black eyes. 'What exactly do you mean by that?' she demanded quietly.

'Wait here while I dress,' Lucas commanded and strode back into the bedroom, leaving Amber standing in an agony of suspense. She considered walking out, but didn't dare. Lucas had been so chillingly confident, she had to know what he meant.

When he returned, Amber's wary gaze swept over him. He looked casually elegant. Light-coloured linen trousers hung easily on his lean hips, a fine knit roll-neck sweater covered his muscular chest and his black hair was brushed firmly from his broad brow. 'Good, you waited. I rather thought you might,' he stated silkily. 'Now, where were we?' he asked, smiling.

She felt like knocking the grin off his face, but instead gathered all the will-power she possessed and took a couple of steadying breaths. 'You were about to tell me why I should not marry Clive but marry you instead. Personally I thought it was my own choice. How silly of me,' she managed to say facetiously.

Lucas's smile vanished. 'You have no choice.' His dark eyes narrowed to angry slits. 'Not if you value your father's good name.' Amber felt a sick feeling in the pit of her stomach as Lucas continued. 'Since Sir David retired, his bank has not, how shall I put it...?' He hesitated; his black eyes, glittering with triumph, clashed with hers. 'His son Mark is not a patch on him. Last year, although it saddened me to do it given the long association between Karadines and Janson's, I had to cut all ties with the bank. It was only out of deference for Sir David that charges were not brought against them.'

'I don't believe you,' Amber said sharply. 'My father is an honest man.'

'Yes, I agree. Unfortunately the same cannot be said for his son,' Lucas opined cynically.

Amber went white, and in a voice that shook she asked, 'You're telling me that Mark has done something illegal?' The horrible part was, Amber realized that she was not completely surprised by Lucas's statement.

Lucas shot her a caustic smile. 'What else would you call using money from a client's account to fund a yacht in the Med and keeping a very expensive mistress?'

Amber turned her head aside, unable to meet his eyes. Mark had bought a yacht, that much was true, and the mistress didn't surprise her much either. His poor wife Mary was the mother of three delightful daughters, and spent her whole time apologising for not producing the son her husband wanted.

Lucas walked over to her, his long fingers clasping her chin. 'If you don't believe me, ask him, Amber,' he challenged.

She had a terrible feeling Lucas might be right, and she hid her confusion with an angry accusation. 'You would use the feeling I have for my father to blackmail me into marrying you?' she derided. 'In your dreams, buster.'

His jaw tensed and something violent flashed in his eyes before he drew a deep breath. 'Not in a dream, but in reality, yes. If that's what it takes to get what I want. Yes,' he reiterated bluntly.

She searched his lean, strong face, sure he must be kidding. Surely no man in the twenty-first century could force a woman into marriage? He didn't mean it. But she could not help noticing the implacable determination in his gaze. How had she forgotten what a ruthless bastard he could be? She'd fooled herself into thinking she could have him for a night and walk away. Amber felt her stomach curl sickeningly with fear as her eyes skimmed over his magnificent physique, the vibrant raw energy of the man that fascinated her even as it repelled her. She had underestimated Lucas. But she'd also overestimated her own ability to control her chaotic emotions. Her eyes widened in horror. 'You're crazy,' she bit out as realisation dawned. He was serious, and, worse, much worse, she was tempted...

One ebony brow lifted while a ruthless smile curved his sensuous mouth. 'Perhaps, but how would you live with yourself knowing you could have saved the reputation of your father's firm? A father who went to great lengths to find you and acknowledge you.'

She was trembling. 'You're a bastard, Lucas,' she said, her strained features reflecting her inner turmoil. 'But I'm not afraid of you. I will ask Mark, and—'

He cut across her. 'You *do* that. I made my decision a while ago, I'll give you until the day after tomorrow to make yours.'

Amber heard the car drive up, the engine stop and the car door slam. Her full lips tightened in an angry grimace as she glanced out of the window of her living room. Lucas was pushing open the wrought-iron gate that led up the garden path to the front door of her cottage.

Since the night when she'd fallen like a ripe plum into his arms, in his hotel suite, her life had become chaotic. The following evening she'd met Mark, her half-brother, for a drink, and as soon as she'd mentioned Lucas Karadines he had gone white, and within minutes she'd had the whole story: it was true. It would have been risible if the consequences had not been so tragic for Amber.

Wednesday morning Lucas had called at her office. Loyalty to her father's family and her guilty feelings over Spiro's legacy had forced her to accept Lucas's proposal. Because she knew she did not deserve to gain by Spiro's death. He had been a good friend for many years, as a student and after. Yet she had not contacted him in over four years because he had invited his uncle to the opening of his art gallery without telling her, and told Lucas that she'd put up the capital for Spiro's venture. Worse, she could not shake the notion that if she had not given Spiro the money to go to New York when he had, he might not have contracted the disease that had killed him. But the fact that Lucas the devil had won did nothing to soothe her anger.

That weekend, at Lucas's insistence, she had taken him to her father's house in Surrey, and dropped the bombshell of her forthcoming marriage the following Saturday. Lucas had charmed Sir David and his wife Mildred so much so that Mildred had insisted on throwing an engagement party. Amber had been glad to get back to work on the Monday and away from Lucas, who had business in New York for a few days. But then she'd had the unenviable task of lunching with Clive and telling him she was marrying Lucas Karadines. She had felt an absolute worm by the time they had parted, because she hadn't been able to tell Clive the real reason for her hasty marriage, and he'd taken her rejection with a brave smile and an honest desire that they remain friends.

Then mid-week she'd discovered Lucas had spoken to the chairman of Brentford's. The firm had given her three months' holiday. When she had discovered from one of the other partners why, she had been furious and deeply hurt in equal proportions.

She heard the doorbell ring. They were flying out to Greece today and tomorrow was their wedding day. 'Unfortunately,' Amber muttered darkly, smoothing the fine buttercup silk summer dress she had chosen to wear over her slender hips, and, taking a deep, calming breath, she walked out of the living room, along the hall and opened the front door.

Lucas stood on the path, tall and dark, and the expression on his strong face was one of amusement. 'I don't believe it—you live in a country cottage with roses around the door. It is not you at all, Amber,' he drawled mockingly.

Put out by his opening comment, Amber snapped, 'How the hell would you know?' Her heart had leapt at the sight of him—she had not seen him since last Sunday.

A green polo shirt fit snugly over his wide shoulders, and outlined the musculature of his broad chest in loving detail. Khaki cotton trousers clung to his hips and long legs. A pair of sunglasses was shoved carelessly back across the thick black hair of his head, revealing his perfect features in stark beauty. It wasn't fair; no man should look so good. Even the summer sun glinting on the silver wings of his hair only enhanced his vibrant masculine charm.

Lucas straightened. 'As I recall I know you very well.' His dark eyes roamed over her face and down over her shapely figure in a blatant sensual caress.

'Only in the biblical sense,' Amber returned, and, turning back into the hall, she grabbed the case she had packed and walked to the door. 'I'm ready. Let's go.' She did not want to invite him into her home, because she knew her marriage to Lucas would only last as long as it took Spiro's will to pass probate. She loved her cottage; she had bought it from her landlord three years ago, and had had great fun renovating it. She wanted no memories of Lucas to haunt it when she returned.

'Is that all your luggage?' Lucas demanded, one dark brow arching incredulously on the single suitcase. 'We are getting married in the morning, we will be in Greece for at least the rest of the summer. Where are all your clothes? Surely not in that thing.' He flung an elegant tanned hand at her admittedly rather battered suitcase.

'Let's get one thing straight here, Lucas. I don't need anything special for a civil marriage that is strictly business and will be terminated as soon as possible; the dress I am wearing will do. Easy-care wash and dry as are the other clothes I have packed. I don't need much to bum around on a Greek beach for three months, which is *all* I will be doing since you took it upon yourself to get my employer to give me a holiday. Understood?' Amber told him belligerently, squaring up to him, her golden eyes flashing. If he thought for one second she was going to socialise with him, or play the part of the loving wife, or climb into his bed like a good little girl, he was in for a rude awakening.

Black eyes clashed with hers, and she saw the glint of fury before he successfully masked it with self-restraint.

'Amber, you can walk around naked, if that is what you want,' he drawled mockingly. 'In fact, I would prefer you to.' His eyes, flaring with sensual heat, roamed over her body. She looked breathtakingly beautiful, the buttercup silk dress outlining her luscious curves in loving detail. Her eyes were wide and lustrous, with just a trace of vulnerability in their golden depths that her anger could not hide. She was nowhere near as confident as she wanted to appear.

'Oh, that is not what I mean and you know it,' she snapped.

Lucas knew now was not the time to argue. 'It was a joke, Amber, I hear what you are saying. A business arrangement.'

Expecting an argument, Amber was surprised at his easy agreement, and for a moment felt ridiculously disappointed. But then what had she expected? She remonstrated with her foolish heart. Lucas had not wanted her five years ago, he was hardly going to be desperate to marry her now. On that sobering thought she brushed past him, dropped the suitcase on the path, and turned to lock the door of her little cottage.

'What exactly do you intend doing with this place?' Lucas asked, picking up her suitcase in one hand, his other hand settling at the base of her rigid spine as he urged her away from the house.

'Why, nothing,' she informed him dulcetly. 'I expect to be back at work in three months.' Lucas wasn't getting it all his own way. He had ridden roughshod over all her objections, charmed her father, and bribed her boss to give her a three-month sabbatical, by the simple expedient of becoming a client of Brentford's. He might have blackmailed her into marriage, but he was definitely not blackmailing her into his bed again.

'Well, it is a bit small, but I suppose I could get used to it,' Lucas murmured.

Amber tensed. 'What do you mean by that?'

His sensuous mouth tilted at the corners. 'Why, Amber, darling, once we are married, what is mine is yours, and what is yours is mine.'

Amber's eyes widened in astonishment at his words. 'You're joking.'

'If you want us to live in a cottage rather than a mansion,' he said, shrugging his broad shoulders. His dark eyes watched the myriad expressions flicker across her exquisite face, and then flicked appreciatively over the soft curve of her breasts, the narrow waist and on down over the slender hips and long legs. 'I don't mind,' Lucas said huskily, his dark eyes dancing wickedly.

He was laughing at her; she should have been furious.

'But—but, I—I mean you have just agreed the marriage is strictly business,' Amber stammered to a halt. He was handsome, a rampantly virile male, and she stared at him, her breath catching in her throat.

'I know *exactly* what you mean, Amber,' Lucas emphasised dryly. 'You are angling for a fight and I flatly refuse to give you one. Business marriage or whatever! If my competitors are to be convinced, we have to live together for as long as it takes. Now relax, the sun is shining, it is a beautiful day, and tomorrow will be even better. Get in the car and let's go.' With a broad grin he urged her out onto the road and into the passenger seat of a black BMW.

She watched him through lowered lashes as he slid into the driving seat after depositing her suitcase in the back. Why had she even imagined for a moment that she would be able to resist Lucas, deny him her body? If he wanted her he only had to smile at her, and she was lost. Why had she even tried to pretend she hated him? She loved him, and the realisation of exactly how vulnerable she was hurt like hell. But it made her all the more determined to defy him.

Starting the car, Lucas turned his dark head and smiled at her again. 'I have a surprise for you when we get to the airport.'

Her own vulnerability to his blatant masculine charm made her respond with biting sarcasm. 'Let's hope it is the same surprise as the last time you said that to me. You are marrying someone else…'

Lucas stiffened, his smile vanishing, his dark eyes staring straight ahead, watching the road. Amber noticed the dull stain of red on his cheekbones and for a second thought he was embarrassed until he spoke. 'No, this time it has to be you. I have no choice.'

Amber opened her mouth to argue and stopped. Shrinking back in the seat, she let her thoughts loose, and winced at her own conceit. She had been so incensed at being conned into marrying Lucas, convinced she was making a great sacrifice for her family; she had never thought for a moment how Lucas had to feel. He had loved his first wife, Christina, and now because of Spiro's will he was stuck with either trusting Amber, or marrying her. His only other alternative was facing a takeover battle for his business.

A very chastened Amber said, 'It is not too late. We don't have to marry. You can trust me to give you Spiro's legacy, Lucas. I won't betray you.'

A large tanned hand dropped from the wheel to curve over her thigh. Involuntarily her leg flexed, electric sensation tingling down to her toes. Lucas shot her a deep and unfathomable look.

'Sorry, Amber,' he said softly, 'but I do have to marry you.' With a brief squeeze of her leg, he returned his hand to the steering wheel.

With her thigh still burning from his touch, she couldn't think of a thing to say. She closed her eyes to be alone with her thoughts. He had said sorry. Did he mean he was sorry for her? Or sorry for himself because he had to marry her?

Trying to fathom out how Lucas's mind worked was doing her head in, and, opening her eyes, she looked out of the passenger window and realised they were approaching the airport.

CHAPTER EIGHT

'SO WHAT is the mysterious surprise?' Amber finally demanded. The long silence, the heightened tension in the close confines of the car, had her nerves stretched to breaking-point.

'You will soon find out,' Lucas said curtly, bringing the car to a halt at the entrance to the airport terminal and, without so much as looking in her direction, he proceeded to unfasten his seat belt. Whatever the surprise was, Lucas obviously had no intention of enlightening her.

'Get out.' The terse command did nothing for Amber's growing resentment at his high-handed manner. She cast him a fulminating glance but it was wasted as he was already sliding out of the driver's seat, his back towards her.

Amber scrambled out of the car with more haste than elegance, and, straightening up, she flicked her mane of chestnut hair back from her shoulders and looked around.

Lucas stood a couple of feet away. She watched as he lifted an elegant tanned hand and, magically, a small, rather wizened man appeared and caught the car key Lucas threw in his direction. The older man looked vaguely familiar to Amber and, walking forward, she stopped at Lucas's side as the strange man withdrew her suitcase from the car, handed it to Lucas and said something in Greek.

Watching Lucas respond in the same language and smile down at the other man, Amber was diverted from her simmering anger by trying to figure out where she had seen him before. Then the old man lifted his head, grinned at her and she remembered.

'Why, it's you,' the asinine comment slipped out, but the man had turned and was already getting into the car. 'That's the man that called at the apartment,' Amber said impulsively, tilting her head to look up at Lucas. 'I remember him.' She beamed, pleased at having placed the stranger.

One dark brow arched sardonically as their eyes met. 'Ah, yes! The symbolic castration! I don't think a trip down that particular memory lane is appropriate, given we are to be married tomorrow,' Lucas drawled cynically.

Instinctively her eyes dropped to a certain part of his anatomy; realising what she was doing, she quickly glanced back up at his face. 'No. No…' she stammered. She had forgotten her vengeful reaction when she'd destroyed the crotch in his trousers, and felt colour burn up through her skin. Through anger, she decided staunchly, not embarrassment.

The look he cast her held a tinge of amusement that was apparent in his voice. 'It was probably no more than I deserved, given the circumstances. Forget it—I have—and give me your passport, we have to get a move on.'

Whether it was embarrassment, anger, or sheer shock that Lucas had actually admitted he might have been at fault, which was surely a first for the great Lucas Karadines, it did not matter. Amber was flustered enough to delve into her bag, withdraw her passport and hand it to him without a murmur.

'Good girl.' And, cupping a large hand around her elbow, he led her through the airport.

Following his broad back up the steps to the aircraft, Amber fumed at the sheer arrogant confidence of Lucas. He had swept them both through customs, with an ease that lesser mortals could never aspire to. She watched him smile at the stewardess waiting at the entrance door to the plane, and saw the stupid girl simpering all over him. By the time Amber reached the door, the same girl simply bared her teeth at Amber.

Walking into the cabin, Amber stopped dead.

'Surprise, surprise,' a cacophony of voices shouted.

Amber's mouth fell open in shock, her golden eyes widening to their fullest extent. Everyone and their granny were on the aircraft, she registered in stunned amazement.

Lucas stepped forward to curve a confident arm around her rigid body. 'This is your surprise...I thought you would appreciate your family attending our wedding.'

She forced a smile to her lips, while her eyes scanned the interior of the cabin. Her father, his wife Mildred, her half-sister Julie, Julie's husband Tom and their son plus Mark's wife Mary and her three girls were all on board.

But the biggest surprise to Amber was Tim's presence. In a flurry of greetings and with the aircraft door closing and the captain announcing take-off, it was some time before Amber caught her breath long enough to look up at Lucas, who had somehow manoeuvred her into a seat and fastened her seat belt.

'Why didn't you tell me? I thought this was supposed to be a quick civil wedding and an even quicker divorce,' she hissed as the roar of the engines signalled lift-off. 'Why on earth involve my family?'

Lucas's dark head bent towards her, one arm resting lightly over her slender shoulders. 'I am Greek, we are very family orientated,' his deep voice murmured against her ear. 'And, though I have lost my family, it would be unthinkable to exclude yours,' he declared, the warmth of his breath against her face sending her pulse-rate rocketing.

Amber stared at him, and Lucas stared levelly back at her, his hooded black eyes giving nothing away.

'But Tim as well, I thought...' She didn't know what she thought.

'He is your lifelong friend,' he explained with a casual shrug of his broad shoulders. Against her will, Amber's eyes were drawn to those same shoulders, straining under the cotton knit polo shirt, and gulped. The popping of a champagne cork was a welcome diversion.

Seat belts were unfastened, and the luxurious comfort of the private jet was enjoyed by everyone. Amber found herself seated on a soft hide sofa, with Lucas apparently glued to her side. She could feel the heat of his thigh through the thin silk of her dress, and almost snapped the stewardess's hand off when she offered her a glass of champagne. Amber needed to cool down quick...

The flight took on a party mood, champagne flowed freely, and toasts were drunk to the engaged couple. Lucas responded by taking the opportunity to sweep Amber into his arms and kiss her thoroughly, much to the delight of everyone except Amber. Who, as soon as she could without it looking obvious, got to her feet and put some distance between them. She engaged Mary in conversation only to have the woman gush all over her, because her three girls were to be bridesmaids.

It was the first Amber had heard of it, and she downed another glass of champagne as more toasts were drunk to just about everyone.

When Sir David raised his glass and offered a toast to his son Mark who unfortunately could not be with them, Amber glanced warily across the cabin to where Lucas was in conversation with Tim. Her fiancé lifted his head, his black eyes clashing with hers as he raised his glass to her, and smiled a chilling smile that was more of a warning.

But, fortified with another couple of glasses of champagne and a delightful cold lunch to settle her nervous stomach, Amber had forgotten the moment by the time the aircraft landed.

'Are you all right?' Lucas asked softly, his hand on her elbow as he guided her towards one of the waiting cars.

'Yes, never better.' Amber flashed him a smile—somewhere over Europe she had given up worrying, or some time after the fourth glass of champagne. 'Where are we going or is that another surprise?' she asked blithely.

Handing her into the back seat of a luxurious chauffeur-driven, air-conditioned car, Lucas lowered his long length in beside her, and, casually throwing his arm over her shoulders, he hauled her into his side. 'We are going to the latest Karadines luxury hotel complex, about an hour's drive up the coast from Athens.' He looked down into her flushed, beautiful face and his eyes gleamed with triumph, and something else Amber was too inebriated to recognise.

'Does that suit you?' he asked with an indulgent smile.

Lucas Karadines could afford to be indulgent. He congratulated himself as he settled her pliant body more comfortably against him; his long fingers lightly squeezed her upper arm. He had her. Amber was here in his car, in his country, and tomorrow she would be his in every way known to man. 'Amber?' he queried, but her eyes had closed and she was fast asleep.

Amber's eyelids flickered half open and closed again. She nuzzled her head into the warm human pillow, blissfully aware of Lucas's arms enfolding her in a warm embrace.

She opened her eyes again, and let her lips brush against the strong brown column of his throat. Her tongue flicked out, and tasted the warm, smooth skin. Amber breathed in the familiar masculine scent of him and sighed with pleasure. She felt the tightening of his fingers at her waist and stirred, tilting her head back to look up into his much-loved face. 'Lucas,' she murmured his name, still in that no man's land between sleep and wakefulness.

Through half-closed eyes, she saw his dark head descending, the mobile mouth with just the hint of a smile, and her tongue stroked out over her softly parted lips in sensual anticipation.

His mouth covered hers, and she sighed her acceptance as his tongue gently explored the soft dark interior, and she reciprocated. His lips were firm yet sensuous, his touch so light, she mused languidly. His strong hand closed over her breast, and she groaned, the nipple peaking in instant reaction to his touch. She snuggled closer and let her own hand drop to his thigh and gently stroke upwards. She heard his hiss of breath and felt his instant reaction. His long, hard body was savagely tense; her slender fingers traced the outline of his rampant arousal through the fabric of his trousers. His dark head bent and he muttered something violent in Greek and captured her mouth again with a raw passion, a ferocious urgency that took her by surprise. Her head swam and she could hardly breathe. Fire scorched through her veins. She heard him moan, and the blast of heat was overpowering. With a violent curse Lucas lifted his head. Amber surfaced abruptly from a whirlpool of passion.

A blast of hot air *had* invaded the air-conditioned interior of the car. The door was open...

'Come on, you two, we are waiting.' A deep masculine voice laced with laughter echoed in Amber's head, and suddenly she was wide awake. Appalled at what she was doing, she jerked back and clasped her hands tightly together across her chest, staring into Lucas's dark face with horrified golden eyes.

'*Christo!* Don't move,' Lucas growled, his arms tightening around her, shielding his body with hers. 'Give me a moment,' he husked with one strong hand stroking slowly up and down her back, his breathing ragged. 'You have the most damnable timing, Amber,' he informed her, slowly withdrawing his arms from around her trembling body.

A rueful smile twisted his firm lips, but the heat in his hungry gaze as he stared into her upturned face was sent wild colour surging over her cheeks. Lucas still wanted her every bit as much as she wanted him. The realisation sent her into renewed shock.

'I must have been drunk,' she muttered, sliding back along the seat to her own side of the car, mortified that she had betrayed herself so publicly. For a moment she had travelled back in time to the younger Amber when she'd fallen madly in love for the first time and had believed her feelings were reciprocated. Hastily she lifted her hands and swept back the wild tumble of her hair behind her ears.

'Then I will have to make sure I feed you champagne for the rest of our lives.' Lucas drove raking fingers through his thick black hair, much the same as she had just done, and stared at her. Dark eyes met her bemused gold, his lips curved back over brilliant white teeth in a dazzling genuine smile, the like of which Amber had not seen in years, and her own eyes widened in wonder. 'But if you keep looking at me like that I think the champagne may be superfluous,' Lucas prompted softly. 'Come on.'

It was a very subdued Amber that stepped out of the car. How had she imagined for a second that she could marry Lucas and not go to bed with him, when a simple smile had her panting? Her knees felt weak and she was actually grateful when Lucas slid a strong arm around her waist as he introduced her to the man who had so casually interrupted them.

'This is Joe, my right-hand man, and tomorrow my best man.'

Amber looked up into the laughing grey eyes of the tall, brown-haired man. 'How do you do?' she said formally.

'Great for having finally met you,' he responded with a trace of an American accent.

'You're American,' Amber said stiltedly. If she had not been feeling so embarrassed she would have immediately liked the man.

'Greek-American and you are very English, and very beautiful, exactly as Lucas described you.' He smiled broadly. 'Pity he saw you first.'

'Cut that out, Joe; the lady is mine,' Lucas said possessively. Amber watched as the two men exchanged an expressive look, and then they were all entering the vast foyer of the hotel.

Immediately Amber's family surrounded them, while Joe, with a few swift commands, had their luggage taken care of. Lucas confidently listed the features of the complex at Sir David's request. Set in two hundred acres with its own golf course, shooting range, and private beach with every kind of water sport available, it was a holiday paradise. Private chalets were scattered all around the complex. But he had arranged for everyone to stay in a number of suites in the main hotel building, as it was more convenient.

Without a word Lucas took hold of Amber's arm and led her towards a lift. The doors swung open as if waiting for his arrival and he urged her inside.

For the sake of something to say, Amber offered, 'Joe seems a really nice man.'

The look Lucas cast her held a hint of wry acceptance and something more she did not recognise. 'Implying I am not?' he taunted gently.

'I never said that.' She tensed, suddenly feeling claustrophobic in the small enclosed lift.

'Relax, Amber—I was joking. All the ladies like Joe. The trouble is, he likes all the ladies. *All* being the operative word.' Lucas, his eyes glinting, flicked Amber a teasing glance, asking her to share his humour.

Lucas in a light-hearted mood was impossible to resist, and a reluctant smile parted her full lips. She could imagine Joe as a ladies' man with no trouble. He had the good looks and easygoing charm, and the banter girls the world over fell for.

'And of course you don't,' she mocked.

His hand reached out and caught hold of Amber's, spreading her fingers as he threaded his own through hers. 'No, I only want one.' And the look he cast down was serious, his black eyes penetrating on her lovely face. 'And I've got you,' he murmured, leading her out of the lift. Amber was powerless to control the sudden acceleration in her pulse, or to deny his hand holding hers was oddly reassuring.

Twenty minutes later she stood in the centre of the elegantly furnished sitting room, and looked around in wide-eyed awe. 'It's magnificent, Lucas.' She turned her beautiful face towards him and grinned. 'It's bigger than my cottage. I could live in here.' He had just given her a tour of the suite. From the long balcony with magnificent views over the bay, through the stylish bedroom with a king-sized bed, from which she had hastily dashed out into the bathroom, with double shower and whirlpool bath all in the finest marble.

'I'm glad you like it. My only regret is I cannot stop and share it with you now. But have patience, tomorrow will be a different story,' he declared with all the arrogance of a supremely confident man. 'And the experience will be all the more erotic for the anticipation, I promise.'

Amber flinched. After her performance in the car it was hardly surprising; he thought she was a pushover. But then Lucas was a typical alpha male, strikingly handsome, lethally sexy, wealthy, sophisticated, and great in bed, and the combination was irresistible. She doubted he'd ever met a woman in his life that would not be happy to fall into his arms at the first opportunity. But it galled her to think he thought she was one, and that he had to apologise for leaving!

She straightened her shoulders, her proud gaze narrowing on his face. 'Providing I am still here. After all, there is nothing to stop me changing my mind, a woman's prerogative and all that,' Amber pointed out. That should give the arrogant devil something to worry about.

Tall and powerful even in casual clothes, Lucas watched her, not a flicker of any emotion showing on his handsome, hard-boned face. 'I'm sure you can leave,' he said softly, moving swiftly across to where she stood. 'But you won't.' Tilting her chin with one long finger, he added, 'That is the second reason for your family's attendance at the ceremony. You might want to walk out on me, but no way will you walk out on them...' He shook his dark head. 'Leaving them dependent on my hospitality. I know you too well, Amber.'

Amber squirmed at her own stupidity. She had actually bought his fairy story on the plane about her family. His second reason was much more believable. The devious devil—in that second she hated him. 'You really are a swine,' she hissed. The fact that his assumption was also correct did nothing for her temper.

His perfectly chiselled features froze into impassivity, but not before she saw the flare of anger in the depths of the hard black eyes that held hers.

'It won't work.' Lucas's fingers tightened slightly on her chin. 'I told you earlier, I am not going to argue with you, so stop trying.' His thumb traced along her full lower lip, and she could not repress the shiver that rippled through her.

'You want me and I want you, so stop fighting it. With our history it is inevitable.'

'No,' she denied, but her body inexplicably swayed forward like a moth to a flame, her golden gaze captured by the simmering sensuality in his night-black eyes.

'Yes.' Lucas smiled a wry sexy twist to his firm lips. His hand dropped from her face. He ached for her with a hunger, a pain she had no knowledge of. But he dared not touch her again. Not yet! He'd made one mistake, and he was not about to risk making another until he had his ring safely on her finger. 'But not now—I have some business to attend to in Athens, but I will be back to take you to dinner at nine. If you need anything, speak to Joe or Reception.' Lucas bent and dropped a swift kiss on her full lips and left.

Tense and frustrated at her own inability to resist him, Amber paced the length of the room and back, her mind a seething mass of conflicting emotions. Was she a woman or a wimp? A few hours ago she'd been determined her marriage to Lucas would be in name only. But one touch and she melted like ice in a desert. And he, damn him, knew it!

By eight in the evening Amber was almost at boiling-point. The first shock had been Reception delivering a wedding dress to her room and a handful of bridesmaid dresses, closely followed by Julie and Mary and her daughters. Amber had stood in the middle of the room like a statue as the other two women had shoved the girls into masses of white froth while Julie had explained it had all been Lucas's idea. He was such a considerate man, she had rhapsodised.

Apparently, he had explained, because it was a second marriage for him Amber was being stubborn and insisting on keeping it low-key—a simple suit had been mentioned. But he did not want to deprive Amber of a white wedding. So he'd asked Julie to choose the gowns for the occasion.

Any thought of depriving the young girls of being bridesmaids or of doing a bunk on Amber's part had been quickly dispelled by the constant visitors to her room: her father, Mildred, everyone, and all in favour of the wedding.

Amber lay in the decadent marble bath, and steamed her temper as hot as the water. Finally she stepped out and, picking up a large fluffy towel, wrapped it around her naked body, and then, using the hair-dryer provided, she spent the next ten minutes drying her long hair. Walking back into the bedroom, she picked white lace briefs from the drawer and stepped into them. She didn't have much time and she wanted to be ready before Lucas arrived. Amber did not want him in her room again; once was enough for one day.

Quickly she withdrew from the wardrobe a blue silk jersey halter-necked dress, and slipped it over her head. Turning, she glanced at her reflection in the wall mirror, smoothing the clinging fabric down over her slender hips. The skirt ended a few inches above her knee, and she adjusted the bodice over her firm breasts, eyeing the cleavage with a wry look. Either she was getting fatter or the dress had shrunk in the wash. With a toss of her head, she dismissed her worries and slipped her feet into matching blue open-toed sandals.

It took only minutes to apply moisturiser to her smooth skin, a touch of mascara to her long lashes, and a plain pink lipgloss completed her make-up. With the ease of long habit, she brushed her long hair back behind her ears and let it fall loose down her back. She fastened the gold Rolex watch, a present from her father, around her wrist. Five to nine, she made it, and, walking into the sitting room, she picked up her purse and left.

Luck was with her, a lift was waiting. Amber walked in and pressed the down button and seconds later she stepped out into the foyer. Julie and her husband and the whole crowd immediately surrounded her. Joe appeared and, heading straight for Amber, he took her arm. 'You look sensational. Where's Lucas?'

'I don't know,' she told the truth. Then she did know, when a strong arm curved around her waist.

'I'm here, Joe, you can unhand the lady now. I've got her.'

Amber tensed, her heart missing a beat. Slowly she turned her head. 'Lucas,' she greeted him.

'Amber, darling, you couldn't wait, you had to come down to meet me—how sweet.' The devilish light in his dark eyes should have warned her. He curved her close into his hard body, crushing her up against him as his dark head swooped and his lips claimed hers.

Amber's pulse went from normal to the speed of light, and then he lifted his head; though he still held her hard against him and she could not help but be aware of his instant, shameless arousal. 'You're sex mad,' she muttered angrily. 'And you had no right to get Julie to buy a wedding dress.'

He silenced her by claiming her mouth again in a long passionate kiss, and when he finally let her up for air she was boneless. It didn't matter how often he touched her, it was always the same. There had always been a devastating chemical reaction between them, and that had not changed in the intervening years. 'What do you think you are doing?' she croaked.

'Not what I want to be doing, that's for sure,' Lucas said bluntly in her ear, and then very slowly eased her away from him.

Her face scarlet, Amber wanted the ground to open and swallow her up. How dared he embarrass her like that in front of her family? Eyes flashing angrily, she looked at Lucas and caught her breath. In a superbly tailored white dinner jacket and narrow black trousers that clung to his thighs and accentuated the long length of his legs, he looked magnificent. A perfect example of a man—the slight dilation of his pupils still evident, although he had controlled his body, only added to his aura of predatory masculine power.

'You look ravishing, Amber.' His dark eyes raked her from head to toe. 'I am a very lucky man.' Lucas smiled— for the audience, Amber thought, but said nothing as he caught her hand and tucked it under his arm.

Dinner was probably superb, Amber decided almost two hours later. It was a pity she had no idea what she'd eaten. The *maître d'* had arranged for a long rectangular table to be set at one end of the elegant dining room so the whole party could eat together. Seated at Lucas's side at the top of the table, she had smiled and chatted and prayed for the evening to end.

'You must try this, *agape mou*.' Lucas's husky drawl

had all the women at the table swooning, while Amber felt like a cat on a hot tin roof. If he put his finger in her mouth one more time she swore she would bite it off.

Finally, when the meal was over and he called her his love for the umpteenth time, and let his long fingers stray over her breast supposedly to smooth back a strand of her hair, Amber turned in her seat and raised her golden eyes to his. 'You are so good to me, Lucas,' she said, and delivered a hard kick to his shin under the table.

Lucas threw back his head and laughed out loud. 'Really, Amber, you are priceless!'

She wasn't priceless, she was furious and frustrated and tingling all over in a semi-permanent state of arousal, because of his tricks.

'Hey, cut us in—what's the joke?' Joe asked with a grin.

'Private, strictly private,' Lucas responded, and settled gleaming dark eyes on Amber. 'It is only between my fiancée and I. Isn't that right, Amber?'

To everyone else it was a casual comment, but to Amber, with his intent gaze lingering on her face, it was very definitely a warning. Their war was private and nothing must upset the success of the evening. She picked up her wineglass and drained it, avoiding his eyes.

'By the way, Lucas, you will have to leave before midnight,' Sir David remarked as they were all being served with coffee after the meal. 'Traditionally it is unlucky to see the bride before the ceremony on the day of the wedding.'

'Well, I am all for tradition, so at midnight I'll make my way back to my lonely bed,' Lucas drawled with mock sorrow, and everyone laughed, except Amber who could only manage a stiff smile.

The urge to smash through the smooth façade he

showed to their guests raged through her. How could they not see the deception behind the clever, striking face? The feeling of being trapped was almost overpowering and she sighed with relief when a trio of musicians arrived and took up positions on the small stage set at the back of the small square dance-floor at one end of the elegant dining room and started to play. Chairs were pushed back, and to Amber's delight Tim appeared at her side.

'Dance with me, Amber. We have hardly had a chance to talk,' Tim asked. With a brief glance at Lucas, he added, 'If you don't mind.'

'Of course he doesn't mind,' Amber answered for Lucas, leaping to her feet. To escape Lucas's overpowering presence for a few moments was just what she needed. Grasping Tim's hand, she almost dragged him onto the dance-floor.

The lights had been dimmed and quite a few people were dancing. Amber slipped into Tim's arms, and felt as if she were home. 'Thank God!' she sighed, and, looking up into his familiar face and sparkling blue eyes, she smiled her first genuine smile of the evening. 'It's great to see you; I had no idea you were coming.'

'Lucas called me last week and told me your good news. My favourite girl getting married! How could I refuse? Then again, your fiancé is a very persuasive man, I doubt anyone dares refuse him.'

'You've got that right,' Amber said with feeling, her smile vanishing.

'Hardly the response I would have expected from a woman in love,' Tim stated quietly, and, tightening his arms around her waist as they moved slowly to the music, he asked, 'What's wrong, Amber?'

'Nothing,' she murmured. It wasn't fair to involve Tim in her problems.

'Come on, it's me, your best pal. I know you better than you know yourself. I've watched you all night—your laughter was forced and your smile strained. That is not like you at all. You're the most genuine person I know.'

Moisture glazed her eyes. 'Thanks for that, Tim.' And suddenly she had the overwhelming need to confess everything. 'You're right, Tim.' And as they moved around the dance-floor she told him about Spiro's will and the consequences of it.

'That's Spiro for you,' Tim remarked dryly. 'Even in death he causes mayhem. But that is not your problem, Amber. All you need to ask yourself is, do you love Lucas? Everything else is superfluous; believe me, I know.'

'Yes, I never stopped loving him,' Amber admitted huskily, the sadness in her voice unmistakable. 'But Lucas had never loved me. I thought he did, and you know what happened. He fell in love with someone else.'

'I'm not so sure about that,' Tim contradicted. 'Lucas Karadines is a very traditional Greek male, and at the time he would have done anything to humour his father—the man was dying. He went to great lengths to hide Spiro's sexuality from the old man. Marrying the girl his father approved of would seem a likely thing for Lucas to do. As for loving her, he might have thought he did, but we men are just as likely as women to mistake our true feelings.'

'Since when did you become such an expert on the sexes?' Amber asked dryly.

'Since I made a huge mistake with Spiro that could have cost me my life.'

'But you did truly love him,' Amber responded. 'I was there, remember.'

'No, it was friendship and infatuation, and the only reason I stayed so long was because Spiro, as the dominant partner, kept telling me we were in love. But once in New York and watching how he behaved, I discovered I didn't actually care enough to even be jealous, and I realised it wasn't real love I felt for him. I know the difference now. I have a new partner, David.' His blue eyes lit up with happiness as he continued. 'He has a picture-framing business in Newcastle and what we share is true love. So you see, Amber, we can all make quite horrendous mistakes.'

Amber looked up into his lovable face, believing him. 'I am glad for you, but it doesn't really help me. Lucas loved his wife—he can't even bring himself to talk about her death.'

'But she is dead, Amber, and she can't come between you any more. Lucas wants a flesh-and-blood woman.' He held her slightly away from him, his blue eyes roaming the luscious length of her, camping it up with mocking male appreciation. 'And you are certainly that!'

Amber grinned at his teasing; she could not help it.

'Look at him—he is watching me like a hawk.' Tim gestured with his head, and, glancing across the room, Amber saw Lucas rising up from the table, his whole attention fixed on her. 'Believe me, Amber, he wants you and badly. He and I had a long talk last week. I'm sure he loves you even if he does not want to admit it. Take a chance.'

'Take a chance on what?' Lucas's deep, melodious voice broke into the conversation. 'You are already taking a big chance, Tim, dancing with my fiancée for so long. If you don't mind.'

'My pleasure.' Tim grinned and, leaning forward, he dropped a swift kiss on Amber's nose. 'Go for it,' he whispered before placing her hand in Lucas's.

'Are you sure that guy is gay? I saw the way he looked

at you,' Lucas queried, slipping a long arm around her waist, and clasping her other hand in his, holding her close to his strong body.

Tilting her head back, she looked up into his oddly serious face. 'Jealous of Tim?' she prompted with a chuckle.

'I'm no fool; if your closest male friend had been straight I would never have invited him in a million years,' he declared bluntly.

Amber couldn't help it, she burst out laughing.

'I'm glad I amuse you,' Lucas said simply. 'I have been trying to all night.'

The hint of a smile quirked the corners of his mobile mouth as his hand laced with hers and raised it to his lips. He brushed a kiss along her knuckles, before moving her effortlessly to the soft strains of the music.

'Is that what you were doing?' Seducing her more likely, Amber thought, and slid a slender arm up around his neck, tangling her fingers in the silky black hair at his nape. 'I would have called it *teasing*.' She pouted and did some teasing of her own, relaxing against him, and moving her hips in an exaggerated sway to the rhythm of the music. Her golden eyes gleamed mischievously up at Lucas.

His black eyes glittered over her lovely face. 'Amber.' One hand caressed her back down her spine, curving her in closer to the hard strength of his body, and heat pooled in her belly. 'Watch it! You're playing a dangerous game,' his husky voice drawled as he curled their joined fists against her breast.

Her sensitive flesh swelled and her nipples peaked into tight buds against the smooth fabric of her gown as desire, sharp and physical, scorched between them. Amber could not drag her eyes away from his. She wanted him so much, she trembled. 'I don't play games,' she whispered, and then, with courage she had not known she possessed, she asked, 'but what about you?' He'd played with her emotions once before; she had no reason to suppose it would be any different this time.

CHAPTER NINE

LUCAS had hurt Amber so much before, it terrified her as she waited for his answer. But Tim had told her to take a chance; after all, Christina was dead and Lucas was very much alive.

Something she was made vividly aware of the next second as, dropping her hand, he placed his through the silken fall of her hair to curve around the nape of her neck and tip her head back. 'No, I never play games,' he contradicted fiercely while his other hand, low on the base of her spine, urged her hard against him. 'Does this feel like a game?' His lean hips moved urgently against her, making her aware of his arousal. 'Do you think I willingly walk around in this state aching for you? The chemistry between us is as strong as it always was, always will be.'

'Not always.' The memory of him walking out on her was ever present.

Lucas stilled, giving up any pretence of dancing. 'Yes, even then,' he confessed harshly. He knew exactly what she meant, and he was ashamed of his behaviour, but at the time he had been too blindly arrogant to see the truth. He had decided it was time he fell in love and married, and had set about doing it exactly the same way as he pursued a business deal. He had been so confident he'd been doing the right thing. Pleasing his father, and expecting it to please himself.

'No,' Amber denied. 'Don't bother lying.' It was all a game to Lucas, anything to get his own way. 'I was *there*, remember,' she prompted scathingly. 'You said I was disgusting, a hedonist. You as good as called me a whore,' she fumed, all the old anger and resentment bubbling to the surface.

Lucas's arm around her waist jerked tighter. His superb bone structure tautened and something that looked almost like pain glinted in his night-black eyes. 'I was disgusted with *myself*, Amber, never you. Spiro's statement after my engagement party that he was going to marry you had enraged me, but deep down I suspected it was a lie. Though it did not stop me using it as an excuse to see you again. I had to make sure, I told myself, and, seeing you so strong and defiant and desirable, I was lost to all reason, consumed by such an irresistible passion that nothing else mattered. I betrayed my fiancée, and I hated myself, so I took it out on you. You have to believe me, and if I hurt you with my brutally callous remarks I am truly sorry.'

If... He'd almost destroyed her, and he had not even realised he'd been doing it...and yet, looking up into his taut, sombre face, she believed him. Plus he had actually done it, actually managed to say *I'm sorry*. For once the arrogant, all-powerful Lucas Karadines was admitting he was as susceptible to making a mistake as any ordinary mortal was.

'Amber, I swear it was never my intention to hurt you, then or now. We are getting married tomorrow.' His sensual mouth twisted wryly. 'Can we at least try to forget the past and make it work? Make it real.'

His strong hand moved restlessly up and down her spine and with the heat, the strength of him enveloping her, she was tempted to agree.

'Please,' Lucas pleaded for the first time in his life. He had behaved like the worst kind of hide-bound, chauvinistic fool when he had let this woman go. Equating great sex with a girlfriend, but talking himself into loving what he had considered an acceptable wife. Now he knew better: love was an illusion; lust was reality. He might not like the way Amber affected him so instantly. But he was not fool enough to believe he could live with her without making love to her. He was no masochist.

Amber saw his eyes darken. She knew what he wanted, what he was asking, and was dizzied by the sensations snaking through her. She placed a hand on his shirt-front to steady herself. Involuntarily her hand stroked up over the front of his chest, feeling the uneven pounding of his heart beneath the fine silk of his shirt. He wanted her, and in all honesty Amber knew she ached for him. She was older now and she no longer saw Lucas as the perfect, infallible, godlike male she had years ago, yet she still loved him.

She was under no illusion as to why he was marrying her. He was not prepared to trust Amber's word she would sell Spiro's shares to him. It was ingrained in his character to trust no one; an asset in the top echelons of the business world, but on a personal level more of a liability, though Lucas would never see it as such. But the real question was, was she mature enough to forget all her old bitterness and anger, and take what was on offer? A few months of sexual pleasure at least, and maybe, just maybe Lucas might come to love her. Dared she take the chance?

'Amber...' his long fingers tangled in the silky gold locks of her hair, he urged her face to his '...what do you say?'

She could say no! And deprive herself of six months of pleasure and probably the only sex she would get in her life. She looked into his eyes, and was fascinated by the tinge of vulnerability that even the sensual hunger blazing in their depths could not hide. Or she could say yes! And pray she was mature enough to walk away with her pride intact when the time came.

Her golden gaze meshed with his. 'Yes, I suppose…'

Whatever else she might have said was lost as Lucas covered her mouth with his own, his tongue prising her lips apart, thrusting and tasting with a simmering sensuality, again and again.

'This is becoming a habit,' a laughing Joe exclaimed. 'Break it up, you two, it is late.'

Lucas groaned, and lifted his head. He eased his hand from Amber's nape but still kept his arm around her waist. 'We appear to be the floor show, sweetheart,' he husked, brushing the long fall of her chestnut hair carefully back off her face.

'Oh, heavens!' Blushing bright red, Amber tried to ease away, horribly aware the music was no longer playing, and everyone was watching them with varying degrees of amusement.

Lucas grinned and, clasping her around the waist with both hands, he stepped back, his dark eyes, blazing with masculine triumph, flicking over her. 'It's all right, you look decent,' he murmured huskily. 'But Joe is right. It is late, and I have to leave you before the witching hour, according to your father. If I want to be lucky, and I *am* going to be lucky tomorrow night…' He arched one ebony brow wickedly.

Amber's blush could have lit the room. She walked back to the table with Lucas on legs that shook. Any thought of trying to pretend she was immune to him was banished for ever from her brain.

'Well, any lingering doubts I had about the haste of this wedding are well and truly put to rest, old man.' Sir David slapped Lucas on the back. 'But in future I would try to be a little more circumspect, if I were you.' He chuckled.

'I will, Sir,' Lucas agreed and the two men exchanged a very masculine smug grin. 'And look after Amber for me until tomorrow.' Bending his dark head, he pressed a swift kiss on her brow. 'Go to bed. It's late.'

She did not need looking after, nor did she need to be told to go to bed. But, then again, after the exhibition she had just made of herself, maybe she did.

Noon the next day Amber stood in front of the dressing mirror, and barely recognised herself. The sides of her long hair had been swept up into an intricate crown of curls threaded through with perfect white rosebuds and tiny satin ribbons, and the rest left to fall in gentle curls down her back. Her make-up was light but perfect. The wedding dress was a dream, the soft fabric draped narrowly across her shoulders, exposing just a hint of the creamy mounds of her breasts. Cut on the bias, it shimmied across the shapely length of her body to end at her ankles in a scalloped border embroidered in a rose pattern. She glanced around the havoc of the room, and smiled at the three young bridesmaids. They were standing in a stiff line, terrified of spoiling their finery; their dresses flounced like crinolines from fitted waists and copied the embroidery of the bridal gown.

Someone handed Amber a posy of ivory roses mixed with baby's breath and her father appeared at her side, resplendent in a pale grey suit.

'You look beautiful, Amber. I am so proud to be your father and I want you to know—I deeply regret all the wasted years when I was not there for you. Especially now when I am losing you again.' Tears glazed her golden eyes, and she sniffed as he took her hand and tugged it under his arm, adding, 'Time to go, Amber.'

Suddenly the enormity of what she was about to do hit her and for a second she panicked. 'But I don't even know where I am going,' Amber wailed.

Hoots of laughter greeted her comment and someone shouted, 'Joe has it all arranged,' as everyone moved towards the door.

Amber gasped—it was like something out of a Hollywood movie. Joe had done a superb job. A secluded corner of the vast gardens of the hotel was set out with chairs for the guests, the centre aisle leading to a raised dais covered with a delicate arched pergola beautifully decorated with hundreds of tiny white roses and vines.

The three little girls were solemnly walking down the aisle sprinkling rose petals from decorated baskets, and then it was Amber's turn.

Straightening her shoulders, Amber took a tighter grasp of her father's arm and stepped forward, her gaze fixed on the tall black-haired man standing with his back to her in front of the celebrant. Then he turned to watch her approach.

The clear blue sky and the blinding sun added to Amber's feeling of unreality and only hazily was she aware of the guests seated either side of the aisle, her glance captured by Lucas's intent, unwavering gaze. He was magnificent in an immaculate pale grey silk suit, and white shirt, and a grey silk tie shot through with blue. His thick black hair had been neatly trimmed and he looked exactly what he was: a mature, sophisticated Greek businessman, while Amber, on the other hand, was shaking like a jelly with nerves.

It was stupid, she knew. She'd lived with the man for a year, for heaven's sake! She should not be intimidated by what was really a simple civil ceremony—it was not as if she were marrying him for life.

But as her father left her at Lucas's side, Amber knew that for her it would be a life sentence. She would never love any man the way she loved Lucas. Looking up into his darkly handsome face, she had to blink hard to stop emotional tears blinding her eyes. 'You've had your hair cut.' She said the first thing that came into her head to cover her emotions.

His black eyes widened in surprise and then his lips parted over brilliant white teeth in a beaming smile. 'I'm so glad you noticed,' he murmured for her ears only. 'I was afraid you might have changed your mind, and not deign to look at me.'

Lucas afraid was a novel notion, but she did not have time to dwell on it as she listened to the celebrant and surprisingly a priest appeared. Amber was too nervous to take much in but she must have made the right response. Lucas took hold of her hand and slipped a gold band on her ring finger, and indicated she should return the favour by placing a ring on his finger. Surprised he would want to wear a ring, she glanced up and was captivated by the blaze of emotion in his dark eyes. She hesitated for a moment and Lucas covered her hand with his free one and helped her slip the ring on his finger.

'My wife at last,' he murmured. Then gathered her into his arms and kissed her. It was a kiss like no other, firm but tender, sensual and seeking. Amber's head swam, her pulse raced, her full lips parting to welcome him.

'Break it up, you two. You still have plenty of time for that later. We have to party.'

To Amber's chagrin, once again it was Joe who'd brought them back to their senses. Flushing scarlet, she glanced wildly around at all the grinning faces, then tilted her head to look up at Lucas.

'You really are a blushing bride now,' Lucas said wryly. 'My fault—I got carried away.' Her heart gave a curious lurch at seeing the glittering intensity of his gaze, igniting sparks of sensual awareness through her whole body. 'But you are the most beautiful bride. I don't have the words to tell you how much it means to me you are mine.' His voice was thickened with emotion and he lifted her hand to his mouth and kissed the wedding band.

Amber wanted to believe his sentiment was genuine but, tearing her eyes from his, she mumbled, 'Yes, well, thank you.' She loved him but trusting him again was something else...

The speeches were over, and the wedding reception had taken on the air of a joyous feast. Lucas led Amber from one table to another to say their goodbyes. Amber was stunned at the number of people. Lucas appeared to have a remarkable number of friends, all Greek, and as she could not speak the language she simply nodded and smiled.

It was a relief when Lucas curved his large hands possessively around her shoulders and murmured, 'It's time you changed, we have to leave in a few minutes.'

'Leave. What for?' Amber queried. She glanced up and saw the amusement gleaming in his black eyes, and she simply stared rather helplessly back at him.

Lucas chuckled. 'Because the honeymoon is the best part of the wedding, my sweet.'

Julie burst out laughing. 'Come on, Amber, I'll help you change.' Before Amber knew it she was back in the bedroom of the suite.

Amber removed her bridal gown, and with Julie's help managed to remove the rosebuds from her hair. Five minutes later her hair was brushed, but a little on the wild side because of the curls. Julie was holding an elegant cream trouser suit up for her inspection.

'A present from your husband. Put it on.'

A silk and linen mix—the designer label told Amber it was incredibly expensive. The tiny silk camisole that left her midriff bare prevented her from wearing a bra, but with the jacked fastened it looked great. Chic casual and Amber wondered again where they were going. Two hours later she knew...

'So. What do you think? ' Lucas demanded, his black eyes alight with pleasure. 'Isn't she beautiful? I only bought her a few months ago, and I have not really had the time to try her out.' The pride and admiration in his voice were unmistakable.

Amber stood on the wooden deck and looked around. They had driven to a marina along the coast, and Lucas had just finished showing her around his latest toy—a thirty-foot motor cruiser.

'The joy of this is...' Lucas continued, his handsome face animated '...it does not need a crew, I can handle it myself, and the two of us will have no problem. Everyone sails around the islands, but I thought we could explore the mainland coastline, stopping off to see the places of interest, of course. It will be fun.'

He was wearing cream cotton trousers and a short-sleeved blue checked shirt. His legs were planted slightly apart on the deck. He looked so sexy, the sheer size and virile strength of him hit her like a punch in the stomach. Amber hadn't the heart to tell him she'd never been to sea before, other than on a ferry. For all she knew, she might get seasick.

'It sounds very nice, but I don't know much about boats,' she managed to say, suddenly realising just what kind of intimacy she was inviting if she agreed. She had seen the galley was small and compact, the saloon was beautifully furnished, and comfortable, but not huge. There was one large cabin with a very big bed, a shower and toilet. One small cabin with a couple of bunks and a lot of computer equipment.

'You don't need to.' Lucas caught both of her hands and cradled them in his own. 'I will teach you everything; you will love it, I promise.'

Standing barefoot on the deck, Lucas had insisted she remove her shoes, declaring they were unsuitable for the wood deck, and, with the warmth of his hands enfolding hers, she felt totally out of her depth in more ways than one. 'Yes, well...'

Lucas drew her into his arms, pulling her close so the top of her head tucked under his chin. 'Great. I had intended taking you to a very exclusive holiday island in the Bahamas, but yesterday when I saw your suitcase and you said you only needed a few clothes because you intended to bum around and do nothing, I thought of this.'

'I missed out on the Bahamas!' Amber exclaimed, flashing a mock protesting glance up at him, only to chuckle when she saw his teasing expression.

'I will take you another time,' Lucas countered, his dark eyes suddenly serious. 'I am going to do everything in my power to make sure you never miss out on anything life has to offer ever again.' He gathered her in even closer, and Amber was utterly transfixed by the burning desire in his eyes. A desire Lucas was doing nothing to hide.

She gasped, a soft sound, her lips parting as awareness shivered though her. Lucas lowered his mouth down to hers, and stole the breath from her body.

The kiss didn't last long, but when he drew away and said gruffly, 'Let's go below,' with a nod of her head Amber mutely agreed.

Lucas wanted her, and, dear God, she wanted him. She wanted to feel that sensuous mouth on her own again, those elegant hands on her naked flesh, feel once more the exquisite pleasure only Lucas could provide. There was no point in denying it.

He didn't give her time to change her mind. Clasping her hand, he led her quickly down into the living quarters. His steps were urgent as he hurried her through the salon and into the bedroom.

Kicking the door shut behind him, he let go of her hand and reached for her, quickly opening the buttons of her jacket, and he slid it down her shoulders to drop unnoticed on the floor.

Amber gasped, her breathing was fractured, her pulse was racing, her breasts swelling against the silk camisole. His smouldering eyes burned a path down her body, taking in the bare midriff; at the same time his fingers deftly dealt with the fastening of her trousers. His dark head bent towards her and her lips parted in anticipation of his kiss, but instead he moved lower, his mouth closing over the tip of her silk-encased breast, sucking on it, then biting and nibbling, and her spine arched on a fierce shock of sensual pleasure.

He dropped to his knees, taking her trousers and briefs with him while his mouth slid from her breast to lick down over her bare midriff, and circle her navel, and lower.

'No, Lucas,' she tried to protest at the ultimate intimacy, even as a low erotic moan escaped her. His head jerked up, his black eyes smouldered. Standing up, he whipped the camisole over her head, and tumbled her naked body backwards onto the bed.

Lucas looked down at her, his passionate gaze roaming over every inch of her body as he swiftly stripped naked. 'You're perfect,' he growled, falling down to join her on the bed.

'So are you,' Amber murmured throatily, the sight of his big tanned body, hugely aroused, sending shivers of pleasurable anticipation arching though her.

He leant over her, his mouth capturing hers in a savagely hungry kiss that she welcomed like a sex-starved slave, her tongue tangling with his, relishing the devouring need that had always been between them. His hand slid down over her breast and stomach, along her slender thigh, parting her long legs. He touched her, and she shuddered, her body responding with a wanton life all of its own. She grasped his broad shoulders, her slender hands tracing down his long back, feeling the satin-smooth skin burning beneath her fingertips. She wanted him, wanted him now with a fierce, primitive need.

He broke the kiss. They fought for breath, his dark eyes holding hers asking the question and he saw the answer in her luminous golden gaze. With a low growl he lowered his head and sucked one rigid nipple into his mouth. Her back arched off the bed, and she was lost in the fiery sensations flooding through her. She never heard her own little whimpering cries of pleasure, as with hands and mouth Lucas ravished every inch of her body.

'You want me.' Lucas shifted his weight between her thighs, his arms straining either side of her pulsing body.

She was lost to all reason, her eyes burning like molten gold clung to his. 'Yes, yes, yes,' she pleaded, and involuntarily she lifted her long legs and wrapped them around his lean waist. Lucas thrust into her in one strong stroke, and she cried out at the power of his possession. He was there, where she ached for him.

He filled her, and moved in her in a wild pagan rhythm. Her legs wrapped tighter around his thrusting body as she soared ever higher and higher. Her arms reached for him, pulling his head down close enough for her mouth to meet his. Her tongue sought to repeat the rhythm of their bodies.

Lucas threw back his head, his battle for restraint evident in the damp sheen on the taut bronzed features. He watched her eagerly, as he drove feverishly harder, his hands grasping her buttocks, holding her in a grip of steel as she reached the peak. Her keening cry rending the air as the incredible tension snapped, her tight, pulsing muscles convulsed inside her taking Lucas with her in a fierce dynamic surge of powerful release that shook his great body, totally out of control.

It was a frantic coupling and together they clung in the shuddering aftermath, until finally, their sweat-slicked bodies entwined, they both fought to breathe air into laboured lungs, the pounding of two hearts together.

Amber let her arms fall weakly to the bed as reality intruded. But it wasn't love and she had to remember that, and she tried to move.

Lucas rolled off her, and, lying down beside her, he gathered her tenderly into the curve of his body. She tried to ease away, but he hauled her closer. 'Lie still and let me hold you for a while,' he rasped in a throaty voice. 'My Amber, my sexy wife,' and the satisfaction in his tone was unmistakable.

'Wife,' Amber murmured, her golden eyes widening in surprise as she glanced up at him. The *sexy* she did not like at all—it reminded her too much of their past affair. But the *wife* she did like. Amber Karadines had a nice ring to it.

'Why the surprise?' Lucas grinned and, leaning over her, he kissed her very gently. 'We have just consummated our marriage, and that does make you my wife,' he drawled huskily. 'And if you give me a moment I will prove it to you all over again.' His eyes held hers, glinting with amusement, and Amber could not look away.

His suggestion of a repeat performance was enough to make her stomach curl and her breasts tingle, in shameful awareness of his promise of more sensual delights to come. 'I thought we were supposed to be going out to sea,' she reminded him, to take her mind off more erotic thoughts.

'I know,' he declared with a rueful grin. 'I'm beginning to wonder if a cruising holiday was such a great idea with only me to steer the boat.'

'Serves you right.' Amber laughed. 'You will be stuck at the wheel all day and night.'

'No way.' His head bent and he captured her mouth with his own.

Her lips parted, and her senses stirred again, a slow, deep, salacious curl of excitement that unfurled from her belly to ignite every nerve-end in her body. Lucas thought she was sex mad, always had. Why try to deny it? she wondered with stark reality—after all, this was what she wanted. She let her hands slide up over the bulging biceps to the wide shoulders and up to tangle in the thick black hair, and she held his head to hers and returned the kiss with equal fervour.

It was dark when Amber opened her eyes. She rolled over onto her stomach and discovered she was alone in the big bed. Then she realised the low noise she could hear was the sound of the engines, and the gentle motion of the boat told her he had put out to sea. Struggling to a sitting position, she surveyed the tangled mass of sheets, and her own slightly bruised naked body. She was just reaching for a sheet to cover her with when a light flicked on. Blinded by the light, she blinked for a moment.

'Good, you're awake. Come on.' Lucas smiled, walking over to the bed and lifting her bodily out of it.

'Wait a minute, what do you think you are doing?'

He lowered her down the length of his long body, and, with her feet on the not-so-firm floor, she glanced up at him. 'What time is it?'

'Time you started work, sailor. Hurry and get dressed

and meet me on the deck. If I stay here much longer—' his sparkling black eyes slid lasciviously over her naked body '—the boat will probably run aground.'

Ten days later, Amber leant on the rail of the boat with a cup of coffee in one hand, idly surveying the approaching shoreline. She had just showered and put on a fine lawn sarong skirt in blue and white with a blue bandeau around her breasts. Her long hair hung down her back in wet strands, because Lucas's precious boat with all mod cons did not possess a hair-dryer.

Stifling a big yawn, she lifted the cup to her mouth and took a sip. She grimaced as she swallowed. She needed the caffeine—an unrestricted diet of sex, sex and more sex could be pretty exhausting. For the first four days of their honeymoon, Lucas had anchored the boat in a secluded cove and they had lived on sex and the provisions on board. Lucas was almost insatiable, more so than she remembered, and, being brutally honest, she was no better herself.

He only had to look at her a certain way and they were straight into bed, or not necessarily the bed—the salon, the galley, the deck, a beach, even the sea, which she was surprised was possible. Maybe Lucas had been right about her all along—maybe she was a sex fiend, but then what did that make him?

She drained her coffee-cup and sighed. He certainly did not love her, the word hadn't been mentioned. Sometimes when she felt him deep inside her, possessing her, devouring her completely, she had to bite her tongue to stop crying out her love for him.

The tour of the Greek coastline had been a joke. The only sites Amber had seen were the sea and a naked Lucas. Her lips curled in a secretive smile—not that she was complaining. Lucas was fun to be with, and an experienced and inventive lover, and no woman could have dreamed of a more passionate honeymoon. And they had actually managed to travel through the Corinthian canal a couple of days ago.

They had stopped in the town of Corinth, and dined out for a change, and now they were heading for Karadines Island, and home.

Home was such an emotive word, and Amber felt longingly of her own little house in England. Amber was beginning to have severe doubts about lazing around all summer. It was all right for Lucas—he was going back to work after the weekend. He had told her last night. He had everything arranged: they would live on the island, and Lucas would travel into Athens most days by helicopter, but when he had to travel further afield Amber would go with him—at least until the children arrived, he'd laughed.

Amber had been stunned to think Lucas was actually considering her as the mother of his children. Or had he been joking…? She wasn't sure and so she'd mumbled something and changed the subject.

Before she'd left England she'd visited her doctor and started taking the pill, because, though loath to admit it, she'd known a platonic marriage was never going to work between them. And she wasn't fool enough to risk getting pregnant, much as she would love to have his child, until she was sure their relationship was going to last beyond the probate of Spiro's will. Lucas had let her down before, and she still didn't trust him…

Two large hands slid around her slender waist. 'Time to take up position.'

'What position would that be?' Amber queried teasingly as she turned in his arms to face him. He looked good enough to eat, showered and shaved and dressed in white tailored shorts, and pale blue short-sleeved shirt, and his sensuous mouth curved in a wicked smile.

'How about over the rail?' Lucas prompted, elevating one dark brow enquiringly. 'I think that's one we have missed.' His head dipped and he kissed her, and in an exaggerated gesture bent her back over the rail.

'No, no,' she squealed with laughter as he nuzzled the side of her neck. 'I was only joking.'

'I wasn't,' Lucas drawled mockingly, allowing her to stand up.

'You're incorrigible.' Amber shook her head, but grinned.

'I know. We will save the rail for later. In the meantime would you go to the stern of the ship and be ready to throw the line? We are going to dock in a few minutes.'

Only then did she notice they were a lot nearer the shore. She could see the tiny harbour, and she was vividly reminded of her other visit here with Tim and Spiro. It seemed a lifetime ago now...

Twenty-two and in love for the first time, the only time. Full of confidence and dressed up to the nines, she'd set out to make Lucas Karadines notice her. Hoping and praying he would fall in love with her, and they would live happily ever after. Then believing he had, she'd been bitterly disillusioned when their relationship had ended.

Who would have thought years later she would be coming back as Lucas's wife? Was she making the same mistake again? Amber wondered. No, because it wasn't the same. She was no longer a young, trusting fool; she no longer wore her heart on her sleeve. She and Lucas had a mature adult relationship based mostly on sexual attraction and a growing mutual respect. She kept her love and her innermost thoughts to herself. Perhaps she had finally grown up emotionally...

How times change, Amber mused sadly, her hazel eyes hazing with moisture. She was no longer the carefree girl who had first arrived on this island, but at least she was here. Poor Spiro was dead, and the woman Lucas had really loved, Christina, was also dead, both long before their time. Amber was the lucky one. She had a chance at a good marriage. It was up to her to take it. Life was too short for regrets.

CHAPTER TEN

'THROW it, Amber. Amber!' Lost in her thoughts, Amber had forgotten what she was supposed to be doing until an irate Lucas appeared at her side, grabbed the rope from her hand and threw it, muttering a string of curses in Greek.

She looked at him, and felt her breath catch in her throat. His hair was rumpled, his big muscled chest was bare and he looked supremely male and infinitely desirable.

'What were you thinking of?' Lucas whirled to face her. 'We almost hit the pier.'

'Sorry.' Amber smiled up at him, and, stepping forward, she looped her arms around his neck and, stretching up, placed a swift kiss on his firm lips. 'Guess,' she murmured teasingly.

His arms clasped her loosely around the waist, his dark eyes lit with laughter. 'I'd take you up on that, but the welcoming party awaits.'

Before she could respond, a heavy-set middle-aged man hurried along the deck to meet them carrying two garlands of wild flowers in his hands.

As he approached Lucas greeted him, and, taking Amber's hand, said, 'This is Tomso, he runs the bar-cum-store, and is in charge in my absence—a sort of mayor.'

Amber smiled as Tomso insisted on placing the garlands of flowers over their heads and leading them ashore. 'What did he say?' she asked Lucas as they stepped onto the old stone pier. The row of about a dozen or more whitewashed houses lined one side of the earth road overlooking the bay were the same. But the twenty or so smiling faces of the locals waiting to greet them were a surprise.

'Every new Karadines bride arriving on the island has to be met with a garland of flowers; it's tradition.' Sliding an arm around her shoulders, and briefly kissing her smiling mouth, he added, 'We also have to walk to the villa.'

A great cheer went up as Lucas led her along the road, and suddenly Amber wondered if Christina had enjoyed the same welcome and her smile dimmed a little.

Sensing her withdrawal, Lucas looked directly into her eyes. 'What's wrong? Tired?'

'No, I just wondered how many other Karadines brides got to do this walk,' she replied flippantly.

'You're the first,' he conceded wryly. 'I should have added if we don't have a tradition we invent one.'

Amber's head jerked around and she looked at him with open-mouthed incredulity. 'You invent...' And staring into his sparkling eyes, she shook her head and grinned.

Hand in hand they walked up the winding path that led to the big rambling Greek-style house. Scarlet bougainvillaea made a brilliant splash of colour against one of the white walls. As they drew closer Amber could see the huge iron gates were open onto the forecourt with an ornate fountain in the centre.

'Come on, let me show you the house.' Lucas urged her inside out of the sun.

'I have been here before,' she reminded him easily.

He looked down at her, his dark glance moving intently over her lovely face. 'As a visitor years ago. Now I welcome you to your home, Amber.'

'And was it Christina's home as well?' She wanted to bite her tongue the minute she'd said it. But to her astonishment Lucas grinned and swept her up high in his arms.'

'Never,' he said adamantly. 'Christina was a city girl through and through. Nothing would persuade her to visit the island. But it's good to know you are jealous.'

Whatever she might have said was lost, as Lucas turned to introduce her to a plump lady waiting in the cool of the interior.

'This is Anna, she keeps the place running. If you want anything you just ask. She does speak a little English.'

Anna shook hands with Amber enthusiastically. 'Welcome, welcome. It is hot for you. You like a cool drink? Lemon?'

'Yes, thank you.' Amber looked around her. The impressive reception hall with its central marble staircase looked different, but she could not immediately think why. She turned enquiring eyes up at Lucas. 'It is different,' she said. 'But why?'

'Let me show you.' Grasping her hand in his again, he gestured with his free hand to ornate double doors set in one wall. 'Remember the sitting room? It has been extended into what was the study. The dining room, the terrace and everything else is the same. But I've had the opposite side extended by about thirty feet.' Then she realised the one wall of the hall that had been blank now had two doors set into it. He led her through one of them.

Amber stared around her in amazement. Pride of place went to a custom-made oak desk fitted with all the latest computer equipment. A long low cream hide sofa overlooked a large window that opened onto a vast expanse of lawn, and in the distance there was what looked like a stone patio area. She turned to look up at Lucas. 'This is your new study,' she surmised.

'No.' He folded his arms around her waist, his black eyes holding hers. 'This is *your* study. I know how much your work means to you and this study has everything you need to keep in touch with the world markets, and your office in London. Mine is next door. I did think of having one big study, but I realised if we shared one neither of us would get much work done. Do you like it?'

Like it! She loved it. Lowering her eyes from his, she swallowed the lump of emotion lodged in her throat. More importantly, she loved what it represented. Years ago he had objected to her work, and now he had done this for her. He was not quite the male chauvinist pig she had thought him to be. He understood her need to work, to be her own woman. Hope grew in her heart for their marriage. Building a study for her was not the act of a man who expected to be rid of her a few months later.

'Well?' he prompted when she took too long to answer.

'I love it,' she said simply. She could feel the threatening prickle of moisture in her eyes, and to hide her emotions she eased out of his embrace and walked back to the window and stared out.

'I knew you would.' Lucas followed, slipping a casual arm around her waist.

Amber leant into him, revelling in the hard heat of his body. 'And of course you are always right,' she teased.

'Not always.' He moved to her side, his eyes catching hers again. 'But I am trying, I want you to be happy here...' he lifted one hand, so he could gently comb his fingers through her long loose hair '...with me,' he husked and she trembled, her breasts swelling against her top.

'I think I will be,' she murmured, wallowing in the wonderful heady sense of elation she was experiencing as she stroked a hand up over his broad chest and felt his muscles ripple with pleasure.

'Good.' His black eyes moved lazily over her small face, the expression in the darkening depths anything but good; wickedly sexual, more like.

'Anna will be here any second,' Amber said, reading his mind.

'You're right.' Lucas grinned, stepping back. 'But I shall continue the guided tour until we reach the bedroom.' Looking out of the window, he added, 'There is no sea view, which is a plus for a study, as it would only be a distraction.' He indicated with his hand the patio area. 'But you do have a view of the heliport so you will know the moment I arrive home.'

Amber couldn't help but burst out laughing. Trust Lucas! He had given her a high-tech study so she could continue to work, but made absolutely sure she would know the second he was home. He hadn't changed that much after all...

'What's so funny?' One dark brow arched in genuine puzzlement.

'Nothing—nothing at all,' Amber said, shaking her head, her long golden hair shimmering over her shoulders.

Anna entered the room carrying a tray with the jug of lemonade and two glasses and, thanking the housekeeper, Amber filled the glasses and handed one to Lucas. 'Drink your lemonade and show me the bedrooms.'

His black eyes flared and he drank down the lemonade in one go. Reaching out to flick her hair back over her shoulder, he implored her to hurry up. Five minutes later he was lowering her down onto an enormous bed, and joining her.

'Nice bedroom,' Amber commented, running her fingers up into his hair, and then his mouth covered hers.

Clothes were ripped off, and with eager hands and hot and urgent mouths they explored and gloried in each other, until finally once more they reached the ultimate pinnacle of passion and then slid languidly into the heated comfort of the aftermath.

'All right, Amber?' Lucas's husky demand vibrated against her smooth cheek, as she lay sprawled on top of him.

'Better than all right,' she breathed against his chest, and, pushing herself up, she looked around. She spied her skirt, her *torn* skirt, and, glancing back down at Lucas, she added, 'But we have to stop doing this or I will very soon have no clothes left!'

'I have to go to Milan next week. Come with me and you can shop till you drop.'

She went to Milan with him, and Lucas bought her a complete new wardrobe, and on returning to the island she modelled the whole lot for him, including the lingerie, with countless interruptions.

It was lucky she had because over the ensuing weeks Lucas spent only three days a week in Athens, but numerous business colleagues arrived on the island. Though she had told herself she would not socialise, she did, and she was too much of a professional to greet smart-suited businessmen in cut-off jeans. She contacted her own office and discovered quite a few of her clients had insisted on dealing only with her. With the compliance of her boss, and the state-of-the-art equipment Lucas had provided, she quickly slipped back into work mode and when Lucas was in Athens she spent the time as hard at work.

As the weeks stretched into two months they developed an enviable lifestyle. They went swimming, sailed, ate together and slept together. They also talked, listened to music or sometimes simply sat companionably in the same room reading. The one thing they did not do was talk about their relationship and underpinning all their activities was the simmering desire for each other. Their love-making was great. They could not keep their hands off each other.

Amber wandered out onto the terrace and sat down on a conveniently placed lounger overlooking the gardens and the pool, and stared out at the sun-drenched blue of the sea beyond. Her marriage was working better than she had ever dreamed possible. She remembered their early-morning romp and a sensual smile curved her wide mouth. But was sex enough? she asked herself, chewing her bottom lip with her teeth. It was Monday and three weeks today she was supposed to return to England. She would have to go back anyway, because, although she could keep on top of her job as well from the island as England, her clients expected some personal contact, as did the other partners in the firm. She would miss this place, lazing around in only briefs and a cotton shirt, with the greatest lover in the world for company. What more could a woman want?

'Hi, beautiful, waiting for me?' Lucas leant over and brushed his lips lightly over her brow before sitting down on the lounger beside her, flicking open the buttons of his jacket and shrugging it off.

'Yes. But I didn't hear the helicopter.' Amber glanced across at him, and watched as he unfastened the buttons of his shirt and lay back with a sigh. He had been in Athens today and he looked tired—sexy but tired.

With his eyes closed, his long lashes curled on high cheekbones, his firm lips curved in a smile. 'That's because I came back by boat. The helicopter is out of service until Saturday.'

'But what about the rest of the week?'

Lucas dealt her a simmering look from half-closed eyes. 'The rest of the week, I am going to stay here with you.'

Amber rose to her feet and, leaning over him, she murmured, 'Promises, promises.' She pressed her lips to his, probing his mouth with her tongue. Lucas responded by slipping his strong hands up under the soft shirt she was wearing to cup her full, firm breasts with his palms, and groaning. 'This is what I came back for,' he confided hoarsely, and moments later they were in the shuttered coolness of their bedroom.

Amber threw off her shirt, and watched utterly enslaved as Lucas stripped off his, and then with a husky growl tumbled her naked onto the bed.

A long powerful thigh nudged hers apart and she wrapped her arms around his neck and kissed his mouth, his eyes, his shoulder, anywhere she could reach.

His long fingers teased her nipples, traced over her stomach and parted the soft folds of velvety flesh between her thighs. Amber groaned out loud, heat flooding through her, and he took her hard and fast, and she was with him all the way until their mingled cries of release left them absolutely sated in each other's arms.

'Do you think the hot climate in Greece has anything to do with making people feel sexy?' Amber asked lazily.

A great guffaw of laughter greeted her remark, and Lucas, propping himself up on one elbow, stared down at her. 'You know what I l…' And he stopped, an arrested expression in his black eyes. He focused on her flushed face, her swollen mouth, thick black lashes screening his gaze. 'What I adore about you, Amber, for all your brains and beauty, you can be so naive.'

Amber forced a grin to her lips, but for a moment there she had been sure he was going to say he loved her. 'Better naive than world-weary, like some I could mention.'

He didn't rise to her teasing but looked at her for a long while with disturbing intensity. 'You're right.' And, rolling off the bed, Lucas strolled over to the bathroom. 'I need a shower.'

Ah, well! Amber sighed happily. They had the whole week together. But she was wrong...

After dinner Lucas retired to his study to make a few calls and Amber headed for bed. Fifteen minutes later, showered and wearing a peach-coloured satin negligée, Amber walked back into the bedroom, the material floating around her as she moved. Tiny shoestring straps supported the bodice—a delicately embroidered web of fine lace revealing tantalising glimpses of her full breasts and dusky nipples. Outrageously sexy, it had been chosen for her by Lucas and Amber felt great wearing it. She crossed to the dressing table, and, opening a drawer, withdrew the small box that held her contraceptive pills, a dreamy smile on her face. Lucas would be joining her soon. Flipping open the top of a delicately lacquered box, she picked up a pill and lifted her hand to her mouth.

'What the hell are you doing?' Lucas's deep voice roared, and the box went flying through the air, pills cascading on the floor, and suddenly her wrist was caught in an iron grip. 'Drop it. Drop it now,' he said in a rough threatening voice, with menace in his dark eyes.

The single pill fell from her fingers, and Amber felt a frisson of fear run down her spine. She had never seen Lucas in such a violent temper.

He pulled her towards him, the strong dark planes of his face contorted with rage. 'What are they?' he demanded, fury in every line of his body. 'Tell me, damn you.'

She opened her mouth to speak but no sound came out. The tension in him was so strong that she shivered at the impact of it. She stared at him, and the violence leaping in his eyes scared her witless. Amber told herself she had no reason to fear him, she had every right to take birth control pills.

'Answer me, woman,' he raged, his hand falling from her hair to curve around her throat, tipping her head back. 'Tell me or so help me I'll—'

'You're hurting me.' She choked, the breath squeezed from her lungs.

Suddenly he released her, but he still held her wrist. She tried to jerk away, shaking from head to foot, but he forcibly pulled her closer.

'Birth control pills,' she muttered in a low, frightened voice.

'Not amphetamines,' Lucas grated between his teeth, some of the anger easing from his body. 'You're sure?' His simmering black eyes fixed on her face.

Some opinion he had of her that he dared suggest she would take drugs. Anger tightened her mouth, and she returned his look with a hard, level stare. 'They are my birth control pills,' she reiterated.

'My wife, and you—'

'Thought I was a junkie,' Amber cut in hardly.

She saw him stiffen 'One cannot be too sure nowadays.' His dark eyes were hooded and curiously blank when he added, 'You'd better pick them up, as you seem to think you need them.' Letting go of her wrist, he spun around and stalked off into the bathroom without another word.

Amber crawled around the floor trying to find her remaining pills, and then, placing the box back in the drawer, she climbed into bed. Lucas's reaction puzzled her—it had been out of all proportion, and totally out of character.

The bathroom door opened and Lucas approached the bed, a small white towel flung precariously around his hips, and with another towel he was rubbing his damp hair. Helplessly Amber's eyes trailed over his magnificent tanned torso, and she forgot their brief argument, her body warming at the sight of him.

Lucas slid into bed and, leaning over her, brushed a few strands of hair from her forehead, his fingertips stroking down the curve of her cheek. 'Do you like children, Amber?'

'Yes,' she murmured, but warning bells rang in her brain.

'So why the pill? You're a married woman,' he asked silkily, his dark eyes intent and a little speculative on her lovely face.

Amber didn't want this conversation, not now, not yet... Easing away from his side, she looked up at him, and, choosing her words carefully, she said, 'You told me to take it the first time we were together, so naturally I do now.'

'And if I told you to stop? If I told you I wanted you to be the mother of my child,' he suggested, 'how would you respond?'

Her heart missed a beat, but her own sense of self-preservation made her cautious. 'That it was not a very sensible suggestion if we are to part in a few months.' She waited with bated breath, hoping and praying for him to ask her to stay for ever, tell her he cared. She was disappointed...

For a space of ten seconds he didn't speak. She saw the muscles bunch at the edge of his jaw, and if she had not known better she would have thought he was shocked. 'That could be ignored,' he finally offered.

'Why?' She had to know. She had swallowed her pride once where Lucas was concerned and she wasn't doing it a second time. It was his turn...

'I'm forty-one, it is time I had a family, and you are twenty-nine next week. It makes sense.'

There was nothing in the world she wanted more than to have his baby, but the cold calculation in his words and his unsubtle reminder of her age were not what she had wanted to hear and her disappointment was intense. 'I'll take it under consideration,' she mocked, evading a direct answer. 'But right now, I'm tired, can we have this conversation some other time?'

'There is nothing more to say.' Amber flinched at the finality in his tone, the cold derision in the eyes that met hers, and when he turned his back on her and went to sleep she had a sinking feeling the honeymoon was over.

Wednesday afternoon she answered the telephone in her study, and smiled at the sound of her father's voice. She needed something to cheer her up, as her marriage was going down the pan fast. Yesterday Lucas had buried himself away in his study, only surfacing for meals. Last night they had lain in the same bed, but as far apart as it was possible to be. Amber could sense him both physically and mentally withdrawing from her and she could do nothing about it. But realistically she knew a relationship built only on sex was bound to fail. The only question was *when*?

Five minutes of listening to all the city and family gossip cheered her up.

'We had visitors at the weekend—your friend Clive.' Her father chuckled.

'Clive?' Amber responded in surprise.

'Yes, he wanted to know if you will be back for your birthday next week.'

'Not next week, but I will be back soon.' Amber didn't see Lucas standing at the open door of her study or the murderous expression on his face as he turned and left. A few minutes later she concluded the conversation.

Turning back to the computer, she tried to work. The

mood Lucas was in there was no point in joining him, she thought acidly.

'Are you busy?' The man occupying her thoughts walked into the room.

Amber swung around on her chair. 'Not if you can think of something better to do,' she teased with determined cheerfulness. He was wearing a beige linen suit, and the desperate thought occurred to her that, if she got him almost naked in the pool, perhaps they could get back to the way they had been. 'It's so hot I thought I might go for a swim.' Rising to her feet, she walked towards him.

'Don't let me stop you,' he said bitingly. Her golden gaze winged to his and she froze at the contempt she saw in his black eyes.

'I thought you might join me,' she said quietly.

His mouth twisted into a mockery of a smile. 'Sorry, but I have to go to Athens after all, something has come up.'

'I thought the helicopter—'

'It is repaired,' he said, cutting her off. Anger gleamed cold as ice in the darkness of his eyes, but there was reluctant desire too, and it was the desire she responded to when he pulled her into his arms and kissed her with a fierce, possessive passion. Then just as fiercely he put her away from him.

'I won't be back until Saturday. If you need anything, call me—Tomso has the number.' He strode out of the room.

What she needed he could not give her, she realised with a despairing sigh, the sound lost in the whirring sound of the helicopter arriving. He had not even said goodbye.

Amber watched from the window as the helicopter rose

in the air and vanished. It was happening all over again—
Lucas running out on her. The truly sad part was, Amber
realised stoically, she wasn't even surprised she had no
faith in him. She'd been expecting it.

CHAPTER ELEVEN

AFTER spending the night alone, Amber was nowhere near as stoic. She missed Lucas desperately. She had not slept. She couldn't work, and finally mid-morning she decided to walk down to the pier. Tomso waved her into the bar and over a cup of coffee he rhapsodised in fractured English over Lucas and their marriage, informing her they had never seen Lucas so happy, and if anyone deserved to be happy he did after the terrible loneliness of the past few years.

Amber presumed Tomso meant the deaths of all Lucas's family members and it made her think. She had acquired a whole new family that had taken her into their home and hearts while Lucas had lost his. His grief must have been horrendous. Strolling back along the beach, she sat down on the hot sand and took a long, hard look at herself, and was not impressed at what she saw.

She claimed she loved Lucas, but she was too proud and too frightened of being hurt to tell him. But she was hurting now anyway. If she truly loved him, and she did, she should be declaring it from the rooftops, not hiding it as though it were something shameful. Was she really so lacking in courage?

As for Lucas, he had an inherent need to be in control at all times. He was a dynamic, arrogant man, but not a man to talk about his feelings or show them. He was a loner; he withdrew behind a cool, aloof mask at the least sign of challenge to his real emotions. Yet when they made love Amber was almost sure he was as overwhelmed as she was, but far too proud to admit it. But then so was she...

Lucas had hinted she stay with him and have his child. Perhaps that was as near as he could get to admitting he wanted her every way a man wanted a woman, and not just as the sex object he had once labelled her. Christina was dead, and Amber was pretty certain there was no other woman in his life. Dared she take a chance and tell him how she felt? Was she strong enough to cope if he rejected her love? The answer to both questions was yes.

The bible said, 'hope deferred maketh the heart sick,' and it was happening to her. Surely it was better to know the truth one way or the other and get on with her life? And, with that thought in mind, she had made her decision.

The following morning Amber dressed with care in one of her Milan purchases. A sleek white linen dress, with a slightly scooped neckline, buttoned from top to bottom and skimming her slender body from shoulder to mid-thigh, with a matching fabric high-heeled sandals and shoulder-bag to complete the outfit. Her long hair was swept up in a twist on top of her head, and even in the late summer heat she looked coolly sophisticated. She had talked Tomso into bringing her to the mainland by boat and he had also arranged the taxi to carry her to the tower block that housed the offices of Karadines International.

Getting out of the taxi, she hitched her bag on her shoulder and took a step towards the entrance and froze. She blinked and blinked again. It couldn't be—she was seeing things. The woman was dead...

'Amber, it's good to see you again. I was sorry to hear about Spiro, but I hear congratulations are in order, and, hey, Lucas isn't a bad old stick. Even after our divorce he still looks after me, though he does not have to. We have just been to see him.'

It was Christina, a slim, beautiful, positively glowing with life Christina, and obviously pregnant, accompanied by a very handsome young man whom she proudly introduced as her husband with love shining in her dark eyes.

The blood drained from Amber's face. She was pole-axed. She said something and it must have been okay, because a few minutes later she was standing on her own, her dazed eyes watching Christina and her husband walk down the street.

'Hi, Amber.' She vaguely heard her name and turned her head; it was Joe. 'Are you okay? You look like you've seen a ghost.'

'Maybe I have,' she said without thinking in her shocked state, her stomach twisted with nausea and sweat dampening her smooth brow.

'Funny! I'm glad to see you haven't lost your sense of humour. Lucas has been acting like a bear with a sore head for the last two days. For the sake of his poor beleaguered workforce, try and cheer him up, will you? You are going up to see him?

'Oh, yes.' See him! She was going to kill him… Lucas had lied…

'Come. I'll show you to his private lift.' With Joe leading the way, Amber stalked into the Karadines building. Joe ushered her into the small lift.

'It opens into his private office suite. I'll probably catch you later,' Joe said with a grin as the doors swished shut.

Amber sank back against the wall, her mind a mass of teeming emotional pain, humiliation, sheer disbelief. It was a horrible thought, but until now she had not realised how much she had counted on Christina being finally out of his life to win Lucas's love. Tim had told her to take a chance, but she had never had one… Lucas had told her his wife was dead. It was a lie of such magnitude no one with any sense of morality could forgive it. Not only was Christina alive and well, but she had divorced Lucas and married a gorgeous young man and was pregnant. But Lucas was still looking after her.

With blinding clarity Amber saw it all. It must have been a hell of a jolt to Lucas's colossal ego to be rejected by the woman he loved, the woman who had lost his child, and then to see Christina happily married and pregnant again.

Amber had felt sympathy for him and had hoped that once the grieving was past he would fall in love with her. Only last night she'd decided to tell him how much she loved him, and all the time the swine had lied to her. His request she have his baby took a much more sinister turn in the light of Christina's pregnancy. Lucas hated to lose at anything. If his ex-wife could have another child, then so could he. Lucas didn't care about her, Amber realised. She was obviously a convenient pawn to be used in the competition with his ex-wife, and Spiro's legacy was an added bonus.

Amber had been second best once in Lucas's life and she was damned if she would be again. She didn't need the lying, conniving pig, and she was about to tell him so. By the time the lift stopped Amber's overriding emotion was murderous rage.

Her golden eyes leaping with fury, she strode out of the lift, and on past a stunned-looking secretary who cried, 'You can't go in there,' as Amber thrust wide the door of Lucas's office, and slammed it shut behind her.

The object of her fury was sitting behind a large desk. His head shot up as the door slammed, his black brows arching enquiringly, and not a flicker of emotion disturbed his hard-cut handsome features. 'Amber, to what do I owe this honour?'

'Honour, honour!' she screeched, striding across to the desk and planting her hands flat on it. 'You don't know the meaning of the word, you devious, lying bastard.'

'Be careful what you say, Amber.' Lucas shoved back his seat and stood up, moving around the desk. 'A Greek will not allow anyone to cast a slur on his honour. Even you, my beautiful virago,' he drawled mockingly, but with a hint of steel in his tone.

'How could you?' she demanded wildly. 'How could you tell me Christina was dead? What kind of sick joke was that? You want to get down on your knees and pray for your immortal soul or you will surely go to hell.' She was in full flood now. Her golden gaze clashed with his. 'The night before our wedding Tim convinced me to take a chance on you growing to love me. After all, you were a man with a man's need and your first wife was dead. So I did.' Amber didn't see the brilliant flare of triumph in Lucas's eyes—she was on a roll. 'The other night when you flung my pills from my hand...' she accompanied the word with the gesture, knocking a desk lamp flying to the floor with a resounding crash, but even that did not stop her '...then you suggested I have your baby, I, idiot that I am, actually felt guilty for denying you. I spent all yesterday thinking how really you were a caring guy, but too shy to show your emotions!' A hysterical laugh escaped her. 'Shy! You don't have any genuine emotions, only devious plans!'

'Amber,' Lucas slotted in, 'you've got it all wrong.' Reaching out, he grasped her upper arms.

'No. I have finally got it right! After five long, miserable years I am over you. I actually came here today to tell you the opposite. What a joke! I got out of the taxi and, low and behold, risen from the dead on your doorstep I meet Christina, the woman you really love. God! How it must have dented your pride to have your young wife discard you. But I am through being a substitute for any woman.'

'Shut up and listen to me.' His hands tightened on her arms. 'You're screaming like a fish wife, and there is no need.'

His eyes were black but there was fire in them that mirrored the violent emotion in her own. 'Need. What would you know about need? Everything is sex and money to you,' she retorted, trying to pull free, but his grip tightened.

Suddenly aware of how close they were, she felt a trembling start deep in the pit of her stomach, and she stared at him in blazing, humiliating anger. 'I am through listening to you,' she said, feeling her hands clenching into fists at her sides. 'I am leaving you. I never want to see you again. As for Spiro's legacy, see my lawyer.'

His mouth curled in a chilling smile. 'Very convincing but don't pretend you're leaving on my account. I heard you yesterday on the telephone talking to Clive, telling him *not next week but soon*. Three nights without sex too long for you, Amber?' he asked with biting sarcasm.

Her hand flew out and slapped his face in blazing anger. His head jerked back and his eyes leaping with rage clashed with hers for a second, before he hauled her hard against him, his mouth crashing down on hers, kissing her with a raw, savage fury that left her with the taste of blood in her mouth.

She tried to struggle, but he was too strong, and when he finally lifted his head she stared at him with bitter, pain-filled eyes, tears burning at the back of her throat because his last crack had told her his opinion of her had never changed. She froze in his arms and pride alone made her tell him the truth.

'I spoke to my father yesterday. He mentioned Clive

had visited him, and as a friend asked if I was coming back for my birthday. A *friend* that is all Clive has ever been. But you,' she said, her lips trembling, 'you never saw me as anything but an easy lay. You have the mind of a sewer rat.' The tears she had restrained for so long filled her eyes; she blinked furiously, but one escaped down the soft curve of her cheek. 'And I am leaving you.' She tried to push him away, the tears falling faster now as the trauma of the last few days, few months, finally caught up with her and Lucas's callous comment had been the last straw.

'Oh, hell, Amber.' Lucas groaned, hauling her tight against him. 'Don't cry. I can't bear to hear you cry.' With one strong hand he stroked her back, while his other hand lifted to her face and his fingers smoothed the wetness from her cheeks.

She choked back a sob. 'I am not crying,' she murmured, but long shudders racked her slender frame.

Suddenly the door opened, and Lucas turned his head and said something violently to his poor secretary, but the interruption gave Amber the strength to break free from him, and, rubbing the moisture from her face, she fought to regain her self-control. She was not shedding another tear over the fiend, and on shaky legs she stepped towards the door.

'No, Amber. Please.' Lucas swept her up in his arms. 'You have had your say, now it is my turn.'

'What do you think you're doing? Put me down,' she demanded hoarsely.

'What I should have done years ago, but never had the guts,' Lucas admitted and, sitting down on the sofa, he held her fast in the cradle of his arms. His face was only inches away from hers, and the black eyes caught hers with brilliant intensity.

Even in her abject misery, to her horror, the scent, the heat of him invaded her senses, reawakening the familiar awareness she always felt in his presence. 'Let me go, Lucas. Your secretary.' She was grasping at any excuse; she had to get away.

'No, I am going to keep you here until you hear me out,' Lucas informed her bluntly. 'Even a condemned man is allowed to speak.' His features were harsh, brooding as he studied her tear-streaked face.

She nodded—she did not trust herself to speak. Better to hear him out and get out, before she broke down completely in front of him.

'Forgive me for what I said about three days without sex. I didn't mean it. But to hear the mention of Clive's name is enough to drive me insane with jealousy.'

He was jealous, and it gave her hope.

'But I believe you, I know you have to go back to London. You love your work, and I had every intention of taking you. I even got your father to purchase the old rectory for us in the village near his home. I thought we could split the year between Greece and England.' And tilting her chin with one finger, he looked deep into her tear-washed eyes. 'But I wanted it to be a surprise for your birthday.'

Surprised! She was amazed. 'You bought a house?' she murmured. He had been planning for their future together, including her career.

He nodded and continued. 'But I don't believe you meant what you said about Christina. Would you really wish her dead? Because that is what you implied.'

'No, never.' She found her voice. Horrified to think how callous she must have sounded. Then she remembered why she had behaved as she had. 'But you lied.'

'I never lied, Amber. That day in your office I told you

my father had died, and Christina had gone the next year. Perhaps my grasp of English is at fault, but since when had *gone* meant the same as *dead*?'

'Then why did you not tell me you were divorced?' she demanded huskily.

'What man wants to discuss the biggest mistake of his life,' he said slowly, and she felt his muscular body lock with tension, 'with the woman he loves?'

She was held in his protective arms, with the warmth of him surrounding her, and for him to suggest he loved her was the cruellest cut of all to her bruised heart. 'Please, Lucas, no more lies: you loved Christina, you told me so. You probably still do,' she said sadly.

His dark eyes locked on hers as if they would see into her very soul. 'No, I lied to you and myself, and I paid for it with the worst few years of my life.' His dark eyes clouded with remembered pain. 'It was my own fault, but the worst part is knowing in my arrogance I hurt you.'

He brushed her lips with his in a bittersweet tenderness that squeezed her heart. This was Lucas as she had never seen him before. 'I got over it,' she muttered.

'You should not have had to.' He eased her off his lap onto the sofa beside him as if she were the most fragile Dresden doll, and placed an arm around her shoulders, holding her turned towards him. 'I need to explain why I behaved the way I did.' His dark eyes clouded with painful memories. 'My mother was a stunningly beautiful woman.' Amber could believe that. Just look at her son!

'Men adored her. She had numerous affairs—her last one ended at her death of a drug overdose when I was thirteen.' Amber gasped—she had not known that.

'Yes, not very pleasant.' Lucas's lips twisted cynically. 'Though the man we were living with at the time was quite good about it. He gave me a thousand drachmas, and told me I was big enough to look after myself and not to think of my mother as a drug addict because she wasn't. She did not need to get high to be the sexiest lady around.'

'It must have been hard for you.' Amber was shocked, the image of Lucas as a young boy living such a life filled her soft heart with compassion.

'I don't want your pity, Amber,' he said hardly. 'I don't deserve it because I let my mother colour my relationship with you. I didn't see it at the time, but I realised it when it was too late.'

Amber sat up a little straighter—this insight into Lucas's character was so unexpected she could not help but be moved and she wanted to hear more.

'When you came to the villa the first time, you were not as I remembered. You had metamorphosised into an elegant, gorgeous girl who made no secret of what she wanted. I, to my shame, had asked you simply so I could fool Father into thinking you were Spiro's girl, and—'

'You don't need to explain—I know all about that.' Amber felt the colour rise in her cheeks; she had been blatant in her pursuit of Lucas.

'Of course, Spiro told you. Anyway, when we became lovers, although you were a virgin, you were so eager, so uninhibited, you were everything I had ever fantasised about. I wanted you morning, noon and night, and it angered me. I vowed never to be like my mother—addicted to sex—and yet around you I was. I had no control where you were concerned. The year we were together I deliberately forced myself to stay away from you for longer than I needed to, just to prove a point. Then, when I did come back early, you had no time for me, so I began to blame you. Stupid, I know, but though I enjoyed everything you had to give I convinced myself you were too sexy, too career-minded, too free-spirited to be anything other than a girlfriend. Too like my mother.'

His mother had a lot to answer for, Amber thought bitterly. She had coloured his view on relationships from a very early age. But she made no comment as Lucas continued.

'The odd occasion marrying you crossed my mind, I quickly dismissed the notion, and not least because I would also have had to tell my father you had never been Spiro's girl. And I had implied it to hide the fact he was gay. I was an arrogant, conceited bastard, I admit it. When the chance came to make a deal with Alex Aristides, I leapt at it. My father was delighted, and when I met Christina, I was at the right age to marry.' He shrugged his broad shoulders beneath his tailored white silk shirt. 'I am Greek; we are strong on tradition and family. I had just had an argument with you about work, and Christina appeared as a sweet, malleable female. Someone I could love and look after.'

'This is all very interesting, Lucas,' Amber cut in, 'but I really don't need to hear any more.' She was not sitting listening to him telling her how much he loved Christina yet again, and, rising to her feet, she was abruptly pulled back down onto Lucas's lap.

'Damn it, Amber. I am putting my pride on the line here.' He held her firm on his lap and his mouth swooped down on hers and he kissed her with a driven urgency that awakened the same response in her, so that in seconds she was flat on her back on the sofa with Lucas lying over her.

'I am trying to tell you I love you. I always have, being brutally honest.' He clasped her head between his large hands, forcing her to look at him, his black eyes dark and glittering with emotion. 'I knew the last time we were together in the loft but I wouldn't admit it, not even to myself.' He kissed her again. 'I knew when I walked into your office three months ago. But still I told myself it was just sex. I had behaved abominably towards you, and I didn't think you would give me the time of day, so I forced you into marrying me.'

'You wanted Spiro's shares,' she reminded him.

'You think so?' His mouth quirked in self-derision as he continued, 'I already have most of them, as you will discover when you hear from the lawyers. You knew Spiro—did you honestly think he would be able to hang onto his inheritance for one year, never mind five? He invested in every crackpot scheme his friends suggested, and then some. At least a dozen times he sold me blocks of his stock.'

'What, you tricked me?' Wide-eyed, she stared at him, her thoughts in chaos.

'Another lie.' His jaw clenched. 'Haven't you realised yet? I would lie, I would cheat, I would do anything to have you.' Lucas groaned, burying his head in the glorious gold hair. 'But, God help me, Amber, I do love you.'

If he did not marry her for Spiro's legacy, then... Amber reached up to him, her slender fingers lacing around the back of his neck, the blood pounding through her veins. 'I think I am beginning to believe you,' she whispered, incredulous hope growing in her heart.

'Spiro's will gave me the excuse to see you again. I took one look at you sitting behind the desk in your office, and I was determined to have you back in my life. When you told me you might marry Clive I was frantic. I freely admit I lied to get you back. I wasn't taking any chances.'

'But you told me you loved Christina.' Amber could not get over that fact. 'I saw you with her in New York—

when she was pregnant you were so crazy about her you asked me to go and look after her.'

A harsh laugh escaped him. 'I had to look after her, but I never loved her. The marriage was over before the honeymoon finished. You can guess what I discovered on my wedding night, you had already hinted as much. But that did not matter. I tried to make the marriage work, though we were rarely together because she refused to travel. Until I discovered the final irony when she was pregnant, and then the gods really laughed at me. Christina was a drug addict, and had been since the tender age of fourteen, which is why she would not go to the island. Too far away from her supplier and, as for sex, she would do anything with anyone for a fix. I never touched her again.'

'Oh, my God, no.' Amber tightened her arms around him, feeling his anguish as if it were her own. 'The night of the party she was rolling her own cigarettes and I wondered why,' she murmured out loud. 'Her little vice, she said.'

'Cannabis was the least of her addictions. Our baby was stillborn two months before the due date because Christina had been taking heroine all along.' Lucas ran a hand over his eyes as if they hurt him.

'And Christina now?' Amber asked.

'I look after her business interests—a promise I made to her father, but I divorced her as soon as my father died. I persuaded her to go into rehab. She met her new husband there. He is a doctor and much more competent to look after her than I. She has been clean for over a year.'

'I see.' Amber looked deep into his night-black eyes and she knew he was telling the truth.

'Do you? Do you really?' His sensuous lips tightened in a grim line. 'Have you any idea what it did to me the other night seeing you with a pill in your hand? Just a few hours earlier I had almost told you that I loved you, and I had to walk away because I suddenly realised the enormity of my mistake. I did not deserve you. You gave me your love once with all the joyous abandonment of a true innocent and I in my arrogance took it as my due and walked out on you for the sake of what I thought would be an easy marriage. I stood in the shower and I could not believe how blind I had been. Then later when I saw the pill in your hand I nearly died. I thought you were on drugs, and after the last few months together I could not live if anything happened to you. When I realised it was a birth control pill I was relieved but I was angry—I wanted you to have my child, but I had not the courage to tell you I loved you. The next day, hearing you talk to Clive, I was gutted.' The expression in his eyes nearly stopped her heart, so full of anguished love that it was almost painful.

'You do love me,' she whispered, hardly daring to believe it was true.

'Believe it.' And he lowered his head, his mouth finding hers in a kiss of aching tenderness. 'You are in my blood, my bones.' His throatily murmured words made Amber tremble inside. She looked up into his darkly handsome face and was stunned by the slight vulnerability in night-black eyes. 'Forgive me, Amber, stay with me, and I swear I will spend the rest of my life trying to win your love.'

'I forgive you, and you won't have to.' Amber smiled. She had a better understanding of why he had behaved the way he had in the past, and if their marriage was to work she had to believe in him, trust him. She moved sinuously against him, her hands reaching up to clutch at his broad shoulders. 'I do love you, Lucas. I always have and always will—there has never, ever been anyone else for me,' she confessed, and pulled his head back down to hers. Her

tongue touched his and she felt the shuddering intensity
of his response.

They kissed and clung to each other, and with shaking
fingers Lucas unfastened the buttons down the front of her
dress, and parted the fabric exposing the near naked length
of her to his view. 'You are so beautiful, so exquisite
inside and out,' he grated, shrugging off his clothes and
dispensing with her briefs in seconds. His great body
arched over her, his eyes glittered down into hers. 'And
you really are all mine at last.' Then his head swooped
down, and his mouth covered hers in a kiss of pure possession before burning a red-hot trail of fire down her slender throat to her swollen breasts.

He filled up her senses as never before, she was drunk
on the wonder of their declared love. Amber moaned as
he found the rosy peaks and licked them with his tongue.
Her seeking hands stroked up over his back, traced his
spine, and her nails dug into his flesh as he suckled the
rigid tips each in turn, until Amber cried out and her back
arched involuntarily seeking more.

Lifting his head, he looked down at her. 'I love you,
Amber,' Lucas groaned, his voice thick with hunger. 'I
want you.' His fingers spread over her flat stomach, caressing all the erotic places he knew so well.

'And I want you always and for ever.'

With a low growl deep in his throat, he slid between
her thighs and made her his. With huskily muttered words
of love and need, Lucas told her everything she had always
wanted to hear fall from his passionate mouth. Their coming together was better than anything that had gone before,
because this time their bodies and minds as one added a
new dimension. Love.

Surfacing from the exhausted aftermath of their love-
making, Amber stirred in Lucas's arms and looked around.

'Get up, Lucas, get off.' She shoved at him and he sat up, allowing her to do the same.

'No regrets, Amber, you are not going to change your mind,' and she was stunned to see a trace of doubt in his slumberous black eyes.

'No.' He loved her, she could feel it in her soul, and she did not like to see her dynamic, powerful husband uncertain. 'But look where we are, is the door locked?' She grabbed the front of her dress and began frantically fastening buttons.

'No.' His dark eyes, brimming with love, held hers. 'But my secretary would not dare disturb us,' he said with all the arrogant confidence Amber recognised.

She smiled. 'I'm taking no more chances,' and, standing up, she continued dressing, glad to see Lucas was doing the same. 'I can't believe we made love in your office.'

Lucas, looking utterly gorgeous with his hair disheveled, his trousers on and his shirt hanging off his shoulders, pulled her into his arms. 'I can, but if it perturbs you so much...' he grinned down at her '...what about trying the rail we missed on the boat? Another honeymoon?'

And they did...

ARISTIDES' CONVENIENT WIFE

JACQUELINE BAIRD

CHAPTER ONE

ENGLAND IN FEBRUARY was not a place he would have chosen to be, Leon Aristides thought angrily as the freezing rain continued to lash down almost obscuring his view of the road. But the letter he had received at his office in Athens yesterday morning from a Mr Smyth, a partner in a firm of London solicitors, and the information enclosed within had totally stunned him.

Apparently the man had read an article in the *Financial Times,* mentioning the dip in the price of Aristides International shares, where Leonidas Aristides had explained it was an understandable market reaction to the tragic accident that had claimed the lives of his sister and his father, the chairman of the company, but the price would quickly recover. The said Mr Smyth had informed him Delia Aristides was a client of his and he wanted confirmation of her death as his firm held a will made by the lady and he was the executor.

Leon's first thought was that it must be a hoax resulting from the mention of his name in the paper, an unusual enough circumstance in itself. The Aristides name occasionally appeared in financial journals, but rarely if ever in the popular press. A banking family, they belonged to the type of wealthy élite that did not court publicity or fame but concentrated on the fortune. Their privacy was so closely guarded that the general public barely knew they existed. But after a telephone call to Mr Smyth, Leon had quickly realised the man was serious and if he didn't act fast that anonymity might disappear all too soon. He had arranged to call him back later. Then he had finally taken the time to go through his sister's safety deposit box, something he should have done weeks ago, but which the constant pressures of business had prevented.

There were the jewels their mother had left her, as he had expected. But there was also a copy of a will drawn up two years ago by the same Mr Smyth of London and officially signed and witnessed. A will moreover that took precedence over the will held by the family lawyer in Athens that Delia had made at the age of eighteen at their father's instigation.

The information the new will contained so outraged Leon his initial reaction had been to tear the document into a million pieces. But only for an instant before his iron-cool control had reasserted itself and he had called one of his lawyers. The resultant conversation had made him think long and hard.

A return call to Mr Smyth and he'd had an early appointment with the man for the following day. At the crack of dawn this morning he had boarded his private jet heading for London. A sombre interview with the lawyer had confirmed the shocking news.

Apparently on Leon's verbal confirmation of Delia's death he had immediately drafted a letter to one Miss Heywood as instructed, informing her that Delia had died and she was a beneficiary of her will. Leon could do nothing about it now, but he had obtained the man's promise of absolute discretion in the matter and they had parted with a handshake. Mr Smyth was an honest man but no fool, a banking company like Aristides International was not one to upset unnecessarily.

Leon manoeuvred the rental car into the short drive. In the

ordinary course of events he usually travelled by a chauffeured limousine, but in this case absolute secrecy was required until he had assessed the situation. He stopped the car and glanced up at the house. Nestling in the Cotswold hills, it was a double fronted detached stone built house, surprisingly set in the corner of the walled grounds of a luxury hotel.

Which was why he had driven past the entrance drive to the Fox Tower Hotel and around the whole damn estate three times without connecting the entrance to the hotel with the home of Miss Heywood: The Farrow House, Foxcovet Lane. So much for satellite navigation systems. Finally, in frustration he had entered the hotel and booked a room for the night; it looked as if he was going to need one if he did not find the elusive Miss Heywood soon. Then with a few casual questions he had discovered where the house was and why it had taken him so damn long to find it.

A light shone from a downstairs window, hardly surprising given the gloominess of the day, and hopefully an indication Helen Heywood was at home. He had considered ringing her, but he did not want to warn her. The element of surprise was the best weapon in any battle, and this was a conflict he was determined to win.

A predatory gleam lightened his dark eyes as he opened the car door and stepped out onto the gravelled drive slamming the door behind him. Unless she had already received the letter from Mr Smyth, which was highly unlikely if the British postal service was anything like the Greek, the lady was in for one hell of a shock. Squaring his broad shoulders, he approached the front door with decisive steps and rang the bell.

No signal again. Helen slowly replaced the telephone on the hall table, a frown pleating her smooth brow. Her best friend

Delia Aristides led a hectic lifestyle but she usually called every week and visited at least once a month. Admittedly since Delia had returned to Greece last July she had occasionally missed a week or two, but now it was over six weeks without a call. What made it worse was Delia had promised her son, Nicholas, she would definitely visit in the New Year after cancelling her last three visits, but once again she had cancelled at the last minute. Helen had heard nothing since.

She chewed worriedly on her bottom lip. It wasn't fair to Nicholas, or to her for that matter. Nicholas had been at nursery school all morning and, after she had collected him and made his lunch, he was now taking his afternoon nap. She knew he would be awake in an hour, if not sooner, and she wanted to get in touch with Delia before that. But she only had Delia's cell phone number. Helen knew the address of the Aristides island home but not the telephone number, she had tried to get the number from enquiries but of course it had turned out to be ex-directory. She was at a loss as to what to do next.

Helen grimaced and picked up the post she had not yet had time to look at from the hall table. Maybe Delia had written, but it was a forlorn hope. Her friend had never written a letter in all the time she had known her, the nearest she got was a card at Christmas and birthdays. Telephone or e-mail were her preferred forms of communication.

The doorbell rang, and she dropped the post and, heaving a sigh, wondered who could be calling in the middle of the afternoon.

'All right, all right I'm coming,' she muttered as the bell pealed out again and continued to ring. Whoever it was they obviously were not big in the patience department, she thought as she walked down the hall to open the door.

Leon Aristides. Helen stiffened, her hand tightening on the door handle, unable to believe her eyes. For a fleeting moment

she wondered if she had forgotten to wear her contact lenses
and he was a figment of her imagination, but only for a moment.

'Hello, *Helen,*' a deep-throated voice drawled, and although
she was slightly myopic there was nothing wrong with her
hearing. Oh, my God, Delia's brother! Here, at her door.

'Good afternoon, Mr Aristides.' She automatically made
the polite response, her shocked gaze flicking up over him.
Six feet plus and immaculately clad in a dark business suit,
white shirt and silk tie, he hadn't changed much in the years
since she had last met him. He was just as big, and dark, and
forbidding as she remembered.

With heavy-lidded dark eyes and angular cheekbones, a
large straight nose and a wide mouth, he looked hard rather
than handsome. But he was physically attractive in a raw, masculine way. Unfortunately for Helen, he still had the same disturbing effect on her as he had the first time they had met,
bringing a sudden fluttering in her stomach that she determinedly put down to nerves. She couldn't possibly still be
afraid of the man. She was twenty-six, not seventeen any more.

'This is a surprise. What are you doing here?' she finally
asked, eyeing him warily.

She had met him nine years ago, the one time she had gone
on vacation with Delia to her family holiday home in Greece,
and she had been left with a lasting impression of cynical arrogance and powerful masculinity.

She had been walking along the beach when a deep voice
had called out demanding to know who she was. She had
understood that much Greek. Glancing towards the sea, she
had seen a man standing on the shoreline. She had known it
was a private beach, but as Delia's guest she had had every
right to be there, and in her innocence she had called out a
response and walked towards him, concentrating on trying to
bring him into focus. As her vision had improved she had

offered her name with a smile, and held out her hand, then stopped and stared, her hand suspended in mid-air.

He had been tall and broad with a white towel draped around his lean hips, and the musculature of his magnificent bronzed body had been so clearly defined Michelangelo himself could not have sculpted better.

His gaze had captured hers, and the breath had stopped in her throat. There had been something dark and dangerous swirling in the black depths of his eyes that had made her heart beat faster. Every primitive sense she had possessed had told her to run but she had been paralysed by the physical presence of the man. Then he had finally spoken, and his sarcastic comment rang in her head to this day.

'Flattered though I am, and available as you so obviously are, I am a married man. You should try asking before ogling.' And he had walked away. She had never been so embarrassed before, or since.

'I would have thought that was self-evident.' The sound of his voice jerked her back to the present. 'I am here to see you. We need to talk.' He smiled but she noticed the smile didn't touch his eyes.

Helen didn't want to talk to him. She shuddered at the thought.

After their first meeting, for the rest of her stay in Greece she had tried to avoid him. It had not been too hard. With the constant flow of sophisticated friends and family to the Aristides home, it had been quite easy for two young girls to go unnoticed. On the rare occasion when Helen had had no option but to be in his company she had addressed him with cool politeness. When his beautiful wife Tina had arrived near the end of Helen's stay, she had only been able to wonder what the happy-go-lucky American woman saw in such an aloof, cynical man.

For Helen his scornful and deeply embarrassing comment to her, coupled with the senior Mr Aristides' distant politeness to both her and his daughter, simply confirmed what Delia had told her when they had first become friends at school.

According to Delia the reason she was at boarding-school in England rather than at home in Greece was because her father and her brother had agreed she needed to improve her English, but the reality was they had both decided she needed the discipline of a girls-only boarding-school. Apparently she had been caught smoking and flirting with a fisherman's son. No big deal according to Delia, who had personally thought it had more to do with the fact that her mother had committed suicide when she was twenty months old, from depression after her birth. Her father had blamed her for the death of his wife, and preferred her out of his sight.

To quote Delia, her father and brother were both stiff-necked chauvinist pigs. Ultra-conservative wealthy bankers totally devoted to the family business of making money, the females in their lives chosen simply as assets to enhance the business.

Delia had had no intention of being married for the benefit of the family company, as her mother and sister-in-law had been. She had been determined to stay single until she was at least twenty-five and then her father could not prevent her from inheriting the banking shares her mother had left in trust for her. Helen over the years had helped her to do just that.

Recalling Delia's low opinion of her brother, Helen stared at the tall, wide-shouldered man in front of her. His black hair was plastered to his head by the driving rain, but he still exuded the same shattering aura of aggressive male power that had so frightened her the first time they had met.

'Are you going to ask me in?' His dark eyes narrowed on her face. 'Or is it your habit to keep visitors wet and freezing on the doorstep?' he mocked.

'Sorry, no, y-yes…' she stammered. 'Come in.' She stepped back as he brushed past her into the hall. She closed the door and turned to face him, and it took all her self-control to say coolly, 'Though I can't imagine what you and I have to talk about, Mr Aristides.'

Why was Aristides here? Had Delia finally told her family the truth? But if so why hadn't she called and told Helen? Suddenly not having heard from Delia for so long took on a frightening aspect. She had been worried for young Nicholas, but now she was more worried for her friend.

'Nicholas.'

'You know!' Helen exclaimed and lifted shocked violet eyes to his. 'So Delia finally told you,' she prompted with a sinking heart.

She had always known that when the time came Delia would reveal to her family that Nicholas was her son and take over the full-time care of the boy, but she hadn't expected it for at least another three months. Nor had she fully expected the extent of the pain in her heart at the prospect of becoming an honoured aunt, a visitor in Nicholas's life rather than virtually his sole carer.

'No, not Delia,' he said curtly. 'A lawyer.'

'A lawyer…' Helen was hopelessly confused and the mention of the legal profession filled her with foreboding. To give herself time to gather her scattered thoughts she crossed the hall and opened the door to the large cosy sitting room. 'You will be more comfortable in here.' She indicated one of the two sofas that flanked the fireplace, where a fire burned brightly in the grate.

'Please take a seat,' she said politely, nervously clasping her hands together in front of her. 'I'll get you a coffee, you must be cold. It is a foul day.' She noted a droplet of water fall from his thick black hair to linger on the slant of his cheekbone. 'And you need a towel.' She was rambling, she knew, and quickly she turned and scurried back out of the room, her legs shaking and her mind racing. She grabbed her bag off the hall table and dived into the kitchen.

Leon Aristides noted her nervousness, in fact he had noticed every single detail from the moment she had opened the door, from the hip-hugging blue jeans to the tight blue sweater that outlined her firm breasts. Her hair was much longer now, otherwise she looked no older than the first time they had met. Then she had been lovely and ripe for the plucking and he damn near had.

He had arrived at the family's island home late in the night and early the next morning had been swimming naked in the sea. Emerging out of the water he had seen her walking towards him. Her fair curly hair had framed a face that was pale with huge eyes, a small straight nose, a full lipped mouth and had been gentle in its natural beauty. She had been wearing a long-sleeved ankle-length white dress in some fine material that should have been demure but instead with the sun behind her had been virtually transparent. Beneath the dress she had been wearing tiny white briefs.

Leon shifted uncomfortably in the seat, as he again saw in his mind's eye the high, round breasts, the tiny waist, the feminine flare of her hips and shapely legs as she had moved towards him, her gaze fixed intently upon him. He had demanded who she was and what she was doing there.

Showing no embarrassment at his nudity, she had called out that she liked the early morning before the sun got too hot. But he had got hot simply looking at her, and whipped a towel around his hips as she had continued to approach him. 'I am Helen, Delia's friend from school.' And she had held out her hand and stopped not a yard away.

The thickly lashed eyes she had lifted to his had been a smoky violet, and full of hidden promise. He had been surprised and tempted to take what she had been so blatantly offering, until it had registered with him that she could only be fifteen, the same age as his sister. He had dismissed her with a few crude mocking words, disgusted with his own reaction more than with her.

When she had answered the door earlier, and looked up at him with those huge violet eyes, he had had the same urge all over again. Remarkable, because she wasn't his usual type at all; he preferred tall, slender brunettes, an image of his current lover, Louisa, a sophisticated French lady, forming in his mind. He had not seen her for two months, which probably accounted for his unexpected sexual reaction to Helen Heywood. She was the direct opposite of Louisa, a pale-skinned ash-blonde who couldn't be much more than five feet tall. Added to which the innocent-looking Miss Heywood had to be the most devious, money-hungry woman he had ever encountered, and he had encountered quite a few.

Still he had her in his sights now and she was no match for him, he concluded arrogantly and briefly closed his eyes. *Theos,* he was tired, and for a man who lived to work that was some admission, but the last few weeks had been hell.

It had started when he had taken a phone call in his office at Aristides International Bank in Athens a month ago. His father and sister had been in an accident and he could remember the day in every minute detail.

He had paced the length of the hospital corridor outside the operating theatre, with a face like thunder. None of the hospital staff who had passed him had dared to speak, but they had all known he was Leonidas Aristides the international banker, with offices in Athens, New York, Sydney and Paris, as rich as Croesus, and about to be more so after the tragic events of the day.

He had stopped outside the double doors and wondered how long it had been. He had glanced at the functional watch on his wrist, and stifled a groan—a meagre forty minutes.

Not even an hour since they had wheeled the broken body of his sister Delia through the metal doors of the operating theatre. Only three hours since the telephone call he had taken at the bank informing him of the car crash that had killed his father instantly and badly injured his sister. Even as he had been informed Delia had been transferred by air ambulance from their island home to the best hospital in Athens.

He had trouble believing what had happened. They had all spent Christmas and New Year's Eve together on the island but he had left early the next afternoon to spend a couple of weeks in New York. He had flown into Athens early that morning assuming his father and Delia had returned to their house in the city a couple of days ago and expecting to meet his father at the bank. Only to be told his father was still at their holiday home.

How the hell had it happened? he had asked himself for the thousandth time, having already demanded the same from the hospital staff and the police right up to the minister. All he had known was Delia had been driving to the harbour with their father when apparently she had lost control of the car and ended up in a ravine. As for the top team of surgeons he had demanded and got, they had been reluctant to give an opinion on Delia's chances other than to say she was critical but they would do all they could.

He had crossed to slump down in a seat facing the theatre doors, and had laid his head back against the wall and closed his eyes in an attempt to block out the reality of the situation.

His father was dead and he had known he would mourn his passing, but his sister had been fighting for her life behind those closed doors, and he had never felt so helpless in his life.

A sense of *déjà vu* had enveloped him. A different couple, a different time, and, he had prayed, a different outcome. Four years ago in June he had sat in a private hospital very like this in New York, waiting while they operated on his wife Tina after another car crash. The passenger then had been his wife's fitness instructor who had died instantly.

A bitter, cynical smile curved his hard mouth. Later the surgeon had told him sadly his wife had died on the operating table, but they had delivered the child she was carrying, a boy. For a moment he had felt a surge of hope until the doctor, who had carefully avoided eye contact with him, had added, 'Although the child was full term he was badly injured and his chances of survival are slight.' A few hours later the child had also died.

'Mr Aristides.' Leon opened his eyes and, silently praying this accident would have a happier outcome, he rose to his feet as the surgeon approached him. 'The operation was a success and your sister is now in Intensive Care.' He heaved a mighty sigh of relief, but it was short-lived as the surgeon continued, 'But there are severe complications, she has lost a lot of blood and her kidneys are failing. Unfortunately the traces of recreational drugs in her system are not helping. But we are doing all we can. You can slip in and see her for a few moments, the nurse will show you the way.'

He was still reeling from the knowledge his sister took drugs when she died two hours later.

Opening his eyes, Leon looked around the very English-looking cosy sitting room. If he had thought the fact that his sister took drugs was the worst thing she could have done in her young life he had been proved wrong yesterday.

The intelligent, educated young lady he had imagined Delia had grown up to be had been leading a double life for years with the help of Helen Heywood. A woman he distinctly remembered his sister telling him she had virtually lost touch with when she had gone to university in London.

Even for a man as cynical as him, particularly where the supposedly fair sex was concerned, the lies and the acting ability Delia had displayed over the last few years boggled the mind. He had loved his sister though he might not have shown it as he should, and her deceit hurt. For a man who never indulged in emotion and actively disdained anyone who did, it was a galling admission and he knew exactly who to blame. His sister was gone, but Miss Heywood had a hell of a lot to answer for, and he was just the man to make sure she did.

CHAPTER TWO

HELEN STOOD IN the kitchen watching the coffee percolate, and trying to think straight. Leon Aristides was here, in her home, and he knew about Nicholas. It wasn't too bad, she told herself. So he knew Delia had an illegitimate son, and obviously he knew that Helen looked after the child. Maybe Delia had finally told her father, and maybe he had consulted a lawyer and maybe he had told Leon. But it was all very odd and there were way too many maybes!

At the very least Delia might have warned her, she thought, miffed with her friend for putting her in such a position. Snatching her bag off the kitchen table, she took out her cell phone and tried Delia's number again. It was still dead.

Five minutes later, after snagging a towel from the downstairs toilet, she walked back into the sitting room carrying the coffee tray. 'Sorry it took so long.' She placed the tray on the occasional table and held out the towel.

He took it from her hand with a brief, 'Thank you,' and, swiftly wiping his face, he began drying his thick black hair. In his dishevelled state the family resemblance to Nicholas was quite startling.

Realising she was staring, she quickly sat on the sofa opposite him. 'Black or white, Mr Aristides?' she asked coolly.

'Black, one sugar and drop the Mr Aristides. Leon will do—after all, we are old friends.'

'If you say so,' she murmured, and poured the coffee, unable to get his name past her suddenly dry mouth. As for being 'old friends,' he must be joking. Lifting her head, she handed him the cup and saucer, and flinched slightly as his fingers brushed hers. Their eyes met and for a second she saw a gleam of something sinister in the depths of his that made her stomach clench, and then it was gone and he was raising the cup to his mouth.

Oddly flustered but determined not to show it, Helen took a much-needed drink of her own coffee, and, replacing the cup on the table, she said, 'Now perhaps you can tell me why a lawyer informed you about Nicholas? Did Delia finally tell her father the truth, and perhaps he contacted a lawyer?' she queried.

He drained his cup, replaced it on the table, and raised his head, his dark eyes resting on her with cold insolence. 'By the truth, I presume you mean that my crazy sister had a child outside marriage, a son that her family knew nothing about. A son that you have taken care of from birth… Is that the truth you are talking about?' he prompted, his cold dark eyes narrowing at the look of guilt that flashed across her pale face.

'That my own sister could be so devious as to deprive her father of a grandson is beyond belief, and that you with the collusion of your grandfather apparently aided and abetted her is downright shameful, if not criminal—'

'Now wait just a minute,' Helen cut in. 'My grandfather died months before he was born.'

'My sympathy, I apologise for maligning the man. But it does not make your actions any less shameful,' he said bluntly.

'The only shameful act as far as I am concerned is your father forcing Delia into becoming engaged to a distant cousin when she returned to Greece last summer. A man of his choosing, to keep the money in the family. She is not crazy, quite the reverse. Delia always knew her father would try and marry her off eventually and prepared for it,' Helen said adamantly.

'She tried to delay it as long as possible—that was why she changed the course she was taking at university after the first year, so she could extend her studies a year. And, for the same reason, once she did graduate she decided to take a teacher's training course for another year.' Helen leapt to defend her friend. She didn't like Leon Aristides and she liked even less his derogatory comment about his own sister.

'You know more than me, it would seem,' he drawled sardonically his eyes narrowing on her small face, and Helen felt inexplicably threatened.

She hesitated and lowered her lashes to hide her too expressive eyes. It was not like her to let her tongue run away with her, and she had the disturbing conviction that she would need all the self-control she possessed around Leon Aristides.

'As to that I don't know.' She gave a slight, what she hoped was a nonchalant, shrug. 'But obviously Delia has changed her mind about Nicholas or you would not be here,' she continued. 'But I spoke to her a few weeks ago and she never said anything to me. As far as I know, she still has no intention of marrying the man and only agreed to the engagement to keep her father happy until she is twenty-five in May and comes into the inheritance her mother left her. Then she has every intention of telling the whole world she has a child when her father can no longer control her.'

'She will never have the chance.' He brushed aside her stalwart defence of his sister with a few cold words.

'My God, Delia was right about you!' she exclaimed. 'You're as—'

'Delia is dead, as is my father,' he interrupted brutally,

guessing her thoughts about him, and deflecting them in the bluntest way possible.

'They were staying on the island, and Delia was driving them to the harbour when the car slid off the road and into a ravine.' He spoke emotionlessly as if he had recited it all a hundred times before. 'Father died instantly, Delia a few hours later in hospital without ever regaining consciousness.'

Helen stared at him in stricken silence. She could not believe it, did not want to believe it.

'Dead…Delia dead,' she murmured. 'It's not possible.' She lifted wide, appalled eyes to the man opposite. 'It has to be a ghastly joke.' Not half an hour ago she had been worrying because Delia had not called; now she was expected to believe she was dead.

'The accident was on the fifteenth of January and there was a double funeral three days later.'

Suddenly, like a tidal wave crashing down on her, the full horror of his revelation swamped her mind, and she knew Aristides was telling the truth. Her heart contracted in her chest, her eyes closing momentarily as she struggled to hold back the tears. But it was a futile gesture as moisture leaked beneath her lashes. She wrapped her arms around her middle in a physical attempt to hold herself together.

Delia, beautiful, brave headstrong Delia, her friend and confidante—dead.

She remembered the first time they had met. Theirs had been an unlikely friendship, the extrovert Greek girl and the introvert English girl.

Helen at sixteen had missed a lot of schooling owing to the accident that had killed her parents. Her father had worked as an IT consultant for a Swiss bank in Geneva and they had been on a skiing weekend in the Alps, when an avalanche had buried her parents and left Helen slammed against a tree chest-deep in snow. Rescued hours later, she had fractured her pelvis, but worse had lost her sight. Whether it had been snow blindness from exposure to the brilliant sun in the hours before she had been rescued, or a psychological reaction at seeing her parents killed, it had taken her a long time to recover.

She had returned to England to live with her grandfather, and slowly recuperate. Finally she had resumed her education as a day pupil at a boarding-school in the countryside near her home. She had been put in the same class as Delia although she had been two years older than everyone else. It had been Delia who had stood up for Helen when others in the class had teased her about the ugly tinted glasses she had worn at the time. From that day forward they had become firm friends and Helen had frequently invited Delia to her home for weekends. Her grandfather had been a classics scholar who spoke fluent Greek and the school had approved the outings.

When Helen had left school early to look after her grandfather, who had been left wheelchair-bound after a stroke, Delia had continued to visit right up until she had left school herself to go to university in London. They had kept in touch by telephone and the odd e-mail, but Helen had not seen Delia for two years until she had turned up unexpectedly one weekend looking pale and sombre. Not her usual confident self at all.

'Obviously the news is a shock to you and I'm sorry to intrude on your grief.' The brisk dark voice cut into her reverie, not sounding the least apologetic. 'But I came here to see my nephew and discuss his future.'

Tight-lipped and clenching her teeth in an attempt to control her grief, Helen lifted tear-drenched eyes to Leon Aristides and shivered at the aloof glacial expression she saw on his face. If this man was mourning the loss of his father and sister it certainly did not show. He was as hard as a block of granite, and suddenly fear for Nicholas and what his future would be overrode her grief.

'Nicholas is asleep upstairs. He attends nursery school in the morning and after lunch he usually has a nap,' she said truthfully, struggling to gather her tumultuous thoughts into some kind of order. Instinctively she knew Delia would not have wanted her son brought up in the same mould as her father and brother, and she needed all her wits about her to deal with the situation. 'I don't think it is advisable to wake him up to tell him his mother is dead.' She choked over the last word.

'I wasn't suggesting any such thing.' He lifted a hand and ran it through his thick black hair, and for a moment she thought she saw a gleam of anguish in his dark eyes.

Helen began thinking maybe Leon Aristides was more upset than he appeared. Suddenly she remembered Delia mentioning that his wife and newborn child had died in an accident. This must be a double blow to him—she had lost her best friend but he had lost his father and his sister—and her soft heart squeezed with compassion.

'But he will have to be told later and in the meanwhile—' Aristides rose to his feet and stepped towards her '—I want to see some proof the boy actually exists and is here,' he declared with a sardonic lift of an ebony brow.

Helen gritted her teeth at his cynical comment and any sympathy for him disappeared. 'Of course.' She stood up and found he was much too close, and sidestepped out of his way. 'If you will follow me,' she murmured and made for the door.

The curtains were closed against the dismal dark day and a small car-shaped night light that Nicholas adored illuminated the bedroom. The bed was also a model of a car, and lying flat on his back was Nicholas wearing white underpants and a tee shirt. With his curly black hair falling forward over his brow, and his thick black lashes lying gently against his smooth cheeks, he was deeply asleep.

Helen smiled down at the infant, and very gently brushed a few stray curls from his brow. She heard a deeply indrawn breath, and glanced back at Aristides. She could sense the tension in every muscle and sinew of his big frame as he stared down at the sleeping boy, totally transfixed.

Helen didn't like the man, she found him hard and cynical. If she was honest she also found him intimidating. He was not only tall, but powerfully built with wide shoulders and a broad chest, lean hips and long legs. Yet right at this moment he looked as vulnerable as the child who held his complete attention.

Silently she moved back a few steps towards the door, to give him some privacy in which to get over the shock of seeing his nephew for the first time. He was entitled to that much, but he was not necessarily entitled to sole care of the child, she reminded herself firmly.

Her eyes misted with tears as she saw again in her mind's eye Delia's face when she had turned up out of the blue on a day in February much like this one four years ago. She had been upset, but determined, and no amount of talking had been able to get Delia to change her mind.

Delia had been pregnant and unmarried at twenty. There had been no way she was going to tell her father, and she had asked Helen to help her take care of the baby until she came into her own fortune. Then she could say to hell with her father and bring her child up as she wished.

Personally Helen had thought it was the craziest idea she had ever heard, and had told her so. She had doubted Delia could keep the pregnancy hidden, never mind keeping a child secret, and what about the father?

The father was a fellow student who had been killed in the London train crash that had been all over the papers a few weeks earlier. But Delia had had it all worked out. She would go home for Easter as usual and return to university in London afterwards. Her father had been ecstatic at the news Leon's wife was finally pregnant so he would pay Delia even less attention than usual.

Delia had been convinced she could get through the holiday without anyone realising she was pregnant. The baby was due on the first of July and it would be simple to book into a private hospital in London to have a Caesarean delivery in mid-June. Then she could leave the child with Helen and still be able to return to Greece for the summer holidays without her family being any the wiser. Helen had thought the whole idea ridiculous, but Delia had been nothing if not determined.

A wry sad smile tipped the corners of her lips. Thinking about Delia now, she realised she had been just as stubborn and autocratic in her own way as her father and brother.

Even so Helen had flatly refused her request and with the help of her grandfather had tried to persuade Delia that she must tell her family the truth. Helen had thought they had managed to convince her to do just that when she had left two days later.

A strong hand grasped her arm shocking her out of her musings.

'He is every inch an Aristides,' Leon said softly, turning towards her and blocking her view of the room. 'You and I really do need to talk.' The pressure of his fingers on her arm and the closeness of his large frame did extraordinary things to her breathing. 'Are you alone here?'

She gasped and tilted back her head to lift her gaze and met his intent black eyes. Her mouth ran dry and her pulse took off at an alarming rate. He saw her reaction and his dark gaze fell to her softly parted lips and then provocatively lower to linger on the proud thrust of her breasts against the soft wool of her sweater, before flicking back up again to her face. 'You are a very attractive woman—perhaps a live-in lover?'

'Certainly not,' she snapped, blushing to the roots of her hair.

'That makes it easier,' he murmured, and settled a long finger over her lips. 'But shh—we don't want to wake the child.'

Her lips oddly tingling from the touch of his finger, before she knew what was happening she was out of the bedroom, the door closed behind her and halfway down the stairs.

'You can let go of my arm now.' Helen finally found her voice, deeply shaken by the startling effect Leon Aristides' deliberately sensual look and touch had upon her.

He let go of her arm without a word, and walked down the stairs and into the sitting room, obviously expecting her to follow. She stopped for a moment at the foot of the stairs to gather her chaotic thoughts into some kind of order. But the resentment burning bitterly in her breast did not help. Who the hell did he think he was, treating her home as if it were his own?

Unfortunately she knew exactly who he was, she recognised with her next breath; a wealthy, powerful man who happened to be Nicholas' uncle. Much as she would like to be rid of him, she realised it wasn't in Nicholas' best interest or hers to antagonise the man, and reluctantly she finally followed him into the room.

He had flopped down on a sofa, his head thrown back and his eyes closed. He had opened his jacket and loosened his tie. The top button of his shirt was undone, revealing the strong tanned column of his throat. His long legs were splayed out in front of him, the fabric of his trousers pulled tight across his thighs and graphically outlining the bulge of his sex.

Flaked out as he was, for a moment his sheer physical impact hit her like a blow to the stomach. Leon Aristides might be one very conservative banker, but there was no mistaking he was all virile male.

Her violet eyes roamed in helpless fascination over his superb body. He was probably a magnificent lover, she thought, and a shaming tide of pink coloured her cheeks.

Helen felt like a voyeur; erotic thoughts about men had never bothered her before. What on earth was happening to her? She rubbed suddenly damp palms down her thighs, and, swallowing hard, took an involuntary step back. She raised her head to find his dark, astute eyes resting on her. Oh, my God! Did he know what she had been thinking? And quickly she broke into speech. 'Would you like another coffee or something?'

'Something...' His dark eyes swept leisurely over her in undisguised masculine appreciation. Suddenly she was horribly conscious of her old denim jeans and the well-washed sweater she was wearing. But even worse was the peculiar swelling in her breasts at his lingering appraisal. 'Yes, the something has more appeal,' he drawled huskily. 'What do you suggest?' and he smiled.

Her gaze dropped from the amusement in his dark eyes to the curl of his sensual lips, revealing gleaming white teeth, and for a second she stopped breathing, mesmerised by the unexpected brilliance of his smile.

Realising she was staring again, she hastily glanced somewhere over his shoulder and blurted out the first thing that entered her head. 'Tea or wine, if you prefer? When my grandfather was alive he kept quite a lot of red wine and I don't drink much so there are a couple of bottles around.' She was babbling again, but nothing like this had happened to her before.

Helen wasn't naive. She knew all about sexual attraction—she had dated Kenneth Markham for almost a year, until he had decided to go to Africa and help the starving, and she had never heard from him again. But this was different—instant and electric—and it shocked her witless.

'I'll go and get the wine.' She dashed back out of the room like a scalded cat.

In the safety of the kitchen she took a few deep, steadying breaths. She was still in shock at the news of Delia's death, she told herself. That had to be why her body had reacted so peculiarly to Leon Aristides. She didn't even like him, and she certainly wasn't attracted to overtly macho men. She much preferred the sensitive, caring type like Kenneth, the type one could talk to without feeling threatened in any way. It had to be the tragic news that had made her hormones go haywire. A physical anomaly brought on by the pressure of the moment. Reassured by her conclusion, she took two glasses from a cupboard, before she crossed to the wine rack and reached for a bottle of wine.

'You're tiny, allow me.' She almost jumped out of her skin as a long arm stretched over her head.

She spun around to find the damn man only inches away. 'I can do that,' she said in a voice that was not quite steady. Disturbed by the ease with which his closeness affected her all over again.

'It is done.' He shrugged his broad shoulders, holding a bottle of red. 'But you can give me the bottle opener, and something to eat would be much appreciated. I was too busy searching for this place to take time out to eat lunch.' His dark eyes flicked down at her. 'Sandwiches will do,' he ordered calmly.

The 'tiny' and his arrogant assumption she would feed him infuriated her, but she didn't argue. It was a relief to move away from him and, opening a drawer, she took out the bottle opener, and slapped it on the bench beside him before crossing to the fridge and extracting a block of cheese.

'Will cheese do?' She flicked him a glance and was further incensed to see he had moved to sit at the kitchen table, a glass of wine in his hand, the bottle of wine in front of him and another glass on the table.

'Perfectly,' he said calmly and took a sip of the wine.

Turning her attention to the task before her, Helen quickly made two sandwiches and put them on a plate, all the time tensely aware of the man behind her.

'Your grandfather had good taste in wine,' his deep voice drawled appreciatively. 'In fact, according to the report my father had on him, your grandfather was a highly intelligent, highly moral, well respected professor.'

'Report!' Helen exclaimed, turning around to stare at him in amazement, the plate of sandwiches in her hand tilting precariously.

'Here, let me take that.' He reached across and took the plate from her unresisting grasp and, placing it on the table, picked up a sandwich and began eating with obvious enjoyment.

He was doing it again, ordering her around, and for a long moment she stared at him, stunned. 'Your father actually investigated my grandfather.' Her indignant gaze fixed on his hard face.

'Yes, of course,' he stated coolly. 'Before my sister was allowed to visit your home my father had checked with the school and privately that you and your grandfather were suitable people to befriend her. Obviously over the years the circumstances had changed, but neither my father nor I for that matter had any idea. Delia was nothing if not inventive.' He took another sip of wine before continuing. 'I distinctly remember three years ago a cartoon Christmas card you sent Delia particularly amused my father. He asked after you both and suggested she invite you over for another holiday. Delia's response as I recall was that your grandfather had suffered a stroke some years before and you stayed at home to look after him. It was unfortunate, but she had not seen you since she went to university in London, and apart from the occasional Christmas and birthday card the friendship had fizzled out.'

An ebony brow arched sardonically. 'I am beginning to realise my innocent little sister was like all women—as devious as the devil and an accomplished liar,' he stated witheringly and reached for another sandwich.

Helen opened her mouth to defend her friend and closed it again. What could she say? From the moment she had taken Nicholas into her home she had silently colluded with whatever story Delia had chosen to tell her family. That Delia had lied about their friendship brought the fact home with brutal clarity. But then why was she surprised? In the first few months after Nicholas was born Helen had been hoping that Delia would see sense and tell her family about the boy, while Delia had obviously been busy covering the trail that led back to Helen.

'Sit down and have a drink. You look completely stressed out,' he observed, his cold dark eyes narrowing on the look of guilt that flashed across her pale face.

She pulled out the chair and sat down, and picked up the glass with a hand that was none too steady. She lifted the glass to her lips and took a long swallow. Helen seldom drank; alcohol went straight to her head. But Aristides was right, she was stressed to breaking-point, the enormity of the deception she had agreed to finally hitting her. Much as she had loved Delia and wanted to help, Helen knew deep down inside her reasons had not been purely altruistic.

Before the death of her parents she had been a happy, confident teenager. She had had all the hopes and dreams of a young girl. School, college, a career, then love, marriage and children. But everything had altered the day of the accident. Her near idyllic life had been shattered and, much as she'd loved her grandfather, he hadn't been able to replace what she had lost.

Delia had been the one bright spot in her life, but when she had first made her outrageous proposal Helen had refused, until the sudden death of her grandfather in late April had changed everything. Delia had turned up for his funeral still pregnant and with her own family still not aware of the fact.

To Helen, grieving and totally alone for the first time in her life, Delia's request that she take care of the baby while she continued her studies suddenly had not seemed so outrageous. If Helen had been honest it was a dream come true.

'More wine?' He interrupted her thoughts, lifting the bottle of wine from the table.

She glanced at him, violet eyes clashing with black, and she knew the dream was about to become her worst nightmare. She lowered her eyes from his too-penetrating gaze and realised she had drained her glass. She also realised she needed all her wits about her for what was to follow.

'No. No, thank you,' she said with cool politeness.

'As you wish,' he replied, and refilled his own glass and replaced the bottle on the table, casting her a mocking glance from beneath heavy-lidded eyes, and then lifted his glass to his mouth.

Unconsciously she watched his wide, mobile mouth, saw the movement in the strong line of his throat as he swallowed. Her fascinated gaze followed the movement lower to where the open collar of his shirt revealed a few black hairs on the olive toned skin of his chest. Suddenly heat flushed through her veins and curled in her belly. Oh, no, she thought, it was happening again and it terrified her.

She raised her eyes to his face and opened her mouth to say something, anything, but she couldn't breathe. She simply sat there, colour flooding into her cheeks, her lips softly parted, paralysed by the sexual awareness that tightened every nerve in her body.

He replaced his glass on the table and was studying her

flushed face. He knew what was happening to her, and why. She saw his heavy-lidded eyes darken with sensual knowledge. She saw the hint of satisfaction in the slight smile that curved his mouth, and suddenly the air between them was heavy with sexual tension.

CHAPTER THREE

IT WAS THE gleam of masculine satisfaction in Aristides' lazy smile that hauled Helen back to sanity. She stiffened and clenched her teeth in an attempt to subdue the tide of heated sensation that had invaded her body. Not something that had ever happened to her before, or ever would again if she could help it.

Taking a few deep breaths, she rationalised her extraordinary reaction to the man. So she had finally realised Leon Aristides was a sexy beast, and could turn a woman on at will. But then why was she surprised? According to Delia, in her family all the men had wives and mistresses, from her great-grandfather who had started the bank, all the way down to Leon. Given that Helen was now bound to have contact with the man over Nicholas, anything of a personal nature between them was absolutely unthinkable. Nicholas' happiness was her top priority.

'Nicholas,' she said firmly. 'You want to talk about Nicholas.'

'Yes, Nicholas,' he agreed, and leant back in his chair, a contemplative look on his dark face. 'But first we must discuss Delia. Starting at the beginning is usually the most constructive way to find a lasting solution to a problem,' he offered and, much to Helen's surprise, proceeded to do just that.

'Delia was the baby of the family. I was fifteen when she was born and for the first three years of her life she was a source of joy to me. I admit after I left home to study and later to live in New York for a number of years I did not see as much of her as I possibly should have done, but I thought we had a good relationship. I saw her at least two or three times a year, usually over the holiday periods. She went a little wild as a young teenager but that was soon sorted out. My father gave her a generous allowance, and almost anything she asked for she could have.' He shook his dark head in disbelief, for once not looking the cold, austere banker Helen knew him to be.

'She always appeared content and well adjusted, so why she thought she had to hide her child from her family I will never understand.' His dark eyes narrowed speculatively on her. 'You obviously knew a different Delia from my father and I, and I guess you were a party to all her secrets.'

She looked away from his curiously penetrating gaze, and coloured slightly. 'A few.'

'How much did she pay you to keep them?'

'She never paid me!' Helen exclaimed indignantly, her colour heightened by the gleam of contempt in his eyes. 'I loved Delia; she was my best friend.' She drew in an audible breath, and lowered her head to hide the tears that threatened as memories of her friend engulfed her. But refusing to give in to her emotions, she continued.

'From the first day I met Delia at the boarding-school your father had banished her to, I would have done anything to help her because she stood up for me. I was a day pupil, which set me apart from most of the class, added to which I was two years older than everyone else.'

Leon tensed slightly at that piece of information, his dark eyes narrowing speculatively on her downbent head. So Helen Heywood was not quite as young as he had thought...interesting. He had intended to take her to court if he had to, though the thought of the resultant publicity was anathema to him. But he had forgotten how very attractive she was and now a much better scenario occurred to him.

He recalled the strange reaction of the hotel receptionist as he had enquired about the Farrow House. The young woman had looked at him rather coyly, then said, 'Of course, you must be a very good friend of Helen Heywood and Nicholas.' After seeing the child, he could guess what the girl had been thinking.

Lost in her memories, Helen was totally oblivious to her companion's scrutiny and continued, 'With the age difference and wearing glasses, needless to say the class bullies had a field-day with me. But Delia waded into them on my behalf and won. I was never bothered again.'

She lifted her head, violet eyes blazing with conviction as they clashed with astute black. 'We were firm friends from that day onward. I would have done anything for Delia, and she would have done anything for me, I know,' she said adamantly.

'Perhaps, but you never will know now,' Leon drawled sardonically. 'But carry on—I would like to know why you agreed to go along with her hare-brained scheme.'

Helen didn't appreciate the 'hare-brained' but she could not exactly deny it. If she was honest, she was amazed the deception had lasted so long. For the first year of Nicholas' life she had encouraged Delia to reveal his existence to her family, but as time had passed Helen had not been quite so eager for the truth to be told. Guilt at her own role in prolonging the situation made her voice curt as she continued.

'When Delia came to visit me four years ago, and told me she was pregnant, she had a scheme all worked out. Easter at home in Greece would be no problem; no one would notice her. According to Delia your father was over the moon because you had just told him your wife was pregnant and the much-wanted grandchild was due in August. How could she, even if she wanted to, disgrace her family and spoil everyone's delight, with the news her own child was due a couple of months earlier?' she queried sharply, so caught up in her own emotions she never saw the flash of anger in his dark eyes.

'Anyway, she didn't want to. She didn't want her child brought up to be like her father, a chauvinistic tyrant who blamed her for the death of her mother.' Leon's head did jerk at that but he did not stop her. 'She didn't think you were much better after you agreed with him to ship her off to boarding-school because of a couple of teenage flirtations.'

His mouth twisted cynically. 'Of course, you agreed with her, and it never entered your head she might have been better served if you had gotten in touch with her family.'

'No, I didn't just agree with her,' Helen retorted hotly. 'I told her to do just that.' She paused, her anger fading at the memory of what had happened next—the death of her grandfather.

'Very laudable, I'm sure, but not very believable given the present circumstances,' Leon remarked cynically.

'You are wrong. I only agreed to help her after she returned from the Easter holiday, and came here for my grandfather's funeral. She told me that no one had even noticed she was pregnant,' Helen shot back scathingly, 'which rather proved her point.'

'Regrettable. But not worth arguing over,' he opined flatly. 'We now have a young boy's future to consider, a boy without parents.' His dark eyes narrowed intently on her pale face. 'Unless you happen to know the name of the father?'

'Delia told me he was dead,' she said, avoiding his astute gaze. She had also made Helen promise never to reveal the man's identity, and she saw no reason to break her word now.

'You are sure?'

'Absolutely,' Helen said firmly, looking straight up at Leon. Delia had shown her a newspaper cutting of the train crash that had killed the man.

'Good.' She had not given him a name, which Leon was sure she knew. Miss Heywood had very expressive eyes and she had avoided looking at him when she had answered, and for the opposite reason he believed her when she said the man was dead. 'Then there is no fear of anyone appearing out of the blue to claim the boy. That only leaves you and I.'

'Before you say anything more—' Helen rushed into speech '—you should know when Nicholas was born Delia made me his guardian, with her, until he is twenty-one. It was necessary in case of emergency and so he could be enrolled with a doctor and the like, and I have the documentation to prove it.' She felt some guilt for what she had allowed to happen, but even so she wasn't about to give Nicholas up to this granite-faced autocrat without a fight.

'I'm sure you have,' he drawled cynically. 'Before I arrived here I visited a lawyer in London, a Mr Smyth, and he is in possession of Delia's last will and testament. In it she makes you a substantial beneficiary of her estate, twenty per cent to be precise, and you and I are now joint trustees of Nicholas' money, as I am sure you know.' Helen's mouth fell open in shock. 'Don't look so surprised—after all, you are now probably the best paid nanny in the history of the world, as I am sure you also know.'

There was a sinking feeling in the pit of Helen's stomach when she heard the absolute decisiveness in his tone, and she knew he was telling the truth.

'Delia left me money.' She gazed up at him in shock and saw the contemptuous expression on his hard face. 'I didn't know, and I don't want it. I love Nicholas. I agreed to be his guardian to help Delia but not for money,' she said, horrified and furious that this man could think so badly of her. 'And I find it incredible that she made you Nicholas' guardian as well, she told me she did not want Nicholas growing up like you,' she blurted out unthinkingly.

Leon's astute gaze narrowed, his needle-sharp brain instantly recognising Helen Haywood in her upset and anger had made a simple mistake. He had said he was a trustee of the boy's estate, not a joint guardian. But he had no qualms about using her assumption to his advantage. Despite her protestations, and the care she had taken of the child, she was nothing more than a little gold-digger. 'It seems my little sister said a damn sight too much and not always the truth,' he drawled. 'But never mind, it is not important. What is important is Nicholas.'

'Do you think I don't know that?' she cried. 'I have looked after him from birth; I love him as my own. Nicholas' future happiness is all I care about.'

'Excellent.' He ignored the flare of anguish in her violet eyes. 'Then you can have no objection to Nicholas coming back to Greece with me.'

'But that's insane,' she responded emphatically. 'You can't just snatch him away from here. This is the only home he's ever known.'

'Then it is way past time he got to know his own. Nicholas is Greek, and he will quickly adapt. He will enjoy living in my home with my staff to attend to his every need. He will certainly enjoy the sunny climate rather than this constant cold grey drizzle. He is an Aristides and as such will have the best education available, and will eventually take his rightful place in Aristides International.' Leon let his hard eyes sweep over her with a calculated arrogance.

'You say you don't want the money Delia left you, yet, according to the receptionist at the hotel where I stopped to book a room for the night, you are employed as a part-time carer in the crèche for the guests' children. While a very laudable occupation, it is hardly going to make you a fortune,' he mocked. 'A fortune I already have, so what can you offer Nicholas to compare?'

Seething that the superior swine had the audacity to discuss her circumstances with a total stranger, Helen had had enough. 'Money is not everything. I love Nicholas—something you, by all accounts, know nothing about.' She did some mocking of her own.

'Ah, Delia again, I presume. You should not believe everything you hear.'

'Well, your marriage was no love match, rather it facilitated the acquisition of an American bank, according to Delia.' She lashed back, her anger overriding her common sense. 'What kind of example are you going to set for a trusting, lovable young boy like Nicholas?'

'A realistic one,' he stated rising to his feet and walking around to where she sat. 'Not the kind of independent, idealistic fairy-tale view of life you and my sister adhered to.' He captured her chin between his finger and thumb and tilted her head back so she was forced to meet the savage darkness in his eyes. 'Look where love and independence got Delia and tell me I am wrong.'

Helen was speechless for a moment, her hands curled into fists in her lap in an effort to suppress the furious urge to hit him. His sister was dead, and his sneering comment was a low blow.

'Oh! And your way was so much better—you managed to lose both your wife and your child,' she snapped. 'At least Nicholas is safe, and you are the most detestable man it has ever been my misfortune to meet. I wouldn't let you look after my pet goldfish.'

As he towered over her his fingers tightened on her chin

and she thought he was going to break her jaw during the taut silence that followed. Belatedly Helen realised she had gone way too far with her personal comment on his private life. If she wanted to keep in touch with Nicholas she had to get along with this man; how, she had no idea.

Then from just inside the kitchen door a high-pitched voice yelled, 'Let go of my Helen, you nasty man.'

A ball of fury spun across the kitchen and kicked out at Leon's shin. His hand fell from her chin and he stepped back and stared down in amazement at the child clinging to his leg.

'It's all right, Nicholas.' Helen jumped off her chair and crouched down beside the boy. 'He is not a nasty man,' she said, slipping an arm around his smooth little body and turning him towards her. 'He is Mum Delia's brother and that makes him your uncle.' Nicholas' chubby arm closed around her neck and, lifting him into her arms, she stood up. 'He is a nice man,' she said, not believing it for an instant. 'And he has come all the way from Greece to see you.'

'Just to see me,' Nicholas said, his big dark eyes, so like Delia's, lifted up to the silent man towering over them. 'You're my uncle.' Then he looked back at Helen. 'My friend Tim has an uncle who stays with him and his mum, and sleeps in her bed. Is this uncle going to stay with you and me?' Nicholas asked and cast a wary glance back up at Leon.

Helen felt the colour surge in her cheeks, and for a moment she was struck dumb. The fact that Nicholas at his tender age was aware of any adult's sleeping arrangements other than her own shocked her rigid. But Aristides had no such problem.

'Yes. I would like us to stay together,' Leon confirmed, speaking for the first time since Nicholas had entered the kitchen. 'If you will let me,' he added with a smile. 'You remind me very much of my sister Delia.'

'You know Delia?' Nicholas demanded.

'Mum Delia,' Helen prompted.

'Mum Delia,' Nicholas repeated. 'She was supposed to come and see us and didn't. But she sent me a car-shaped bed for Christmas, and lots of toys.' He wriggled free of Helen's hold to stand on chubby legs and glance shyly up at Leon. 'Would you like to see them?'

Speechless with anger, Helen simply stared as Leon knelt down and took Nicholas' hand in his. How dared he tell Nicholas he was staying with them?

'I'd be delighted, Nicholas. May I call you Nicholas?'

'Yes, come on.' Nicholas tugged on his large hand impatiently.

'Wait a minute.' Helen finally found her voice. 'For a start, Nicholas, what are you doing down here? I have told you not to come downstairs on your own.'

She felt guilty as hell. With the shocking revelations of the past hour she had forgotten he was no longer in his cot but in the new bed and could get out in a second, and she had also forgotten to fasten the child gate at the top of the stairs. 'You might have fallen.'

'I'm sure Nicholas is too big a boy to fall down the stairs,' Leon declared rising to his feet. 'Isn't that right, son?'

Since when had his nephew become his son? Helen thought furiously.

'Yes,' Nicholas responded, and by the smile on his face he didn't mind being called son at all. 'What's your name?'

'Leon Aristides.' The big man grinned down at the boy. 'You can call me Uncle or Leon, or both, take your pick.'

Two minutes later she watched man and boy walk out of the kitchen to view the new bed and a sliver of fear trickled down her spine. Her protestation that Nicholas needed a drink of juice and a biscuit, their usual ritual, was brushed aside in typical male fashion by Nicholas.

'You get it ready while I show Uncle Leon my car-bed.'

Her suggestion he needed dressing was brushed aside equally bluntly by *Uncle* Leon with, 'No problem, I can mange.'

Controlling her instinct to follow the pair, she glanced around the empty kitchen with a heart as heavy as lead as the enormity of the news hit her. Delia dead and Nicholas had yet to be told.

Oh, God! She groaned and slumped down in the chair she had recently vacated. She eyed the wine bottle and for a second was tempted to drown her sorrows, but only for a second. She had to be strong for Nicholas. She owed it to her friend to make sure the boy was happy, never mind what the indomitable Leon Aristides wanted.

Rising to her feet, she picked up the glasses and washed them in the sink. No way was she going to quietly slip to the sidelines of Nicholas' life, she silently vowed. She had dealt with enough sorrow and death in her life and she was not going to let this latest tragedy beat her.

Contrary to what Leon Aristides obviously thought with his dig about money and his patronising comment about her job at the crèche, at five feet two she was not a *tiny* ineffectual woman. The 'tiny' still rankled as she picked up the bottle from the table and put it on the back of the bench. She had a core of inner strength that had seen her through a lot of adversity that would have defeated a lesser woman.

She had nursed her grandfather for four years and continued her studies at the same time, eventually enrolling for a home-study degree. A few months after his death she had taken on the full-time care of baby Nicholas and continued her studies and last year she had obtained a degree in History of Art. Plus she was nowhere near the poor little woman Aristides thought.

Her grandfather after his first stroke at the age of sixty, had sold off the fifty acres of land that surrounded their home to an international hotel chain for development while making sure they kept the house and right of way. It was his way of ensuring there was money for his long-term care and Helen.

On inheriting her grandfather's estate after his death, and the life insurance from her parents that had been held in trust, Helen was hardly penniless.

While she was nowhere near as wealthy as Aristides, the money she had invested assured her of a reasonably comfortable living and left her free to indulge her own interests. As a freelance illustrator she had already completed the illustrations for three best selling children's books, and had a lucrative deal with the author and publisher to complete the illustrations on the full series of eight, her time spent at the crèche was a personal pleasure, but her greatest love was looking after Nicholas. Under the circumstances her life was as near perfect as she could have wished. Until today.

She opened the fridge and took out a carton of juice, then reached for Nicholas' favourite plastic mug from an overhead cupboard. She placed them both on the table with the biscuit tin, and straightened up, wondering what to do next.

Quietly she walked into the hall and stood at the foot of the stairs. She could hear the murmur of voices, and then childish laughter. She wanted to go upstairs and join them, but instead she walked the length of the hall and halfway back. She stopped at the hall table and picked up the post she had dropped earlier and looked through it. A couple of circulars and a letter. She turned it over in her hand and did not recognise the sender's address but tensed as she realised it was a solicitor's firm. She read the letter three times, and then slipped it in the table drawer.

Back in the kitchen she stared sightlessly out of the

window. The finality of the situation hit her; Aristides was telling the truth. The solicitor's letter was brief but informative, simply confirming Delia was dead and Helen was a beneficiary of her will.

Sighing, she turned. She needed something to do, something mundane so she didn't have to think of what might lie ahead. Perhaps if she began preparing supper. They always had their meal about six, then bath and bed. Scrambled egg with crispy bacon and grilled tomatoes was a favourite of Nicholas' and she was reaching for the china chicken that held the eggs when Nicholas and Leon walked back into the kitchen.

'Uncle Leon likes my bed,' Nicholas said, a broad grin on his face. 'He said he is going to get me another one just like it for when we stay at his house in Greece.' His eyes were huge with wonder. 'Isn't that great?'

With a malevolent glance at the tall dark man hovering over the boy, she bent down and picked Nicholas up. 'Yes, marvelous,' Helen got out between clenched teeth and deposited the boy on his seat at the table. 'Now drink your juice and have a biscuit, while I get supper ready.' She could do nothing about the stiffness in her tone; she was so angry it took all her self-control to speak civilly.

And it only got worse.

CHAPTER FOUR

THREE HOURS LATER Helen sat on the side of Nicholas' bed and read him *Rex Rabbit and the Good Fairy*. The first book she had illustrated. Nicholas loved the stories about Rex, a rather naughty rabbit, and the fairy that helped him out of his troubles, and the original drawing of the fairy hung proudly on his bedroom wall.

Usually this was her favourite time with Nicholas. But with Leon Aristides sitting like some huge dark spectre on the opposite side of the bed listening to every word tonight was different. She came to the end of the story and nervously glanced across at him.

His dark eyes rested on her. She watched them narrow in silent command, and she knew what he meant. She glanced quickly back at Nicholas, her nerves on a razor edge.

'Now your prayers,' she murmured, smiling softly down at him. It was their usual ritual, but tonight it held only sadness for Helen. She knew she had to tell Nicholas his mother was dead. Not least because Leon had told her so earlier in no uncertain terms when Nicholas had been otherwise occupied with his toys. If she didn't he would.

The childish voice ended with, 'God bless my Helen and God bless Delia. Amen.'

'Mum Delia,' Helen murmured automatically, and was ignored.

'Oh, and God bless Uncle Leon,' Nicholas said with a grin. Then he added, 'When is Delia coming? I haven't thanked her for my bed yet.'

No time was good for what Helen had to say, but she had no choice, and, reaching out a finger to stroke his smooth cheek, her eyes moist with tears, she told him, 'Mum Delia will not be coming back, sweetheart,' and, moving, she slipped an arm around his small shoulders.

'You know she lived a lot of the time in Greece. Well, so does Uncle Leon and that is why he is here today. He came to tell us Delia was badly hurt in an accident and she died.' Her voice broke. Saying the words out loud seemed so final.

'You mean she is never coming back?' Nicholas' bottom lip trembled, and the big dark eyes so like Delia's filled with tears. 'But why not?'

Helen tightened her arm around him and snuggled him closer. 'Remember when your hamster died and you and I had a little service and I told you he had gone to heaven where he would still be able to watch you even though you could no longer see him?'

He looked up into her face and then glanced at Leon and back to Helen. 'Has Delia gone to heaven?' he asked, big fat tears rolling down his soft cheeks.

'Yes, but she will still be watching over you.'

'But I want to see her again.' He began to sob in earnest.

'Shh, it's all right,' Helen husked.

'You won't leave me like Delia?' he gasped between his sobs, his little hands clinging to her shoulders, his body shaking.

Whether he understood the meaning of death, Helen wasn't sure, or whether he was simply picking up the enormity of the news from the tension in the two adults, she could not say. She simply held him close and stroked his dark curly hair, murmuring soothing words of love and reassurance, telling him not to worry, she would always be there for him.

Eventually the sobbing ceased and Helen laid him gently down in the bed and kissed his brow.

'Promise you won't die and leave me?' he pleaded, his eyes huge in his flushed damp face. 'Promise.'

'Don't worry, my love, I will always be here for you,' Helen said softly, brushing her lips against his brow again, and she saw exhaustion overtake him as his eyes closed and she kissed the slightly swollen lids, the smooth cheeks, and tenderly placed his car-printed duvet around his shoulders. 'I promise.' And a tear dropped from her eye to his cheek. His little nose wrinkled and he sighed and slept.

Ten minutes later at Leon's insistence Helen was seated alone in the living room while he went to make coffee. She had been too emotionally exhausted to argue and now she laid her head back against the soft cushions of the sofa and closed her eyes.

Grief and guilt washed over her in waves, and her mind spun like a windmill in a gale. What a mess, and most of it of her own making. She should never have agreed to Delia's mad idea, she should never have let her own circumstances influence her judgment, but then she would never have known the deep love she felt for Nicholas. To lose him would break her heart, yet she had always known Delia would claim him one day and somehow that had never felt so bad.

'Here, take this.' She opened her eyes to find Leon looming over her with a cup of coffee in his hand. 'I've laced it with a little cognac I found in a cupboard. You look like you need it.'

She took the mug from him and raised it to her lips and swallowed down a mouthful of the hot liquid. She grimaced as the spirit caught her throat, but the warmth seemed to spread through her veins inducing a kind of calm. Slowly she sipped the refreshing brew until she had drained the cup and put it on the coffee table in front of her.

Finally she glanced across at Leon reclining on the sofa opposite. He had finished his coffee and he was watching her from beneath heavy-lidded eyes, a brooding expression on his rugged face, and she wondered what he was thinking. A moment later she found out.

'Did you mean what you told Nicholas about never leaving him?'

'Yes, of course,' she asserted. 'I know it will be difficult, and obviously I don't expect to be physically with him all the time,' she said gathering her thoughts into some kind of order. 'I understand you will want to spend some time with him. You could take him for the holidays, as I know it is a custom in your family, plus apparently you have already told him.' She couldn't resist the dig. 'Given the circumstances it is in-evitable Nicholas and I will be apart for some periods, but I will still keep in touch with him by telephone on a daily basis so he will never feel I have left him,' Helen offered and thought she was being reasonable.

'I hear what you are saying, but I don't agree. I can see Nicholas is happy with you and you don't want to part with him. But as his uncle, his only blood relative, I think we should share his upbringing. Nicholas can live with me for six months of the year and you for the other.'

'Don't be ridiculous,' Helen exclaimed, her eyes widening in astonished disbelief on his darkly attractive face. 'That would be absurd. Nicholas switching home every six months, switching schools, doctors everything—only a man could come up with such an idiotic suggestion,' she declared, for once feeling superior to the arrogant devil.

His mouth hardened. 'Exactly.'

'Then why suggest it?' she queried warily, no longer feeling superior as she realised he had set her up for something, but what?

'Don't get me wrong. I think you have done a wonderful job with Nicholas, with little help from my sister, though his knowledge of the Greek language is quite good, so she did do something right. But I have noted he calls you *my* Helen. But he rarely adds the prefix Mum to Delia's name unless you prompt him. He is upset at the news of her death, but, though it pains me to say it, nowhere near as upset as he would be if he lost you. To all intents and purposes you are his mother, and I think it would be in his best interest if he stays with you.'

'You mean you agree he can stay with me? ' Helen asked, hardly daring to believe Aristides could be so reasonable.

'No, I mean the boy has had a confusing start in life with you as the only constant adult and he deserves more. He deserves two parents and a stable home and I can provide that.'

For a moment she was confused, then the full import of his words hit her and her heart sank. Obviously he had a new wife.

'So you married again; I didn't know,' she murmured. Why hadn't she thought of that? A wealthy, virile man like Leon Aristides who could take his pick of women, of course he had a wife. Suddenly the possibility of losing Nicholas completely became very real. How could she possibly deny the young boy two parents?

'No, I am not married yet.'

'You have a fiancée. You mean to marry and make a home for Nicholas?' she found the courage to ask. While her heart was breaking at the thought of losing him, her own innate honesty told her she could not deny Nicholas the chance of being part of a normal family.

Leon did not answer immediately. He placed his glass on the table between them and lounged back on the sofa, his dark eyes, piercing in their intensity, focusing on her ashen face. 'No, I do not have a fiancée. But with one condition you can marry me, and we can share Nicholas' upbringing at my home in Greece.'

Helen stared at him in stunned disbelief. 'Marry you! Are you mad?' He had to be joking. She didn't like the man. But something in the ruthless curl of his mouth, in the black unfathomable eyes that held hers, sent a prickling sensation down her spine. Her heart beat like a sledgehammer in her chest. She felt again the fear she had known as a teenager the first time they had met, and she knew he was not joking.

His mouth twisted sardonically. 'I have been accused of many things, but mad was never one of them. However, you and my sister obviously were, to have hatched such a ridiculous plot and denying a child his right to grow up in the bosom of his family. I was informed when she died that Delia had taken drugs, which might account for her perverse behaviour. So do you have the same problem? I need to know before I marry you,' he demanded arrogantly.

'I certainly do not,' she exclaimed furiously. 'And I don't believe for one minute Delia did either, she was perfectly fit and healthy the last time I saw her.'

'Then you are even more naive than you look.' His night-black eyes mocked her. 'I have the doctor's report to prove it.'

Helen was stunned into silence, her mind at first rejecting the truth, and then it slowly dawned on her she had not seen Delia since last summer. Maybe the pressures of returning to live in Greece and her engagement might have led Delia into doing something so stupid. It certainly explained her erratic behaviour over the last few months. The cancelled visits and dwindling telephone calls, suddenly it all made a horrible kind of sense. Why had she not noticed something was wrong? She had failed her friend when she had needed her. 'I never knew; I never guessed,' she murmured.

'I am inclined to believe you. Preliminary investigations seem to suggest Delia only got involved in recreational drugs last year when she returned to Athens and began to socialise in the party crowd—tragically for her.'

'Surely her fiancé could have stopped her,' Helen exclaimed.

'Her fiancé was blissfully unaware of what she got up to when he wasn't around, and when he found out after her death he was horrified. His father sent him to Japan to work and get over his loss, and I would guess by now his main feeling is that he had a lucky escape,' Leon drawled. 'Delia was more devious than any of us imagined. But as she is no longer here, you now have to pay the price for your foolishness. Unless you want to traumatise Nicholas by leaving him, you will have to marry me.'

Put like that, Helen had no defence. She had failed to recognise Delia had needed help. Helen could not, would not, compound her fault by failing Nicholas as well. But marriage to Leon Aristides…

Searching for the words, she began hesitantly. 'Surely there must be some other way that would fulfil all Nicholas' needs that does not involve marriage?' she appealed to him,

Leon Aristides saw the flicker of helplessness in her violet eyes, the slight perceptible slump of her slender shoulders, and he knew he had won. 'Nicholas has just lost his birth mother—not a very good one, I will grant you,' he said dryly. 'He sees you as his mother and he needs the reassurance of your constant presence more than ever now. You have known my nephew from birth. I have not had that privilege. I am not a brute, but there is no way I will allow you to have sole custody. Marriage between us is the only answer.' And, rising to his feet, he crossed to sit down beside her on the sofa.

'Believe me, Helen, if there was any other way I would take it.' And he reached for her hand, clasping it against his thigh. 'I have married before and I have no real desire to do so again.' He let his thumb idly caress her palm. 'But for Nicholas' sake I will.'

He felt her tremble and saw the flash in quick succession of two different emotions in her huge violet eyes. The first was fear, but the second was one a man of his experience could not fail to recognise, and he felt a surge of triumph go through him. She had tried to hide her awareness of him all afternoon, but he had seen it in her hastily lowered lashes, her pink cheeks. He could feel it in the rapidly beating pulse in her slender wrist. It would be no hardship to bed the lovely Helen and his body hardened perceptibly at the thought.

But now was not the time, besides which he still had Louisa. Nicholas was his first priority, and he must not forget Helen Heywood was as deceitful a woman as any he had ever met. As she was Nicholas' official guardian and a trustee of the boy's estate, he needed her in Greece and tied to him by the legal bond of matrimony. As her husband it would be much easier to protect the boy's interests and his own.

Ever since the death of his father he had naturally assumed complete control of the company. He had dealt swiftly and fairly with the odd objection from various distant cousins who had through inheritance retained an interest in the business. He'd had everything under complete control until the discovery of Delia's new will. Suddenly Helen Heywood's involvement posed a threat—a very slight threat, it was true. But he was a man who left nothing to chance.

Lifting her hand, he folded her slender fingers into her palm and placed it in her own lap, and sat back.

'You must see, Helen, whatever personal sacrifice you and I have to make, it is the only sensible solution,' he told her with just the right amount of wry acceptance in his tone. He let his eyes slide over her and he gave an inward smile. She was flustered, and trying very hard not to show it. 'You told me you have no man in your life at the moment, and I am unattached, so no one else will be hurt, except Nicholas if we don't marry and provide a stable home for him.'

'But we hardly know each other, never mind care,' she argued faintly, and he saw the confusion in her eyes.

His hard mouth twisted in a sardonic smile. 'Courtesy of Delia you seemed to think earlier you know a lot about me.' A guilty blush stained her cheeks, which didn't surprise him in the least, he thought with a flash of anger. She had a hell of a lot to feel guilty about, but he let none of his anger show as he continued, 'As for me, I know you are great with Nicholas and that is enough for me. A convenient marriage is not that unusual, and with the goodwill of both parties can be quite successful. We have the added incentive of Nicholas to ensure our marriage will be amiable.'

For the count of a few heartbeats Helen simply stared at Leon Aristides. The genuine concern in his steady gaze was undeniable, and not something she had thought him capable of. Maybe he was not as hard as Delia had made out, she didn't know any more. It didn't help that she could still feel the warmth of his thigh against her skin, the stroke of his thumb against her palm, and she clasped her hands together trying to control her rapidly beating pulse.

'A marriage of convenience, you mean?' She finally managed to speak. Of course that was all he was suggesting, and she knew it made sense, so why did she feel oddly deflated?

'Yes,' he said with a determination that left her in no doubt. 'Obviously we will have to live in Greece as my headquarters are there. But there is no reason why you should not keep this house, and visit your friends occasionally. Business takes me abroad quite often so it won't be a problem.'

He rose to his feet and looked down at her, a hint of cynicism in the depths of his dark eyes as they held hers. 'And there is another compelling reason why we should marry. When we spend time together with Nicholas, as is inevitable, how would it look to an outsider? Nicholas is innocent and does not understand, but the first words out of his mouth when I met him were about his friend's live-in "uncle." You and I both know what connotations people put on such a relationship and I am not having him exposed to that kind of speculation on top of the fact he is illegitimate. I know in your country a child outside of marriage is quite acceptable and fast becoming the norm. But in Greece it is still frowned upon.'

Embarrassment and, yes, guilt, she acknowledged, made her blush, and she tore her troubled eyes away from his. 'Nothing can change the circumstances of Nicholas' birth.' She made a helpless movement of her hands. 'But I hadn't thought of that,' she said shakily.

'Well, think about it now, and say you will marry me.'

'I don't think I could live with myself if I let Nicholas down.'

'Good, so that is a yes.'

He was towering over her, tall, dark and formidable. She had to tilt back her head to look at him again and reluctantly she nodded. 'I suppose so.'

'You can leave everything to me.' He reached down and wrapped his large hand around her arm and hauled her to her feet. Before she could protest his dark head swooped down and she felt the firm pressure of his mouth against her own. She caught the faint scent of his aftershave mingled with clean, slightly musky male, felt the heat of his body enfolding her and the subtle intrusion of his tongue between her softly parted lips. She swayed slightly in shock as unfamiliar electric sensations surged through her, and then abruptly he released her.

'What did you do that for?' she demanded when she could catch her breath, still reeling from the effect of his brief embrace.

'Get used to it.' And the look he levelled at her held none of the concern she had noted earlier, but a cold determination that she found oddly threatening. 'As you yourself said, Nicholas is a loving boy, and for him to feel secure with us he will expect to see some signs of affection between us.' His voice was cool and edged with mockery. 'And you could use the practice.'

She lowered her lashes over her luminous eyes. From burning with heat, Helen was burning with rage and humiliation. So in the kissing stakes Leon Aristides thought she was useless. Given his no doubt vast experience of the female sex it was hardly surprising, and why was she angry? She should be thankful. Now she knew without a doubt she need have no fear of their marriage of convenience being anything more than just that.

'I must leave now.' Leon interrupted her thoughts and she glanced back up at him. 'I am staying at the hotel for the night, and I have a few calls to make.' He spoke impatiently as though he could not get away fast enough. 'But I will be back in the morning to see Nicholas, before work commitments dictate I return to Greece, but I will keep in touch. You concentrate on getting packed up here. I will arrange the wedding ceremony for two weeks on Saturday in Athens.'

Helen gasped. 'But it is already Thursday.'

'Don't look so worried. I'll call with all the details and be back to collect you both in good time. Everything will be fine.' He turned towards the door.

A knock on the door—a coded knock: one, two, and one again—stopped Leon Aristides in his tracks. He turned and lifted an enquiring brow in her direction. 'You have a late caller, it would seem—one who sounds as though he is expected.' He saw Helen's mouth curve in a genuine smile.

'Yes, he is,' she said, walking towards him.

'Who is it?'

'It's only Mick. He works for the hotel security. I'll see you out and let him in. He always stops on his rounds for a cup of tea and to check Nicholas and I are okay,' she offered and walked past him.

Two minutes later Leon Aristides climbed into his car, a deep frown on his hard face. It was a new experience for him, being ushered out of a woman's house without a second glance while a good-looking young security guard was ushered in, and he didn't like the feeling.

Still, he thought coldly as he started the car, it was no more than he had expected. Helen Heywood was a very attractive woman in her mid-twenties; it was only natural she had a sex life. Her denial earlier of a live-in lover was disingenuous, and confirmed once again her devious nature. But what did he care? She had a shapely little figure and it would be no hardship to bed her.

He was a banker first and foremost, and he had achieved what he had set out to do. Soon he would have Nicholas in his home and Helen Heywood as his wife. The family fortune would be protected and his position as head of Aristides International Bank would be indisputable. With a bit of luck he might even be able to protect his sister's name.

He stopped the car and handed the keys to the parking attendant. A smile of ruthless satisfaction curved his hard mouth as he entered the hotel. The same girl was on reception as he asked for his key.

'Did you find Helen and Nicholas?' she asked.

The girl was friendly and obviously a gossip. Leon glanced down at her name tag and his smile morphed into one of utter charm. 'Yes, Tracy, I did, and Helen is even more beautiful than I remembered; as for Nicholas, he is a delightful boy.'

He bent his dark head slightly. 'In fact I will let you into a secret; I have asked Helen to marry me and she has agreed.'

'Oh, how romantic.'

'I think so.' Leon smiled again, ordered a meal, and left. Once in his room, he opened his laptop and began to check his messages, finding an e-mail from Louisa in Paris complaining about his long absence. Louisa was a problem he had to solve quickly, and surprisingly he realised he was rather relieved at the thought.

Helen had just seen Mick out, when the telephone rang. She listened in stunned silence as Tracy congratulated her on her forthcoming marriage. Aristides had wasted no time. She was so shocked that she agreed with everything Tracy suggested without anything really registering.

Helen went to bed with her mind in turmoil. She cried into her pillow as the full horror, the finality, of Delia's sudden death finally sank in. Then she lay red-eyed and sleepless, her mind spinning at the thought of actually marrying Leon Aristides.

She must have been mad to agree; the shocking news must have momentarily short-circuited her brain, she decided as the first rays of dawn lighted the sky. However much she wanted it to be, Nicholas was not her child, and she couldn't marry Aristides simply to keep the boy. By the time she finally fell asleep her mind was made up. She would tell Leon Aristides she had changed her mind. There had to be another way.

'Come on, Nicholas, eat your yoghurt.' He was being particularly difficult this morning. She had dressed and washed him, and settled him at the kitchen table with his breakfast, but she was still wearing a fluffy red towelling robe with eyes to match.

A pealing of the doorbell made her groan. Oh, God, what

idiot called at eight in the morning? She opened the door
with Nicholas at her side to see Leon standing there, looking
wide awake and vibrant in the same dark suit but with a dark
grey shirt and tie that made him look even more forbidding
to her tired mind.

Nicholas looked warily up at the man. 'I'm having my
breakfast.'

The words were superfluous as his mouth was covered in
strawberry yoghurt, and Helen, after the conventional greeting,
added in an urgent aside to Leon, 'I need to speak to you.'

One look was all it took for Leon Aristides to realise Helen
had changed her mind. She was hovering in the hall wearing
some shapeless red robe, with her hair falling in a tangled
mass around her shoulders.

'I will look after Nicholas.' He kept his tone light. 'You run
along and get dressed and we will talk later.' Then, dropping a
brief kiss on the top of her head, he grinned down at the boy.
'Back to the kitchen for you—I could do with something to eat.'

Fifteen minutes later, washed and dressed in jeans and a
pink cashmere sweater, her hair loose, Helen entered the
kitchen. But she was definitely superfluous to requirements,
she realised resentfully some time later.

Leon, with a skill she would not have attributed to him, had
patiently overcome Nicholas' rather sombre mood. In a stroke
of brilliance he had told him amusing stories of Delia as a
child, making him laugh and quietening all his fears. Within
an hour Nicholas had returned to his usual sunny disposition,
and was chatting happily and confidently with his new uncle,
totally captivated by the man. Talk about male bonding, Helen
thought, watching the pair lay out a train set on the bedroom
floor. How Leon Aristides had obtained one so quickly in the
rural depths of the Cotswolds, she had no idea.

By the time she finally got Leon on his own for a moment while Nicholas visited the lavatory she discovered she was too late.

'Mr Aristides,' she began, glancing down at him balanced on his haunches fixing the damn train. 'About yesterday—I've changed my mind. I don't want to relocate to Greece and I don't want to marry you. We will have to come to some other arrangement,' she finished in a rush.

Leon rested his eyes on her, his gaze running over her slim shapely body, and for a moment said nothing. He saw the determination in her expressive face and something more—the slight fear she could not hide.

'Too late,' he said softly. 'I have already told Nicholas we are all going to Greece. If you want to tell him you have changed your mind, and you don't want to go with him, fine. But if you do, you run the risk of upsetting him all over again, and maybe losing him altogether, so be warned.'

'You had no right to do that,' she gasped.

Leon rose to his feet, and grasped her arm. 'I had every right; we had an agreement,' he said coldly and saw her go pale. 'I am a man of my word. You, on the other hand, like most females, don't seem to grasp the concept. But we will marry.'

'Are you fighting?' a plaintive voice asked, and the two adults both turned to look at the small boy. Leon reacted first.

Dropping back down on his haunches, he held the boy by his shoulders. 'No, we were discussing our future together. '

Helen could do nothing but watch and agree as Leon explained Helen was going to marry him, and they were going to be his new parents and all stay together in Greece.

By the time Leon had finished Nicholas was clearly a little boy whose every dream had just come true and was suffering from a severe case of hero-worship.

Not surprisingly Helen was suffering from a severe tension

headache. The man had used emotional blackmail without a moment's hesitation to secure her co-operation and, while she bitterly resented it, she was powerless to do anything about it. When Aristides, after insisting on arranging a meeting for her with Mr Smyth for the following week, finally left around noon, claiming pressure of business, she was relieved to see the back of him.

What had she done?

CHAPTER FIVE

HELEN LOOKED AT her reflection in the mirror, and almost groaned out loud. She looked like a child in fancy dress; why on earth had she given in to Nicholas? He was a little boy—what did he know about clothes?

The answer came to her as quick as a flash. She had given into him because she loved him and always would. He was the reason she was standing on her own in a huge bedroom suite in this nineteenth century mansion, set in elegant gardens overlooking a tree-lined square in Athens, about to be married to a man she didn't love, and who certainly didn't love her.

The past couple of weeks had been chaotic. Tracy and the friends Helen had made on the hotel staff had turned up at her door at the weekend and insisted on throwing a wedding shower for her. They had pooled their resources and given her a present of some skimpy lace briefs and the most revealing negligee she had ever seen, well aware of her penchant for delicate underwear. Not that Leon was likely to see her wearing them, but just the thought made her blush. If that was not bad enough Tracy had brought a bridal magazine and declared she must choose a glamorous wedding dress. When Helen had said no, it was to be a simple civil ceremony, Tracy had declared that as she was marrying a filthy rich man the least she could do was look the part, and had left the magazine behind when she'd left in case Helen changed her mind.

Which was why she now looked so juvenile. Nicholas had seen the pictures in the magazine and decided one model was wearing the exact same dress as the fairy on his bedroom wall. He could be as stubborn as a mule and she knew where he got that from, she thought dryly. He had gone on and on about wanting to see her wearing the fairy dress, until finally she had given in. On a visit to London to keep her appointment with Mr Smyth the lawyer, she had bought the gown.

Leon had telephoned frequently and visited them again earlier in the week. With ruthless efficiency he had made a deal with the hotel management to take care of her house and arranged for the transportation of all the items Helen had decided were essential for their relocation to Greece. Then he had spent most of the afternoon with Nicholas before leaving at six for a pressing engagement in Paris.

Helen had not seen him again until late yesterday afternoon. His PA, Alex Stakis, had arrived yesterday to escort her and Nicholas to Athens in the Aristides private jet. Apparently Leon had been too busy. Well, that was fine by Helen; the less she saw of him, the better.

He had the uncanny ability to make her very aware of him and, worse, aware of herself in the most peculiar way. Her body seemed to have taken on a life of its own at odds to the dictates of her brain, and she didn't like the feeling. Last night, after charming Nicholas into agreement, he had ordered an end to her early suppers with the boy and insisted she dine with him later after Nicholas was in bed. Bitterly resenting his overbearing attitude, but powerless to argue with him in front of Nicholas, she had reluctantly agreed.

Dining alone with him had been an ordeal. Leon had been perfectly polite, the conversation mostly confined to the wedding arrangements for the following day with a few social niceties thrown in. But somehow every time his dark eyes rested on her she had to battle down the embarrassing heat that threatened to colour every inch of her pale skin.

It was galling to have to admit that Leon could make her feel physically conscious of him without any effort on his part. Her only comfort was the knowledge that he wasn't in the least attracted to her. He had as good as told her so the one time he had kissed her. All she had to do was control the odd feeling of panic that he aroused in her and concentrate on Nicholas, and everything would be fine.

She glanced at her reflection again, a wry smile curving her lips. She certainly had no fear of inciting the interest of any male over the age of seven in this gown. Fashioned in silk, the sleeves were long and wide at her wrists. The bodice embroidered with silver thread skimmed her breasts and narrow waist ending in a point over her flat stomach. The skirt of the gown fell in fine panels of cobweb silk of varying pointed lengths around her ankles. Not something Helen would ever have chosen. Plus the jewel encrusted satin slippers with upturned pointed toes she wore on her feet instead of the high heels she usually favoured did nothing for her lack of height, but at least Nicholas would be happy. She was totally unaware of how the gossamer fine fabric sensuously caressed her slender body with every move she made.

The door opened and the housekeeper, Anna, a tall, grey-haired woman of about sixty, walked in, closely followed by Nicholas.

'Oh, Helen, you look beautiful.' He gazed up at her, his dark eyes shining like jewels. 'Exactly like my fairy picture.'

'Thank you, darling.' She bent down to give him a hug.

'Uncle Leon sent me to get you 'cause it is after two,' he said, puffed up with importance. 'Everyone is waiting.'

Anna looked at her. 'He is right, madam, and there has been a slight change of plan. The ceremony is to take place inside instead of in the garden,' she said with a telling glance at the rain lashing the window.

Helen smiled. So much for Leon's assertion that the sun always shone in Greece. 'That's fine,' she reassured Anna, glad that at least she spoke excellent English. The other members of staff she had met last night did not.

'Lead on, Nicholas.' She grinned down at him and taking his hand in hers, she headed for the door.

Standing in the hall, Leon greeted the last guests, and glanced around the group of about thirty people. He had invited only those friends and business colleagues that he deemed absolutely necessary. To the distant relatives and acquaintances he had excluded, he had used the valid excuse of the recent deaths in the family as the reason for keeping the ceremony small and low key. At some later date he knew he would have to host a party to introduce Helen and Nicholas, but right now business came first. His priority was to make sure his marriage to Helen Heywood was completed without a hitch and she was legally tied to him as his wife. For that he did not need a great show. He had already had the huge society wedding with Tina; he didn't need another one.

He moved to speak to his PA, Alex Stakis, who was also acting as his witness, and was suddenly aware of the strange silence that had fallen over the assembled guests. His PA was staring straight past him, an expression of avid male appreciation lighting his face. Leon turned and followed the line of Alex's gaze and stiffened.

Descending the marble staircase was a vision of loveliness, a girl that looked as if she had just stepped out of any red-blooded man's dream. Helen Heywood, his soon-to-be wife, and the knowledge sent a surge of pleasure through his powerful frame that had nothing to do with business and everything to do with the tightening in his groin in anticipation of the night ahead.

Her ash-blonde hair was loose and fell in ringlets around her slender shoulders. Her gown was a fantasy in white and silver, long-sleeved with a deep vee neckline that revealed the creamy curves of her breasts, and faithfully followed every exquisite line of her body. The skirt skimmed her hips and floated in a stream of flimsy panels around her legs and thighs revealing tantalising glimpses of pale flesh as she descended the marble staircase. Her small feet were encased in harem styled slippers and to top it all off on her head was a silver garland of tiny rosebuds. She was laughing down at the little boy holding her hand and he was grinning back.

For a long moment Leon simply stared, and he had a fleeting sense he had seen Helen like this before. But he couldn't have, she looked ravishing, and he certainly had not seen her wearing make-up; even though she wasn't wearing much, the effect was stunning.

Her sparkling violet eyes were accentuated by a misty shadow and a touch of mascara exaggerated her incredibly long lashes. Her full lips were coated in a deep rose gloss and her pearly white skin was tinted by the faintest of natural blushes. She looked bewitching, the perfect bride. Innocent, and yet sensual, and the way the flimsy material clung to her petite body was as sexy as hell.

But she also looked as out of place in the small, sophisticated civil ceremony he had arranged as snow in summer, he realised grimly and frowned.

He had told her it was to be a simple ceremony, and it had never occurred to him she would dress as a bride. But this was her wedding, the only one she was ever going to have if he had his way, and he always did.

Inexplicably Leon felt guilty. His mouth tightened as he walked forward, his eyes focused on her lovely face. 'Helen you look beautiful,' he stated, and bared his teeth in a smile.

'Thank you.' She glanced at him and didn't bother to return the smile. Instead she immediately gave her attention to the little boy holding her hand. 'Nicholas chose my dress, didn't you, darling?'

A wry smile quirked his mouth. If that was true the boy had a heck of a precocious view of the female form for one so young. Then abruptly he stiffened as he saw more of her breasts than was safe in his semi-aroused state. And the luminous look of unconditional love in her eyes as she bent towards the boy as he cheerfully agreed didn't help his condition.

No woman, not even his own mother, had ever looked at him like that. Not that he would want them to, he thought cynically. He had all he wanted, or he would have tonight, he amended, and reached for her hand, enfolding it firmly in his own. 'The celebrant is waiting.'

Helen listened to the bearded little man reel off the service in Greek with a little English thrown in for her benefit and responded appropriately, not looking at Leon unless she had to. When he had taken her hand at the foot of the stairs she had felt a sudden quickening in her pulse and almost panicked. But one glance at his set face, his broad shoulders and solid, muscled body immaculately clad in a sombre dark suit had been enough to calm her nerves.

Leon Aristides looked about as happy as the condemned man heading for the electric chair, his attempt at a smile a mockery. However, this was a marriage of convenience, they had both agreed, so she had nothing to worry about.

Finally when the gold band was firmly on her finger, and

surprisingly a gold band on Leon's as well she heaved an inward sigh of relief. Then the little man instructed Leon to kiss his bride.

Leon took her chin in his hand and tilted her face up to his. Their eyes met and for an instant she saw a flare in the ebony depths of his that made the hairs on the nape of her neck stand on end. It took all her self-control not to flinch when his dark head lowered and he brushed her lips briefly with his own.

'Now that wasn't as bad as you expected,' he said softly, his eyes gleaming with sardonic amusement as he curved an arm around her waist and turned her to face the guests, well aware of her initial reluctance.

And it wasn't so bad, Helen conceded a few hours later. She had managed to control her urge to flinch every time Leon looped an arm around her waist, reminding herself it was necessary for Nicholas' sake. If she had to grit her teeth occasionally to subdue the little nervous tremors that afflicted her when he laid his hand on hers at the table or touched her cheek in an apparently affectionate gesture for the benefit of the guests, nobody seemed to notice. And after a long, leisurely meal and two glasses of champagne Helen was convinced she was over the worst and her self-confidence was restored.

Alex Stakis had made a speech, and Leon had said a few words, and then the party had moved from the dining room into a huge drawing room and become more informal.

She had met Leon's friend and lawyer, Chris Stefano, and his wife Mary who was English and also a lawyer before her marriage. Helen liked her and quickly discovered Mary was the proud mother of an eight-year-old boy, Mark, and twins, a boy and a girl who were the same age as Nicholas, and, as they were all bilingual, the children quickly made friends.

Alone for a moment, Helen allowed herself a sigh of relief. Thankfully Leon had finally left her side and was deep in discussion with Chris Stefano and another man. She glanced around the room. Sophisticated, elegant people stood around in groups chatting and drinking. Not really her scene at all, and thanks to Nicholas she was hopelessly overdressed.

'You look a little lost.' Mary Stefano approached her. 'Don't worry, you will get used to it,' she said with a glance across to the group of men. 'I have been married to Chris for nine years and in all that time I have never been to a party, wedding or baptism where the men haven't ended up discussing business, especially Leon and Chris.' She grinned.

'I can see that.' Helen smiled back.

'Well, look on the bright side—at least you will have Leon to yourself on the honeymoon.'

'We're not having a honeymoon,' Helen declared quickly, the very thought made her inwardly shudder. 'Leon is far too busy, and I have to take care of Nicholas.'

'Not much of a wedding night with your son around to wake you at the crack of dawn.'

'Oh, Nicholas is not my son,' Helen declared swiftly. 'He is Delia's child, but I have always helped to look after him while she studied.' A sad smile curved her lips. 'Now with Delia gone—'

'Delia's, you say?' Mary cut in and gave her an odd look. 'I see, well, I'd better go and find my brood. It is almost seven, time we left.'

Puzzled by Mary's comment, Helen paused for a moment. Surely Leon must have told his friends Nicholas was Delia's child. She was about to follow Mary and ask her, but before she could move the celebrant appeared at her side and began a long conversation in a mixture of English and Greek. Good manners dictated she stay and listen. Her own command of Greek was slight, only what she had picked up from her grandfather and Delia when she had been teaching Nicholas.

He, on the other hand, being so young, had grasped the language remarkably well, and Helen had no doubt after a few weeks living in Greece he would be speaking it like a native.

Finally the celebrant left to refill his glass and Helen turned towards the door, intending to look for Nicholas.

'Helen.' A long arm snaked around her waist. 'Going somewhere?'

She stiffened automatically and tilted back her head to glance up into the hard face of Leon. 'I'm going to find Nicholas, it is past time he was in bed.'

'There is no need. Mary and Chris are taking him to stay at their house for the night.'

'Whatever for?' And not giving him time to respond, she said swiftly, 'Nicholas has never been away from me for a whole night before.' She felt his hand tighten on her waist and saw the mockery in his dark eyes and suddenly the old tension Helen felt around him returned.

'Then it is about time he was. I know you love him, but you are in danger of smothering him,' he told her bluntly. She opened her mouth to object but he cut in dryly, 'Before you say anything else, Mary offered to take him after *you* told her we had no honeymoon planned. Nicholas is delighted at the idea, and here they come.'

Helen walked into her bedroom and closed the door behind her. It was over. She pressed a light switch and the room was dimly illuminated by a couple of bedside lamps. For the first time in over three and half years there was no Nicholas to check on, and the knowledge was saddening. From being virtually the centre of his universe she had to accept he was growing up; his life, his horizons, were expanding, which was as it should be.

Leon had been right about Nicholas; with a kiss and a hug

for Helen, he had left happily with Mary and her family. It had taken another few hours and another buffet-style meal before the final guest had departed, and she had been left alone with Leon. She had refused his offer of a nightcap pleading exhaustion, which wasn't far from the truth.

Sighing, she pulled the garland from her head, a brief smile curving her lips. Well, at least Nicholas had got his wish. She walked into the huge *en suite* bathroom that was bigger than her bedroom at home. Along with the usual luxurious fixtures there was a huge circular spa bath almost big enough for her to swim in.

Helen slipped out of the dress and her briefs, dropping them on the floor. She piled her hair into a shower cap, and took a quick shower, before wrapping a huge bath sheet sarong-style around her naked body. She crossed to the double vanity basin where she had left her toiletries and picking up a brush, swiftly brushed the carefully contrived ringlets out of her hair until it fell in its usual soft waves around her shoulders. No sign of a bride remained, she thought, tucking her hair behind her ears, and picking up her discarded briefs, she dropped them in the laundry bin before gathering up her dress and entering the adjoining dressing room.

They were the only rooms, plus the nursery suite across the hall that was Nicholas' that she could safely say she knew how to find. Tomorrow morning she really must get Anna to give her a guided tour of the house. There had not been time yesterday and today she had merely gone where she was told.

Helen opened the closet where her clothes had been stowed with Anna's help the night before and hung the dress up. Opening a drawer, she ignored the flimsy negligee and withdrew a knee-length cotton nightshirt she usually wore around Nicholas. A tender smile curved her lips as she glanced at the print of the two teddy bears on the front. Nicholas had told her the first time he had seen her wearing it that the shirt made her look doubly cuddly.

She was smiling as she wandered back into the bedroom, and tripped over the bottom of the bath sheet.

'Careful.' Two strong hands grasped her shoulders and steadied her. 'There is no need to kneel at my feet just yet,' a deep voice drawled mockingly.

'You!' she exclaimed, looking up into the amused dark eyes of Leon. 'And I wasn't,' she snapped, shrugging his hands off her shoulders and stepping back. 'This sheet is too big.' And so was he.

Helen's heart skipped a beat as her startled gaze swept over him. His tall, lithe body was clad in only a black towelling robe that exposed a large area of hair darkened chest and ended mid-thigh, revealing his long legs. For a banker, a man who did no physical work, he had a magnificent physique, the thought came unbidden to her mind.

Then suddenly she realised the only thing protecting her own naked body was a towel—a towel that, following her tripping over it, had slid perilously south. She dropped her nightshirt and hastily hauled the bath sheet as far up as it would go.

'This is my room and I would like you to leave,' she declared a little shakily.

'It is also mine, the master suite,' Leon said with a soft, husky laugh and she was struck dumb by his outrageous dec-laration. Before she could even get her head around the fact, never mind object, his strong hands spanned her waist and he swung her off the floor.

With her feet dangling in the air, she instinctively reached out and grasped his broad shoulder to steady herself. With her free hand she hung onto the knot in the towel as if her life depended on it. She had never been on eye level with him before, his face suddenly only inches from her own. Her shocked gaze met the glittering intensity of his night-black eyes and her heart lurched in panic. Her position had just become a heck of a lot more perilous, she realized, swallowing hard. His hands were burning into her waist, and her breathing was suddenly erratic.

'What on earth do you think you are doing?' Red-faced with embarrassment and something more she refused to recognize, Helen tried to wriggle free. 'Put me down.'

'Certainly.' He moved and somehow instead of his hands on her waist one long arm held her clasped firmly against his big body. His other hand twisted in the waving mass of her hair, tipping her head back.

She stared at him like a mesmerised mouse. She saw his dark head lower. He wouldn't...he couldn't be going to kiss her...

'But first...' Even as her own lips trembled in expectation of his kiss his firm lips brushed the tender skin of her throat.

The warm moist flick of his tongue seared her skin, sending a starburst of tiny tremors racing along every nerve in her body. His sensuous mouth closed over the suddenly racing pulse in her neck and paused to suck lightly before trailing a string of kisses up her throat in a slow, seductive path to her lips.

'No.' Helen choked and tried to resist but a strange warmth began to unfurl in the centre of her being, her body betraying her as a rising tide of totally new emotions flowed through her.

'No,' she murmured again, but it was more of a moan, her lips helplessly parting beneath the heady pressure of his mouth to accept the subtle penetration of his tongue. His hand tightened on her nape and he kissed her with a slow, seductive passion that stoked the unfamiliar warmth into a flame that seemed to melt her bones. She had never known a kiss could be so exquisite she thought dreamily, never known anything so pleasurable existed.

She sighed when he broke the kiss, and groaned as he bit

the soft lobe of her ear, his warm breath curling around the inner whorls.

'Do you still want me to put you down?' His deep, husky voice resonated through every cell in her body.

Helen stared dazedly into the smouldering blackness of his deep set eyes, and the temptation of total capitulation to the unknown pleasure he was offering urged her to say no. His hand at her nape stroked down to splay over her bare shoulder blades holding her close to the muscular wall of his chest, her breasts inexplicably tightening at the contact. His mouth covered hers again and he was kissing her as she had never been kissed before, deeply, erotically. She shuddered and clung to him, the flames of desire burning ever higher, and when he finally lifted his head she was helpless against the storm of heated sensations roaring like wildfire through her.

He lifted his head and drawled thickly, 'Well, Helen, must I put you down?'

The 'no' of surrender hovered on the tip of her tongue. His hand slipped down and drew her into the hard heat of his lower body. Crushed against him, she felt the rigid length of his masculine arousal against her churning stomach, and in a moment of clarity she realised what she was inviting.

'Yes. You—you…' She panicked, and, lost for adequate words, she shoved her hands against his chest and began to struggle like a deranged idiot. 'You animal.'

Something deadly flickered in the depths of his eyes, then it was successfully masked. 'All right, I heard you,' he drawled mockingly and lowered her to the floor.

CHAPTER SIX

HOT AND FLUSTERED, Helen staggered back a few steps and frantically tried to assimilate what Leon had just said and done and why. He had told her she was hopeless at kissing, she wanted to yell at him, her body strumming with the opposing emotions of fury and a frustration she had never experienced before.

He had said their marriage was one of convenience...but whose? She asked the question she should have asked herself the minute he'd suggested marriage. Certainly not hers. She had left her home and come to live in a foreign country to accommodate him and his lifestyle, and if he thought for one second she was going to accommodate him in bed as well he was in for a rude awakening.

She grasped the bath sheet tightly around her. 'What do you think you are playing at?' Her eyes blazed a brilliant violet up to his. 'Ours is a marriage of convenience and don't you forget it.'

'A convenient marriage, yes, but also a legal marriage, and as such you must know it is usual to consummate the union.' His dark cynical gaze held hers and she stared back in appalled amazement. 'If anyone is playing around here it is you.'

'Me?' she screeched. She could not believe the turn of events. 'Are you out of your mind?'

He shook his dark head dismissively. 'Oh, come on, Helen,' he drawled as he lessened the space between them. 'Who do you think you are kidding? I am no fool. Your earthy little moans, the soft flush of arousal colouring your skin are a complete give-away,' he declared throatily, and reached out to brush a strand of hair over her shoulder, not the least fazed by her angry outburst. 'You want this just as much as me. In some cases I believe a bit of game-playing can spice up a jaded sex life, but in our case it is not necessary, I can assure you.'

Helen stilled, her eyes widening in confusion on his ruggedly attractive face. She could not believe what she was hearing. His strong hands curved over her shoulders and he stared down at her, his firm lips curling in a knowing, sensual smile, all confident, virile male.

'I will make it great for you, believe me.'

It was his colossal conceit that finally got through to her and from being confused she was instantaneously contemptuous. 'No, you arrogant jerk.' She hissed like a spitting cat and shoved him hard in the chest, catching him unawares and ducking free from his hands.

His face darkened, all traces of humour vanishing from his granite-like features. 'It is a bit late for outraged virtue,' he drawled derisively, his dark eyes narrowing on her flushed furious face. 'You can't pretend you are an innocent, Helen. You are an adult woman, with a woman's needs. True, Nicholas might have curtailed your love life a little, but I saw the very convenient arrangement you had with Mick the security guard. And as for the outfit you wore today, it simply screamed sex. So no more games.'

He thought Mick was her sexual partner, and her fairy styled dress was sexy. She almost laughed out loud. The man must live on another planet. She shook her head in amazement at his misconceptions. 'I am not—' was as far as she got.

'Oh, yes, you are.' He looped an arm around her waist and deftly swept the towel from her body.

For the first time in her adult life she was totally naked in front of a man, and the shock held her rigid. Protectively she closed her eyes against the flush of embarrassment colouring her skin and instinctively she leant away from him. But that was a mistake.

'Exquisite. Helen of Troy could not have been more beautiful.' She heard his deep-throated murmur and her eyes slowly opened.

'All my fantasies in one perfect little package,' he husked, his incredibly dark eyes lifting briefly to hers and she was paralysed by the intensity of his gaze as he subjected her to a slow, raking appraisal.

For what seemed an age he just looked at her. Then his hand lifted and the pad of one finger traced the upper curves of her breasts and the valley between with a tactile sensuality that stopped her heart. She drew in a much-needed ragged breath. How could such a slight touch be so seductive? she wondered desperately. But in a second her desperation turned into helpless capitulation as he urged her closer. Her body leapt in response at the brush of his naked thighs against her own, her legs suddenly losing the power or will to support her as she swayed against him.

Her breasts felt oddly swollen, and a heady sensation seemed to thicken and slow the blood flowing through her veins. His long fingers splayed to cage the fullness of one breast in the palm of his hand and slowly, very slowly, trailed to the burgeoning rosy tip to nip ever so gently.

He murmured something in Greek but she barely heard as he delivered the same erotic delights to her other breast. A stomach curling thread of exquisite sensation pulled from her breasts to the juncture of her thighs and obliterated any lingering will to resist from her mind. She moaned low in her throat as a sensory pleasure she had never felt in her life before totally beguiled her.

His mouth replaced his fingers, and from new sensations of wondrous pleasure she was transported into the realms of aching need as she felt the flick of his tongue on her breast, his lips curling over the rigid peaks to suckle and savour each in turn. She gave an audible gasp, her back arching involuntarily as he gathered her closer still, trailing a line of fire from her breasts to her lush mouth.

'Ah, Helen, you are beautiful and responsive, everything a man could want,' he whispered softly against her lips, taking possession of her mouth with a deep kiss, his tongue probing with a skilful eroticism that was nothing less than a deliberate seduction of all her senses.

She closed her eyes, her hands of their own volition stroking over his broad shoulders and wrapping around his neck in complete surrender to the magic of his mouth. As if it was a signal he had been waiting for he scooped her up in his arms and carried her to the bed.

Her lashes lifted, her huge violet eyes met the smouldering intent in his, and for a brief confusing moment she wondered what was happening to her. He laid her on the bed, and shrugged off his robe, and her wonder changed to awe.

His body loomed over her, outlined in the glow of the bedside light. Naked, he was magnificent. Tall and golden, his broad chest shadowed with black body hair that arrowed down the centre of the hard muscles of his abdomen to widen and frame the proud strength of his fully aroused sex. Helen gazed almost with fear but mostly in helpless fascination, and when she lifted her eyes to his face she saw the slow, sensual burn in his smile as he lay down at her side.

'You look as though you have never seen a naked man

before, and yet we both know you have.' He chuckled and leaning over her he caught her hands in one of his and placed them above her head. 'But it is still a hell of a turn-on,' he husked, his dark gaze roaming leisurely over her naked body, his free hand stroking down over her shoulder to cup her breast.

She didn't know what he was talking about and suddenly fear overtook her fascination. 'You mustn't,' she breathed, like someone waking from a dream. 'You can't,' she cried, but her cry turned to whimpering moan as he lowered his head and sucked a taut nipple into the heat of his mouth again, while his long fingers toyed with the other.

He lifted his dark head. 'I can and I must. I promised you it would be great, *ma petite.*' He squeezed her breast and rolled the rigid tip between finger and thumb, tugging ever so slightly until a helpless groan escaped her.

'And for that I must take you slowly.' His dark head bent and his skilful mouth tormented and teased one breast and then the other before returning once more to take her mouth in a kiss that was a deliberate sensual onslaught designed to drive her mindless with pleasure, while his hands continued to caress her aching breasts.

'You like me playing with your breasts,' he taunted softly, raising his head, his dark eyes skimming down her writhing body. 'I wonder how much more your perfect little body enjoys.' His fingers traced the fine scar low on her belly. 'Appendix?' he prompted.

Helen tensed; should she tell him? But even as she pondered her answer his dark eyes lifted to hers.

'Ah, Helen.' The hand holding her wrists stroked down her arm and a thousand little nerves quivered at his touch. 'No need to be embarrassed; so much perfection needs an endearing blemish.' And he flicked her lips with his tongue, a glimmer of humour in his teasing caress.

Then with slow deliberation he kissed and licked his way down her throat, his strong hands forming and caressing her hot little body with a teasing tactile skill that made her burn. He nudged apart her legs and settled between her thighs, his dark head trailing lower to taste her aching breasts yet again, and down over her navel until his lips traced the slim white scar. The slightly rough scrape of his jaw against her soft skin was electrifying and she gasped and writhed beneath him, hungry for more.

Deep in her mind the thought of resistance flickered and died as she felt the heat of his mouth glide lower, his fingers touch the curls at the apex of her thighs. Her pelvis arched instinctively and she was lost, lost to everything except the incredible urge to lose herself in the drugging excitement, the hunger consuming her.

But Leon refused to be hurried. His hand traced her inner thigh and down her trembling legs, but avoided the one place where she ached for him.

Helen's hands were now free to lash out at him, but she no longer had any desire to, utterly captive to the wildly exciting pleasure he aroused in her. She reached for his broad shoulders, her fingers delighting in the sleek, smooth feel of his skin. And when he lifted his head to take her mouth again she welcomed his kiss, her tongue twining with his in a greedy, untutored passion.

The clear male scent of him filled her nostrils. The expert touch of his mouth and hands, and the breathtaking eroticism with which he continued to explore her body, incited a fevered response in her she could never have imagined herself capable of. Hesitantly she drew her fingers down the indentation of his spine to his firm buttocks, then up over his belly to his chest. Her fingers curled in his body hair, audaciously scraping the pebble-like male nipples. She heard him groan and bit lightly where her fingers had been, felt his great body jerk, and, fascinated by the discovery she could affect him, she greedily raked her hands and nails over the hard sleek muscle and sinew of his magnificent body.

For Helen place, time and reality ceased to exist. She was totally consumed by the man and the torturous pleasure he aroused in her to the exclusion of all else. She moaned when his long fingers finally parted the velvet lips of her sex and found her hot, wet and wanting. The subtle mastery of his fingers stroking and exploring the moist centre of her femininity made her groan out loud as she experienced for the first time in her life the incredible tightening sensation, the intense build up of physical pleasure that the most intimate touch of a man could arouse.

'You want me?' Leon demanded, teasing her swelling bud with his fingertip. He needed to hear her say the word although he knew the answer with every tremor, every moan that escaped her lush mouth as he skilfully deepened the rhythmic pressure until she writhed beneath him like a wild thing.

With a shaking hand he donned protection. He was rock-hard with the need to be inside her, and he stroked her again and saw her violet eyes purple with desire. She was amazing, her perfect little body a firehouse of passion, and he didn't think he could hold out a second longer. 'Say the word, Helen.'

'Yes, yes,' she moaned.

Only then did he lift her and in one fluid movement thrust into her. She was small and tight and as he surged inside her he felt the unexpected resistance and heard her cry of pain. With every muscle and sinew in his body straining with a super human effort of control, Leon managed to still inside her. He covered her mouth with his, absorbing her cry, kissing her long and deep.

Helen went from frenzied to frozen in a second. Her body

arched in an instinctive attempt to throw him off, and she tried to bite his tongue, her only thought to escape.

'Stop it, Helen, don't fight me,' Leon husked against her lips. 'Trust me.' His hands flexed and gentled on her hips, and he withdrew ever so slightly and advanced again a little more.

Incredibly Helen had still been a virgin. His wife a virgin and, along with an overwhelming need to possess her completely, he was aware of a shockingly basic feeling of primitive male posession. She was his and only his. Using all his considerable experience, he stroked and caressed her. His tongue searched the moist interior of her mouth with a sensuality that reflected what he ached to do with her body. Knowing he had to give her time to accept him.

'No, don't,' she moaned.

'Shh, Helen,' he husked softly against her mouth, his hand stroking up her trembling body to cup one lush breast. 'I promise seconds from now you will be begging me to continue.' He ran the tip of his tongue slowly around the outline of her mouth before seeking again the hot sweet passion within, while his agile fingers teased the tip of her breast.

A moment later Helen realised Leon was right. Miraculously the pain subsided and a quiver of renewed pleasure lanced through her as he continued to kiss and caress her. With a subtle thrust of his hips he moved in her, slowly stretching and accustoming her to his thick fullness, arousing her with ever-lengthening strokes.

Helen was quickly oblivious to everything except the strength, the power of him filling her, driving her inexorably once more to that torturous brink of ecstasy she could only imagine. She clung to him as though he were her world. Then with one deep, powerful thrust he sent her over the edge, her body convulsing around him in a tidal wave of earth-shattering mindless delight. She cried out his name, her legs locking fiercely around his waist, never wanting to let him go, never wanting the cataclysmic feeling to stop. She felt him tauten and heard his answering cry as his great body shuddered violently with the powerful force of his own orgasm.

His weight pinned her to the bed, but it was a weight Helen relished as the tempestuous waves of their loving gradually subsided, bringing her quivering body down to a state of languorous fulfilment.

She gazed up at her lover—her husband—utterly awe-struck. Nothing she had experienced, or imagined, in her life had come close to the intense, raw emotion he had aroused, the overwhelming power of his possession.

'Leon, I never knew, never imagined,' she murmured, 'making love could be so intense, so mind-blowing—pure magic.' She smiled a slow soft curl of her lips and reached out a finger to trace the outline of his mouth.

'Leon,' she husked softly. 'Leon.' From never calling him by name if she could help it, now she wanted to shout it from the rooftops.

His name on her lips was a sensual invitation but, mindful of her recently lost innocence, one Leon knew he should not accept. But amazingly his body was telling him otherwise, and abruptly he rolled off her.

'Helen,' he responded with humorous indulgence, and, leaning up on one elbow, he surveyed his beautiful wife's slender body, her tousled mass of silken hair, and soft, swollen-mouthed, blissful smile.

God! She was good—better than good, amazing. How he could have thought she was not his type was unfathomable to him now. She was everything a woman should be and the urge to kiss her lush lips and start all over again was incredibly instant.

Accustomed to sophisticated women who knew the score and to whom having sex was not much more than a pleasurable workout, he found it a novel experience to see genuine wonder in her huge violet eyes, and Leon almost succumbed. In all his thirty-nine years he had never known a woman like her, an innocent and a sensualist rolled into one. Then cynically he reminded himself she might be innocent in the sexual stakes, but in every other way she was as cunning as the rest of her sex.

Still, it was a terrific ego trip to know he was her first, and with that in mind his conscience told him he needed to give her time to recover, though his body was telling him otherwise. His dark eyes narrowed speculatively on her lovely face. She was made for sex, as of today she was his, and there would be plenty of other times.

With that happy thought uppermost in his mind he told her, 'You are now my wife.' A smile of sheer masculine satisfaction glinted in his dark eyes. 'You are also full of surprises. Who would have imagined a sexy little lady like you, still a virgin?' He shook his head in amused amazement, and slid off the bed to stand looking down at her. 'I'm flattered you enjoyed your first taste of sex, Helen, and I must confess I am delighted to discover you have a remarkable natural aptitude for the act.' And, turning, he headed for the bathroom before he lost control and succumbed to the temptation she offered and joined her in bed again.

He disposed of the condom and washed his hands. Another bonus with Helen, he thought complacently, after years of protection, he need never use another condom as he introduced her to every aspect of sex. His big body tightened at the prospect. He glanced into the mirror above the basin and rubbed his hand against his cheek, her skin was as soft as silk, and he could do with another shave. A wry grin twisted his mobile mouth. Not tonight, though—a rough chin might help him control his basic urges in consideration of his very new wife. He had a lifetime to enjoy the pleasures of the flesh with Helen, and surprisingly the idea of being tied to one woman for years did not faze him at all.

Helen's dreamy gaze followed his retreating form as he headed for the bathroom, all long, lithe, muscular male. Her eyes widened in disbelief as the scratches on his back and tight buttocks finally registered in her love-hazed mind. Had she done that? Oh, God, yes. What had possessed her?

Leon, her convenient husband.

His departing words replayed in her head, and she came down to earth with a thump.

He hadn't sounded very flattered, and 'enjoyed your first taste of sex' was not how Helen would have described the act. The very word 'act' offended her sensibilities, and in that moment with sickening clarity she realised what an idiot she had been. The most emotional, momentous experience in her life had meant little to Leon. It had been just that, an *act* on his part. A way to ensure the absolute legality of their marriage, he had told her so.

For a while she had allowed herself to forget he was a hard, cynical banker, a man who controlled vast amounts of money, a man born to take account of every eventuality to control everything, Nicholas and herself included.

She cringed at her own naivety, at her own wholehearted surrender to the man. His reference to her natural ability filled her with shame and humiliation. How could she have responded to him so shockingly?

The answer was in every pore of her body, the swollen fullness of her lips and in the tender tips of her breasts, because she wanted Leon in the most primitive way possible, but had never recognised the fact.

Instinctively her awareness of him had scared her from the

very first time she had set eyes on him. She had told herself when they had met again it was silly to be afraid of the man. First impressions were usually correct, she should have remembered that, and run as far and fast as she could when he'd reappeared in her life.

It was too late now, she had married the man, and for Nicholas' sake she was going to have to live with him, but not here in his bed. She leapt off the bed, her frantic gaze flying around the room. She had to live with him, but she did not have to sleep with him. He had said they had to consummate the marriage. My God! He had certainly done that, but she wasn't hanging around for a repeat performance.

Finally finding her nightshirt on the floor, she picked it up and pulled it over her trembling body. Nicholas' room was free, she would spend the rest of the night there, and find a room of her own in the morning. Brushing her hair from her eyes, she turned towards the door.

With all the arrogant confidence of a very self-satisfied man, Leon wrapped a towel around his hips and sauntered back into the bedroom. Not only did he have Nicholas, a true Aristides, an heir to inherit his fortune, it was a pleasurable bonus to have the lovely Helen as his wife. He looked at the bed, the empty bed, and his pleasure turned to cold anger in an instant.

He glanced across the room. She was almost at the door, her glorious hair falling in a tumbled mass of waves halfway down her slender back. 'Going somewhere?' he demanded, striding towards her, and he saw her shoulders stiffen as she slowly turned to face him. Her violet eyes that had looked at him with such awe not long ago now sparkled with defiance.

'Yes, I am going to find a room of my own.'

'This is your room,' he stated angrily, not appreciating her rebellion. She had to know her place was in his bed, and he reached for her shoulders, his eyes raking over her. The cotton shirt was shapeless and ended mid calf. But it was the pattern that really caught his attention and diffused his anger somewhat. For a man accustomed to his ladies dressed in the finest silks and satins it was a real shock.

'What on earth are you wearing?' he asked incredulously. Two ridiculous teddy bears danced across her chest.

Helen hoped it was the picture holding his attention and not her breasts, but much to her shame she could do nothing about the sudden swelling in those same breasts. Leon with a slip of a towel slung around his lean hips was a breathtaking sight to any female between the ages of eight and eighty, she thought, and much to her chagrin she was no exception.

'It's my doubly-cuddly nightshirt,' she blurted. The air between them was fraught with tension and she dragged in a slightly unsteady breath before continuing. 'Nicholas likes it, he named it, and anyway it has nothing to do with you what I wear.'

'Maybe not, though your exquisite body deserves the finest silk and satin,' he opined as his hands tightened on her shoulders and he drew her closer, his dark eyes gleaming with such blatant sexuality it made her heart leap in her breast. 'But it has everything to do with me where you sleep, and that is in my bed.'

She lowered her lashes over her too-revealing eyes. She could barely look at him without blushing. 'No, thank you,' she said with all the cool she could muster. 'I want my own room.'

An amused smile played around his firm mouth. 'So polite, but that is not possible, Helen, and anyway all your clothes are here. Surely you would not want to upset Anna by demanding she move them from our suite after one night,' he prompted mockingly.

She didn't appreciate the mention of Anna or his amusement. She glanced at the rumpled bed. Obviously what had just happened there was one big laugh to him, whereas to her it was the scene of her downfall and totally humiliating.

'There is no "our" suite,' she snapped. He was so damned arrogant, nothing dented his massive male ego, and she continued defiantly, 'I'll apologise to Anna for the inconvenience tomorrow, but I am not staying here with you.'

'You don't have a choice.' His mouth tightened, his great body tensed, and all trace of humour vanished. 'You're my wife and your place is in my bed.' His eyes narrowed on her flushed, mutinous face. 'Don't try my patience. I have told you before, I don't like women who play games.'

Her face grew hot with renewed humiliation and fury. 'I am not playing a game,' she lashed back. 'You said we had to consummate the marriage—well, we have. And I have no desire to repeat the exercise.'

One eyebrow rose with derisive scorn. 'Oh, but you do.' And a hand left one shoulder to curve around her waist and draw her hard against him. 'And if you were honest you would admit that it is that desire that has you running scared.'

The contact with his big muscular body sent the blood pounding through Helen's veins. She looked up at his ruggedly attractive face. His dark eyes held a wealth of intimate, sensual knowledge that shamed and excited her, but also infuriated her beyond words.

'No,' she cried. 'I hated it. I hate you,' she flung angrily and twisted furiously against his steel-like grip, but to no avail.

His lips twisted in a humourless smile. 'You don't know me well enough to hate me. That may come later—one never knows with women,' he said dryly, his hand snaking up her back, pressing her to him from chest to thigh. 'But what you hate now is the fact that it was I who showed you what a rampant little sensualist you are, and you hate yourself for enjoying sex with someone you don't know very well.'

Her eyes glittered with angry resentment. 'That is not true; you deceived me—you behaved like an animal.'

'A male animal you thoroughly enjoyed and I have the marks to prove it,' he stated with undisguised satisfaction.

Helen blushed scarlet and lowered her lashes to disguise her vulnerability from his discerning gaze. But she could not refute it.

Lifting a hand, he cupped her chin. 'Don't let it bother you, Helen, I enjoyed receiving every one. I enjoyed you.' His thumb brushed her jaw line and the fullness of her bottom lip. 'Your problem is you enjoyed me but do not want to admit the fact.'

'No.' Her eyes glittered in angry rejection. 'I was shocked—you caught me by surprise.' And his husky chuckle did nothing for her overstretched nerves. The musky male scent of him tantalised her and the pressure of his hard body against her own overheated flesh made her tremble.

'You certainly surprised me. I could never have imagined a beautiful woman of your age would still be a virgin. Which leads me to believe that rather naively you have been labouring under the popular female illusion that some day you would fall in love and live happily ever after? Tonight was your first time and, while your body wantonly delighted in the experience, your untried emotions received a shock perfectly natural under the circumstances. I'll give you that.' His hand burrowed through her hair and he tilted her head up to his. 'You made the discovery that love, not that I believe it exists,' he drawled with cynical humour, 'is not a prerequisite for great sex, and your childish illusions are shattered.'

Her eyes blazed angrily. 'At least I had some, but you are an unfeeling, insensitive oaf.' That he was right about her did not make her feel any better, but the fact he didn't believe in love did not surprise her at all.

'Insensitive maybe, unfeeling never,' he drawled. His hand

stroked caressingly down her spine to press her into the hard strength of his thighs, so she could be in no doubt of exactly how he *felt*.

'As for taking you by surprise—' his smile was decidedly feral as he tilted her head back '—well, this time, my sweet wife, I am giving you fair warning. I am going to kiss you.'

Dark eyes merciless in their intent burned into hers. Helen wanted to look away, to break the spellbinding power of his sexuality. 'No, please.' But as his arm tightened around her all her traitorous body wanted was to surrender once again to the powerful virile strength of his.

She made a weak attempt to struggle free. But his dark head bent and his mouth covered hers, his tongue delving between her parted lips with a devastatingly skilful passion that plunged her straight back into the same state of sensual overload as before.

Her arms of their own volition wrapped around his neck. Her fingers sought the thickness of his hair, raking her fingers through its silken length with sensuous delight. She fell into his kiss like a starving woman, oblivious to everything except the man holding her, kissing her. Spinning in a whirlpool of pure pleasure over which she had no control.

'Is that please yes?' Leon husked against her mouth, sweeping her up in his arms.

Helen groaned her agreement. The first time she had felt fear, but not now. Now she was burning up with a hunger she knew only Leon could satisfy.

And when he laid her down on the bed her glittering eyes were bold as they roamed over his magnificent body. Bronzed and sleek-muscled, his skin gleamed satin in the soft light, and when she looked into his eyes the molten desire in the inky depths blinded her to everything in the world but him.

Leon stared down at her, fighting with his conscience, but

her soft, pouting mouth, her wide, inviting eyes, and the firm outline of her rigid nipples against the cotton were too tempting to resist. In one deft move he removed her shirt and gathered her into his arms, his hands moving urgently over her silken flesh. He bent his head to kiss and lick each taut nipple before returning to take her mouth with his own.

Eventually taking everything.

CHAPTER SEVEN

HELEN LAY CURLED up in a ball in the big bed, as far away from her indomitable husband as she could get. The even sound of Leon's breathing told her he was deeply asleep.

But sleep would not come for Helen; shame and humiliation burnt through her aching body at the thought of what she had allowed to happen.

How could she have been so weak willed? How could she have been so wanton? Kissing, touching, scratching.

How could her body have betrayed her so totally, not once, but twice?

Quite easily, she groaned the answer and buried her head in the pillow. She had been seduced by an expert.

The first time she had been swept away in a torrent of undreamed of pleasure as he had kissed and tasted every inch of her. Sweeping away all her virginal fears with a skill and mastery that had overwhelmed her. And when he had finally surged inside her the fierce pain had been obliterated in moments by stroke after stroke of ever-growing torturous pleasure. She had clung to him greedily, her legs locked around his waist as with all his power he had possessed her utterly, the hard strength of him filling and pulsing inside her. Until mindlessly she had cried out as her body convulsed around him in an explosion of emotion so extreme the boundaries of her self were absorbed by his.

Squirming, Helen tried to blank the memory of her second spectacular downfall from her mind. If anything her behaviour had been even worse. Boldly she had caressed and touched him, exploring him with the same intimate detail he had devoted to her. Until finally all that mattered had been the two throbbing, sweat-slicked bodies, touching, tasting, in an orgy of ever-increasing wild abandon that had culminated in a mutually explosive climax.

She heard Leon groan, and tensed, her fingers digging into the edge of the mattress. She didn't want him to wake up.

Because, painful as it was for her to admit it, for some inexplicable reason she was fast becoming incapable of resisting the man, and it could not go on. She was wise enough to know that way lay only heartache. Leon Aristides was the most autocratic, cynical man she had ever met, verging on misogynistic if his comments on the female sex were to be believed, and certainly not the sort of man to fall in love with.

Closing her eyes tight, she silently vowed to herself she would never let her arrogant husband touch her again. Tomorrow she was going to speak to Anna, and have her own room whatever Leon said, and on that thought she fell into an exhausted sleep.

Helen blinked and yawned widely, the distant sound of a door closing echoing in her head. She rolled over onto her back, and stretched, her body aching in unfamiliar places. Then she remembered, her eyes flew wide open and for a moment the sunlight streaming into the room dazzled her.

'Good morning, madam.'

Blinking again, her eyes focused on Anna standing by the bed, a laden breakfast tray in her hands,

'The master said to let you rest, but it is almost twelve and I thought you might like coffee and a little snack.'

'Twelve?' Helen squeaked and sat up in bed, her eyes straying to the indentation on the pillows next to hers. He had gone, thank heaven. Then suddenly realising she was naked, she grasped the coverlet and pulled it up under her arms, before turning a scarlet face to Anna again. 'I am sorry for oversleeping and thank you, Anna.' She took the tray from her outstretched arms. 'I certainly need something,' she muttered under her breath. 'Like a brain transplant.'

'Now, madam, no need to hurry, the master has gone to collect Nicholas and they won't be back for a while. You take your time, pamper yourself.' Anna surprised Helen by smiling broadly at her.

'And may I say, madam, I have known Master Leon since he was an eight year old, and I was first employed as his nanny. I have watched him grow into the man he is today, and I can honestly say I have never seen him look happier than he was this morning. For that I thank you. The man deserves a little happiness in his life. His mother was a difficult woman and rarely cared for him and as for his first wife...' Anna frowned. 'Still, I suppose you already know all about her and I should not waste your time gossiping. But anything you want you only have to ask.' And with another smile she left.

I wonder if that includes a separate bedroom, Helen mused darkly as she drank the coffee and ate the dainty little pastries provided. Somehow she thought not.

Her worried gaze strayed to the other side of the rumpled bed, and she was vividly reminded of last night, reminded of Leon's great golden body over her, in her, taking her yet again as the light of dawn filled the room. And placing the tray on the bedside table, she jumped out of bed and headed for the bathroom.

She turned on the shower and stood beneath the soothing

spray, trying to wash the haunting memories of last night from her mind, and determined to avoid any repeat.

Thirty minutes later with her hair dried she studied her own reflection in the mirrored wall. She looked different; her lips were still slightly swollen from Leon's kisses. Red blotches marred the pale skin of her breasts and lower over her stomach, testimony to her husband's passion.

She spun away from the mirror and quickly dressed. She didn't want to think about his passion; she didn't want to think about him, full stop. Donning a pair of blue jeans and a crisp lemon shirt, she brushed her hair back. She slipped her feet into soft flats, and ventured out of the bedroom.

Rather gingerly Helen walked down the marble staircase. She was sore in a way and in places she had never been before and it was all Leon's fault.

And there he was standing at the bottom of the stairs like a replay of yesterday, only this time he was casually dressed in a cream wool sweater and dark trousers and Nicholas was at his side rather than hers.

'Uncle Leon said we had to let you rest,' Nicholas chirped up, and Helen turned scarlet and her new husband smiled, and today the smile did reach his knowing eyes, and made her blush even more.

'Yes, well,' Helen murmured, reaching the bottom of the stairs and giving Nicholas a big hug. 'Now tell me all about your night away.'

Nicholas duly obliged while Anna served lunch and Helen's tension eased somewhat. Afterwards Leon, much to her surprise, insisted on taking Nicholas upstairs for his nap and promised to play football with the boy later, while Anna gave Helen a guided tour of the house.

The eight bedrooms and five reception rooms impressed Helen but she could not help thinking it was a bit soulless.

Immaculate with high ornate ceilings, brilliant frescos and marble floors, and the furniture to match it was perfect. A little too perfect, a typical stiff-necked banker's abode.

But she did take the opportunity to confide in Anna that she was an illustrator and ask her if she could have a room for a study, preferably not too far from Nicholas' room, because she usually worked when he was asleep. Anna quite happily obliged and showed her to a bedroom, along the corridor from Nicholas'. When Anna went downstairs Helen swiftly unpacked her portable easel and sketch books and removed some essential items of clothing from the master suite. She didn't care what Leon thought. She was having her own room.

Surprisingly the rest of the day was quite fun. She joined Nicholas and Leon in the garden; after yesterday's rain it was pleasant to be outdoors in the sunshine. She was cajoled into playing a game of football, and burst out laughing when her usually imposing husband fell over the ball in his haste to take it off her and sprawled at her feet. Nicholas immediately jumped on his back and demanded he pretend to be a horse and give him a ride.

There was something very satisfying in seeing Leon on his knees. 'Ride him, cowboy,' Helen shouted encouragement.

But when Nicholas tired of the game, Leon slanted a wicked look up at her.

'Your turn, Helen,' and glancing at Nicholas he added, 'What do you think—should I give Helen a ride?'

'Yes. Yes,' Nicholas shouted, his little face wreathed in smiles.

'No, you should not,' Helen declared, blushing scarlet at the sexual connotation that flew right over the child's head. But she was secretly pleased at how well they all got along. Leon looked almost boyish and more relaxed than she had ever seen him when Nicholas was around, which was a good sign for the family she hoped they could eventually become.

Turning her back on the laughing duo, she flung over her shoulder, 'And now I think it is time for tea.'

'Sorry, Nicholas, Helen thinks she is too old to play.'

She heard his mocking comment and spun back round to find him grinning down at her.

'Old, *moi?*'she exclaimed, her violet eyes sparkling with humour. 'You have some nerve at your age.' She saw his dark eyes flash a warning, and, turning, she sprinted for the house with both Nicholas and Leon chasing her.

Bath time was a joint venture and when Nicholas was finally in bed Leon left to return some business calls and Helen stayed to read him a story.

When she walked into the dining room two hours later, Helen immediately sensed the easygoing atmosphere of the afternoon had gone. If it had ever existed except in her mind. Leon wearing a black shirt with a button down collar and black trousers, was standing by the drinks cabinet, a glass in his hand, a brooding expression on his hard face. Casually dressed, he looked incredibly attractive and nothing like a banker, more of a bandit, Helen thought fancifully.

She frowned. His shirt was probably tailor-made by Turnbull and Asser and his trousers similarly designer-labelled. He could afford the best that money could buy, so why wouldn't he look amazing? she told herself, determined to deny her growing attraction for the man.

Leon saw her frown, his own expression one of cool indifference, but inside he was anything but indifferent. For a man who prided himself on his rigid self-discipline it was disturbing to realise he had absolutely no control over the instant reaction of his body. Not since he was a teenager had he felt anything so urgent, if then, and it bothered him.

She was wearing a soft blue wraparound dress that emphasised her tiny waist and moulded her hips and thighs like a second skin. Her legs were covered in silk stockings and on her feet she was wearing high-heeled navy shoes. Her long fair hair was piled up on top of her head in a loose knot, a few stray tendrils framing her small face. She looked exquisite and elegant and she had surprised him again.

The wedding dress yesterday and now this, his image of her, first as a young Lolita, devious and money-hungry, and then as an earth-mother type in jeans and sweater, was constantly changing and it worried him.

He was a man renowned for his brilliant analytical brain, a man without emotion who made decisions in the realms of big business on a daily basis with an absolute conviction that was always successful. So why could he not read his own wife so easily?

'Would you like a drink?' he demanded curtly.

'No, thanks. I'll have a glass of wine with dinner.' She glanced at him and sat down at the table, ignoring him.

Taking the seat opposite her, he filled their wineglasses and as Anna served the first course he watched Helen through thoughtful if frustrated eyes. She was an enigma to him. Like no other woman he had ever met. Beautiful and surprisingly innocent, caring and compassionate as was evident from watching her interaction with the boy. Then add secretive and avid little sensualist and the mixture was dynamite and dangerous to his peace of mind.

He ate the seafood starter deep in thought. He had never given the women in his life more than a passing thought outside the bedroom. But Helen troubled him, and he did not like the feeling.

As Anna removed the plates and set down the main course he thanked her and, glancing at his silent wife, he had the distinct impression she was here on sufferance, and he did not like that either. Nor was he entirely comfortable with the semi-aroused state that afflicted him every time he set eyes on her.

'Tomorrow, Helen, I am in meetings all day until the evening,' he said decisively. She was his wife and he was worrying about nothing, he decided. All he had to do was carry on as before, working all day, only now he could look forward to sating himself in her luscious little body all night. 'I have arranged for Mary Stefano to take you and Nicholas to see the nursery school I have enrolled him in. Mary's youngest children already attend and they love it.'

After eating in silence Helen was surprised when Leon spoke. She looked across the wide expanse of the formal dining table to where he sat. He was forking steak into his mouth with obvious enjoyment, completely unperturbed by her presence. Unfortunately she did not have the same luxury. The tension she always felt around him had returned in spades as soon as Nicholas was tucked up in bed asleep.

'And have I no say in the matter?' she demanded.

'In this case, no, it is done.'

'And if I don't like it?' she asked coolly, but inside she was burning with anger. He was so damned autocratic. 'I am his guardian just as much as you. You should have at least consulted me first.'

He looked over at her, a frown crossing his broad brow. 'Take my word for it, the nursery school is the best in Athens, and as the boy already knows Mary's children he will have no trouble settling in quickly.'

'Why should I?' What he said made perfect sense, but Helen was spoiling for an argument. From the minute Leon had walked into her life he had taken her over, as he did his blasted banks, with a forceful, single-minded determination it was almost impossible to fight. Resentment bubbled up inside her, as much at her own weakness as his strength, and changing tack she said bitterly, 'You railroaded me into having dinner with you rather than with Nicholas the night I arrived.' She shoved her plate away.

'Well, I don't want to do it your way. I don't like to eat late. I prefer to have a light lunch and an early supper, not huge meals twice a day, and I can't eat another thing.' She knew she was being petty but she couldn't seem to stop herself, and, reaching for her glass of wine, she took a long swallow.

'How we got from choosing schools to what time dinner is served I won't even try to discern. The female mind is a mystery to me.' His dark eyes roamed slowly over her, lingering on the shadowed cleavage displayed by the neckline of her dress, before he raised his gaze to capture hers. Something flashed in his eyes that looked like amusement.

'But in case you had not noticed I am a large man, Helen. A cheese sandwich and scrambled eggs on toast and a bit of bacon does not come anywhere near to satisfying me for a day.' His dark eyes gleamed with rueful amusement. 'Though I can see how it would satisfy Nicholas and someone of your stature.'

She resented the dig about her size—though she hadn't minded the *ma petite* when he made love to her, the treacherous thought popped into her head. Then Helen recalled serving him just the food he had mentioned the day he had turned up at her house and she was mortified and angry at the reminder, a telling tide of pink washing over her pale cheeks.

'You should have said at the time if you were still hungry. You are certainly not shy of saying exactly what you want in every other respect,' she declared bluntly.

'True.' He chuckled. 'But as soon as I reached the hotel I ordered room service, so don't beat yourself up about it.'

She saw the humour in his dark eyes and was infuriated. 'As if I ever would over you,' she snorted. She might have guessed Leon was not the type of man to do without anything he wanted.

'Stranger things have happened,' Leon remarked. Her violet eyes were bright as sapphires against her flushed skin, the blue dress folded low between her pert breasts revealing the blush covered more than her face and was not solely with anger, and his body responded accordingly.

'You never know—one day when you get to know me a little better you might feel differently. But in the meantime finish your meal. I don't want you weak with hunger for what I have in mind.'

His taunting, none-too-subtle innuendo was the last straw for Helen. 'I have finished,' she shot back, flashing him a furious glance. The dark eyes that met hers gleamed with a sensuality she could not help but recognise. Her heart raced and her mouth went dry and she hated her own weakness. Leaping to her feet, she pushed back her chair. 'I am going to check on Nicholas—after all, that is the only reason I'm here.'

'As you say.' He cast a knowing look up at her, before glancing down at the watch on his wrist and then back to her flushed face. 'I have a few calls to make to the Far East. I will be up in an hour or two.' And with a dismissive nod of his dark head he returned to his steak.

Helen hoped it choked him, and slammed the door behind her as she left.

She looked around the huge reception hall and sighed. She had probably overreacted slamming the door, but she didn't care. She stopped by the kitchen and told Anna she had had enough to eat and was going to bed with a mug of cocoa, much to Anna's disgust.

She made her way upstairs, and, ignoring the master suite, she glanced in on Nicholas, and then continued along the hall to the room at the end. Closing the door behind her, she quickly undressed and then had a quick wash in the small *en suite* and, slipping on a plain white nightshirt she crawled into the queen-sized bed.

Settling back against the pillows, she cast a satisfied glance around the room and took a sip of her cocoa. It was much smaller than the master suite, but it had a small bathroom and was subtly decorated in cream and buttercup yellow. Along one wall was a chest of drawers, dressing table and a wardrobe. A sofa and chair and small table had been arranged by the window, but she had pushed them to one side and set up her portable easel and placed her sketch books, pencils, pastels and paints on the foot-deep window sill. It wasn't perfect, but the light was good and it would do, she thought complacently.

She eased back against the headboard and took another sip of hot chocolate feeling calmer than she had done since the moment she had set foot in Greece two days ago. She had to accept this was her life now if she wanted to stay with Nicholas, and she did. She loved him to distraction; he was the only child she would ever have and it would kill her to be parted from him.

As for her hard-headed husband, surely he would see the sense in keeping their relationship one of friendship rather than sex. From her very limited experience sex simply caused unwanted tensions in a relationship, which could not be good for Nicholas.

After all, he was the only reason for their marriage. She was under no illusion that Leon cared for her. She was probably a novelty to him, an inexperienced little innocent that happened to live in his house. He was a man of the world who could take his pick of beautiful women. It would be no hardship for him to find someone else to sate his overactive libido with. For all Helen knew he probably had a mistress or two waiting for him somewhere.

Why her heart sank at the thought she didn't want to examine too closely, and sipped some more cocoa.

CHAPTER EIGHT

THE SUDDEN CLICK of a door opening made Helen's heart skip a beat and she looked warily across the room. Fury rippled through her as she saw Leon's tall frame outlined in the opening and unconsciously she pulled the cover up higher.

'What do you want?' she demanded and silently cursed her choice of words as one dark brow arched eloquently in her direction. But defiantly she held his gaze as he walked towards her.

'Now that is a leading question if ever I heard one,' he drawled, and stopped by the side of the bed. 'And one I am sure you can answer if you care to try,' he prompted silkily.

Leon's hard black eyes swept over his errant wife. He noted her scarlet face framed by the silken mass of her ash-blonde hair tumbling over her shoulders, the prim cotton nightshirt skimming over her firm breasts, and he wanted to strangle her.

How dared the little witch try to defy him again? Last night he had taken her innocence with perhaps not as much finesse as he would have liked. But after the initial shock she had been with him all the way and later he could have sworn he had calmed any virginal fears that still lingered. He had the marks to prove it, so what the hell was her game? A cold, disdainful smile twisted his wide mouth. He had had more than enough with his first wife trying to tie him in knots with sex. He had soon disillusioned her and he was damned if he was going to let this one try the same tricks.

With each passing second Helen was conscious of the building tension. She could feel his barely leashed anger almost physically, but she refused to respond to his suggestive jibe. Instead she simply stared up at him. Her heart was pounding in her chest, her conviction of moments ago that Leon would see reason taking a nosedive. And what had happened to the calls he was supposed to be making? He'd said hours and it was barely thirty minutes.

'Nothing to say, Helen?' His black eyes, cold and hard as stone, stared down into hers.

'You said you were going to work,' she snapped back and tried to ignore the trickle of fear snaking its way down her spine.

'So I did, but Anna, while berating me on allowing my very new bride to go to bed on her own, also let slip that you had chosen a bedroom for a study.' His hard mouth twisted in a derisive smile. 'She is a trusting soul and I doubt it ever crossed her mind you would sleep in the room. But, surprise, surprise, I am nowhere near as trusting and decided to check.'

'Oh.'

'*Oh.*' His dark eyes mocked her ruthlessly. 'Is that all you have to say for yourself?'

Helen swallowed down the nervous lump in her throat and said bravely, 'I told you last night I was not sharing your room again.'

'Why?' he demanded with an arrogance that maddened her. 'After last night there is not a part of your body that I don't know intimately.'

It was true. But it did not help her precarious hold on her temper to be reminded and she dragged an angry breath into her oxygen-starved lungs. 'You are disgusting,' she spat, and tore her gaze away from his harshly attractive face.

Leon moved closer, his big body looming over her intimidatingly. His black shirt was pulled taut across his broad shoulders, the top three buttons were undone, revealing his black curling body hair. At least he had not undressed, she thought, a sudden shameful image of him naked flashing through her mind. 'Go away.' And she meant from her mind as much as the room. 'Just go away.'

Without a word he reached down and wrenched the covers from her grasp.

'Don't you dare,' she cried, grabbing the cover with her free hand before flinging the mug of cocoa straight at him.

The mug bounced off his chest, spreading hot chocolate all over him. She saw his head jerk back and she stared in absolute horror at what she had done. Usually she was the calmest, most even-tempered of women. She had never committed a violent act in her life. Oh, my God! She might have scalded him; a little higher, she could have scarred his face.

'I'm sorry, so sorry,' she said, her guilt ridden gaze fixed on his.

Leon's face was as black as thunder, his dark eyes hard as jet.

'You damn well will be.'

He swore and hauled her out of the bed, throwing her over his shoulder. She tried to struggle, suddenly very afraid, but he was far too powerful for her. He stormed straight into the bathroom and, dropping her to the floor, he locked the door behind him.

Dizzy from being held upside down, the blood pounding in her head, she took a moment to focus. When she did she saw he had removed his shirt and his chest hair was damp and sticky with cocoa.

'I really am sorry.' She tried to apologise, but she was too late.

He gave her a killing look. His arm clamped around her waist, and, kicking off his shoes, he herded her into the shower.

He turned on the water, and spun her around to face him. He grasped her hand and slapped the soap in her palm. 'Now you are going to wash off every drop of your crazy handi-work,' he hissed with a sibilant softness that was more fright-ening than his anger.

The water pounded down on her, and she stared at him wide-eyed and terrified. He was only inches away from her and she did not need her contact lenses to see every muscle and sinew in his great body was taut with rage. For once she thanked the Lord she was small. Her head barely reached his shoulders and she did not have to look at his hard, furious face. But her embarrassment was acute as the water plas-tered her shirt to her skin revealing every curve and hollow of her body.

'What are you waiting for?' His hands caught her wrist and lifted her hand to his chest. 'Wash.'

She swallowed down the refusal that sprang to her lips, and began lathering his chest. The feel of his warm, wet skin beneath her palm, the hard musculature of his chest, were a sensual torture that made her heart race.

'Use both hands. I am a big man,' he ordered harshly.

She closed her eyes and, rubbing the soap between her palms, she splayed her hands on his chest and moved them in ever-widening circles. He felt so good and, appalled at where her thoughts were taking her she gasped.

'There.' Her eyes flying open, she moved back until the wall of the shower stopped her. 'It is done.'

Drenched and battling to keep his rage under control, Leon stared furiously down at her. She was done when he said so. He caught the shimmer of sexual awareness in the darkening depths of her violet eyes. Saw her small, perfectly formed

breasts peaking against the wet shirt and suddenly, from being
rigid with fury at her wild action, he felt his body hardening
with a totally different emotion.

'Not yet, it isn't,' he told her. 'Not to my satisfaction.'

Shedding his trousers, he reached for her and stripped the
shirt from her body.

'No,' she tried to object.

But her denial was weak. Triumph surged though him
along with a devilish desire to possess her so completely and
utterly that she would never again try to defy him. Sliding an
arm around her back he drew her against him.

'Yes, Helen,' he drawled and, taking her chin between his
fingers and thumb, he forced her to look at him.

'The chocolate flowed down my body. You need to wash
lower,' he commanded silkily, stroking a hand up her back
before trailing down the indentation of her spine to finally
curve her pert rear. For a moment he felt her slight resistance.
He pressed her closer against his now throbbing arousal and
felt her shudder in helpless response.

Wet, naked and held against his big body, Helen was vitally
aware of the hard strength of him against her belly. She stared
up at him and the mocking eyes that held hers gleamed with
a molten sensuality that made her stomach somersault. With
her whole body reacting treacherously to the sliding caress of
his hand against her naked flesh, she could barely breathe.
Desire lanced through her, weakening her resistance, still she
tried to shake her head free from his hold. But his grip tightened on her chin.

'Every action has a reaction. Remember that, Helen, and
we will get along fine.' He moved his hand from her chin to
sweep the wet hair from her face.

'But I'll spare your blushes this time,' he declared softly
his dark eyes gleaming with an unholy light. Taking the soap

from her unresisting hand he stroked it down his chest and lower between their bodies.

She was pressed against the impressive length of him, and the back of his hand trailing down her quivering stomach ignited a burning desire in her trembling body that shook her to the depths of her being. She did not want to feel this way about him. Then, turning his hand, he cupped her between her thighs and it was so shockingly intimate Helen couldn't hold back a moan.

He gave a low laugh and proceeded to lather her there, everywhere. She closed her eyes as he explored and caressed her hot, wet flesh, all thought of resistance banished from her mind. She shuddered as his hand stroked back up over her stomach and on to massage the fullness of her breasts. When he had dropped the soap she had no idea. The water blinded her and her whole body pulsed with pleasure.

'I am almost done,' he said roughly. 'You really do have the most delectable body.'

A helpless moan escaped her and she reached for his broad shoulders. His dark head bent and he urged her against the strong power of his thighs as his mouth took savage possession of hers. Her head was impelled back against the shower wall at the force of his kiss, but she didn't notice as she shook with need and responded with a blind hunger of her own.

His tongue explored her mouth with a white-hot sexual force that drove her out of her mind. When he lifted her, his strong hands cupping her buttocks, she instinctively crossed her legs around his waist, frantic for him to fill her, possess her, wanting him with a passion that was almost pain.

He looked at her, his dark eyes glittering with a primitive pagan light as he thrust into her hard and deep.

She cried out, her body moving instinctively in the fast and furious rhythm he set. His mouth sought her breast and dragged hungrily on the straining nipple as he plunged harder and faster until she thought she would die from the pleasure. She dug her fingers in his neck. She felt her whole body lock in incredible tension, then shatter into excruciatingly exquisite spasms that went on and on. She dimly heard the animal growl as his great body bucked and shuddered violently, his seed spilling inside her as he joined her in an explosive climax. She buried her head in the curve of his neck as the seemingly endless tremors very slowly receded.

'Helen, are you okay?'

Helen heard the question and lifted her head. He was watching her from beneath heavy-lidded eyes, waiting for an answer, and suddenly she was terribly self-conscious. Wrapped around him like a clinging vine, she felt the reality of the situation hit her. But her own innate honesty would not let her deny her response to him, he only had to touch her and she melted like ice on a fire.

'I'm fine,' she murmured.

It was the answer Leon wanted and slowly he lowered her to her feet. He turned off the water and cupped her head in his hands and gently swept back the tangled mass of her hair from her face before placing a soft kiss on her lush lips.

'Good. Me too,' he admitted huskily. 'So no more arguments about sharing my bed, hmm.' He lifted her out of the shower and, taking a towel from the rail, he wrapped it around her back.

She was everything he remembered from the very first time he'd set eyes on her years ago. Her breasts were high and firm with perfect pink tips, her waist tiny, and now he knew she was a natural blonde. She was so much more than he had expected. From the very beginning he had sensed her awareness of him, known he could have her, but he had never imagined she would be so wildly responsive to him.

'And no more flinging cups of chocolate.' He knotted the

towel between her breasts and stepped back. 'I am not easy to anger, but I do have a temper,' he admitted and, taking another towel, he wrapped it around his hips.

Helen gazed at him helplessly. He was so cool, so in control it was incredible, whereas she did not know herself any more, her emotions were all over the place. Honesty forced her to admit it was her temper that had started the confrontation and his temper that had got them in here. As for what had happened afterwards, it was as much her fault as his, she thought, glancing around the small, steamy room.

'Oh, my God! I can't believe I did that in a bathroom.' Not realising she was speaking the thought out loud.

'I won't tell anyone if you don't,' Leon mocked, his lips parting in a broad grin, his dark eyes sparkling with amusement colliding with hers.

'Hardly,' she cried, shocked, but his humour and his grin were irresistible and her own lips quirked at the corners in a reciprocating smile. 'I wasn't thinking.' And she was fast losing her mind again; Leon looking relaxed and happy was a seductive sight.

'Let me do the thinking for both of us, and in future I think we should stick to our bedroom,' he declared, swinging her up in his arms. 'That way we will have a long and contented marriage.'

'That is the most chauvinistic comment I have ever heard,' Helen stated. 'And will you stop sweeping me off my feet all the time? I can walk,' she almost wailed.

Held in his arms she felt helpless and vulnerable and a whole host of emotions she did not want to face. So much for her vow never to let him touch her again.

'I love the way you walk, but it is so much quicker carrying you to bed,' he said with a wicked grin, carrying her out of the bathroom.

'Please put me down. I need to pick up my clothes.' She glanced around the room and began to struggle. 'Anna will be horrified at the mess we have made.'

'You worry too much,' he mocked. 'Anna won't mind; she has plenty of staff to help her clean up.'

He glanced around the room, and paused. He had been too angry to notice the room when he had stormed in, his whole attention on the woman in the bed, but now he looked around. Some furniture was shoved against one wall, and an easel stood in front of the window with books, paints and other stuff littering the deep window sill.

'You paint,' he said in astonishment, and some memory niggled at the back of his mind. 'Why didn't you tell me?'

'I'm an illustrator,' she snapped, wriggling in his arms. 'I thought it was obvious. I told you my wedding dress was Nicholas' choice. It was the same style as the one the fairy is wearing in the picture on his bedroom wall at home, the one I did for a children's book. I am not the useless little woman you seem to think, and will you put me down?'

Leon's eyes flared. Of course, the drawing in the boy's room. He looked down into her flushed face with barely concealed amusement in his. That was why he had thought she looked familiar on their wedding day, her dress had been a replica of the one the fairy wore, he realised, though on Helen it had looked sexy, but, yes, a little fey.

'I didn't believe you when you said Nicholas had chosen your dress.' He shook his head in wonder. His wife was a talented artist along with her more obvious talents. She never ceased to surprise him.

He tightened his hold on her and pressed a swift kiss on top of her head. 'You and I need to talk. I want to know what other secrets you are keeping from me. But not here.' He strode forward.

She glanced around the messy bedroom as he headed for the door and for some reason she felt as if she owed him an explanation. 'I asked Anna for a room for a studio. She didn't know I was going to sleep here.'

'I am sure she didn't,' Leon drawled, striding into the hall. 'Anna is a hopeless romantic and I see no reason to disillusion her.' He glanced down at her flushed face. 'Luckily you and I have no such illusions, correct?'

'I am not sure I know what you mean,' Helen murmured as he elbowed the door open into the master suite and gently lowered her to her feet, his hands loosely clasping her waist.

His dark eyes narrowed astutely on her guarded face. 'Anna has romantic notions of love and marriage out of all proportion to reality. Probably because she has never married,' he said cynically. 'Take it from one who knows: what you and I have is so much better.'

'And what exactly do we have?' Helen asked, her heart sinking. The passionate lover of moments ago, the man who had awakened her body in a way she had never dreamt possible, was once again looking at her with cold, mocking eyes. And it crossed her mind to wonder why he was so hard-hearted, or if he had a heart at all.

'We have a child to care for, and we have this.' As his mouth took hers in a kiss that left her lips tingling and her temper rising.

'Sex,' she spat.

'Don't be so quick to knock it, Helen. Great sex is a hell of a lot more than some so-called love matches ever achieve,' he stated decisively.

'And however much your conservative little mind wishes it was otherwise, the physical chemistry between us is dynamite.'

For her, yes, but for Leon she wasn't so sure. He was a sophisticated, experienced lover and he had not got that way being celibate, she thought bitterly.

'I have to take your word for that as I have no experience except you to draw on. According to Delia, not something the Aristides men ever suffer from much past puberty. They are noted for their obedient wives and countless mistresses,' she drawled derisively.

'Damn Delia,' he swore. 'She got an idea in her head and stuck with it to the end, just like our mother.'

'Your mother?' she queried, momentarily diverted from her seething resentment of the man.

His mouth twisted in a cold smile. 'Your interest in my family has been long but flawed, sweetheart. Maybe it is time you heard the truth.' Leading her to the bed, he sat down and pulled her down beside him, a long arm sliding around her waist to keep her there.

'You and I need to have a talk to get a few things straight. As you said I was labouring under the illusion you did nothing except look after children, and now I know different. You're an artist in your own right. Tomorrow a proper studio will be provided for you. But by the same token your concept of me is totally coloured by Delia's opinions of her family and not necessarily true.'

'Says you,' she snorted.

He ignored her jibe and continued, 'Contrary to what you think, my father never blamed Delia for our mother's suicide. If anyone was to blame it was probably me.'

'You?' His statement surprised and intrigued her.

'Yes. After I was born she had a mental breakdown.' A wry smile twisted his hard mouth at her shocked expression. 'She was in and out of hospital for years. Why do you think there was a fifteen-year gap between Delia and I?'

Not waiting for her response he continued. 'My father

worshipped her. At that time postnatal depression was a relatively new concept and was suggested by the top consultant my father had hired to treat her. My father believed the diagnosis and was determined not to get her pregnant again, although later the consultant diagnosed bipolar disorder as well.' He threw out his hands. 'But mistakes happen. As for him having a mistress—he never looked at another woman until long after mother had died.'

'But Delia...' she began, and stopped as she realised Anna's comment earlier today that his mother never cared for him gave credence to Leon's explanation. And it went a long way to explain his hard, emotionless attitude towards women. It was hardly surprising for a young boy who was never shown love by his mother to grow up not believing in the concept.

'Listen for a moment,' Leon said curtly. 'Hard as it is for me to admit, with hindsight I think maybe Delia was heading for the same problem.'

'You really think that?' Helen exclaimed.

'Yes.' He nodded with a grim look about his firm mouth. 'Did it never occur to you that Delia gave her baby into your care remarkably easily? And from what I can gather she wasn't around very much.'

'No, certainly not,' Helen shot back. She didn't want to think Delia could have been wrong in her assessment of her own family, because if she did it made her own actions indefensible. 'She asked me to care for Nicholas before he was born. She told me—'

'I know what she told you,' he cut her off. 'And you're probably right—forget I said anything and let's get back to us.'

For Leon to agree with her was a shock to her system, and paradoxically not one she could fully accept, but what happened next was an even bigger shock.

He placed his hand on her cheek and tilted her head

towards him. 'As for me—' his dark eyes locked on hers with piercing intensity '—I am older than you, and naturally there have been a number of women in my life. But I can assure you I have always been monogamous for as long as a relationship lasted, and I was never unfaithful to my wife as long as she was faithful to me.'

'I see,' Helen murmured, quietened by the thought of his first wife. Tina had been very beautiful and had died tragically along with her baby. Maybe that was another reason why Leon did not believe in love any more. Because maybe, contrary to what Helen had been led to believe, he had loved Tina and she had been cruelly taken from him.

'Do you, I wonder?' He raised his black brows over his deep-set dark eyes and caught her hand in his and lifted it to his lips, kissing the gold band on her finger. 'Ours may have been a convenient marriage, Helen, but there is no reason why it can't be mutually beneficial. You and I have a lot more in common than you seem to think.'

That she didn't believe. 'You are joking—a wealthy world banker and a stay-at-home illustrator. I don't see the connection somehow,' she observed dryly.

'We both adore Nicholas and want what is best for him— agreed?' She nodded her head. 'We both do work we enjoy?' She nodded again. 'The sex is great, and so long as you remember I am the only man you are going to sleep with there should be no problem.'

'What about you?' Helen shot back. 'You as good as told me you could not count the number of women you have known and in true chauvinist fashion you have the nerve to demand my fidelity.'

'Yes, absolutely.' He looked at her with amusement and something else in his black eyes. 'But you can demand the same from me, and I will happily comply.'

His firm lips quirked at the corners and he smiled down at her. 'Is that what you want?'

Twenty-four hours ago she would have told him she didn't give a damn what or who he did. But now, with his hand still clasping hers, and held in the strong, protective curve of his arm with the warmth of his naked thigh pressed against her own, she knew it would be a lie.

She did care. Because right or wrong she wanted him, and the very thought of him taking another woman to his bed made her sick to her stomach.

'Yes, fidelity cuts both ways,' she said flatly and, determined not to let him know she cared, she qualified her response sanctimoniously with, 'We need to set a good example for Nicholas.'

'You're right, of course. I bow to your superior wisdom,' he drawled with mock solemnity.

'Very funny.' She tried to pull her hand from his but he tightened his grip.

'I am deadly serious, Helen. I am a hundred per cent in favour of a mutually exclusive relationship. I don't need any other woman with you in my bed. So let's call a truce. You stop resenting the fact that you enjoy sex. Relax and stop trying to fight me. And I will stop, what was it you said?' He grinned. 'I will stop sweeping you off your feet all the time. Agreed?'

His dark eyes smiled confidently into hers. The conceited devil knew he only had to look at her to figuratively sweep her off her feet, never mind physically, she thought wryly, but she could not help smiling at his audacious deal, and nodded her head in agreement.

She did not have a choice, because, whether it was just sex as Leon believed or something more as she feared, he had aroused a hunger in her, a need that she wasn't ready to give up just yet. If ever, she thought as he tipped her back on the bed.

CHAPTER NINE

HELEN STIRRED, LAZILY conscious of the warmth of a hard male body pressed against her back, and the gentle caress of a hand at her breast. Her eyes flickered open and dreamily she registered the firm lips nuzzling her neck and instinctively turned towards the source of pleasure.

Her eyes widened. 'Leon.'

His broad chest was angled towards her, a question gleaming in his dark smouldering eyes. A swift tug of desire plucked at her heart strings and she could no more deny him or herself as the events of last night flashed through her brain and, equally quickly, a blush covered her whole body.

'I should hope so, Helen,' he mocked, and his lips brushed lightly against her mouth sending a shiver through her. 'I am your husband.' He chuckled softly.

As if programmed to his touch her lips parted, her eyes drifted shut and she helplessly surrendered to the exquisite temptation of his kiss.

'What the hell?'

She groaned at the abrupt withdrawal of his mouth from hers. She heard the roar and opened her eyes to see Nicholas scrambling up over Leon's thighs towards her.

'Helen.' Chubby arms reached out to her, his little face all smiles. Immediately she raised her arms to cuddle him, but Leon sat up and took a firm hold on the boy.

'Good morning, Nicholas,' he greeted dryly, pressing a swift kiss on his small head. 'You and I, young man, have to have a talk. First rule of the house is you do not barge into our bedroom at the crack of dawn. Understand?'

'What are you doing in my Helen's bed?' Nicholas demanded.

'We are married and married couples share a bed.'

'So why can't I come in at dawn?'

Helen glanced at Leon and hid a smile. He looked so adorable with his black hair curling haphazardly over his brow, and so magnificently male. His broad, muscular chest gleamed in the morning light and the swiftly placed coverlet he had dragged over his thighs did not quite hide the embarrassing state of his sex. The perplexed, frustrated expression on his dark face said it all. He was about to discover sex was not everything in a marriage. He was being thrown into fatherhood at the deep end and he hadn't a clue, she thought, and waited to hear her very new husband's answer.

'Because Helen is my wife now, and I said so.'

What a cop-out. She watched with interest as the man and boy with almost identical eyes stared at each other, fully expecting Nicholas to yell his displeasure at being denied his early-morning cuddle.

But to her amazement he rested a hand on Leon's chest and turned his big eyes to her. 'Mark said that now you two are married that makes you my mum and dad. Is that right?'

It was Helen's turn to be lost for words. But Leon had no such problem.

'Mark is right,' he said. 'We are officially your mother and father.'

'Then I can call you Mum and Dad?'

Helen was stunned and watched as Leon simply ruffled the boy's hair with a gentle hand and smiled.

'If you want to call us Mum and Dad, that is fine.' Turning his head, he fixed dark eyes on Helen's, a challenging light in the inky depths that she could not ignore. 'Isn't it, Helen?'

She tore her gaze from his and pushed a shaky hand through her hair, sweeping it from her face, and looked at Nicholas. His big eyes were dark and softly pleading and she knew she had reached the ultimate point of no return.

She had married Leon so she could stay with Nicholas, be a mother to him, but she had not really considered Leon as anything other than his uncle. In the back of her mind she had thought a man like Leon would not want too close a commitment to another man's child—after all, he would probably want to father a child of his own one day.

He had shocked her with his instant acceptance of Nicholas' request. Some day maybe she had thought Nicholas would accept them as his mum and dad. But that it had happened so quickly surprised her. His biological mother had died only two months ago, and though she knew Delia would only ever have wanted what made Nicholas happy she could not help feeling guilty. The death of her best friend had given Helen her dearest wish and the thought played on her conscience, life seemed so unfair.

Not just because of her guilt that Nicholas had accepted her as his mum so swiftly, but also because it had suddenly occurred to her that Leon had not used any protection after the first time they had made love. If he harboured some misguided belief that she would provide him with a child he was in for a big disappointment.

She would have to tell him.

'Helen.'

She heard Leon prompt, and knew now wasn't the time.

And unless she wanted to look like a wicked witch of the west to Nicholas, she had to agree, and in her heart of hearts she knew it was what she wanted, and with a silent prayer of thanks to Delia she agreed.

'Yes, darling.' She reached for Nicholas and cuddled him against her, tears of sadness and joy stinging her eyes. 'Uncle Leon and I love you very much and we would be honoured to be called Mum and Dad, if that's what you want. But you do understand you must always remember Delia with happiness and joy as the mother who gave you life. Okay?'

'Yes, great…Mum,' he said with a grin, and hugged her back.

'Come on, Nicholas.' Leon slid off the bed, tucking a discarded towel from last night around his lean hips, much to Helen's relief, and plucked Nicholas from her arms.

'I will help you get dressed, and Helen can have a rest. She needs it.' He winked at her. 'And you need a nanny.'

'What is a nanny?' Helen heard Nicholas ask as Leon swept him up on his shoulders and headed out of the room.

His answer was lost to Helen by the closing of the door. At the same time she realised another door had closed. Leon had laid down the rules and Nicholas saw them as his mum and dad who shared a bed. Unless she was prepared to upset him, that was how it must stay. The hoary old saying that she had made her bed and now she had to lie in it sprang to mind.

And being brutally honest she was not averse to the idea any more. It had been very pleasant to wake up in Leon's arms.

That evening over dinner she was convinced she had made the right decision when Leon suggested they should legally adopt Nicholas, and make him truly their own. He reckoned it would be quite straightforward as he was the boy's uncle and she was already his guardian and he would get Chris to look into it straight away. Helen thought it was a marvellous idea. She would be Nicholas' mother, not just his guardian until he was twenty-one but legally for life, and later in bed that night she didn't think of resisting when Leon took her in his arms.

The next six weeks were a revelation for Helen. On better acquaintance with Anna, she very quickly realised her help was not needed in the well-oiled running of the house. A young girl, Marta, was hired as Nicholas' nanny, much against Helen's wishes. But Leon simply overrode her arguments, pointing out as his wife she would have social commitments to fulfil and it was unfair to expect Anna or any of the other staff to take on the extra work of babysitter. Plus, he had added with a gleam in his dark eyes, he didn't appreciate the boy crawling over him first thing in the morning, not when he was with her. Then kissed her senseless.

The one job Helen insisted on was taking Nicholas to nursery school, but as a chauffeur-driven car transported them there and back it wasn't really necessary. The high spot of her morning was meeting Mary after dropping the children off and sharing a leisurely coffee and gossip with her at a local café.

At first she had felt guilty at keeping the chauffeur waiting but Mary had quickly disabused her of the notion, telling her it was normal in Leon's world to have a car waiting at all times, and did she really want to put the driver out of a job for the dubious pleasure of driving through the chaotic Athens traffic herself? And though she was a good driver her answer was a resounding no.

Usually, after collecting Nicholas from nursery school, they had lunch together and she spent some time playing with him, before spending an hour or two on her artwork. Sometimes she left him in the nanny's care and worked some more or went on the occasional shopping trip with Mary around the expensive stores and boutiques of Athens, as she was doing today.

As for her husband, she knew him a little better now than

when they had first met and she was cautiously hopeful for the future. He appeared rather austere to most people, which she conceded was hardly surprising given he seemed to have had a pretty loveless childhood. She didn't doubt he had genuinely cared for his sister, but the age gap between them probably accounted for the misconceptions they had had of each other. Yet Leon was brilliant with Nicholas when he had the time, and when the three of them were together usually at weekends, she could almost believe they were a family.

But Leon was a difficult man to truly know except in the biblical sense. There was an aloofness about him and the strict control with which he compartmentalised his life was daunting to behold. Business was his top priority; he thought nothing of flying off to New York or Sydney for a few days and had done so three times in the short period they had been married. She had tried to tell herself she didn't mind. She was glad to have Nicholas to herself for a while, but her own innate honesty forced her to admit she did miss her husband.

Last Wednesday it had been brought shockingly home to her just how much. He had left on the Monday for New York and she hadn't been expecting him back until Thursday at the soonest.

After dinner, with Nicholas fast asleep in bed, Helen, feeling oddly restless, had wandered out onto the veranda to lean against the ornate balustrade in the darkness with only the moon and stars for company.

'Well met by moonlight, fair Helena.' The deep, husky drawl made her heart lurch in her breast and, turning her head, she saw Leon.

'You aren't supposed to be back yet,' she exclaimed. Their eyes met and she shivered as one long finger brushed against her cheek, then his hand curled around the nape of her neck.

'And taking liberties with Shakespeare is frowned upon,' she tried to joke.

His hand raked up through her hair and he smiled, his dark head bent towards her. 'You're right, I would much rather take liberties with you.' Sliding his other arm around her waist, he kissed her. When they finally came up for air his dark eyes held hers, and she was powerless to look away, powerless to hide her own need.

'Ah, Helen, my sweet Helen, I missed you.' His sensuous lips curled in a soft, tender smile, the sort she had only ever seen him bestow on Nicholas. Emotion threatened to choke her and she could not speak. 'And I do believe you missed me,' he prompted huskily, and her answer was in the luminous depths of her violet eyes.

They made love that night with tenderness and a passion that Helen had never experienced before. Later, cradled in his arms with her head on his chest, the steady, rhythmic beat of his heart music to her ears, she finally accepted what she had known deep down all along.

She loved Leon. The desire, the passion might be just sex to him, but it was never just sex to her. She loved him with every breath she took and she knew she always would.

He was not the hard, uncaring man she had imagined him to be. Anna and all the staff adored him, and as for Nicholas, he worshipped him. The cold, austere persona Leon presented to the world vanished as soon as he set eyes on Nicholas. He was wonderful with the boy, and lately she had the growing feeling his relaxed, caring side was extending to her. God, she hoped so! She vowed to do everything in her power to make a success of their marriage in the hope that eventually Leon might grow to love her as she loved him.

Thinking about that night now, standing in a shop waiting for Mary, Helen sighed. Her husband was a hard, complex man and a complete workaholic, but to give him his due he did always kiss her awake, and sometimes more, before descending to the basement gym for a workout. He was terrifically physically fit, but he had to be for his punishing schedule. By the time Helen got down for breakfast with Nicholas he was usually leaving or had already left, returning in the evening to spend at least an hour with Nicholas before he went to bed.

Dining alone with Leon was no longer the ordeal she had once feared. But underneath the casual conversation there was always a simmering sexual tension that Helen could not deny, didn't want to. The thought of the night ahead was ever present in her mind, for in Leon's arms she became vibrantly alive and under his tutelage increasingly sexually adventurous in a way that she had never thought herself capable of.

Helen had tried to convince herself it was simply a natural response to a long overdue sexual awakening on her part, and had nothing to do with love, but after last Wednesday night she couldn't pretend any more.

She loved him, she could not help herself. He was a wonderful, inventive lover, generous to a fault, concentrating on her pleasure in myriad ways she had never imagined possible, before seeking his own.

When he wanted to be, she had discovered much to her surprise, he was an intelligent, witty conversationalist. He had an uncanny knack for giving a thumbnail sketch of people with a subtle humour that appealed to her. She had also discovered they had the same taste in music and shared the same love of books, Leon preferring political thrillers while Helen preferred a good detective novel.

When he had realised while reading Nicholas a bedtime story that they were her humorous illustrations all the way through the book he had laughed aloud.

'My God, Helen, your talents are truly limitless,' he had quipped and kissed her, much to Nicholas' disgust.

Their conversations were naturally quite often about Nicholas, and of course discussing any arrangements Leon had made for their social life. So far they had shared Sunday lunch with Mary and her family and sometimes they went out as a foursome for dinner, all of which Helen had enjoyed, and a couple of formal dinners with some of his business acquaintances and their wives, which she had not enjoyed quite as much.

The party he was hosting tomorrow night was to introduce Helen to the distant relatives and social élite of Athens who had not been invited to the wedding. It was to be held in a top Athenian hotel and Leon had given her strict instructions this morning to buy something new to wear, which she had rather resented.

She had given up on the practical cotton nightshirts weeks ago, and indulged her secret pleasure in delicate underwear, and she had a perfectly good wardrobe of classic clothes. Helen was not quite the prim little stay-at-home Leon seemed to think she had been. She had led an active if limited social life, Nicholas permitting, as a member of a local drama group and book club. When her parents were alive they had led a busy social life in Switzerland, and Helen had learnt how to behave in any society. Her mother had taught her the fundamentals of style for a small woman when she was a young teenager and in fact she still had quite a few of her mother's classic designer clothes, which she had kept originally as mementoes and now wore. In fairness to Leon, he always complimented her on what she did wear. Plus the first time he had been away on business when he had returned he had taken her to the bank, opened an account for her, and presented her with a limitless credit card.

She had tried to refuse but, for once his cynicism not in

evidence he had rather dryly confessed he hated shopping and was hopeless at buying presents, but he wanted her and Nicholas to have everything they desired. Then he had presented her with a fabulous emerald and diamond ring he'd told her he had bought as he'd happened to be passing Van Cleef and Arpel in New York. That Leon, her workaholic husband, who by his own admission hated shopping, had found time in his busy schedule to nip into Van Cleef's just for her was what delighted her, and gave her hope that their relationship was growing into something more than just a convenience.

'So what do you think? Will I knock Chris' socks off at the party tomorrow night?' Mary did a twirl as she walked out of the dressing room.

'It won't be his socks coming off, but that apology for a dress.' Helen laughed, eyeing the clinging full-length, backless indigo-blue dress that Mary was almost falling out of.

'Too much, hmm?'

'Too little,' Helen shot back.

'You're right, but it would be great on you. Come on try it on. You have to impress the guests tomorrow night.'

Helen kissed Nicholas goodnight, and left, his comment that she looked like a lovely purple lollipop, good enough to eat, echoing in her head. She stood in front of the mirror in the master suite and eyed her reflection. Why did she let first a child and then Mary tell her what she should wear? Because she was a sucker when it came to pleasing the people she cared about, she concluded. Though no one could call this gown childish she thought ruefully; she had never worn anything so revealing in her life.

The spaghetti-strapped dress cupped her breasts, exposed her back to the waist and clung to her hips and thighs like a second skin. The fantail pleat in the back was there out of necessity, allowing her to walk. But at least this time she was wearing a pair of four-inch high-heeled diamanté sandals, favourites of hers. And with Anna's help her hair was piled in an elegant concoction of curls on the top of her head, making her look quite tall, she told herself bracingly.

'*Theos,* you are not going out in that.' Leon's voice cut into her musings, and she turned her head to see him exit the dressing room and walk towards her.

The breath stopped in her throat. He looked strikingly attractive in a formal black dinner suit, and the predatory expression in the dark eyes that roamed blatantly over her set her pulse racing.

'Don't you approve?' She pouted and did a swift twirl. 'Mary said it was definitely me.' She grinned cheekily up at him.

Leon gasped, a certain part of his body leaping to immediate attention. The view of her back naked to her pert bum was enough to make a strong man weak at the knees.

'Mary wants her head examined,' he said when he could finally speak, taking in her beautiful smiling face and the shining mass of fair curls pinned on the top of her head. She was wearing a shimmering sort of purple-blue dress that curved across her perfect breasts, revealing more of the creamy smooth fullness than any man except him should ever see, he thought proprietorially. And what was left of the gown clung to every curve of her delectable body.

A wry smile quirked his mouth. 'That dress is verging on the indecent, but you look absolutely stunning.' Moving towards her, he dropped a kiss on the tip of her nose.

'Thank you, kind sir,' she quipped. 'But Nicholas thinks I look like a purple lollipop and good enough to eat.'

'That boy has great taste for a child.' Leon chuckled and reached for her shoulders. 'And I definitely agree with him,' he husked and drew her gently against his tall frame. 'I wouldn't mind eating you right here and now.' The thought of lowering his head to the delta of her thighs and tasting her sweetness rendered him rock-hard.

She lifted sparkling eyes to his, and he saw her pupils darken and dilate. He slipped a hand around her neck and watched as her eyelids drifted down, her lips softly parting in anticipation of his kiss.

'I don't dare or we will never get out of here,' he groaned, and abruptly he dropped one hand to her tiny waist and spun her back to face the mirror.

'What do you think?'

Helen felt the coldness on her skin and upon seeing her reflection in the glass her eyes widened in amazement at the fabulous fall of diamonds strung around her throat. She lifted her hand and touched the jewels, lifting her eyes to meet his in the mirror.

'Leon,' she murmured his name, overwhelmed by his gift. 'You bought this for me?'

He smiled slightly. 'Yes, our six-week anniversary. Do you like it?'

'I love it,' she said truthfully, stunned that he had cared enough to actually remember how many weeks they had been married. 'It is the most fabulous gift I have ever received. Thank you.'

She had to blink away an emotional tear. Then she remembered. 'But I thought you never went shopping for presents.'

'I had some help,' he confessed ruefully, and, wrapping his arms around her stomach, he pulled her back against the hard warmth of his body. 'I asked Mary to make sure you bought a dress and to tell me what kind of jewellery would match. She said to stick to diamonds, making it easy for me.' Loosening his hold on her, he slipped his hand in his jacket pocket. 'I bought the earrings and bracelet to match.' He clipped the bracelet around her slender wrist. 'You can manage the earrings yourself, I hope.' He placed them in her hand. 'Because if I hold you much longer that is it, we will be going nowhere.'

Helen had felt the pressure of his arousal against her and a gleam of mischief sparkled in her eyes.

'That's fine by me.'

She turned and looped her arms around his neck. 'I would much prefer to stay here.' She pressed up against him and tilted back her head to look up into his darkening eyes. 'Parties are not my scene. I much prefer one to one,' she declared softly, her full lips curving in a slow, sensual smile.

'No, you don't, you little witch, I am not being side-tracked,' he declared with a reluctant smile. 'But hold that thought until we return, hmm?'

His unexpected gift and commanding presence at her side gave her the confidence to stand at the entrance to the grand ballroom and greet all the guests.

With Leon's arm around her Helen glanced up at him, her violet eyes sparkling. 'I feel like royalty standing here. Do we have to do this?'

'Not for much longer,' he murmured, and then someone called his name and his arm suddenly tightened around her waist.

'Takis, nice to see you. I wasn't sure you would make it.'

Helen cast a sidelong glance at Leon, immediately sensing he was not pleased to see the man at all. Then she looked at the man standing in front of them, her eyes widening in instinctive female appreciation. He was of medium height, slim with black hair and strikingly handsome in a rakish kind of way.

'I wouldn't miss your wedding party for the world. I attended your first one, remember?' the man drawled.

He looked Greek, but he spoke with an American accent, Helen noted, and then he smiled and his brown eyes gleamed golden as they met hers.

'So this is Helen.' Taking her unresisting hand, he lifted it to his lips. 'It is a pleasure to meet you, and a surprise. I never thought Leon had such good taste, stick-like models are more his scene. But you, babe, you are exquisite, a perfect little Barbie doll.'

Helen was still trying to decide if it was an insult or a compliment to be called a babe and a Barbie doll in the same sentence when he turned his attention back to Leon.

'A beautiful wife and a son as well—you are a lucky bastard, cousin.'

'Thank you, Takis,' Leon said smoothly. 'I knew you would be pleased for me. Now if you will excuse us, it is time we mingled.'

She wasn't imagining it; the tension between the two men was palpable. Helen glanced curiously at her husband but before she could utter a word he was urging her into the crowd.

'Wait a minute.' She stopped. 'What was all that about? Why didn't you tell that man Nicholas isn't your son, but Delia's?'

'Why bother?' He shrugged one shoulder. 'He is our son now, or had you forgotten at the sight of a handsome face?' he prompted silkily.

'No...' Helen shook her head. 'And don't pretend you're jealous,' she mocked, while secretly hugging the thought to her. 'But I am surprised. I mean, he is your cousin—surely he knows.'

'Actually, strictly speaking he is my late wife's cousin, and I am sure he does know. He is the sort who makes it his business to know everything. But Nicholas is no concern of his.'

'If you say so,' Helen murmured, but she could not help recalling quite a few odd glances from different people over the past few weeks that she had put down to natural curiosity, now she wasn't so sure.

'I've noticed some peculiar looks from a few people, even Mary on our wedding day.' She raised puzzled eyes to his. 'I suppose it is the family likeness between Nicholas and yourself. But shouldn't you deny the assumption? I mean, we don't want to mislead people.'

'Helen, darling,' he drawled with a sardonic lift of one ebony brow, 'it is public knowledge that both you and I have stated Nicholas is my sister's child. But people believe what they want to believe.' His firm lips twisted in a wry smile. 'As far as I am concerned I couldn't care less what other people think. The boy knows the truth, that is all that matters.'

'Yes, but—'

'So they assume you're his mother—what difference does it make?' And his arm tightened around her. 'In life as in business it is sometimes beneficial to muddy the waters a little. And if it is your reputation you are worried about, forget it. As my wife you are beyond reproach, and if the confusion helps Delia's reputation in other people's eyes—why not? Nicholas might thank us for it in years to come.'

Helen frowned. He sounded so reasonable, but he was protecting the memory of his sister at the expense of hers. Well, not exactly, she conceded. He hadn't actually lied. Leon just manipulated the situation, allowing people to think what they wanted to think. Much the same as he had with her when he had suggested a marriage of convenience. He had to have known what she'd thought, and she wondered how many more false assumptions he had allowed her to make.

Not much later she found out.

Helen glanced around the glittering throng not feeling quite so confident. Waiters circled the crowd with drinks and canapés, a quintet played dance music and everyone looked to be enjoying themselves.

'Love the necklace.' The familiar voice of Mary drew Helen's attention to the couple who had stopped in front of them. She saw her friend flick a glance at Leon.

'It is perfect, Leon,' Mary declared and grinned at Helen. 'I gave him such detailed instructions even he could not fail. You really have me to thank for his choice,' she declared outrageously. Everyone laughed, Helen included, relieved at Mary's timely interruption.

Leon was right. She was worrying about nothing, what did it matter what a few people thought? Helen shot him a teasing glance. 'Surely you are not going to let Mary get away with insulting you.'

'Her husband is my lawyer. Trust me, if I say a word to Mary he will sue me,' Leon replied drolly, and more laughter ensued.

Chris stopped a passing waiter and champagne was served all around. He then insisted, as this was an official wedding party, albeit the second one, he had to make a toast.

'To two good friends, Helen and Leon, may you have a long and happy marriage.'

'Thank you,' Leon replied sincerely and, looking into the vividly sparkling eyes of his wife, he suddenly realised he didn't care that she had kept his nephew hidden for years, didn't care if she had known about the money she was to inherit. She was worth every penny and more. He thanked God and Delia that he had found her, and had had the good sense to marry her.

She gave him a brilliant smile, and his chest tightened as his hand automatically flexed on her waist with the sudden stirring in his groin. How she did this to him he couldn't explain and he didn't care, he simply relished the feeling.

A strong sense of elation gripped him. The nearest he had

ever come to feeling like this was when he clinched a particularly good deal. But even the best deal of his life did not compare with the heady pleasure he felt right now with Helen openly gazing up at him with adoration in her gorgeous eyes for all to see.

He was not a demonstrative man, never had been. His mother had knocked that tendency out of him as a child with her violent mood swings, one day loving him and the next day cursing him, so he had learnt very early in life not to trust emotions of any kind. But now with all his friends and acquaintances around him he declared, 'And the biggest thank you must go to my beautiful wife for being brave enough to take on a cynic like me for her husband.' And dipping his head, he kissed her. He felt her sway against him, tasted the melting sweetness of her mouth, and very reluctantly broke the kiss, while quickly calculating how much longer they would have to stay for propriety's sake.

CHAPTER TEN

A MINUTE LATER Leon cursed silently under his breath. Dropping his hand from Helen's waist, he squared his broad shoulders, and went still. There was tension in every line of his body, his grin fading to a grimace as his dark eyes rested on two late arrivals. The French Ambassador to Greece, who had been invited with his wife, but instead had turned up with a different companion, a very tall, striking-looking woman... Louisa...

What the hell was she doing here? He had broken up with her the week before he'd married. And she had done very well out of the deal. He had given her a luxury apartment in Paris and a considerable amount of money in consolation for his ending their affair.

'M. Distel, a pleasure to see you again.' Leon shook the man's hand. 'Louisa.' He nodded at his ex-lover but he could do nothing to prevent the usual French greeting of a kiss on both cheeks by the woman, one of which darted to his mouth. Then reluctantly but smoothly he introduced the pair to Helen.

Helen had immediately stiffened sensing danger the minute Leon's hand had fallen from her waist. She had felt his tension, and, following the direction of his eyes had watched the very tall, glamorous-looking woman walking towards them. Her hair a mixture of brown and red stripes, was perfectly cut in a short asymmetrical chop, and the black dress she wore was obviously the latest in designer chic and very short too, exposing her incredibly long legs.

But it was her face Helen noticed most. Her dark eyes, kohl-rimmed and narrow, were fixed on Leon like heat seeking missiles, her lush lips, obviously collagen-enhanced, Helen thought distastefully, curved in an intimate smile just for him. And when Leon said her name the red-nailed hand she laid on his arm screamed possession. The kisses she planted on him confirmed how close they were.

Feminine intuition, every instinct, told Helen that this woman had known Leon in the most intimate way possible, and the happy little bubble she had been floating in for the last few weeks burst, pierced by the dual monsters of suspicion and jealousy. It was easy to forget locked in her husband's arms that he had quite a few lovers in his past, but to be faced with one of them made it impossible to ignore. She accepted the congratulations of the French ambassador in a cool calm voice, but when Louisa took her hand and smiled with dark, spite-filled eyes her composure almost deserted her.

'So you're the lucky lady, not at all what I expected.' The woman stared down at Helen, making her feel like a midget, and it only got worse as she added. 'You are really quite small.'

'Ah, small but perfect.' The Frenchman intervened with true Gallic charm. 'And you also have a son, I believe, a great gift for any man.'

Helen heard Mary gasp at her side, but by a terrific effort of will she retained her self-control, while inside she was fuming.

'Not my son—' she glanced up at Leon her eyes diamond bright '—is he, darling?'

Leon let his eyes rest for a moment on Helen. She was angry and hurt and he didn't blame her. He had dismissed her worry over the parenthood of the boy quite casually after Takis' comment, and now Distel was implying the same. She was so lovely and so naive in a worldly sense he should have realised she was sensitive about the boy's parenthood, whereas he didn't give a damn one way or the other. But if he wasn't very careful the sophisticated French pair would make mincemeat of her in a second if he let them. Louisa had already insulted his wife with her crack about her height; he knew Helen was touchy on the subject. Why, he had no idea, she was perfect in his eyes.

But for once in his life he felt fiercely protective and embarrassed at the same time, not emotions he was familiar with. He knew most of the people here recognised Louisa as his ex-mistress, and he felt guilty that his past affair had put Helen in this position and was determined to remedy the situation, before she had a chance to find out.

With that in mind he said, 'No, of course not, Helen. Everyone knows he is my sister Delia's child. But the ambassador's English is not so good.' He smiled gently down at her. 'Excuse me for a moment while I explain to him in French, hmm…' She nodded her head and he returned his attention to Distel and Louisa.

The patronising swine, Helen thought, and shook her head, too enraged to speak. Instead she took another glass of champagne from a passing waiter, and listened. Her face paled and the blood turned to ice in her veins, her suspicions confirmed. She needed to sit down or she would fall down, such was the extent of her shock. Swiftly she drained the glass and when Mary moved to visit the powder room Helen jumped at the chance to go with her. She had heard enough, more than enough.

'That woman is Leon's lover,' Helen said flatly as they entered the powder room.

'No, you're wrong,' Mary quickly denied—a little too quickly.

Helen looked at her friend with cold, dull eyes. 'Please don't bother to lie on my account, it is not necessary.'

'I'm not exactly lying.' Mary sighed. 'But I'm not surprised you guessed they had had an affair. Louisa made it pretty obvious she couldn't take her eyes off him. But really, Helen, you have nothing to worry about. Leon married you. He loves you and I know the affair is over. Chris told me so.'

'And you believed him.' Helen shook her head and sank down on the nearest chair, not sure her legs would support her. She was numb with shock. She knew Leon did not love her, but to be so callous as to allow his mistress to kiss him in front of her was beyond belief. But then what did she know about men, or the society Leon moved in, other than it was far too sophisticated and blasé for her? she thought bitterly, and glanced up at her hovering friend.

'I hate to tell you, Mary, but your husband lied, and before you say anything else I should tell you I speak excellent French and I understood every word they said.'

Mary collapsed in the chair beside her. 'You speak French. Oh, no. But wait a second, he only spoke for a moment, then the ambassador and Louisa chipped in,' Mary exclaimed. 'They'd only been speaking for a few minutes before we left. So what on earth was said that upset you so quickly?'

Helen folded her arms across her chest, her hands rubbing her upper arms. She was shivering and the cold went bone deep.

'Enough, more than enough. Leon explained Nicholas was his sister's child and then asked Distel if his wife was indisposed.' Helen relayed the gist of the conversation in a harsh, colourless voice. 'The Frenchman said yes, and rather sarcastically added he didn't think Leon would mind him bringing Louisa because he knew they were such old close friends.' She glanced back at Mary. 'The French language lends itself beautifully to sarcasm—did you know that?'

'I'm not interested in the language. Tell me what happened next.'

'Louisa intervened, and said to Leon, and I quote, "Really, *mon cher,* you have nothing to worry about. I would not dream of upsetting your little wife by telling her about us. I know you only married her for the child. I remember in every intimate detail the last night we spent together the week before your wedding. And ten days ago when you gave me the deeds to the apartment, such an extravagant gift…"'

Helen paused for a moment and blinked to hold back the tears that threatened, then carried on stoically. '"I knew it was to ease your conscience, after almost four years I understand you perfectly, *cher,* and when you come back as usual I can promise you will enjoy seeing and removing what your generosity bought." At which point she laughed and you gave me an excuse to leave to come to the powder room, for which I am eternally grateful,' Helen concluded.

'What a bitch.'

'My sentiments exactly,' Helen agreed. 'But a perfect match for my lying bastard of a husband. He is obviously still seeing her. He told me he was going to New York, but according to that woman he saw her in Paris ten days ago.'

'You don't know that.' Mary tried to comfort her. 'You never heard Leon's reply. He probably denied Louisa's whole scenario. Why, only moments earlier Leon, who has never been given to overt displays of affection in his life, thanked you for marrying him and kissed you in front of everyone. That must mean something; you have to give him a chance.'

Helen rose to her feet, her face white and her usually expressive eyes curiously blank. 'I don't think so,' she responded bluntly.

'Oh, come on, Helen, you can't believe for a minute Leon would prefer a hard-faced, stick-thin glamour puss like her to you. You are beautiful and caring and kind. Whereas that one is so up herself I wouldn't mind betting her Brazilian wax is striped red to match her hair.'

'That is terrible.' But the picture Mary painted did make Helen's lips quirk at the corners.

'But you almost smiled.' Mary stood up and rested her hand on Helen's arm. 'Come on, let's get back in there. You are not going to let a bitch like Louisa upset you. And if there is anything I can do…'

'Don't worry, Mary.' Helen glanced at her friend, and, seeing the compassion in her gaze, almost gave in to the pain of the grief that she knew was waiting for her.

But she had too much experience of life's hard knocks to succumb. The loss of her parents, the loss of her eyesight for over a year, the loss of her ability to bear children, the loss of her grandfather and the loss of her best friend had taught her all the tears in the world did not help. 'I will be fine and I won't cause a scene. You're right, it is time we rejoined the party.'

'You're sure?'

'Positive,' Helen said, and opened the door. She felt curiously detached as she walked back into the ballroom. The sound of the crowd, the laughter, the music, could not penetrate the coldness that had settled around her like an invisible cloak. Nothing had really changed she told herself. She still had Nicholas. She had always known Leon was a womanising devil; his own sister had intimated as much. As for loving the man—not any more.

Leon was right: love was an illusion, an illusion she had suffered from for a brief period of time, and could now forget. She had cried at the loss of her family and her friend. All worthy people who had cared for her, but her husband wasn't worth a single tear.

* * *

There was no sign of the French couple when they re-entered the ballroom. Chris and Leon were standing to one side of the dance floor, deep in conversation, but both male heads turned in unison as Mary with Helen behind her entered the ballroom.

Leon's dark gaze sought Helen's and in the very next second he realised something was wrong. Her lips parted over her small white teeth, but the smile she gave him was brittle and never reached her eyes.

He stepped towards her and looped an arm around her waist. 'I missed you,' he whispered softly and brushed her lips with his own. She did not respond, she simply stood still in his hold. 'I have a strong desire to dance with you.' He tried again, lowering his head to breathe against her small ear. 'I simply want you in my arms.'

'Sorry. Mary and I were talking.'

He put both arms around her and drew her onto the dance floor, and she made no objection. She placed her small hand on his shoulder and let him guide her to the music, but something was different.

'Are you all right?' He nuzzled her ear, and she turned her head away.

'Of course. Why wouldn't I be?'

She kept her beautiful face averted, she wouldn't look at him. He tightened his hold on her but her gorgeous body wasn't softening against his as he had come to expect. She was physically in his arms, but mentally miles away.

'Did Mary say something to upset you?' he demanded.

'No.'

He stroked a hand up her naked back, his fingers trailing the indentation of her spine, but she stayed rigid in his arms, and for a moment an unknown emotion went through him—primarily anger, but incredibly laced with fear. No, he was imagining things. Helen was putty in his hands, but she was also quite shy in public. This glittering affair was probably a bit of an ordeal for her, he rationalised her odd behaviour. Of course she was tense as the object of all eyes.

He folded her closer into him. 'Relax, you are the most beautiful woman here and everyone adores you.'

You certainly don't, Helen wanted to scream. But instead she said curtly, 'I doubt that.'

She flicked a cold glance at his hard face and just as quickly away again. Did he really think she was such a wimp she needed reassurance from an arrogant, lying toad like him? Though in one respect Leon had been right all along; the fever in her blood when he touched her was as he had said, just sex. Thankfully she no longer felt anything in his arms. His betrayal had killed every finer emotion in her stone-dead.

His hand curved around her nape, and tilted her head back so she was forced to look at him.

'Are you sure you are okay? We don't have to stay much longer if you don't want to.'

'I wouldn't dream of leaving early. I intend to dance the night away.' She sent him a glittering smile and linked her hands behind his neck. When what she really wanted to do was choke the faithless swine. Anger was the only emotion she had left.

Helen slid into the limo and as far away from Leon as she could get and, leaning back, closed her eyes. She didn't want to look at him, and she certainly didn't want to speak to him. She had danced and laughed all night, and he had had the nerve to tell her she had been the belle of the ball. What a snake. He had the emotional sensitivity of a boa constrictor, but she was determined he was not going to squeeze the life out of her.

She was her own woman, deserving of honour and respect,

and without that they had nothing. She had been fooling herself for weeks, but no more.

When the limo stopped she leapt straight out and into the house and upstairs without stopping. Once in the master suite she took the diamonds from her throat and dropped them where she stood along with the earrings and bracelet, and, turning, headed for the dressing room. She heard him enter the bedroom as she removed the pins from her hair, and shaking her head, she let it fall down to her shoulders. She opened a drawer and avoiding the more glamorous night-wear, she selected a nightshirt. Discarding the dress, she pulled it over her head and walked back into the bedroom.

Leon was standing in the middle of the room, without his jacket and tie, his shirt unbuttoned to his waist and in his hand the jewels she had dropped on the floor. She glanced at his face but when he came towards her she backed away in-stinctively.

He stopped, his chiselled features hardening with some-thing like anger. 'Rather careless, dropping these on the floor. Are you going to tell me what this is all about, Helen? I don't appreciate a woman who blows hot and cold. I was beginning to think better of you, but obviously I was mistaken, unless you have some explanation for acting out of character all evening.'

'And what would you know about my character? You think you know me so well simply because we share a bed and body fluids, but you don't know me at all,' she shot back with scathing bluntness. 'If you did, you might have realised I spent the first fourteen years of my life in Switzerland. They speak four different languages there, and I am fluent in two of them: Italian and French. Need I say more?' She saw a dark flush spread across his high cheekbones. He had a good right to look guilty, the no-good, cheating waster.

'Ah.' He shoved the jewels in his trouser pocket. 'You

heard Louisa.' His dark, compelling eyes held hers as he lessened the space between them. 'That was careless of me and bad mannered, but I switched to French thinking to spare you any embarrassment.'

'You're all heart,' she jeered.

His reply was to reach for her and pull her against him. 'You heard she was once my mistress and for that I am sorry.' His lips curved in a hateful smile. 'But you have no need to be jealous, Helen. I put an end to it before we married, and as long as I have you I don't want any other woman, I swear.'

His truly astounding, unbelievable conceit was too much for Helen and she exploded with rage. 'You must think I am crazy if you expect me to believe a word you say. You are the most devious, manipulative, arrogant swine it has ever been my misfortune to meet. My God, you have been having an affair with that woman for years. What kind of fool do you take me for? The week before you married me you were in her bed. You actually told me you had a pressing engagement in Paris. You didn't mention pressing the flesh, but I should have known. Delia told me what a faithless lot the men in her family were, and, by heaven, she was right. You even had the cheek to tell me you were going to New York and then visited that woman straight from my bed ten days ago, a bed where you had the gall to call me *ma petite,* a French term, when we first had sex.' She would not call it love.

'Now I know why—force of habit,' she jeered. 'Then to cap it all I discover you have given your lover an apartment and Lord knows what else. And you wonder why the jewels you gave me ended up on the floor.' She shook her head in utter rejection of him.

'Are you quite finished assassinating my character?' Leon

demanded harshly, placing a steel-like arm around her waist and hauling her hard against him.

She looked up at him with blazing violet eyes. 'God help Nicholas with you as his father; you haven't a moral bone in your body. As for me, I never want you to touch me again.'

Her last crack was too much for Leon. He was no saint, and he was guilty of having sex with Louisa the week before his wedding. Mainly because when he had made it very clear their affair was finally over she had stripped naked and begged him to make love to her one last time. He had certainly not slept with her, and had left before midnight. Ungallant maybe, but true. Her appearance tonight at the party had been none of his doing, but that his wife should think so badly of him, to believe that he had lied when he'd said he was going to New York, was an insult too far.

He hauled her closer and plunged his hand into her hair and jerked her head back to capture her angry mouth with his. He thrust into the hot, moist depths with an urgent, angry passion. He felt her resistance and fought down the primitive urge to bury himself deep inside her, and make her realise she was his in the most basic way.

Instead with a terrific effort he gentled the fury of his kiss. But still she remained rigid in his arms. Fired by anger and frustration, he slipped a hand beneath her shirt, tracing the line of her leg and thigh while he lowered his head and caught her breast through the fine fabric of her shirt.

Suddenly the cloak of detachment, the numbness that had helped Helen through the evening, shattered, leaving in its place a raw, aching pain. Her heart thundered in her breast and she lashed wildly out at him, but it was like hitting a brick wall. Though she fought like a wild woman, when his mouth and teeth fed on her breast the dampness of the fabric rubbing against her sensitive nipples made every sensual receptor in her body quiver and burn. The savage sensuality of his kiss as he captured her mouth again and the caressing stroke of his hand roaming over her hip and the apex of her thighs with a familiarity her body recognised ignited a burning need inside her, even as her mind rejected him.

He picked her up and dropped her naked on the bed, when she had lost the nightshirt she had no idea. All she was aware of was the heat, the weight, the scent of him above her. A muscled leg parted hers, his hungry mouth clamping on her pouting breast, and finally her body arched convulsively and she was conscious of nothing except the thick length of him thrusting, filling her with ever-deeper strokes, until she was swept away in a maelstrom of shuddering ecstatic sensations that culminated in an explosion of the senses so heart stoppingly intense that for a moment she ceased to breathe.

She felt Leon's weight roll off her, and wondered if that was the little death she had read about as they lay beside each other in silence, the only sounds the heavy pounding of hearts and ragged breathing.

Helen had nothing to say. Her body had made a liar of her.

Leon rose up on one elbow and looked down into her shadowed eyes. 'I think we can safely forget your, "I never want you to touch me again,"' he taunted softly. 'You can no more resist the passion, the desire, that flares between us than I can.'

'That is your conceited opinion,' she shot back.

'Not an opinion, fact, and to prove my point I won't touch you again, until *you* ask me,' he stated, his lips curling in a derisive smile. 'And I doubt I will have to wait long. Some women, once they get a taste for sex, can't do without, and I have a feeling you fall into that category, Helen.'

'In your dreams,' she spat. Shamed at her own weakness and hating him all over again, she wanted to hit out at him, dent his massive ego. 'I am here for Nicholas and nothing else, and, just to set the record straight, the scar on my belly is not from an appendectomy, but from an accident. So if you are nursing any illusion I might get pregnant one day, forget it. I can't have children.'

In her distress and anger she revealed her deepest secret, but his reaction was not what she expected.

His dark gaze narrowed to rest on her face for a long moment and then his hand stroked gently down her body, one long finger tracing the scar, and when he lifted his head again the dark eyes that met hers held a strange light, and his mouth had an ironic twist to it for all that it was set in a straight line.

'A biological child of my own really does not matter to me. We have Nicholas,' he said coolly. 'What happened tonight was unfortunate, and I don't expect you to believe me unreservedly. But if you had listened a little longer you would have heard me reminding Louisa that our affair was definitely over, as she knew perfectly well, and she had been paid off quite handsomely for her friendship. You have nothing to worry about; forget it ever happened.'

His easy dismissal of her confession infuriated Helen still further. Her inability to have a child was and would be a lifelong regret to Helen, but Leon was so cool, so unfazed by her announcement, he obviously didn't give a jot for her feelings. She could almost feel sorry for the French woman, but not quite.

'Is that what your first wife did when she found out about your lovers? Or did Tina never find out what a two-timing bastard you are? Did you simply lie to her as you lied to me when you said you were faithful to her?' she asked bitterly.

'I never lied to you, or Tina, not that she would have cared if I did,' he stated with a slightly cynical smile. 'Tina was a law unto herself. I was twenty-three when I met her and I married her because she would not let me into her bed until I did.'

And for her father's bank, according to Delia, Helen thought distastefully.

'Before you ask,' Leon continued, accurately reading her mind, 'the merger with her father's bank was of much greater benefit to him than it was to us. We were looking to expand into America, true, but there were much more viable options on the table than his, and I had to work like a slave to make the merger profitable.

'As for the rest, I told you the truth when I said I was faithful to Tina as long as she was to me.' His wry mocking glance seared through her as he continued. 'What I didn't tell you, as I do not like to malign the departed, was that although Tina was a lovely lady I was not her first lover and I certainly was not her last. The concept of monogamy was totally foreign to her nature.'

Helen's lips tightened. *And his,* she thought savagely.

'I am not in the habit of explaining my past actions to anyone, but in this case I will make an exception, because I can tell by the expression on your face that like all females you are never going to let the matter drop until I do,' he said cynically. 'By the time you met Tina in Greece we had been married seven years and she had had at least three lovers that I knew of, Takis, her cousin the party animal, being one of them. Adultery is not the sole prerogative of the man in any marriage. We stayed married mainly for the sake of our fathers as they were great friends, and also as I had no intention of ever marrying again I saw no compelling need to divorce. If that offends your prim little mind, tough, but it is the truth.'

Helen's eyes widened incredulously on his face. Tina unfaithful to him? Why would any woman want another man once they had him? was the first thought that popped into her mind. Her second that for a man with a massive ego like Leon to freely admit his wife had cuckolded him and with her own cousin was unbelievable.

She stared up at him contemplatively. His black hair was rumpled and falling over his forehead, his great body gleamed golden in the dim light and his dark gaze was curiously intent on her face. For a moment she had the fanciful idea he actually needed her to believe him.

No. Leon didn't need anyone. As for believing him, she didn't know what to believe any more. Leon had turned her life upside down, and here she was lying beneath him sated from sex. When, if she had a grain of common sense, she would be packing her bags and leaving. So what did that make her?

A fool, she thought, but it did not stop her murmuring, 'If that is true, I am sorry.'

'No need to be, and I don't need your sympathy. It changes nothing. You and I are married with a child to care for and that is all that matters.'

He was right in one respect. Unless she left Nicholas, and she would never do that willingly, everything else was irrelevant. She had not married Leon for his character, or for the sex. Because that was all it was or ever could be, she recognised now. Her dream of Leon growing to care for her was just that—a dream.

'I need to get up and shower, if you don't mind.'

'Ask me nicely and I'll join you.'

'Hell will freeze over first,' she snarled and rolled off the bed and raced to the bathroom with his mocking laughter ringing in her ears.

When she returned to the bedroom Leon was sprawled across the wide bed, flat on his back and sound asleep. She looked at him for a long time. He really was quite magnificent—on a sexual level, perfect. But was she mature or jaded enough to accept sex for fun, and nothing more? She was still worrying the thought in her mind when she crawled into bed.

When she awoke the next morning he was gone, and she

realised for the first time he had slept beside her without touching her, and left without the early-morning kiss he usually gave her. Obviously he had meant what he had said about not touching her until she asked him. Well she never would, she silently vowed.

When he returned that night it was as if nothing had changed. Over dinner he told her they were leaving for the island the following day for two weeks over the Easter holiday, and the nanny was having a few days leave but would join them later.

When he joined her in bed he simply said goodnight, turned his back on her and within minutes the deep even sound of his breathing told her he was asleep. Sleep did not come so easy for Helen. The seed of hope that had taken root in her heart and begun to grow in the last few weeks had, like a tender shoot caught by a spring frost, been killed stone-dead.

The next day they boarded a much smaller aircraft than the company jet necessary to land on the island's private runway. Nicholas was ecstatic, Helen subdued and Leon his usual aloof self.

CHAPTER ELEVEN

'I HAVE TO go to the mainland this morning.' Leon addressed his wife over the breakfast table set on the terrace of the villa. She looked up at him her violet eyes wary, and he wanted to shake her. No, what he actually wanted to do was make mad, passionate love to her, and he cursed for the hundredth time the asinine challenge he had made that she had to ask him first. He must have been mad, but his pride would not let him back down.

She would come around he knew. He could see the desire in her eyes, when she watched him covertly beneath those incredible long lashes, in the way she backed away from him when they were alone in the bedroom or when they messed about near naked on the beach with Nicholas. Helen was frightened to touch him, and he was man enough to know she was more afraid of herself than him.

It was only a matter of time before she gave in and begged him to make love to her. In the meantime, unless he wanted to end up looking like a prune from the countless cold showers, he needed to get off the island and away from temptation for a few hours. Thankfully, he had some business to discuss with Chris.

'I have meetings lined up with Chris. You can come with me if you like.' Where the hell had that come from? And he told himself he was relieved when she refused.

* * *

After over a week of Leon's constant company, it was with a relieved sigh that Helen stretched out on a towel on the beach.

She had spent a fun day with Nicholas, a visit to the harbour and an attempt at fishing, followed by lunch outside the local café. A slow walk back to the villa, and a short nap, and now it was three in the afternoon and she had given in to his demand to play on the beach.

She glanced at Nicholas happily building a sandcastle a few feet away and sighed. At least he was enjoying the holiday, but the sight of a Leon wearing a tee shirt and shorts day after day, or even less on the beach with them, had her nerves in shreds. It was bad enough she had to fight the temptation to touch him in the huge bed at night, without being faced with his great bronzed body all day as well.

'When is Dad coming back?' Nicholas demanded, coming to slump down on the towel beside her. 'I want him to give me another swimming lesson.'

'I can do that,' Helen declared and got to her feet. She threw off her sun hat and caught his hand in hers. 'Women are just as good as men at swimming, you know. I don't want you growing up to be a chauvinist.' Like Leon, she thought as she led him towards the water.

'What is a chauvest…chauvinct…?'

'Yes, what is a chauvinist?' a light voice called.

Helen spun around, her eyes widening. 'Mary, where did you come from?'

She was walking towards her with her eldest son Mark at her side.

'Leon brought us all over, along with the nanny. He thought you might like some female company for the Easter weekend and the children would enjoy playing together.'

'It's great to see you, and he's right, I could use the company, but he never said anything to me.'

'Maybe he wanted to surprise you.' Mary grinned and, with an order to Mark to watch Nicholas, turned her keen gaze on Helen. 'I can see why, you are not looking very well at all. What's with the dark circles under the eyes? You are on holiday, you're supposed to be relaxing, not wound up as tight as a drum.'

Helen grimaced. 'What do you expect?' She glanced at Nicholas and saw he was happily engrossed with building the sandcastle again with Mark supervising. 'And to answer your first query, a chauvinist is a man like Leon, a man who thinks women are an inferior species, and the only place for them is in bed.'

'That bad, hmm?' Mary took her arm. 'Come on, sit down I have something to tell you.'

Helen sat back down on the towel and Mary flopped down beside her.

'You love him, I can see that, and I can understand why you don't trust him after what you overheard. As a lawyer I know I should not betray a confidence, but I like to think of you as my friend and you deserve to know.'

'That sounds ominous.'

'Not at all. Chris is not just Leon's lawyer, he's also his friend. Leon called him last night to tell him he was coming over to go over some family business they had been dealing with. But he also told Chris that, although he enjoyed every moment here with you, he thought you might appreciate some female company for the weekend. Now for Leon to actually consider how a woman might feel outside of the bedroom is definitely a first in all the time Chris has known him. Chris is convinced Leon is totally smitten with you.' Mary lifted her eyebrow elegantly in Helen's direction.

'You don't need me to tell you Leon is a cynic where women are concerned. But even more crucial information I discovered later, in bed.' She grinned wickedly. 'It was Chris who visited Louisa in Paris a couple of weeks ago. It was Chris in his capacity as Leon's lawyer who presented Louisa with the deeds of the apartment, and a cheque for a large sum of money. Not very nice, I know, but not grounds for divorce. Now, whether Leon slept with Louisa the week before he married you, I don't know, but he definitely did not afterwards. He wasn't even in Paris when Chris clinched the less than salubrious deal, and that is the absolute truth. Pillow talk can be a mine of information.' Mary chuckled. 'But you must never tell a soul I told you this or Chris will kill me.'

Thinking about the conversation she had overheard, Helen realised what Mary was saying could be true. Louisa had not actually said Leon had handed the gifts over personally. Helen had just jumped to that conclusion. She looked into the eyes of her friend and saw the honesty and genuine care there and sighed.

'I believe you, Mary, but it changes nothing. Leon does not believe in love. I will never be anything other than a convenient body in his bed, and not even that now,' she confided. 'In the fight we had after the party the conceited devil declared he would not touch me again unless I asked him, and that is never going to happen.'

'Talk about cutting off your own nose to spite your own face—are you crazy?' Mary declared. 'Heaven knows, Leon has never had much love in his life and he probably would not recognise the emotion if it hit him in the face. But if you really love him, show him. What are you, a woman or a wimp? You can easily make him change his mind. It's up to you to try, and now I am taking these two boys back to the villa and you can stay here for a while to think what you really want to do.'

If Helen believed Mary, and she did, Leon had been faithful at least since they had married. But with the image of his magnificent virile body flashing though her mind, she recognised he wasn't a man cut out to be celibate, and there were hundreds of willing women out there. Was she such a fool as to deny what her body craved, and maybe push him into the arms of another woman? Not a pleasant thought, and one that made her realise sadly that she still did not trust him. Her heart told her love and trust were indivisible, but her head and her achingly frustrated body were telling her to go for the love and hope the trust came later.

Helen was still thinking what she wanted to do, or more to the point whether she dared do what her heart was telling her to, when she walked into the bedroom to shower and change. She slipped off her shirt and grimaced as the sand stuck in her bikini irritated her skin. Then her answer walked out of the bathroom, all six feet plus of vibrant male, his black hair wet from the shower and wearing only a towel slung around his lean hips.

'Leon, I thought you were with Chris and the children,' Helen blurted, her heart hammering against her breastbone, her gaze roaming helplessly over his near-naked body. In front of her fascinated gaze he whipped the towel off his hips and began rubbing his hair dry.

'The nanny is looking after them.' Leon slung the towel around his neck, his dark eyes flicking appreciatively over her bikini clad figure and up to her scarlet face. The pupils of her wide eyes were dilating with desire, and her lush little breasts were firm, the rigid nipples peaking against the scrap of blue fabric just begging to be touched.

The fact she could still blush after all they had shared was a source of amusement to him and rather endearing. He took the towel from his neck and draped it around his hips as he walked towards her and battled to control the urge to take her in his arms. With a little verbal encouragement he would not need to, she would be asking him in no time at all.

'You have the same expression on your face as the very first time you saw me naked on the beach,' he reminded her softly. 'I wanted you then, but I was married. I remember saying you should ask before ogling, that was perhaps a little unkind of me.'

He stepped forward so their bodies were only inches apart, and saw the slight tremor that shivered through her. She wanted him.

'I never saw you naked,' she returned. 'Not until we married.'

'Liar.' He smiled down into her incredible eyes. 'I saw you staring at me as you walked towards me, before I slung a towel around my waist.'

He wasn't touching her but Helen was hypnotised by his closeness the heat of his body reaching out to her. It was so long since she had felt his touch, the glory of his possession, and her whole body was flooded with heat. Mary was right, and all she had to do was ask. She opened her mouth to do just that when he continued speaking.

'Now I really appreciate you ogling me.' He let his appreciative gaze roam sensuously over her lush little body. 'And I will forgive the lie, if you say the words I want to hear. You know you want to. The tell-tale press of your perfect little nipples against your bikini top are screaming for my touch.'

Helen heard what he said and it was his damned arrogance that froze the words he wanted to hear in her throat.

'I do not lie and I did not see you naked,' she snapped. 'I was blind for over a year and I had just had my last eye operation a few weeks earlier. I was staring because I was trying to bring you into focus, and when I did you were wearing a towel,' she told him furiously.

Leon's startled gaze leapt to her face. He knew she wore disposable contact lenses and he could see she was telling the truth. *Theos,* he was fifty kinds of fool. Was he never going to get anything right with this amazing woman? Swallowing his pride, he reached for her.

'To hell with you asking, I am taking,' he declared, and hauled her against his hard body, finding her mouth with his own, and kissed her with all the pent-up frustration that had gnawed away at him for a week. He savoured the taste of her, felt her body melt against him, heard her low moan, and wondered why he had waited so long.

He swept her up in his arms, and carried her to the bed.

'What are you doing? I am covered in sand,' she squealed.

Leon grinned at her stunned expression and changed direction to head for the bathroom. 'I am going to bathe you, pamper you and make love to you, not necessarily in that order.'

Held against his broad chest Helen ran her tongue over her suddenly dry lips, and swallowed hard. He had actually said make love, and she had not had to ask him.

Unbelievably her proud, indomitable husband had relaxed his iron control and given in to his feelings. Whether it was love or lust didn't really matter. As Mary had said, it was up to Helen to teach him the difference. She looked at his hard, chiselled features, the determination and passion blazing in his eyes, and she knew even if it took a lifetime she would try, because she loved him.

When he lowered her to the cool marble floor she stood still as he deftly removed her bikini and turned on the shower. Her hungry gaze swept helplessly over him as he shed the towel and joined her.

With a gentleness that enthralled her, he bathed her from head to toe. His hands lingered in certain places and she made no objection as his lips pressed soft kisses on her sensitised flesh, igniting a familiar heat inside her. She returned the favour and ran her hands up his strong arms, caressing his wide shoulders, and clung as he lifted her from the shower to wrap her in a huge towel and tenderly dry her body.

Finally when he lowered her onto the bed, and came down on top of her, his arms either side of her supporting him, his muscular thighs trapping her legs, she felt the hard strength of his arousal against her belly and she was no longer dry, but hot, moist and wanting. His mouth covered hers and she opened to him with a passionate sigh of relief.

He lifted his head, his smouldering gaze sweeping over her. 'Have you any idea how beautiful you are?' he husked.

For a long moment she looked up into his dark, attractive face, and she knew he could no more deny the compulsive desire that flared between them than she could. She reached for him then and drew his head down to hers, and kissed him. Her tongue seeking the magical depths of his sensuous mouth, her hands stroking and kneading his sleek bronzed skin. Discovering again the familiar strength and contours of his great body.

'Ah Helen, you have no idea how much I need this,' he groaned, trailing an exquisite line of kisses to her aching breasts. He closed his mouth around a rigid peaking nipple, suckling her hungrily.

Helen gave a gasping cry and arched into his mouth, her hands raking through his hair as he bestowed the same savage pleasure on the other. His tongue gently laved each straining nipple, his hands stroking, shaping the line of her waist, hip and thigh. Then he curved a strong arm round her to splay across her back, his mouth trailing lower, never ceasing the exquisite torment. His free hand reached to trace her lips, her throat, her breasts. Her legs parted eagerly, wanting, aching for him there. She felt the touch of his tongue in her navel and groaned her delight as his mouth dipped lower still and found those other lips and his skilful tongue teased the small, swelling bud of her passion.

'Please, Leon,' she cried out as her whole body shuddered in instant violent response. But still he continued until the pleasure was almost pain.

'Please,' she begged.

Leon heard her cry and lifted his dark head, feeling her hands rake up over his back, her teeth nipping his shoulder. He saw the blind hunger, the passion on her beautiful face, and with one powerful thrust plunged into her moist, tight, silken sheath and stayed. He wanted to make this last, but he could not. The sweet taste of her was on his tongue, the fiery heat of her consumed him, and for once his incredible control deserted him as her inner muscles clenched around him, drawing him on. And with a shuddering groan he thrust again and again, driving her, driving him, on a wild, primitive ride that exploded into a mutual orgasm that shattered anything he had experienced before.

Helen clung to Leon, her hands instinctively stroking his broad back as the trembling aftershock of their ferocious passion slowly faded away. The weight of his body pinned her to the bed, but it was a pleasurable weight and one she had missed the past week. She sighed languorously, her mind and body at last in accord.

Leon eased his weight off her and leant on one forearm looking intently down into her beautiful face.

'Finally defeated,' he stated huskily.

Her mellow mood shot to hell with two words, Helen shoved at his chest and he fell onto his back and she sat up. 'I was not defeated; I never asked you.'

It was her turn to stare down at him, breathless but infuriated by his arrogant assumption, the fact she had been going to ask him conveniently forgotten.

'You grabbed me,' she declared hotly and he had the nerve to laugh out loud.

'I meant I was admitting defeat, which you may not realise is an unheard-of occurrence for me.'

'Oh.'

Leon admitting defeat was too incredible for words. He was sprawled back on the bed with his hands behind his head. His black hair sexily tousled, a sensuous smile on his face. Anyone looking less defeated would be impossible to find, she thought wryly. He looked what he was: a supremely confident, sexually sated man.

'Though I suppose,' he drawled musingly, 'in the interest of married harmony we could call it a draw. I seem to recall you begging me not once, but twice.'

His dark eyes lit with laughter twinkled up at her and she could not help the laugh that bubbled out.

'You are impossible, and if we don't get dressed and downstairs our guests are going to come looking for us.'

'Okay.' He sat up and slid an arm around her shoulders. 'Are we okay now?'

Helen noticed he said 'we' and not 'you.' And for a moment she wondered if Leon really did care.

'If you have to think of an answer, forget it.'

'No, I mean, yes, we are fine,' she admitted blushing scarlet.

'Good.'

He gave her a brilliant smile and a swift, hard kiss on her mouth before leaping off the bed gloriously naked.

'Give me a couple of minutes and you can have the bathroom.' And she had the strongest feeling he was relieved by her answer.

'Hurry up, you lot,' Leon yelled from the foot of the steps of the aircraft. 'The holiday is over; get on board.'

'Is that any way to speak to our guests?' Helen demanded, walking up to him, Chris, Mary and the nanny bringing up the rear with the four lively children.

His dark eyes smiled wryly down at her as he snaked an arm around her and tucked her possessively against his broad shoulder. 'Probably not, but, much as I have enjoyed our holiday, I have discovered friends and family can seriously curtail one's sex life. The next time we go away we are going on the honeymoon we never had when we married.'

'That sounds promising,' Helen murmured, her heart singing as he bent his head and kissed her.

The last few days had been a revelation. Everyone had thoroughly enjoyed themselves; the days had been warm and fun with the children, the nights still cold in April, but hot for the adults in bed at night. Leon relaxed and loving was a sight to behold. Helen was almost sure it was love, though he had never said the words, but then neither had she.

'Yucky,' a little voice cried. 'I'm never going to kiss a girl.'

And the adults were all laughing as everyone boarded the aircraft.

'I have to get up,' Leon groaned.

'I rather thought you just had,' Helen returned wickedly, leaning up to rest her arms on his broad chest, her legs straddling his strong thighs.

'You, madam, are getting very risqué,' he chuckled, and in one deft movement Helen was on her back and Leon was looming over her. 'Not something I expected from the innocent I married.' His deep dark eyes smiled into hers. 'But then I never expected to…' And he stopped.

'To what?' Helen asked, lazily running her hands up over his broad chest.

'Nothing. I have to go.' He leapt off the bed, and paused

for a moment to stare down at her. 'There is something I have to tell you, but it can wait until tonight.'

'You sound serious.'

'I am about you.' Bending over, he brushed a tender kiss across her brow. 'Tonight.'

Spinning on his heel, he headed for the bathroom.

Helen hoarded his words like a treasure in her heart. She was sure he was going to tell her he loved her. Amazingly he had said he was serious about her, and after the last three weeks of what she could only describe as sheer bliss what else could it be?

Hopefully it would be the icing on the cake to a perfect day, Helen thought dreamily as she washed and dressed with care in a slim fitting natural linen skirt and matching short fitted jacket. On her feet she wore high heeled tan sandals and carried a matching purse. She was not taking Nicholas to school today, the nanny was, as Helen had an appointment at eleven.

At first when she had begun to feel tired and slightly nauseous she had put it down to the change in country, in food, and the much hotter weather in Greece than she was used to. It had been Mary who had pointed out that it could be something else. Helen hardly dared to hope, but she had made an appointment with Mary's gynaecologist for this morning.

She asked the driver to wait, and entered the private clinic.

Dr Savalas was a woman in her fifties with three children of her own, and immediately Helen felt at home with her, and told her the story of her accident and apologised in advance for probably wasting her time.

'So, let me get this straight, Mrs Aristides: you think you might be pregnant, but at the age of fourteen you had an accident. The doctor in Geneva told you the operation to repair your fractured pelvis was a success. Then added he was sorry but it was unlikely you would ever have a child. Have I got that right?'

Helen nodded her head.

'Well, give me his name, and let's see, shall we?'

An hour later Helen sat looking at Dr Savalas, her eyes swimming with tears of happiness. 'I really am pregnant?'

'Most definitely. I have checked with your doctor in Geneva and there is no real medical reason why you should not carry the child to full term. Though your pelvis has been weakened and you are quite small. To err on the side of caution, they suggest and I agree you should not attempt to have a natural birth, but opt for a Caesarean delivery.'

Helen floated out of the clinic on cloud nine, and climbed into the waiting car, a smile a mile wide on her face. When the driver asked her where to, without a second thought she said the bank. She had to tell someone or she would burst and Leon had the right to know first.

She skipped out of the car twenty yards from the bank, and told the driver to take a lunch break and she would call him later if she needed him. She felt like laughing out loud, but controlled the impulse, but could do nothing about the broad smile on her face.

CHAPTER TWELVE

'WELL, WELL, SOMEONE looks happy, and very pleased with themselves.'

Helen looked up in surprise at the handsome man who had stepped in front of her. 'Hello, Takis.'

'Let me guess, you're on your way to see Leon and the lawyers to collect the inheritance Delia left you.'

'No, with a bit of luck I am going to try and persuade Leon to take me out for lunch,' she said with a smile. After what Leon had told her she was wary of the man, but nothing could dent her euphoric mood today. Though she was slightly surprised by his comment. Why would Takis know anything about Delia's will? Not that it mattered. As far as she was concerned the inheritance was for Nicholas, full stop.

'You're a lucky lady and soon to be a very wealthy one. But nowhere near as lucky as Leon. He has control of everything and you as a beautiful bonus. I have got to hand it to him—he is brilliant and ruthless when it comes to business.'

There was something in his golden eyes that looked very like envy, and his less-than-flattering description of Leon dimmed her smile somewhat.

'I'm sorry, I have no idea what you are talking about,' she said slowly.

'Oh, come on, Helen, you may be blonde, but you're not an air-head. You must know that old man Aristides died before his daughter. Which meant Delia inherited forty per cent of her dad's fortune and according to my information she left eighty per cent of her estate to her son, and the rest to you. Surely you must have realised you and the boy stood to gain a heck of a lot more than if Delia had died first, much to Leon's dismay.'

Helen's smile vanished along with her sense of euphoria. 'What exactly are you trying to say?' she asked with a queasy feeling in the pit of her stomach.

'You don't know, you really don't know.' Taking her arm, he urged her towards a small pavement café. 'Join me for a coffee and I will explain.'

Over a cup of coffee Takis did just that.

'Leon and his father have always kept the majority of shares in Aristides International in the immediate family. They always had Delia's voting rights, though it might have been different if she had lived long enough to inherit the ones her mother had left her at twenty-five. But after the double tragedy and the discovery of Delia's will and her illegitimate child—you, Helen, became the wild card in the pack. As executor of the boy's estate Leon would not have had a problem, he could simply vote the child's shares the way he wanted to. But you could be a real problem for him.'

'This is all way over my head,' Helen muttered, taking a sip of her coffee with a growing feeling of dread.

'It is quite simple: you inherited twenty per cent of Delia's estate which includes eight per cent of the company shares from her father. I hold some, as do a host of other people whose family members have been involved in mergers in the past or simply bought them. The rest are held by big investment companies that are more than satisfied with Leon's leadership. To give the devil his due he has a phenomenal business brain. But technically if we all joined together Leon would now no longer have a majority and your holding could be instrumental in voting him out of office.'

'I see.' Helen nodded.

'Don't get me wrong, Helen. You are a very beautiful woman, but you are in a very strong position, particularly as the child's guardian.'

'Leon is as well,' she cut in swiftly, and saw the look of pity in Takis' eyes.

'Are you sure about that? Check with your lawyer. I think you will find Leon is an executor of the boy's estate, not his guardian.' He shrugged his shoulders. 'It is not important. You're a lovely lady, and I hate to be the one to tell you but Leon had very compelling reasons to marry you, and not just for the boy. Your inheriting Aristides shares posed a threat— a very slight threat, it is true—to his absolute control of the bank. You must know what a control freak he is. So be careful.' And with that he up and left.

For a long time Helen simply sat and stared at the table with sightless eyes, Takis' revelation running though her brain, not wanting to believe the evidence before her. She recalled the appointment Leon had set up for her with Mr Smyth. He had congratulated her on her inheritance and on her forthcoming wedding and told her Leon was the executor of Nicholas' estate along with her and suggested he read the will in its entirety. But she had been in a hurry to go and buy her wedding dress, and refused his suggestion. She had told him she wanted to give the money to Nicholas. And then she recalled he had advised her to hold back on any decision until the will had passed probate. Had he been trying to warn her?

The adoption of Nicholas, which Leon had suggested and which had been instrumental in dissolving her resistance to him after only two days of marriage, suddenly took on a much more sinister light. If he was never the boy's guardian, as Takis had said, it made sense for Leon to press for adoption, then he would have exactly the same rights has her. How could any man be so ruthless, so Machiavellian?

'Would madam like anything else?'

Helen looked up at the waiter. 'No. No, thank you.' And he gave her the bill. A bitter smile curved her lips. Takis had left her to pay.

She walked through the streets of Athens her head bent and her mind in turmoil. When she finally reached the house it was after four. She heard the sound of childish laughter from the garden, and walked around the house to where the swimming pool was situated.

'Hi, Mum, watch me swim,' Nicholas yelled.

She watched him, blinking back the tears. Marta, the nanny was in the pool with him while Anna was sitting at the patio table with the driver, and both were keeping a watchful eye on the boy.

'Come on in,' Nicholas shouted.

'Not today,' she called back. 'I'm going upstairs to change.' And waving, walked indoors.

Not any day, she thought sadly, putting a protective hand on her still-flat stomach. Nicholas was Greek. Leon had been right about that. He was well looked after by people who adored him. He didn't really need her, she decided sadly. She didn't belong here, and she was going home.

She stopped halfway up the stairs, appalled at where her own selfish thoughts were leading her. Nicholas was her child as much as the child she carried in her womb, who would also be half Greek. She had no more right to deprive the child of its heritage than she had Nicholas. They would physically be cousins, and, in her heart, brothers.

She stripped off her clothes and flopped down on the bed and cried her eyes out. All her hopes and dreams shattered by a casual meeting and a few choice words from a man she barely knew.

A long time later she stood up and walked into the bathroom. She was mind numbingly frozen. She stepped into the shower and turned on the tap and let the hot water rush over her. But she felt as if she would never be warm again.

How could she have been such a blind fool? Such an idiot? she berated herself. She was still asking herself the same question when she sat before the dressing table in her bra and briefs to dry her hair.

'Hello, sweetheart.' Leon strode into their suite, a broad smile on his face. 'Wear something glamorous—I am taking you out to dinner.'

He wrapped an arm around her, pulling her gently up to her feet, his appreciative gaze sweeping over her scantily clad body, his eyes darkening as he would have pulled her close to kiss her. But Helen put her hands against his chest and pushed him away.

The veil of love had been torn from her eyes, and at last she was seeing him as he truly was. The ultimate tycoon. Tall and powerfully built, clad in a perfectly tailored pearl-grey suit. His hard, angular face and high cheekbones exuded an aura of ruthless power and absolute authority. How had she been so blind? she thought, seeing the flicker of impatience in his eyes. He hated to be thwarted in business or sex.

'I don't want to go out to dinner with you,' she said flatly. What should have been the most wonderful moment of her life was now a travesty. Scantily clad as she was, she wanted to get it over with and out of his sight as quickly as possible. 'I am pregnant.'

'You said you could not have children,' Leon declared harshly.

She stared at him. He didn't look delighted at the prospect. His face was more austere than she had ever seen it, his heavy lidded eyes were narrowed suspiciously on her, and a muscle flickered in his tanned cheek. Why was she surprised at his response? He had told her he didn't care about having a biological child; he probably did not want to split his wealth another way, she thought contemptuously.

'I was wrong; apparently a fractured pelvis does not preclude me getting pregnant after all, though it will prevent me from having a natural birth. The doctor told me I must have a Caesarean delivery.'

She could not believe she was talking to him so calmly when inside she was a seething mass of pain and fury. And she had been wrong about never feeling warm again; the few brief moments held against his long body had warmed her instantly, and she hated herself for it.

'Is it mine?'

That had to be the cruellest cut of all Helen thought savagely after a day that had seen her emotions go from dizzying happiness to absolute despair. She could not take any more.

'Leave me alone.' He disgusted her. 'Just leave me alone.'

She brushed past him. She had to get away.

'Sorry,' he said roughly, catching her by the arm and turning her back into the warmth of his body. 'Of course it is mine; I don't know what I was thinking of. Put it down to my natural cynical nature and forgive me.'

Held in his arms she could feel herself weakening. So what did it matter why he had married her? The irony of the situation suddenly hit her. In the beginning he had accused her of caring for Nicholas for money and the inheritance he had been sure she knew about, and had had the gall to call her the best paid nanny in the world. Yet all along it had been Leon who had been guarding his own incredible wealth.

'Helen, please, I really am sorry for doubting you for a minute. I would trust you with my life,' he said solemnly.

The shock of his repeated apology made her head spin. Too little, too late, she thought bitterly.

'Well, I sure as hell wouldn't trust you as far as I could throw you,' she lashed back. 'I met a friend of yours today and he was most informative. It seems the only reason you wanted Nicholas and I was to keep overall control of your bloody bank.'

His mouth hardened into a thin line as he demanded, 'What friend?'

'I bumped into Takis on the way to see you. Dr Savalas had confirmed my pregnancy and I wanted you to be the first to know. More fool me.' She glared at him. 'Takis stopped to congratulate me on becoming a wealthy woman and to warn me about you. We had a coffee together, and after chatting to him I suddenly found I had no desire to see you. Instead I decided to come back here.'

'Don't try my patience,' Leon said softly, his dark gaze roaming over her face and down to where her breasts were barely covered by the lace bra. 'What exactly did Takis say to you that changed the very willing wife I left in bed this morning into the tense angry woman before me now?'

She briefly closed her eyes against the pull of sensuality his blatant masculine look had aroused. The happiness of this morning felt like a lifetime ago now, Helen thought sadly.

'Takis told me the truth—something you seem to have an aversion to.' She shook her head, she hadn't the strength to yell at him and it took all her willpower to continue coolly, 'Ironic, isn't it, Leon? When you arrived at my home you accused me of being a gold-digger, when all the time it was you that was driven by money.'

She looked at him then and was slightly shocked by the

ferocious anger on his hard face, but not totally shocked. Like most powerful men he probably did not like to have his faults revealed.

'I know all about the wills,' she said flatly. 'The fact your father died first meant Delia inherited from his estate and consequently Nicholas and I got a lot more than you bargained for. Discovering we existed must have been one hell of a shock to you. No wonder you hotfooted it to England—your absolute control over Aristides International was threatened.'

She saw his face darken and thought he had a good right to look guilty. 'And your oh, so sensible offer of a convenient marriage while carefully avoiding telling me you were not named as Nicholas' guardian was a hell of a lot more devious than anything I ever did. As for adopting Nicholas, that was a master stroke.'

Helen stopped, unable to go on for a moment as the full extent of his deception struck her all over again. 'You were so efficient and considerate, even to arranging a meeting for me with Mr Smyth.'

She glanced up, her challenging gaze roaming over his hard face.

'Tell me, how much did you pay him?' she asked scathingly, recalling when he had asked her the same thing and flinging his own words back at him.

'That is enough,' he grated between clenched teeth. 'I never paid him a penny. And I never said I was Nicholas' guardian, I said I was a trustee of his estate.'

Thinking back she realised he was right, but it didn't alter the fact he had let her think it—his *muddy water* principle, no doubt.

'Maybe not.' She shrugged. 'He did tell me to read the will, but I was in a hurry to buy my wedding dress and didn't bother. How's that for a sick joke? But to give Mr Smyth his due he did tell me not to sign away my inheritance until I had thought about it for a few months. So he was honest, unlike you. Amazingly I was naive enough then to believe what you told me, but not any more.'

'If you shut up I can explain,' Leon began, lifting a hand towards her, and she knocked it away.

'Oh, please, spare your breath,' she said with a sarcastic lift of a finely arched brow. 'You tricked me into marriage. You tricked me into bed, and you would have quite happily let me trick myself out of the inheritance Delia left me.'

'No,' he growled and wrapping an arm around her waist, hauled her against him. 'That is not true and the main reason Takis has gone to such lengths to try to poison your mind against me is because I confronted him today with the final result of the investigation into Delia's drug taking. Takis is the party animal who handed out drugs like candy to his friends, Delia being one of them. The police can do nothing about it, because they can't prove it. But I told him if I ever saw him in Athens again I would destroy him.'

Helen believed him, but it didn't make any difference; it simply confirmed what a ruthless bastard Leon was. She drew in a deep, shuddering breath and suddenly she was intensely aware of his great body hard against her own. The scent of him, a mixture of tangy cologne and musky male, was clouding her senses and her cool control took a serious knock.

'You're probably right but it doesn't really matter any more,' she said flatly, determined not to be blinded by sex again. 'You don't need to worry; I have not changed my mind. I will still sign everything over to Nicholas. Now, if you don't mind, will you please leave?' Her head was suddenly spinning, her legs felt weak and she could not take any more.

'I want to get dressed,' she murmured, and felt herself falling against him.

* * *

Helen opened her eyes, and for a moment wondered where she was. She glanced around and realised she was lying on the bed. How did she get here? The door opened and Anna appeared with Nicholas by her side and a cup of tea in her hand. Helen pulled herself up to sitting position, wiping her damp hair from her face.

'What happened?' she asked.

'You fainted.' Anna smiled and stopped by the bed. 'Not unusual for a girl in your condition. Master Leon caught you and put you on the bed. He told me you were pregnant and now he is calling the doctor.' Handing her the cup, she added, 'Men are helpless at times like this. Now, drink that tea, and tell Nicholas you are fine.'

The little boy climbed on the bed.

As the events of the afternoon came back to her in all their horror, she hugged Nicholas close and with a few words and a cuddle she reassured him she was fine, and he was off like a shot to resume playing.

'Have you eaten today?' Anna questioned as he left. 'The chauffeur thought you were lunching with Master Leon, but he said you did not, and you are eating for two now, remember.'

'No, I'm afraid I missed lunch.' Helen shook her head and Anna left to return five minutes later with a ham salad, and left again.

After eating the salad Helen was about to get up and dress when the door opened again, and Leon walked in. He was the last person she wanted to see, she thought, her eyes flicking bitterly over him. He had lost the jacket and tie, his shirt was unbuttoned and if she had not known better she might have thought he was upset. A small grey haired man followed behind him, whom Leon introduced as the doctor.

'I don't need a doctor,' she began. 'I—'

'I will be the judge of that,' Leon said grimly, striding over to the bed and lowering her back down. 'You are too damn volatile to know what you need,' he muttered, pulling the sheet up over her thighs.

The doctor took her temperature, felt her pulse, asked a few questions, and nodded his approval when she mentioned Dr Savalas, while Leon stood in brooding silence listening to the whole proceedings.

'I will see the doctor out,' Leon declared, looking down at her with cold, hard eyes. 'Then I will be back.'

Helen inwardly shivered sensing the threat in his tone, and began to get up again. She needed to be dressed and on her feet to face him.

'Don't even think about getting up,' Leon commanded, and the doctor agreed. Helen silently fumed. Defying her autocratic husband's orders didn't bother her one bit, but the doctor was a different proposition. Nothing and no one, herself included was going to do anything to harm the precious life inside her.

Punching up the pillows, she eased her body up the bed. She had to stay in bed, but she didn't have to lie down. She had lain down enough for Leon Aristides, but not any more. Once she got out of this bed she was never sharing another bed with the man again.

For the sake of the child she carried and Nicholas she would stay and willingly sign everything over to the child or children. Leon was hard-headed and ruthless enough that once he got what he really wanted she knew he would leave her alone. It would not be a problem for him. He had told her himself his first marriage had been just such an arrangement for years; as for her, she could get used to anything in time. God knew, she had had enough practice, and this time she had the compensation of not one, but hopefully two children to love.

The door opened yet again and a glimmer of humour lightened her eyes. She was beginning to feel as if she were in the middle of Grand Central Station. But one look at the grim expression on Leon's hard face as he strode over to the bed and her amusement vanished. Suddenly she did not feel quite so brave, or so sure.

'The doctor said you must rest for a half an hour and then you can get up. Is there anything I can get you?'

'No.' She just wanted him to go. 'I think you have done quite enough for me already,' she drawled facetiously. 'I have nothing more to say to you except terms. If you wish to remain married, I am prepared to stay in this house for Nicholas' and our unborn child's sake, but not in this room. If you want a divorce I will give you one, but I keep the children.' At last she was taking back control of her life.

For a long tense moment there was silence. 'You really don't trust me at all. But this conversation is not over.'

His black eyes raked over her with insulting arrogance that did not help her budding confidence. 'We will discuss your terms later in my study after Nicholas is in bed. Don't make me have to come and fetch you.' He left, slamming the door.

Helen stood outside the study, reluctant to go in. Nicholas was safely tucked up in bed, and she had not seen Leon since he had stormed out of their room. She squared her slender shoulders, and nervously adjusted the neckline of the blue silk wrap around the top she had opted to wear. With not quite steady hands she smoothed the fabric of her slim fitting navy skirt down over her hips and drew in a deep steadying breath. She had to face Leon some time and she could no longer delay the confrontation.

The door opening interrupted her thoughts and Leon was standing in the aperture, a glass of what looked like whisky in his hand. He had changed, she noticed, into a crisp blue tailored shirt and dark blue trousers. They were a matching pair, the thought struck her. Not anymore, she amended swiftly, and lifted her head to fearlessly meet his gaze.

'Come in, we are expecting you,' he said smoothly, and stepped back to allow her to enter.

What did he mean 'we'? Helen was immediately thrown into confusion, her startled gaze sweeping around the room to rest on Chris Stefano standing by the desk.

'Chris. Hello,' she managed to get out through suddenly dry lips walking into the middle of the room. 'Nice to see you.'

'Take the social exchange as read,' Leon said curtly. 'Chris has some documents for you to sign and he is in a hurry.' And raising the glass to his mouth, he drained the contents.

Helen stopped, her slender body tensing. Chris was Leon's lawyer. Leon had said documents, plural. Had he already decided to take her up on her offer of, not just the inheritance, but a divorce as well? The sudden stab of pain in her heart made her wince.

'Are you sure you are all right?' Leon placed a hand on her arm.

She felt the pressure of his fingers against her bare skin and glanced up at him. His hard face looked drawn, his lips tight, and his deep set eyes had a troubled look about them. Concern for her? No, Leon was a man who had never truly cared for a woman in his life.

'Yes, I am fine.' She shrugged off his hand and walked to the desk. 'Show me where I have to sign.'

She forced herself to smile at Chris and picked up a pen from the desk.

'Sorry for the rush, Helen, but Mary and I are supposed to be going out to dinner. But you know your husband—if he wants something done, he wants it done yesterday.' He chuckled, and placed two papers in front of her. 'I am sure

Leon has explained everything to you, but if you want to read them go ahead.'

It took every bit of self control Helen possessed to smile back at Chris. 'No, that won't be necessary. But you could run the important points by me again.'

Was it a divorce Leon was going for? She cast a sidelong glance at her husband. He had moved to the opposite side of the room, where he was refilling his glass from a decanter. 'They are perfectly straightforward,' Chris said, and she quickly turned her attention back to him. 'The first is simply your acceptance of the money and shares, et cetera, Delia left you. I will need the name and number of the account you want them held in and the transfer will be through in five days.'

'Wait a minute! That's not right. I told Leon I want everything to go directly to Nicholas,' Helen exclaimed.

'I know, but he wouldn't hear of it. He told me before Easter to make sure everything was transferred into your name.'

'Before Easter, but...'

That could not be true, and yet she trusted Chris, and if it was true she had made the biggest mistake in her life today. She had believed everything Takis had told her, a man she hardly knew, and she had condemned Leon without giving him a chance to explain. She turned shocked eyes to Leon. He was leaning against the fireplace glass in hand, his expression inscrutable.

She thought back over the twelve weeks she had been married, and realised the preconceived notions she'd had of Leon had coloured her thinking the whole time. Being brutally honest, she knew it probably would not have mattered what he did. The wonderful lover, the great father, the magnificent diamonds he gave her, and most importantly his explanation of Louisa, while not pleasant to hear, had been truthful.

But still she had not credited him with an ounce of trust.

Instead she had believed a virtual stranger over him. What had she done?

'I am in a bit of a hurry, Helen,' Chris prompted. 'The other document is the first stage in adopting Nicholas.'

'No. I am not signing anything,' she stated, looking back at Chris. 'I thought...'

What she had thought was shaming and she stopped in mid-sentence.

'Like most women, my wife has trouble thinking clearly.' Leon addressed Chris as he crossed the room to Helen's side, closing his hands on her shoulders and turning her round to face him.

'I've told you before. Let me do the thinking.'

She was so heart-stoppingly beautiful both inside and out, and so thoroughly confused, and he knew he was to blame.

'You must sign the first document, Helen, to close the estate, afterwards you can do what you like with the money. As for the second document it can wait if you prefer. But Chris can't; he is in a hurry.' He held her shocked gaze, the air between them thickening with tension. He saw the kaleidoscope of emotions flickering in the violet depths of her eyes. Unlike him, she never could hide what she was feeling and he knew the moment she made her decision.

Helen signed both documents quietly.

'Why, Leon?' she asked quietly as Chris departed. 'Why did you not stop me this afternoon? Why did you ignore what I said about giving everything to Nicholas? I misjudged you so dreadfully. I didn't trust you an inch and I feel such a fool,' she admitted bleakly.

'No. I am the fool,' Leon declared, his dark gaze raking over her with a burning intensity that made her pulse race and her heart beat loudly in her breast. 'I ignored what you said, because I wanted you to have everything.'

'You said that once before,' Helen murmured. 'A couple of weeks after we married, when you took me to the bank.'

'I meant it then, and I mean it now,' he said simply, and, bending towards her, he had swept her up in his arms before she knew what was happening.

'What are you doing?' Helen cried inanely, flinging her arms around his neck.

'What I should have done weeks ago.'

He carried her to the sofa and, dropping down, he held her firmly on his lap. His dark gaze narrowed intently on her pale face.

'Told you I love you,' he said thickly.

Stunned, Helen stared at him like a woman transfixed.

'Me… You love me.' She had to be dreaming, or she had finally flipped and she was hearing voices.

'Yes, you, Helen. I never thought love existed until I met you.'

A great surge of hope swept through her. She wasn't crazy, Leon had said the words she had longed to hear.

'Oh, Leon, I—'

He lifted a finger and laid it against her soft lips.

'Say nothing. I have to do this now or I may never have the courage again.' He stopped her, a self deriding smile curving his mouth.

'From the day we met again in England I wanted you sexually. But you were right, and so was Takis in a way—my main motivation was to get you and Nicholas under my control. Technically I could have lost control of the company, but it would never happen. Some of the small shareholders like Chris and Alex and a few more would never vote against me. But I like to be thorough and when you offered to sign everything over to Nicholas, I said nothing and married you for my convenience, not yours,' he confessed in a rush.

Helen stirred restlessly on his lap, this was not what she

wanted to hear, but his arms gathered her closer. His dark eyes held hers, serious in their intent.

'I am trying to be honest, Helen—not pleasant, I know. I decided you were a clever, conniving woman, but on our wedding night I discovered in one way at least you were completely innocent. I was amazed and delighted, and in my arrogance I told myself I had a willing, sexy woman in my bed and an heir to inherit after me. What more could a man want?'

'That is so chauvinistic.' Helen shook her head. But she wasn't surprised. Leon was never going to be the new age man women's magazines raved about.

'I know, and I am ashamed to say I carried on thinking that way for quite a while. I told myself the incredible urge to make love to you every time I looked at you was just sex, I couldn't admit it was more.'

'And was it more?' she asked, willing him to say he loved her again, because she still could not quite believe him.

Leon smiled and buried his lips in the silken scent of her hair for a moment.

'Oh, I think you always knew it was more,' he husked, his dark gaze returning to her upturned face. 'It was more the first time I had to leave you to go to New York and I bought you a ring. It was more every time I held you in my arms and made love to you. It was more when I told Chris to make sure you inherited everything you were entitled to. I loved you but I was too much of a coward to tell you.'

There was no doubting the sincerity in his dark eyes, and she ran a gentle finger down the side of his face, her heart swelling in her breast. He caught her hand in his and raised it to his lips and she was powerless against the softness of his small caress and the flood of emotions it evoked. She stirred restlessly on his lap and was aware of the hard strength of his aroused body beneath her. And wriggled again.

'Don't do that.' Leon tightened his grip on her hand. 'Let me finish. I finally admitted to myself I loved you the night of the party. I stood with you in my arms and knew you were my world. I thanked you for marrying me and I had never felt such happiness in my life. Then like Nemesis, Louisa arrived.'

'She does not matter.' Helen lifted her other hand to curl around the nape of his neck and brought his face towards hers. She finally believed Leon loved her; this big, beautiful, austere man loved her.

'All that matters is that you love me, and I love you,' she said unsteadily, her eyes swimming with tears of joy.

'Helen,' he husked, 'I don't deserve you but, God help me, I will never let you go.'

He kissed her with a reverence, a deep tender passion that touched her very soul.

'You love me.' He lifted his head to look deep into her eyes, a gleam of uncertainty in his own.

'You really love me?' he asked in a voice that was raw with feeling. 'Can you can forgive my less than honourable intentions in the beginning?'

'I truly, passionately love you,' she said adamantly. She did not like to see her proud, arrogant husband looking humble. Well, maybe just this once, she thought, happiness bubbling inside her. 'And I will forgive you anything because I love you.'

So much had happened in the past three months. So many misunderstandings and misconceptions, mostly held by her, and on a more serious note she added hesitantly, 'But can you forgive me?' The past could not be changed, but to go forward she knew she had to face and resolve her own demons. 'I think I knew I loved you from the day we married. I admitted as much to myself when you came back from New York the last time. But I never trusted you as I should. I believed the worst over Louisa, and I believed Takis instead of listening to you.'

'So long as you listen to me in future I don't give a damn,' he stated fiercely, and she laughed out loud. Her arrogant, powerful husband was back. 'As I said before I would trust you with my life. Which reminds me—' he speared a hand through her hair, a solemn expression on his darkly attractive face '—are you sure that this pregnancy is safe and what you want? I don't want you put at the slightest risk. I can live without a biological child, but I can't live without you.'

His sentiment was heart-warming but his unspoken suggestion of a termination horrifying. 'Don't be ridiculous. Of course I want our child, and I will be fine, and so will the baby. You're probably worrying because you lost your first child.'

'Actually this will be my first child. After years of marriage when nothing happened Tina said she was fine, so I thought I could not have children, and by that time the marriage was basically a sham anyway. I finally decided to seek a divorce, thinking Tina would leap at the chance to have a family with someone else, but I was wrong. I had not slept with her in over a year when she turned up in Greece for Christmas and crawled into my bed. I am ashamed to say I was quite drunk at the time, and later when she said she was pregnant I could do nothing about it.' He shrugged a shoulder.

'The car accident that killed her was in New York in June, the baby the doctor delivered was full term, so could not possibly have been mine.' An ironic smile twisted his firm mouth. 'The baby survived for a few hours and bore a striking resemblance to her African-American fitness instructor who died with her.'

Helen was speechless. It was the same ironic smile he had given her when she had told him she was sterile, and now she knew why. This strong, proud man had suffered the same pain as her. She placed a tender hand either side of his head and kissed him with all the love and compassion in her heart.

'Ah, Helen.'

Leon groaned and deepened the kiss as passion took over, and within moments Helen was beneath him on the sofa. His hand swept over her breast and thigh to the hem of her skirt, and he froze.

'You're pregnant; is it allowed?'

'Well, some of your more erotic positions might not be viable after a while, but right now anything goes.'

Later that night in bed, with all barriers down and the freedom to reveal their deepest emotions, they made love with soft words, subtle caresses and a tenderness and passion and hunger that superseded everything that had gone before until finally they fell into an exhausted sleep wrapped in each others arms.

Seven months later Leon, all gowned up, walked beside the gurney, holding Helen's hand as they wheeled her towards the operating theatre.

She looked so small even with their child in her body and he had never been so terrified in his life. He loved her so much with a depth of passion that seared his soul. The last few months had been the happiest he had ever known. She was his life, his soul mate, his reason for living, and if anything happened to her his life would be over. But he let none of his fear show as he gently touched her soft cheek.

'Don't worry, I am here.' She looked at him with wide trusting eyes and her beauty tore at his heart. For a man who had never known emotions until she came into his life, Leon's suddenly threatened to get the better of him and he had to blink away the moisture in his eyes.

'I love you and I am going to stay with you every step of the way. Hold onto me and you will be fine.' She gave him a beautiful smile and squeezed his hand as they entered the theatre.

* * *

'Congratulations, Helen, Leon, you have a perfect little baby girl.'

Helen's violet eyes blazing with joy roamed delightedly over the baby. 'A girl. A daughter.' She smiled and glanced up at a hovering Leon. 'Our daughter.'

'I can't believe it,' Leon declared, his dark eyes luminous with tears of happiness and love as they moved from the tiny baby to his wife. 'She is beautiful, just like you—thank you, my love,' he husked, and bent his head to place a soft kiss against her lips. 'I swear I will love and protect you and Nicholas and our miraculous little girl with the last breath in my body.'

Helen saw a tear slide down the sharp blade of his cheekbone. She grasped his hand in hers, her lips parting in a slow, beatific smile. 'I know you will, Leon. I love and trust you totally and I thought we might call our daughter Delia. What do you think?'

'Delia... Yes, of course, I think it is perfect,' Leon agreed, his heart overflowing with love for this tiny, tough, compassionate woman, his wife. 'Delia brought us together and gave us our son, Nicholas. It is fitting.'

'Then you better go and find Nicholas,' Helen murmured drowsily. 'So he can meet his sister.'

Leon did not go immediately; he waited until the doctor was finished, and stayed by her side until she fell into an exhausted sleep. Then he bent to kiss her lips once more, and smooth some silken strands of hair from her brow.

'Sleep well, my love, and when you awake Nicholas and baby Delia and I will be by your side, I promise. Now and for ever more,' he vowed, his voice thick with emotion and pride. Only then did he straighten up, and leave to fetch Nicholas. A man with a dazzling, determined gleam in his dark eyes. A man on a mission for life.

THE BILLIONAIRE'S BLACKMAILED BRIDE

JACQUELINE BAIRD

CHAPTER ONE

'I STILL can't believe you chose this for me,' Emily Fairfax said with a shake of her head as she sat down opposite her older brother Tom and his wife Helen at their table in the vast ballroom of the deluxe London hotel. 'I feel terribly conspicuous.' Embarrassment coloured her face almost as red as the outfit she was wearing.

'Oh, lighten up, Emily. You look great.' Tom grinned at her. 'This is a costume ball for Dad's favourite charity, The Children of Africa's Guardian Angel Project; he would have appreciated the Devil and Angels theme. Dad had a great sense of humour. Remember Mum's fortieth when he insisted everyone dress as Knights and Squires? I think he would have seen the funny side...'

'All too well. Most of the women ended up looking like young boys, dressed in doublet and hose. I wondered at the time if Dad had secret gay tendencies,' she quipped and then turned her sparkling blue gaze on her sister-in-law, a petite gamine-faced brunette. 'But this is different, Helen. There is nothing funny about being squeezed into a red latex suit that is a couple of sizes too small. What on earth were you thinking of when you ordered it?' she demanded, and saw the mischief dancing in Helen's brown eyes and her lips twisted in a wry smile.

Tom and Helen had met at university and had married two

years ago at the age of twenty-three. They were now the proud parents of a one-year-old daughter, who had been born the week before Tom and Emily's father had died suddenly of a massive heart attack. The child was named Sara after their mother, who had died three years earlier after a long battle with cancer.

'I don't know what you are complaining about. You look fine, and I went to a lot of trouble to get that costume in the right size. At four and a half months pregnant I am actually the same bust measurement as you and I tried it on to make sure it would fit,' Helen said with a grin.

'Did it never occur to you that you're five feet nothing and I am five nine—that it would have to go a little further on me?' Emily groaned. 'You damn near broke my neck pulling the hood over my head. It is still aching.' She slipped a hand beneath the heavy fall of her hair and rubbed the nape of her neck to emphasize the point.

'Don't blame me. If you had come back to London yesterday as you were supposed to, you would have had time to get your own costume. But instead you spent another day on site and only arrived a couple of hours before the event. Plus it is April Fool's Day,' she said with an impish grin. 'And be fair— I did cut the hood off and twist it into a braid so you could wear the horns as a head band.' She burst out laughing.

Emily bit her lip to fight down the answering grin that threatened. She had totally forgotten it was the first of April, and Helen was right—she should have returned from Santorini yesterday instead of flying into London this evening. She really had no one to blame but herself, but she wasn't going to let her beloved sister-in-law off too easy.

'Anyone with a grain of common sense would have ordered an angel costume for me. The same as yours, I might add. It is only logical that the women dress as angels and the men as devils. Like my idiot brother T—'

'Excuse me.' A deep, slightly accented voice cut into Emily's good-natured tirade. 'Hello, Tom, nice to see you again.'

'Anton, glad you and your friends could make it.'

Emily looked over at her brother as he greeted the new arrivals he had invited to make up their table of eight.

She glanced up at the man who had so rudely interrupted her. His back was turned to her and he was pulling out a chair for his companion, a stunning brunette who naturally was dressed like an angel in a diaphanous gold and white fabric that seemed to reveal a lot more flesh than Emily imagined any self-respecting angel would reveal.

At least her outfit covered her from neck to toe, she consoled herself, though she had been forced to undo the front zip a few inches to prevent the damn thing crushing her chest so tightly she could barely breathe. It wasn't her usual style, that was for sure, but it didn't really faze her. She knew she had a decent enough body, she just wasn't used to displaying it quite so dramatically.

'Allow me to introduce my friend Eloise,' the deep voice continued as the brunette sent a social smile around the table, 'and my right-hand man, Max.'

Emily glanced at the middle-aged burly man and smiled in welcome as he took his seat at the table next to Helen. Then the stranger turned to her.

'Emily, isn't it? Tom has told me a lot about you. It is a real pleasure to finally meet you. I am Anton Diaz.' A large strong hand was held out and she politely put her hand in his, while her mind busily wondered how Tom knew the man, and why her brother would have mentioned her to him.

Then suddenly her mind went blank as a bizarre sensation a bit like an electric eel snaking up her arm had her skin breaking out in goose-bumps under the latex. Hastily she pulled her hand free and slowly looked up.

Emily had a long way to go... He had to be at least six feet four, she reckoned, and then her curious blue gaze collided with deep brown eyes and she simply stared...

The man was like a sleek black panther: poised, powerful and predatory.

She grimaced inwardly at the fanciful notion, really not her usual style.

The introductions moved on and Emily supposed she had made the right response, though she could not be sure. Her mouth felt dry and she had trouble tearing her fascinated gaze away from the tall, striking man.

He was dressed all in black. A black silk-knit roll-necked sweater outlined the impressive musculature of his broad chest. A short black cloak covered his wide shoulders and flowed down like bats' wings to broad cuffs around strong wrists, set off by tailored black trousers. He should have looked ridiculous in costume like the majority of the people present. Instead, if ever a man looked like a devil it was this one...

Dark and dangerous, she thought, her heart inexplicably tightening in her chest, and for a moment she had difficulty breathing that had nothing to do with the latex suit she wore.

His straight black hair worn slightly longer than was fashionable was swept casually back off his broad forehead. Distinctive arched brows framed deep-set almost black eyes, high cheekbones, a large hawklike nose and a wide sensuous mouth completed the picture. As she stared his lips parted to reveal even white teeth. He was smiling down at her. She lifted her eyes to his and even in her stunned state she recognized the humour did not entirely mask the cool remoteness of his dark gaze.

The man was not conventionally handsome, his features too large and harshly chiselled for classic male beauty.

Brutally handsome…was a better description.

There was something insulting about the way his dark eyes slid casually down to her cleavage and lingered for a long moment. But even as she recognized his insolent masculine appraisal for what it was her skin prickled with shocking awareness. The breath caught in her throat and she gave a shaky inward sigh of relief when he casually pulled out the chair next to hers, and lowered his long length into it.

It could be worse, Emily told herself, at least with Anton Diaz seated at her side, she did not have to face him.

Instinctively she recognized he was a man who was supremely confident in his masculinity and totally aware of his effect on the opposite sex, and discreetly she crossed her arms over her suddenly hardening nipples. A sophisticated charmer with an aura of ruthless power about him that would intimidate anybody, man or woman, she concluded. Not her type at all…

Even so, there was no escaping the fact he was an incredibly sexy man, as her body's unexpected response confirmed.

'I could not help overhearing your comment, Emily. Shame on you, your chauvinism is showing.' The devil spoke in a deep, dark, mocking voice that made her hackles rise.

'What do you mean, Mr Diaz?' she asked him with cool politeness, flicking him a sidelong glance, and was once again captured by the intensity of his dark eyes.

'In today's world of equality between the sexes isn't it rather politically incorrect to assume all the women should dress as angels and the men as devils? And, given the very striking outfit you are wearing, just a little hypocritical,' he drawled mockingly.

'He has got you there,' Helen piped up and everyone laughed.

Everyone but Emily.

'My costume was my sister-in-law's choice, not mine. She has a warped sense of humour,' she explained, forcing a smile to her lips. 'And I see you are dressed as a devil, rather upholding my theory. Though you do seem to have forgotten the horns,' she prompted smoothly.

'No, I didn't forget. I never forget anything,' he asserted, his dark eyes holding hers with an intimacy that made her pulse race and she could do nothing about the pink that tinged her cheeks. 'I am supposed to be an angel, admittedly a dark angel, but an angel nevertheless.'

Emily saw what he meant, her blue eyes sweeping over him. It was the perfect costume for him. Unrelenting black and somehow threatening… She glimpsed a darkening in his deep-set eyes and something more. Anger… Why? She had no idea, and in an attempt to control her overheated imagination and body she looked somewhere past his left shoulder. She took a deep steadying breath, but for a long moment was incapable of making a response. No man had ever had such a startling effect on her in her life, and she had met plenty, and been attracted to a few, but never quite like this.

She was a twenty-four-year-old freelance marine archaeologist and had spent the last two years since qualifying gaining experience in her field. She had been on a few seagoing explorations. Her colleagues were mostly men, explorers, divers and fellow archaeologists with the skills needed to search and map out underwater wrecks and artifacts. Yet never once had she felt the sudden heat, the stomach-churning excitement that this man aroused in her with one look.

Get a grip, girl, she told herself. He was with his very beautiful girlfriend and, while Emily considered herself passably attractive, she was no competition for the lovely Eloise.

What was she thinking of?

At twenty-one, after a disastrous engagement that had ended abruptly after three days when she had found her fiancé in bed with her flatmate at university, she had sworn off men.

Nigel had been an accountant in her father's firm. A man she had fallen in love with at sixteen, a man who had kissed her at her eighteenth birthday party and declared he felt the same, a man who had offered her comfort and support when her mother was ill and died, a man whose proposal she had accepted shortly after. A man who, when she had confronted him in bed with her flatmate, had actually admitted the affair had been going on for a year. Her flatmate, her supposed friend, twisted the knife by telling her she was a fool. Nigel's interest in Emily had only ever been for her money and connections.

Which was a laugh. Admittedly the family home was probably worth millions in today's market, but they lived in it, had done for generations. The business earned the shareholders a decent dividend each year but not a fortune by any means, but at the time she had felt utterly betrayed. She would no more compete for a man than fly to the moon, and, to be honest, over the intervening years, she had never felt the need. Which was probably why she had never since had a long-term relationship? she thought wryly.

'Yes, of course, I see it now, a silly mistake on my part,' she finally responded.

'You're forgiven,' he said with a smile that took her breath away all over again.

But at that moment the last two guests making up the table arrived and Emily smiled with relief. It was her aunt Lisa, her father's older sister, and her husband, James Browning, who was also the Chairman of the Board of Fairfax Engineering since her dad's death. She felt the light brush of Anton's shoulder against hers as, like a perfect gentleman, he stood up until Lisa was seated, and she determinedly ignored it.

Her equilibrium thankfully restored…

James took the seat on the other side of Emily. 'Aunt Lisa, Uncle James, it's good to see you,' she offered, her wayward emotions firmly under control.

But it was the *sotto voce* comment that Anton Diaz made among the flurry of introduction as he sat back down that threw her off balance yet again. 'But if a devil is more to your liking I'm sure something can be arranged.'

Her mouth open, her face scarlet, she stared at Anton. One dark brow rose in sardonic query, before he turned to respond to Eloise's rather loud request for champagne.

Was she hearing things? Had he actually made such a blatantly flirtatious comment or had she imagined what he said?

She did not know…and she did not know whether to feel angry or flattered as dinner was served. Emily's emotions stayed in pretty much the same state of flux until it was over; she was intensely aware of the man at her side.

The conversation was sociable, and when the meal ended and the band began to play Emily could not help watching Anton and Eloise as they took to the dance floor. Both Latin in looks, they made a striking couple and the way Eloise curved into her partner's body, her arms firmly clasped around his neck, left no one in any doubt of the intimacy of their relationship.

Emily turned to James and asked what she had been dying to ask all evening. Who exactly was Anton Diaz?

According to her uncle, Anton Diaz was the founder of a private equity business that made massive profits out of buying, restructuring and then selling on great chunks of worldwide businesses. It made him a man of enormous influence and power. It had also made him extremely rich. He was revered worldwide as a financial genius, with a fortune to match. His nationality was hazy, his name was hispanic, yet some considered him Greek because he spoke the language like a native. Rumours about him abounded. Her aunt Lisa offered the most colourful speculation that his grandmother had been the madam of a high-class brothel in Peru, and her daughter had been a wealthy Greek's mistress for years and Anton Diaz was the result of the affair.

Her aunt also informed her archly that he owned a magnificent villa on a Greek island, a vast estate in Peru, a luxurious apartment in New York and another in Sydney. Recently he had acquired a prestigious office block in London with a stunning penthouse at the top, and there were probably more. Plus the parties he held on his huge luxury yacht were legendary.

James attempted to steer the conversation back to less gossipy ground by continuing that he knew Anton was multilingual because he had heard him employ at least four languages when they had first met at a European conference a couple of months ago. Since then they had become business acquaintances and friends of a sort, hence Tom inviting Anton and his party to join them tonight. In fact, Anton Diaz's expert advice had been instrumental in them deciding to diversify and expand Fairfax Engineering, James informed her in an almost reverential tone.

It was news to Emily that the firm needed revising or expanding, but she had no time to dwell on that revelation as her aunt chimed in again. Apparently Anton was a confirmed bachelor and as famous for the women he had bedded as he was for his financial skills. His countless affairs were apparently well documented by the press, actresses and models featuring prominently.

Emily believed her uncle and aunt and in a sense felt relieved. Her earlier reaction to Anton Diaz had been normal under the circumstances. The man exuded a raw animal magnetism that probably affected every woman he met the same way, and if his press was to be believed he took full advantage of the fact. He was not the type of man any self-respecting woman would want to get involved with.

After her one disastrous relationship Emily had very firm ideas on the type of man she eventually wanted to marry. She wanted a like-minded man she could trust. Certainly not a womanizing, globe-trotting billionaire, plus she was in no hurry to marry—she enjoyed her work far too much to think of curtailing her career for any man for years yet.

Draining her coffee-cup, she smiled at James and Lisa affectionately as they decided to dance. Then looking around the table, she saw only the burly Max was left.

Emily was naturally a happy, confident girl with a successful career and a growing name in her field of expertise. She was also a realist and never let anything she could not change bother her for long. She was a firm believer in making the best of any situation. Neither the blatantly sexy costume she wore nor her strange reaction to the indomitable Anton Diaz was going to prevent her enjoying the evening.

'So, Max, would you like to dance?' she asked with a broad smile. She watched him blink, then grin and leap to his feet with alacrity.

'It will be my pleasure,' he said as he pulled out her chair. His brown eyes widened as she rose to her feet, sweeping over the length of her body with unconcealed admiration. 'You are a very lovely lady, señorita,' he said, taking her hand and leading her to the dance floor.

Max was about an inch taller than Emily, and quite a lot wider, but for a heavy man he was a very good dancer and surprisingly light on his feet. Emily relaxed in his hold and began to have fun.

* * *

Anton Diaz allowed a small satisfied smile to curve his hard mouth. True, the man he had really wanted to meet, Charles Fairfax, had died a year ago. But his family and firm still existed, and would do just as well for his purpose.

He glanced around the glittering throng. London's social élite letting their hair down in a costume ball in aid of African children, and apparently a favoured charity of the Fairfax family. The bitter irony of it did not escape him and for a moment his black eyes glinted with an unholy light.

Last December when his mother, as if sensing the end was near, had finally told him the truth about the death of his sister Suki twenty-six years ago it had given him one hell of a shock. Actually Suki had been his half-sister, but as a child he had never thought of her like that. To him she had been his older sister who took care of him.

He had believed Suki died in a car accident, tragic but unavoidable. But apparently she had deliberately driven her car off a cliff and left a note for his mother that she had immediately destroyed.

Suki had committed suicide because she had been convinced it was due to her family name and her illegitimacy that her lover, Charles Fairfax, had left her and married someone else. Then his mother had made him promise never to be ashamed of his name or his heritage.

Bitterness and bile rose in his throat just thinking about it now. He had named his company in memory of Suki, but the name had an added poignancy now. The letter he had discovered among his mother's papers after her death had confirmed she had told him the truth and more, and he had vowed on his mother's grave to avenge the insult to his sister no matter how long it took.

He was not a fan of costume parties and usually avoided them like the plague, but on this occasion he had an ulterior motive for accepting the invitation to share a table with the Fairfax family.

A deep frown marred his broad brow. Never in his hugely successful career had he ever had any trouble taking over any company he wanted and Fairfax Engineering should have been an easy acquisition. His first idea had been a hostile takeover bid and then the destruction of the company, but on studying the firm's set-up he was reluctantly forced to the conclusion that plan would not work.

The problem was the company was privately owned by family members and a small portion was diverted into a share scheme for the workforce. Also unfortunately for him it was well run and profitable. It had originally been based on the ownership of a coalmine, but a previous Fairfax had had the foresight to expand into engineering. Now that coalmining was virtually defunct in Britain the firm had found a niche market building a specific type of earth-moving equipment that was used in most countries in Europe.

With a few discreet enquiries it had become obvious none of the principal shareholders was prepared to sell even at a very generous price, and, while not giving up on a buyout, he had been obliged to adopt another strategy.

He had planned to persuade the company it would be in their best interest to expand into America and China, with his expert advice and generous financial backing, of course. Then when they had overextended themselves financially he could step in and pull the rug from under them and take the firm, in the process virtually bankrupting the Fairfax family. With that in mind he had deliberately made the acquaintance of the chairman of the board, and the MD, Tom, the son of Charles Fairfax.

The only downside to his strategy was it was taking him a hell of a lot longer than he had anticipated to grind the Fairfax name into the dust. Three months of manoeuvring and, while he was closer to attaining his goal, he wasn't there yet. The problem was the son and uncle that ran the business were both competent but very conservative businessmen and, again unfortunately for Anton, neither of them appeared to be particularly greedy or the type to take unnecessary risks.

But why would they be? he thought cynically. The company was over a hundred and sixty years old and they had never had to fight to make a living or to be accepted by their peers.

'Anton, darling, what are you thinking?'

He disliked the question, though he had heard it often enough and experience had taught him where women were concerned it was best ignored or answered with a white lie. Exasperated, he looked down at the woman in his arms. 'The latest figure on the Dow Jones—nothing that would interest you.'

'My figure is the only one you should be thinking of,' she responded with a pout, plastering herself to him.

'Save the flirting for your husband. I'm immune,' he said bluntly. Eloise was very beautiful, but she did nothing for him except remind him of his sister. That was why he had helped her out of a bad situation twelve years ago in Lima when her manager at the time had signed her up for what was undeniably a porn movie. He got her out of the contract and found her a reputable manager and they had been friends ever since. She was married to a close friend of his and yet given the chance she wasn't above trying to seduce him.

He supposed it was his own fault in a way because once, a decade ago, he had succumbed to her charms one night, though he had very quickly realized he had made a big mistake. Their friendship had survived, and now it was a game she played whenever they met, and he could not entirely blame her. He should have got tough with her long since.

Eloise was her husband's responsibility now. He had to stop pandering to her constant whims this time to hold her hand while she auditioned for a lead in a West End musical. Actually it had been no hardship because he was staying in London a lot more than he had at first anticipated. He had Fairfax Engineering firmly in his sights… He almost felt sorry for the son and daughter; they were young and no competition for him.

He thought of the report he had got from the investigator some months ago. The only photo of the daughter was of a woman standing on a deserted beach with the ocean behind her, wearing a baseball cap that masked her eyes, an oversized shirt and combat trousers. There had been no point of reference to say if she was tall or short, fat or thin.

He had been surprised when he saw her seated at the table. The photo had not done her justice. A ridiculous horned headband held back a shinning mane of blonde hair that fell smooth as silk down past her shoulder blades. Whether the colour was natural or dyed he didn't know, but it looked good. She had the peaches and cream complexion of a stereotypical English rose with magnificent big blue eyes, a full-lipped wide mouth and her breasts looked just about perfect. As for the rest he could not tell, average height maybe. But as a connoisseur of women he would reserve judgement until he saw her standing up. She could quite possibly have a big behind and short stumpy legs. Not that it concerned him; he wasn't going there. The fact she was a Fairfax was a huge turn-off; he wouldn't touch her if she were the last woman in the world.

Charles Fairfax had married the Honourable Sara Deveral in what had been the society wedding of the year twenty-six years ago. His wife had borne him a son nine months later, Tom, and a daughter, Emily, a year after that. The perfect family…

Emily Fairfax had led a charmed life. She had the best of everything. A loving family, a good education, a career of sorts as a freelance archaeologist, and she moved in London society with a confidence that was bred in the bone. The likes of Charles Fairfax were big on breeding, and the thought brought back the bitter resentment that had simmered within him since the death of his mother.

'I don't believe it.' Eloise tilted back her head and Anton glanced down at her. 'Max is actually dancing the tango...'

Anton was diverted from his sombre thoughts and followed his partner's gaze, his dark eyes widening in shock and something more as they settled on his Head of Security and erstwhile bodyguard, though Max, at fifty, was more of a friend than anything else. He hadn't registered the band was playing the tango.

When Anton had a woman in his arms he held her close and naturally moved to the rhythm of the music, the steps not important. But Max was old school and was dancing the tango with all the passion and arrogance of a real aficionado. Incredibly his partner was with him every step of the way.

His eyes narrowed, absorbing the picture she presented. Emily Fairfax was stunning, and the only reason Anton had thought she was average height was instantly apparent. She had fantastically long legs in proportion to her height, a round tight behind, narrow waist and high firm breasts. The red suit was glued to her like a second skin leaving absolutely nothing to the imagination and as Max swung her around Anton doubted there was a man in the room who wasn't watching her. Her blonde hair swung around her shoulders in a shimmering cloud as she moved. And what a mover... An instant pleasurable though inconvenient sensation stirred in Anton's loins.

'Don't they look ridiculous?' Eloise tugged on his neck. 'No one dances like that these days.'

'What…? Yes…' he lied, for once less than his suave self, while silently conceding the pair looked superb, and the majority of people on the floor had stopped to watch. Max dipped Emily low over his arm, her hair touching the floor as the music drew to a close. Anton saw Emily grin as Max lifted her upright and then burst out laughing as the applause echoed around the ballroom.

The woman was not afraid of making an exhibition of herself, and, given the fire and passion in the way she danced, she was definitely no innocent. Such passion could not be confined solely to the dance floor; he recalled that she had been engaged once, according to the report he had read, and there had probably been quite a few men since.

Suddenly, having decided he would not touch her if she were the last woman on earth, Anton was imagining her long, lithesome naked body under his, and it took all his self-control to rein in his rampant libido—something that hadn't happened to him in years.

Deep in thought, he frowned as he led Eloise back to the table. He had set out to destroy Fairfax Engineering, everything Charles Fairfax owned, but he had to concede it was going to take him some time. But now an alternative scenario, a way to hedge his bet on gaining control of the company, formed in his Machiavellian mind. The solution he reached had a perfect poetic justice to it that made his firm lips twist in a brief, decidedly sinister smile.

Marriage had never appealed to him before, but he was thirty-seven, an ideal time to take a wife and produce an heir to inherit his fortune. He bred horses in Peru, and at least physically Emily Fairfax was good breeding stock, he assessed sardonically. As for her morals, he wasn't bothered about the past men in her life, with what he had on her family, she would dance to his tune and disruption to his life would be minimal. He frowned again; maybe Emily Fairfax had a man in her life now. Not that he was afraid of competition—he never had any trouble getting any woman he wanted. With his incredible wealth his problem was the reverse: fighting them off. And Emily had no partner with her tonight, which left him a clear field.

'Thank you, Max.' Emily was still smiling as her dancing partner held out her chair for her. 'I really enjoyed that,' she said as she sat down.

'It is good to see the fortune the parents spent on sending us both to dancing classes wasn't completely wasted,' Tom said, grinning as he and Helen sat down.

'The lessons were certainly wasted on you,' Helen quipped. 'I don't think my feet will ever recover.'

Lisa piped up with, 'Join the club—after forty years of marriage and countless attempts at dancing James still has two left feet.'

Emily laughed at the friendly banter between her family and friends, unaware that the other couple had returned to the table.

CHAPTER TWO

IT WAS a shock when into the cheerful atmosphere Anton Diaz laid a hand on Emily's arm and asked her for the next dance.

She wanted to refuse, but, glancing at Max, she saw he had taken Eloise's hand and was obviously going to dance with her. The hostile look the other woman gave Anton said louder than words she wasn't delighted at the change of partner.

'Go on, Emily,' Tom encouraged. 'You know you love dancing.' He grinned. 'And if our wives are to be believed James and I are useless. Anton is your only chance.'

'Thanks, brother.' Emily snorted and reluctantly accepted and rose to her feet.

Anton gave her a wry smile. 'Your brother lacks a little subtlety,' he drawled as if he knew exactly what she was thinking. 'But I am not complaining if it gets you in my arms.'

Then, rather than taking her arm, he placed his own very firmly around her waist, his strong hand curving over her hip-bone as he urged her towards the dance floor. His touch was much too personal and his great body much too close for Emily's comfort and it only got worse...

As soon as they reached the dance floor he turned her to face him, his arm tightening around her waist as he drew her closer, and at that moment the band began playing a dreamy ballad. She stiffened in his hold, determined to resist a sudden inexplicable desire to collapse against him as he took her hand and linked his fingers with hers and cradled it against his broad chest.

'You surprised me, Emily,' he said, his dark eyes seeking hers. 'You dance the tango superbly—I was quite envious of Max,' he admitted. 'Though to be honest, dancing is not one of my talents. I could not tango to save my life. I am more a shuffle-to-the-music man,' he said with a self-effacing grin that lightened his saturnine features, making him look somewhat approachable. 'So I hope you won't be disappointed,' he concluded with a querying arch of one black brow.

Disappointed… It was a rare occurrence for Emily to dance with a man she had literally to look up to and it turned out to be frighteningly seductive. He fitted her perfectly and, enveloped in his arms, the black cloak enfolding her created an added intimacy. Disappointment was not an emotion troubling Emily, though a host of others were. With his long leg subtly easing between hers as he turned her slowly to the romantic music, her pulse raced, her heart pounded and every nerve end in her body was screaming with tension as she battled to retain control of her wayward body. The damn latex suit was no help; it simply emphasized every brush of his muscular body against hers. And she seriously doubted Anton Diaz had ever disappointed a woman in his life. Certainly not the lovely Eloise, and the thought cooled her helpless reaction to him enough for her to respond.

'Oh, I think not,' she said with blunt honesty. She knew she was reasonably attractive and she had been hit on by many men over the years, but since her failed engagement she had learnt to put men off with no trouble. 'I also think, Mr Diaz, a man of your wealth and power is perfectly well aware of his talents and exploits them quite ruthlessly for his own ends.' Anton might make her heart beat faster—her and the rest of the female population—but she had no intention of falling for his charm. 'As I'm sure the tabloids and your friend Eloise could confirm,' she ended dryly.

'Ah, Emily, you have been listening to gossip. What was it? I was brought up in a brothel surrounded by willing women,' he mocked. 'Sorry to disappoint, but it is not true, though my grandmother did own one,' he admitted, 'and it is a poor reflection on the male of the species that she made rather a lot of money. Enough to send her daughter to the best school in the country and on to a finishing school in Switzerland.'

Emily's blue eyes widened in surprise at his blunt revelations, her tension forgotten as she listened intrigued as he continued.

'When she was in Europe she met and fell in love with a Greek man who was unfortunately married with children. But he was decent enough to set her up in a house in Corinth where I was born. Their affair lasted for years, he died when I was twelve and my mother decided to return to Peru.'

'That is so sad. Your poor mother, you poor boy,' she murmured. Totally absorbed in his story, she compassionately squeezed his hand.

'I might have guessed you would feel sorry for me.' His dark head bent and his lips brushed her brow. 'Ah, Emily, you are so naive and so misguided. As a wealthy man's mistress my mother was never poor in the monetary sense and neither was I.' He looked into her big blue eyes, his own gleaming with cynical amusement. 'I hate to disillusion you, but your sympathy is wasted on me.'

'So why did you tell me all that?' she asked, puzzled. He did not strike her as the sort of man who would bare his soul to a relative stranger.

'Maybe because it got you to relax in my arms.' He smiled.

'Was it all lies?' she shot back, her body stiffening again, this time in anger.

'Not all...I actually am a bastard.' He grinned, the hand at her waist stroking slowly up her back, drawing her closer still. And she involuntarily trembled in his hold. 'And as you so rightly said,' he drawled softly, 'I use all the talents I have to get what I want. And I want you, Emily Fairfax.'

Stunned by his outrageous comment, she stared up into his night-black eyes, and saw the desire he made no attempt to hide. 'You devious devil,' she exclaimed.

'Angel,' he amended, his dark head dipping, his warm breath tickling her ear as he urged her hard against him, making her intimately aware of his aroused state. 'And the way you tremble in my arms I know you want me. The attraction between us was instant and electric so don't pretend otherwise, Emily,' he commanded, and straightened up.

'You're unbelievable,' she gasped. Though she could not deny the trembling, or the attraction, she had no intention of succumbing to such blatant seduction. 'Coming on to me when you have the beautiful Eloise with—'

He cut her off. 'Eloise is a very old friend, nothing more I can assure you, and so could her husband,' he said, his dark eyes holding hers, a wicked gleam in their ebony depths. 'She is quite a famous television star in Latin America, but she has ambitions to be famous worldwide. Which is why she is over here to discuss the possibility of starring in a musical production in the West End next year. She is going back to her husband tomorrow so you have nothing to be jealous about.'

'Jealous. Are you crazy? I don't even know you,' Emily spluttered.

'That is soon remedied. I will call you tomorrow and arrange a time for our dinner date,' he declared, and stopped dancing, his hands sliding to span her waist, and hold her still. 'But now I think we'd better get back to the table, before people start to gossip. The music has ended.'

Emily had not noticed, and, embarrassed, she followed him like a lamb to slaughter, she realized later…much later…

'For heaven's sake, Emily, will you stop devouring that disgusting fry-up—it is turning my stomach—and listen to me,' Helen declared. 'You have to put the poor man out of his misery and have dinner with him. He has sent you roses every single day and the housekeeper is fed up with taking his phone calls. The house is overflowing with blooms and in my pregnant state I might very well get hay fever.'

Emily popped the last bit of fried egg into her mouth, chewed, then grinned at her sister-in-law. 'You know the solution—I told you to throw the flowers away. I'm not interested.'

'Liar—the woman is not born who would not fancy Anton Diaz. Your trouble is you're afraid to get involved after the hateful Nigel. You haven't dated any man for more than a couple of weeks in years.'

'*Moi*?' Emily quipped, placing a hand on her heart. 'I am not afraid of anyone, but I know a devil when I see one, and Anton Diaz is not the kind of man any sensible woman would ever get involved with.'

'Forget the sensible, and live a little. You're at home for the next few months and your research at the museum does not take more than a couple of days a week. It is spring, when a young woman's fancy turns to love.'

'A young man's fancy, you mean, and Anton Diaz is no young man,' Emily responded dryly.

'So what if he is a dozen or more years older than you? You

have plenty of spare time and a wild passionate affair with an experienced man would do you the world of good.'

'I don't think so, and I have no time right now. I am going to view another apartment today,' Emily said, hoping to change the subject, because the subject of Anton Diaz had taken up a great deal of her waking thoughts since the night she had met him. His phone calls she had refused after the first day as just the sound of his deep accented voice made her temperature rise and her whole body blush; the daily roses she could do nothing about.

'Oh, for heaven's sake, Emily, forget about buying an apart-ment. It's a stupid idea. This is your family home, has been for generations since the first Fairfax made his fortune as a coal baron in the nineteenth century, and it is big enough for all of us and half a dozen more.'

Helen rolled her eyes around the spacious breakfast room of the ten-bedroomed double-fronted Georgian house in the heart of Kensington. 'I would hate it if you left and you would hate living on your own. Admit it. And you might as well admit you fancy Anton Diaz something rotten. I have seen the way you try not to blush every time his name is mentioned. You can't fool me.'

Emily groaned. 'Your trouble is, Helen, you know me far too well.' She rose to her feet and smiled wryly down at her sister-in-law. 'I am still going to look at the apartment, though. After all, if I am going to have a wild, passionate affair I will need a place of my own. I'm sure you wouldn't appreciate my bringing a lover back here where your gorgeous child might see and hear more than she should.' She grinned.

'You're going to do it—you're going out with the man?'

'Maybe if Anton calls again and asks me out I will accept. Satisfied?'

'You will accept what?' Tom demanded as he walked into the room, with his daughter in his arms.

'Emily is going out with Anton Diaz,' Helen declared.

'Is that wise, sis?' he asked Emily, his blue eyes serious as they rested on her. 'He is a hell of a lot older than you. Are you sure you know what you are doing? Don't get me wrong, he is a great guy and his business knowledge is second to none—his input and advice to Fairfax Engineering has been exceptional. But he is the type of man that makes other men want to lock up their wives and daughters. The man definitely lives in the fast lane and has a poor track record with women.'

'I don't believe it!' Emily exclaimed. 'Much as I love you two, you should work at coordinating your opinions and advice.' And, grinning, she walked out.

Fate, kismet, whatever it was, but as she entered the hall the telephone rang and she answered. Anton…

'You're a very hard lady to get hold of, Emily. But I like a challenge. Have dinner with me tonight?'

So, she did what she had wanted to do for days and said yes…

Emily viewed the apartment and decided against it. Then spent the rest of the morning at the museum, and the afternoon shopping for a new dress.

Emily smiled, happy with her reflection in the mirror, and, straightening her shoulders, she picked up her dark blue wrap and matching purse from the bed and left the room. She was nervous, butterflies were fluttering in her stomach, but none of her inner emotions showed as she opened the drawing-room door and walked in. Anton Diaz was picking her up at seven and it was ten to.

'Well, Helen, will I do?' She smiled at her sister-in-law reclining on a sofa, a glass of juice in her hand, and saw the embarrassed expression on her face just as a deep dark voice responded.

'You look beautiful, Emily.'

Emily turned her head, her eyes widening as Anton walked towards her from the far side of the room, Tom trailing in his wake.

'Thank you.' She accepted the compliment politely, but it was an effort. She had thought he looked dangerous dressed as a dark angel, but in a perfectly tailored light grey suit with a white shirt and silk tie he looked gorgeous. 'You're early,' she added, raising her eyes to his face. He had stopped barely a foot from her, and his dark gaze slid slowly over her from head to toe, then he lifted his eyes to hers and what she saw in the smouldering black depths made the breath catch in her throat.

For the second time in a week Anton Diaz could not control his instant arousal at the sight of a woman. He had seen a photo of Emily in baggy clothes, and seen her in a very sexy latex suit with her hair down. But the Emily who stood before him now was something else again. She was the personification of sophisticated elegance.

Her blonde hair was swept up into a knot on top of her head, her make-up understated, but perfect. Her big blue eyes were accentuated even more by the clever use of cosmetics, her full lips a soft glossy rose. As for her gown, it was designer; he had bought enough over the years to know. Ice-blue to match her eyes, it was cut on the bias, the bodice, supported by slight straps, clung faithfully to her high firm breasts and subtly shaped her narrow waist and hips to flare ever so slightly a few inches from the hem that ended on her knees. Not too short to appear tacky, but short enough for a man to fantasize about slipping his hand beneath it.

'Beautiful does not do you justice—you look exquisite, Emily. I will be the envy of every man in the restaurant.' Reaching for a cashmere wrap that she held in her hand, he gently took it and slipped it over her shoulders. 'Shall we go?'

It was definitely going to be no hardship to bed the lovely Emily, the finer details of when and where were all he had to decide on, he thought as he battled to control his libido.

Amazingly, Tom Fairfax, despite his usual easygoing nature, had taken him to one side when he had arrived and told him quite seriously he expected Anton to behave himself with Emily and return her home at a reasonable hour. No one had attempted to tell him what to do in years, if ever, and he had been too stunned to reply when Emily had walked into the room.

He could understand the man's concern, but it simply reminded him that he had been unable to take care of his own sister, and the memory cooled his wayward body in an instant.

Emily was too flustered to do more than take the hand Anton offered her. She felt his hand tighten on hers, and caught a flicker of some strange emotion in his dark eyes, gone as he turned and said goodnight to Tom and Helen.

He opened the passenger door of a silver Bentley and ushered her inside. She watched as he walked around the bonnet and slid behind the wheel. He glanced at her, one brow arched enquiringly, and she realized she was staring like a besotted fool.

'Where are you taking me?' She blurted the first thing that came into her head.

He chuckled a deep dark sound. 'To dinner, Emily.' Slipping a hand around her neck, he tilted her face to his dark eyes dancing with amusement. 'But ultimately to my bed.'

His provocative statement had her lips parting in a shocked gasp, and Anton's mouth covered them, firm, warm and tender. Her lips tingled and trembled as his hand trailed around her throat, his fingers curving around her small chin to hold her firm as the tip of his tongue sought hers with an eroticism that ignited a sudden warmth deep inside her. Her eyes closed and her hands slid up to clasp his nape, her fingers trailing involuntarily into the silken blackness of his hair as he deepened the kiss, his tongue probing the moist interior of her mouth, and the slow-burning heat ignited into flame.

'Emily.' He raised his head, and lifted her hands from their death-like grip around his neck. 'Emily, we have to go.'

She looked dazedly up at him, then down at his hands holding hers. Had she really flung her arms around him and clung like a limpet? And suddenly the heat of arousal became the heat of embarrassment.

'What did you do that for?' she asked.

'I believe in getting the first kiss over with quickly, instead of wondering all evening, and to be blunt you have kept me waiting a week already.' He grinned.

'I'm surprised you persisted.' She grinned back, suddenly feeling wonderful, all her doubts and fears about Anton wiped out by his kiss.

'I surprised myself. I am of the W.C. Fields train of thought. If at first you don't succeed, try, try, and then give up—there is no point in being a damn fool about it. Usually two approaches with no response and I move on. But in your case I made an exception. You should be flattered.'

Emily chuckled. 'You are impossibly arrogant, Anton.'

'Yes, but you like me.' He grinned and started the car.

The restaurant was exclusive, the food superb and Anton the perfect dinner companion. His conversation was witty and gradually she relaxed. He told her he spent a lot of time travelling between his head office in New York, and the subsidiaries in Sydney, London and Athens, where he had an island villa within commuting distance by helicopter. But he tried to spend the winter months on his estate in Peru.

Without being aware of it, Emily was already half in love with him by the time he took her home.

'Admit it, Emily, you enjoyed yourself tonight,' Anton prompted as he stopped the car outside her home and turned to look at her. 'I am not quite the ogre you thought, hmm?' And he slid an arm around her shoulders.

'I concede you really are very civilized and, yes, I did enjoy myself.' The champagne she had consumed making her ever so slightly tipsy, she smiled up at him and added, 'But you are still arrogant.'

'Maybe, but will you allow me to take you out again tomorrow night?' he asked formally, but there was nothing formal about the sensual gleam in the black depths of the eyes that held hers as he drew her close.

'Yes,' she murmured, and watched in helpless anticipation as his dark head bent and his wide mouth covered hers.

The second kiss was even better than the first and she leant into him with bone-melting enthusiasm, her arms eagerly wrapping around his neck. She felt his great body tense, felt the brush of one hand against the fabric covering her breast as he deepened the kiss, his tongue searching her mouth with a skilful eroticism that sent shuddering sensations of pure pleasure coursing hotly through her slender body.

She inhaled the unique masculine scent of him, trembled with wild excitement at the pleasure of his kiss, a kiss so deep, so passionate, she never wanted to come up for air. When his fingers closed around the strap of her dress she quivered, but made no objection as he peeled the fabric down over her braless breasts.

He raised his head and she didn't understand his husky

words as he palmed her breast, his long fingers grazing over the rosy tip. Her whole body jerked and her head fell back as he lowered his head and his mouth closed over an exposed nipple. Fierce sensations lanced from her breasts to her loins, moisture pooling between her thighs. She groaned out loud as with tongue and teeth he teased her rigid nipples, until she was a quivering mass of heated sensations she had never experienced before, never believed existed until now.

She threaded her hands through his dark hair, and held him to her aching body, wanting more. She felt the gentle trail of his strong hand sliding beneath her skirt, stroking up the silken smoothness of her thigh, felt his long fingers trace the thin strip of lace between her legs. Involuntarily her legs parted and one long finger edged beneath her panties.

'My God!' Anton exclaimed, rearing back. 'What the hell am I doing?'

She stared up at him, her body sprawled back against the seat in total abandonment, her blue eyes glittering wildly and her pale skin flushed with the heat of arousal at the hands of a man for the first time in her twenty-four years. Quickly he smoothed her skirt down over her thighs and hauled her up in the seat, slipping the straps of her dress back over her shoulder, and placing her wrap carefully around her, folding it over her still-tingling breasts.

'That's better,' he said, his dark eyes suddenly shadowed.

Emily's body still pulsed with sensation, but slowly it dawned on her Anton was no way near as affected.

'Sorry, Emily, I never meant to take things so far in the car of all places.' He smoothed a few tendrils of hair from her brow. 'Damn it to hell, I promised your brother I would look after you.' He swore.

That did get through to Emily. 'You promised my brother...'

she exclaimed. 'You mean Tom had the nerve... I'll kill him.' She could not believe her own brother, and her embarrassment at her helpless capitulation to Anton was overtaken by her anger at Tom. 'He seems to forget I am a grown woman and perfectly able to look after myself.'

'I'm sure you are,' Anton agreed. 'But right now you better get indoors, before I lose control completely,' he added with a self-derisory grimace as he got out of the car and walked around to open the passenger door. He slipped an arm around her waist and led her to the imposing front door of her home. 'I won't come in, I don't dare.' Dropping a swift kiss on the top of her head, he added, 'I'll call you in the morning.' He waited as Emily, her head in a whirl of chaotic emotions—embarrassment, anger and, most telling of all, frustration—found her key, opened the door and walked in.

CHAPTER THREE

THE weeks that followed were like a fairy tale to Emily. She was head over heels in love with Anton Diaz. The love she had thought she had felt for Nigel was nothing compared to how Anton made her feel. There was no point in denying it. She only had to hear his deep, melodious accented voice to go weak at the knees, and when he touched her excitement buzzed through every nerve in her body. She wanted him in ways she had never dreamed of before, but now kept her hot and restless in bed at night.

Thinking about that first night now, four weeks later, as she sat in front of the dressing mirror applying her make-up, ignited a slow-burning heat in the pit of Emily's stomach. But then that was something that pretty much happened every time she thought of Anton these days. A secretive smile curved her full lips as she ran a brush through her hair and rose to her feet.

Anton had been in New York for almost a week, and she ached to see him again. In fact she ached for him, because for some reason there had been no repeat of that first steamy episode except in her head.

They had enjoyed themselves over a few dinners and a trip to the theatre. She had accompanied him on several high-profile social occasions that included his business acquaintances, and the one time they had attended a film première he had quite proudly confirmed to the waiting photographers that they were an item.

But it was their relationship on the sexual front that puzzled Emily. Innocent though she was, she knew deep in her heart she wanted him with every fibre of her being. Given his reputation, she knew the best she could hope for was an affair, and she had confidently expected to be invited to his London penthouse. Within a week of meeting him, she had prepared for their relationship to progress to the physical, but it had not advanced at all. On the contrary, Anton had never even suggested taking her to his apartment, and made a point of drawing back after a kiss or two, while she was left aching for more...

Still, perhaps after a six-day separation tomorrow night would be the night, she thought as she clipped the diamond studs in her ears and stood back to view her reflection. But first she had to get through tonight. A family party for her uncle Sir Clive Deveral's birthday.

Her mother's brother was a bachelor and it was a bit of a tradition that he dined with them all on his birthday before heading off later to his club and his old navy mates to reminisce and get drunk. She had made a determined effort to dress up for her uncle because she knew he really appreciated glamorous women.

He had told her so when, in his own bumbling way, he had tried to comfort her after her disastrous engagement. He had confided that years ago he had lost his fiancée to another man, but he had soon got over it; with so many glamorous women to choose from he preferred to play the field. Then realizing what he had said, he had exclaimed, 'Not that I mean you should play the field. Heaven forbid. I simply meant there are plenty more fish in the sea,' and made her laugh.

He was a real sweetie and Emily adored him. She had spent

many a school holiday at his home, Deveral Hall in Lincolnshire, or at his rather dilapidated villa in Corfu. When her childhood dreams of being a ballerina were dashed by her increasing height it was her uncle who had taught her never to waste time hankering after things that she could not change and move on. Then he had got her interested in archaeology and sailing and swimming in the warm waters off the Greek island and had been instrumental in her decision to be a marine archaeologist.

She smiled at her image in the mirror. The dress she wore was a strapless silver lamé that clung to every inch of her body like a second skin to end six inches above her knees. She had left her long hair loose and she was wearing ridiculously high-heeled diamanté sandals that showed off her legs to the max.

Emily was still smiling to herself as she walked down the stairs to join the family for pre-dinner drinks. Her uncle would love her outfit—he was always telling her that the latest generation of men on the Fairfax side of the family needed shocking out of their staid conservatism once in a while. For that reason he always turned up at any family dinner in a velvet dinner jacket and outrageous waistcoats. The rest of the family would probably have a fit.

She reached the bottom of the stairs and headed towards the sound of talk and laughter coming from the drawing room, and then turned again as the doorbell rang.

'I'll get it, Mindy,' she said as the flustered housekeeper popped out of the kitchen.

She opened the door and her mouth fell open with shock. 'Anton, what are you doing here? I thought you weren't due back until tomorrow.'

'Obviously I got back not a minute too soon.' His dark eyes glittered with some fierce emotion as they swept over her. 'You look unbelievable, though I find it hard to believe you dressed like that for an evening at home. Who is my competition?' he demanded, his dark eyes narrowing with anger on her face. Then without a word he hauled her into his arms and covered her mouth with his own in a hard possessive kiss that knocked the breath from her body.

When he finally allowed her to breathe again she looked up into his burning black eyes. 'What was that for?' she gasped.

'To remind you, you are mine. Now who is he?'

'You're jealous—you think I am going out with another man,' Emily prompted, ridiculously delighted, and, lifting a finger, she stroked the firm line of his jaw. 'You have no need to be, Anton. There is no other man, and we are having a birthday party for my uncle,' she explained, a broad smile curving her slightly swollen lips. 'Come and join us. You will make the dinner table up to an even number.' And she watched as what looked surprisingly like a blush stained his high cheekbones.

'What can I say?' He groaned, holding her away from him. 'Except I've missed you.' His eyes roamed hungrily over her and then, grabbing her arm, he urged her inside. 'I have to speak to Tom.'

'Why?'

'I want to marry you, and I need to ask his permission.'

'What?'

'You heard.' He folded her against his long body. 'Marry me, Emily. I can't wait any longer.'

Not the most romantic proposal in the world, but Emily's blue eyes filled with tears of happiness. Suddenly everything made sense. Anton, wonderful Anton, the man she loved with all her heart, the man she had been worrying would never take her to bed, actually wanted to marry her. Now his behaviour made magnificent sense. She had heard the rumours of his many mistresses, but with her he had behaved with admirable restraint because he wanted more, he wanted her to be his wife, he loved her.

'Yes, oh, yes,' she cried, and flung her arms around his neck.

'What is going on out here?'

Anton raised his eyes and looked at Tom over the top of Emily's head. He had shocked himself by proposing marriage so precipitously. He had had it all planned, the ring in his pocket, a romantic dinner, a skilful seduction; instead he had blurted it out in the doorway like an idiot. But hell! If ever a woman looked like sex on legs and ready to bed it was Emily tonight, he reasoned, so naturally he had to get in quick. And Emily had said yes, mission accomplished. Not that he had doubted for a moment she would say yes, and he refused to admit it was the thought of Emily seeing another man that was responsible for his hasty proposal. He straightened his broad shoulders and tightened his arm around Emily's waist.

'I have just asked Emily to marry me, Tom, and she has agreed. But we would like your blessing,' he said, once more in complete control.

'Is this true, Emily? Is Anton the man for you?' Tom asked quietly, his eyes on his sister.

'Oh, yes.'

'In that case you have my blessing.' Anton met his soon-to-be brother-in-law's eyes and saw the slight reservation in the blue depths. 'But you are a lot older than Emily.' For that, read *You have a reputation with women*, Anton understood instantly. 'And if you hurt her in any way you will have me to answer to.'

'I'll guard her with my life,' Anton declared, and he meant it, though not necessarily for the reason Tom Fairfax thought...

'Knowing Emily and given her career choice, I don't envy you,' Tom teased.

'Tom—please…' Emily groaned. 'You are going to put Anton off before I get the ring on my finger.'

'Never.' Anton glanced down at the woman by his side. 'As your husband I will support you every which way you want, Emily.'

'So stop making cow's eyes at her, and come and meet the rest of the family.' Tom grinned. 'We can make it a double cele-bration and you will have some idea of what you are getting into, my friend.'

Anton knew exactly what he was getting into, he had engi-neered the whole thing, so he was surprised that he actually felt something suspiciously like guilt as the introductions were made. Tom and Helen, he knew of course, and James and Lisa Browning. The Brownings' two adult sons and their wives seemed pleasant enough. Another aunt, Jane, was the younger sister of Sara Fairfax, a widow with twin sons about twenty. Then there was the birthday boy, Sir Clive Deveral, wearing a deep blue velvet dinner jacket, a ruffled yellow shirt and a bril-liant scarlet waistcoat with a face to match.

Although he had seen all their names on the report his in-vestigator had presented, meeting them in the flesh was a little disconcerting. As the dinner progressed he found it impossible to dislike them. Everyone without exception made him welcome and congratulated him on having won Emily's hand in marriage. The conversation was lively and funny and in-evitably reminiscences of other family parties were laughed over. For the first time in years he wondered if there was some-thing to be said for a large close-knit family.

'So what did you think of them?' Emily asked Anton, her arm linked in his as she walked him to the door at one in the morning.

'I think your uncle Clive is deliberately outrageous but a great character and the rest are all lovely just like you,' he murmured as he slipped his hand in his pocket and withdrew a small velvet box.

Emily stared in wonder and a happiness so profound she could not speak.

'I meant to do this over a romantic dinner for two.' His lips quirked at the corners in a wry smile as he opened the box. 'But events rather overtook us.' And grasping her hand, he raised it to his lips and pressed a soft kiss on the backs of her fingers, before sliding a magnificent sapphire and diamond ring onto her finger.

Tears of joy sparkled in Emily's eyes as she looked up into his darkly handsome face. 'It is beautiful. I love it and I love you,' she declared. Anton was everything she wanted, and the fact he had said in front of Tom he would support her in her career banished the faintest doubt, and she kissed him.

They were married quietly on a Wednesday a month later in the church adjacent to her uncle Clive's home, Deveral Hall. Uncle Clive considered Tom and Emily as close to his own children as he would ever get and was delighted to throw open his once elegant but now slightly shabby home for the occasion.

On a brilliant day in late May the old stone house glowed mellowly in the sun. Emily was a vision in white and Anton every inch the perfect groom, tall, dark and strikingly attractive. The fifty-odd guests, mostly family and friends of Emily, were all agreed it was a wonderful intimate wedding.

Anton stared down at his sleeping bride, a slow satisfied smile curving his firm lips, his dark eyes gleaming with triumph.

Emily Fairfax was his... His wife...Señora Diaz...or Mrs...whatever. He considered himself a citizen of the world, and it was only the Diaz that was important. He had applied for a passport weeks ago in her married name, and on production of the wedding certificate Max pulled a few strings and obtained the new passport and delivered it as they boarded the plane for Monte Carlo. Anton had accomplished what he had set out to do from the first time he had set eyes on her. He had married Charles Fairfax's daughter, the niece of a knight of the realm. Not that he cared about titles, but Charles Fairfax certainly had.

Anton's expression darkened. According to his mother, over twenty-six years ago Charles Fairfax had been on holiday in Greece and had seduced Anton's eighteen-year-old sister, Suki. Anton had been eleven at the time and attending boarding school so had known nothing about it. When his sister had died a few months later in a car accident he had been devastated, but it was only after his mother had died he had pieced together the full extent of Charles Fairfax's betrayal, from the letter addressed to Suki he had found among his mother's things.

Charles Fairfax had left Suki pregnant and returned to London. When she had contacted him about the child he had written back saying he did not believe the child was his. Then added he was well aware that Suki was the illegitimate daughter of a Frenchman, and that her mother was the daughter of a Peruvian brothel-keeper, and was now the mistress of a wealthy Greek and had yet another illegitimate child. With such a pedigree there was no way, even if he were free, which he was not, that the proud old name of Fairfax would ever be associated with the name Diaz.

Five months after Fairfax had left her, Suki had picked up a copy of *The Times* newspaper and read the announcement of the wedding of Charles Fairfax to Sir Clive Thomas Deveral's sister, Sara Deveral, and she had given up all hope and committed suicide. Killing herself and her unborn child.

Anton shook his head to dispel the dark memories. Today he had righted the wrong done to his family in a way he knew his mother would have appreciated. Emily Fairfax was now a Diaz, a very fitting revenge.

As for Emily, he glanced back at her sleeping form in the seat beside him. She really was exquisite; in fact, if he had met her without the past to consider, while he would not have married her, he would certainly have bedded her and kept her as his mistress until he tired of her. But looking at her now with her silken blonde hair falling loosely over one side of her face, her soft lips slightly pouted in sleep, he was glad he had.

Emily was intelligent, well educated with a career of sorts and she was not likely to interfere in how he ran his life. Certainly not after he told her why he had married her, and the thought made him pause. Somehow the revenge he had achieved did not give him quite as much pleasure as he had expected. The soul-corroding bitterness that had consumed him since his mother's death had faded slightly. Probably because of Emily—she really was delightful.

Her constant avowals of love, rather than irritating him, he was beginning to find quite addictive. He had known a few women, and he was realistic enough to recognize that, great sex aside, the biggest part of his attraction was his wealth. Personally he thought love was an excuse the female of the species, Emily included, used to justify having sex with a man. Wryly he amended that thought, with the exception of the three generations of females in his family who had imagined themselves in love and suffered for it.

His grandmother had been the daughter of a wealthy Spanish Peruvian rancher, a Señor Sebastian Emanuel Diaz. Her father had disowned her after she had disgraced the family by getting pregnant and running away to Lima with a ranch hand. They never married and he left her when their daughter was barely a year old. His own mother had repeated the same mistake twice over, first by falling in love with a Frenchman who had left her with a baby girl, and then with Anton's father, a Greek who was married, and she became his mistress. While not a complete tragedy, his mother had not made the wisest of choices. As for his sister—to kill herself for love didn't bear thinking about.

No, if love existed then it was a destructive emotion and not one Anton was prepared to embrace. He lusted after Emily, but he had no illusions about the female of the species. He knew his wealth and power were probably just as much an aphrodisiac to Emily as they had been to the countless other women he had known.

The wedding had gone perfectly and they were now on his private jet heading for the South of France to board his yacht anchored off Monaco.

His dark eyes narrowed as they roamed over her lovely face, serene in sleep. He noted the fantastic sweep of her lashes over her eyes, the sensuously curved passionate mouth, the slight curve of her breasts revealed between the lapels of the wild blue silk suit she wore, and his body tightened.

Pity he had not been able to remove the exquisite white wedding gown. The image of her as he had turned to watch her walk down the aisle would live in his mind for ever. Beautiful was an understatement; her sparkling blue eyes had met his and for a long moment he had not been able to breathe, such was her effect on him. Even now remembering made his heart beat faster and he fought the temptation to kiss her awake. He had waited this long, he could wait a little longer until they reached the comfort of his yacht. He did not want to rush what he had promised himself would be a long night of passion.

A light flashed in the gathering darkness, and he heard the sudden change in the engine noise; they would be landing soon. Good, he was getting impatient. He could not remember the last time he had waited so long for a woman, if ever...though it had all been part of his plan.

Emily was a passionate woman, and as an experienced man of the world and a skilful lover Anton had recognized that immediately. He had quickly decided his best policy was to give her just a taste of what she wanted and no more. To build up her frustration until she was so desperate to have him she would accept his proposal of marriage without a second thought. Which of course she had.

Anton shifted uncomfortably in his seat. The trouble was he had suffered just as much if not more from the enforced celibacy, as the stirring in his groin could testify. He had ended his last affair a month after his mother's death when the woman he was involved with at the time had started hinting at marriage now he was alone in the world. He grimaced painfully. He had never gone so long without sex since he was a teenager, but thankfully the wait would soon be over.

A slight frown creased his brow as, thinking back over the past few weeks, he suddenly realized every time he had stopped after a kiss or two Emily had looked at him with desire-dazed eyes, and yet she had made no attempt to seduce him, no attempt to touch him intimately. Not the usual reaction of a sexually sophisticated woman. In his experience they normally made their desire very clear. Odd...or maybe not so odd, he corrected cynically. She had probably been playing the same waiting game as he had to make sure of getting a ring on her finger...

'Anton.' A throaty murmur had his eyes flying back to her face.

'You're awake. Good.' He lowered his head to taste the soft

sweetness of her luscious mouth. 'We are landing soon,' he murmured, lifting his head, and, taking her hands in his, he folded them on her lap. 'Another half-hour and we will be on board the yacht.'

'It can't be too soon.' Emily smiled up at him, her brilliant blue eyes dazzling him. 'My love. My husband.'

'I agree, wife.' Anton smiled back. Yes, she was his wife, he had succeeded, he thought complacently as, with a sexy Emily firmly clasped to his side, he led her off the jet to the waiting helicopter.

His mother must be smiling down on him and that snobbish swine Charles Fairfax must be spinning in his grave, or burning in hell. He didn't care which. Because his daughter was now a Diaz, the name he thought not fit to be connected to Fairfax. A result all around…

His hand tightened possessively around her slender waist and in that moment he decided… Actually there was no pressing need to tell Emily what a two-timing dirty swine her father was, the real reason he had married her. It was enough for Anton to know he had kept the vow he had made on his mother's grave.

Emily staggered out of the helicopter into Anton's arms. He swung her off her feet and she wrapped her arms around his neck as, ducking his head under the still-swirling blades, he carried her to the stairs leading down from the helipad and into the body of the yacht. He didn't stop until he reached the main salon and lowered her slowly to her feet.

'Welcome aboard.' He grinned down at her and Emily registered the swell of his arousal as he dipped his head and kissed her.

She felt the earth move, or maybe it was just the yacht, but either way she flung her arms around Anton's neck again and clung.

'I want to make it to the bed at least,' she heard him groan, his hands roaming restlessly down her spine and over her bottom.

Emily shivered with excitement and, glancing around her in awe, she laughed out loud. 'This is huge!' she exclaimed, turning back to Anton, and saw his lips twitch. 'I have been on expeditions on ships half this size.'

'Emily—stop talking,' Anton commanded, his ego slightly deflated. His lips sought hers once again, and she closed her eyes in willing surrender as his tongue slipped between her softly parted lips in a long drugging kiss.

Finally when she was breathless he raised his head. 'I have waited too long for this.' He peeled off his jacket and hers as he walked her backwards in what she hoped was the direction of the master cabin.

She felt her breasts swell as his hand stroked one lace-covered breast, his thumb grazing the tip over the fine fabric, and her nipples tightened into hard pulsing points of pleasure. His mouth caught her soft gasp of delight, then moments later he nudged a door open with his shoulder.

She barely registered the bedroom; she had eyes for nothing but Anton.

Without a word he cupped her face and bent his dark head, covering her mouth with his at first tenderly. Then, as she opened her mouth to him, with a fast-growing passion that she returned with helpless fervour.

'Emily.' He said her name, and, lifting his head, he locked his dark eyes with hers, black with a hunger, a passion, that burned through to her bones. His hand slid around her back to dispense with her bra and stayed to hold her to him. For a long moment he simply stared and just his gaze on her naked breasts made her tremble with excitement.

'Exquisite,' he murmured throatily as he lowered his head

to trace the slender length of her neck with his mouth and suck on the rapidly beating pulse there. Then trail lower to her breast.

His tongue licked one pert nipple and the tightened tip engorged at his touch. She cried out as his teeth gently tugged, and her head fell back over his arm, her back arching in spontaneous response as she offered herself up to the incredible pleasure only Anton could arouse. He suckled first one and then the other with a skill that drove her crazy with need and had her writhing in his hold.

She felt her skirt slide to the floor, and suddenly he was swinging her up in his arms again and lowering her gently to the bed. She whimpered as he straightened up and looked down at her.

'You have no idea how much I want you,' he grated, his black eyes ablaze as he divested himself of his clothes in seconds.

She stared at the wide tanned shoulders, the muscular, slightly hair-roughened chest, the strong hips, the powerful thighs and long legs. Totally naked and fully aroused he was almost frightening in his masculine beauty, and nervously she crossed her arms over her throbbing breasts.

'Let me look at you,' he growled and, leaning over her, he grasped the top of her minuscule lace briefs. 'All of you.' He slid them down her long legs and dropped them. Then his hands curled around her ankles and slowly stroked up her long legs tracing the curve of her hips, the indentation of her waist. She was trembling all over by the time he reached for her wrists and, unfolding her arms from her chest, pinned her hands either side of her body.

'There is no need to pretend shyness,' he husked. 'You are exquisite, more than I ever dreamed of.'

Excitement arced through her like an electric charge, her blue eyes as bright as sapphires as his dark eyes dropped to her breasts and lingered before roaming over her from head to toe once more. Emily had thought she might be embarrassed naked for the first time before Anton, but instead she was wildly excited, her slender body reacting heatedly to his intense scrutiny.

'I can't take my eyes off you, Emily, my wife. And soon to be my wife in every way.' Taking protection from a bedside table, he lowered himself down beside her, his magnificent body sliding against her, flesh on flesh.

What followed was so outside anything Emily had ever imagined it was unreal. The odd time she had imagined the act of love she had thought it would be some magical meeting of heart, body and soul, sweet, tender love reaching a joyous climax. But the violent emotions flooding through her were nothing like that.

'You can touch me, Emily,' he murmured, his dark eyes gleaming down into hers as his mouth covered hers. She reached for him in an almost desperate haste, the masculine scent of him, the sleek slide of his skin against hers, the devouring passion of his mouth igniting a white-hot heat inside her.

With tentative hands she explored the width of his shoulders, the strong spine. She shuddered as his dark head lowered and found her pouting breasts once more. No longer tentative, but eager, she stroked up his back and raked her fingers through the black silken hair of his head, holding him to her. She groaned out loud as he lifted his head and moaned her delight as he found her mouth again. The sensuality of his kiss made her head spin and her body burn.

She closed her eyes and savoured the slight masculine scent of him, and wreathed helplessly as his hands slid down the length of her body caressing, stroking and finally settling between her parted thighs.

His long fingers found the moist, hot centre of her femininity and a low aching moan escaped her, and she wanted more, much more, her hips lifting, her whole body throbbing. She was helplessly in thrall to the wonder of his expertise and her own uninhibited response. She clutched desperately at him and looked up into his taut dark face, saw the black passion in his eyes and revelled in it.

Wild and wanton, she caught his hair and pulled his head back to her mouth. She was panting with frustration and an incredible need to feel all of his long, hard body over her, in her, joined with hers. She groaned as he paused to slip on protection and then kissed her. The sensuous pressure of his lips, the thrusting of his tongue mimicking the sexual act and the fire in her blood turned her whole body into a flame of pure sensation. He settled between her thighs, and she cried his name, burning with a fever for more. His hands on her hips tightened and she arched up as he thrust home.

Emily felt a stab of pain and winced. She saw the shock in his dark eyes as he stilled and began to withdraw. But she could not let him go, not now as the thick fullness of him made her inner muscles clench, and instinctively she locked her legs around his waist, slid her arms around his back. 'Please. Please, I want you. I love you.'

She heard the sharp intake of his breath, felt the heavy beating of his heart and the tension in every muscle of his body. Then he moved, slowly thrusting a little deeper, and then withdrawing and sliding deeper still.

Miraculously her silken sheath stretched to accommodate him, and Emily was lost to everything except the pure physical wonder of his possession. The indescribable sensations beating through her, the sleek skin beneath her fingers, and the heated scent of two bodies joined. The wonder as in seconds she matched the rhythm he set, driving her ever higher to some unknown destination she ached…was dying for.

Her nails dug deep into his satin-smooth skin as great waves of ecstasy rippled through her and then roared as he thrust hard and fast and she cried out as her body convulsed in exquisite rapture, and she was flung into a hot, mindless oblivion. She heard Anton groan, and she forced her eyes open and felt his great body buck and shudder with the force of his own release.

Loosely she wrapped her arms around him as he buried his head on her shoulder. The heavy pounding of his heart against hers and his weight were a solid reminder of the power and passion, the love he had given her. A soft smile curved her lips. Anton truly was her husband.

CHAPTER FOUR

EMILY had never imagined such ecstasy existed, and as the rippling aftermath of pleasure receded and her breathing steadied a beauteous smile curved her swollen lips. She savoured the weight of Anton lying over her, the heavy pounding of his heart against hers.

'I am too heavy,' he rasped.

'No, perfect,' she murmured and felt the warmth of Anton's breath against her throat as he rolled off her.

Her blue eyes misty, she watched him walk to the bathroom, and return moments later, his great body bronzed and glistening with beads of perspiration. 'Come back to bed.'

He lay down beside her, supporting himself on one elbow, his dark eyes searching hers. 'Anton.' She lifted a hand to brush the damp fall of hair from his brow. 'I never knew love could be so…' She was lost for words except to say, 'I love you.' She couldn't stop saying it. 'I love everything about you.' Her finger traced the line of his cheekbone, his strong chin shadowed with dark stubble. She sighed. He was so magnificent…so perfect…and incredibly she felt slow-building warmth once again in her slender body.

'Why didn't you tell me you were a virgin?' He shook his head, and her hand slipped to his broad shoulder, relishing the feel of his smooth skin beneath her fingers.

'Does it matter? We are truly married now,' she said, but her smile faded a little as she looked into his eyes. They were no longer gleaming with desire, but narrowed in angry puzzlement on her face.

'But you were engaged to be married once before. How could it be?'

Emily was surprised and intrigued. How did Anton know she had been engaged before? She was sure she had never told him, and without a second thought she asked him.

'Someone must have mentioned it,' he dismissed, and she had the oddest notion he was avoiding a direct answer. 'But that is not important; you should have told me I was your first.'

'Why? Would you have refused to make love to me if I had?' she teased, and stroked a slender finger down his chest. Slowly, sensually...

'Yes... No... But I could have been more careful if I had known.'

She lifted both her hands and ran her fingers through his black hair, holding his head firmly between her palms. Her blue eyes were sparkling with devilment. 'Well, you can be careful the next time.' And pulled his head down, wanting to kiss him.

She heard the husky rumble of his laugh and suddenly he turned, and in one fluid moment he pulled her on top of him. She wriggled a little, her legs parting to enclose his strong thighs, and heard his sharp intake of breath with feminine satisfaction.

'For an innocent I have a feeling you are going to be a very fast study,' he said with husky amusement in his tone.

'I hope so,' she quipped, and ran her hand over the soft curling hairs of his chest, her finger grazing a very male nipple. 'When does the next lesson begin?' she asked mischievously, resting her chin on his breastbone and looking up into his darkly handsome face.

His sensuous grin sent a delicious shiver the length of her spine. 'I think I have awakened a sleeping tigress, and the first thing you need to know is the male takes a little longer to recover than the female, though it is a known fact that with a little encouragement the waiting time can be reduced.'

'Like this, you mean,' she prompted softly, and dipped her head to brush his lips with hers, and then his throat, and finally her tongue slipped out to lick a hard male nipple. She loved the musky male taste of him; she could not get enough of him, revelling in the strong hard body beneath her. She trailed one hand down over his rock-hard diaphragm, her slender fingers tracing the slim line of black body hair down to the flat plane of his belly, and lower to explore his essential maleness, and very quickly the waiting was over.

Time had no meaning as they explored the hunger, the depths of passion and the exquisite tenderness of their love. They bathed and made love again, slept and made love again…

Emily yawned and opened her eyes to find Anton standing over her dressed in khaki shorts and a white polo shirt, and holding a coffee-cup in his hand. Sleepily she looked at him, a slow beautiful smile curving her full lips.

'You're up,' she murmured and her stomach gave a distinct rumble. 'What time is it?'

He grinned and placed the cup and saucer on the bedside table. 'One.' Then he bent his head to drop a swift kiss on her brow.

She frowned. 'It's the middle of the night. Come back to bed.'

'It is one on Thursday afternoon.'

'Oh, hell!' she exclaimed and stretched, then winced as muscles she never knew she had stung. 'I must get up.' She started to, then realized she was naked, and, finding the cotton coverlet, she tugged it over her body.

* * *

Anton winced guiltily with her, his dark eyes roaming over her lithe, shapely form. She looked so delectable, her blonde hair tousled around her beautiful face, her lips pink and swollen from his kisses, and the sheet barely covering her luscious breasts.

He had bedded some of the most stunning women in the world, but none came close to Emily. She was perfection incarnate, and he knew the image of her naked body, the wild passion they had shared, would be for ever etched in his brain. She had been a virgin, and he should have had more control, and he had *tried*.

After the second time, he had carried her to the bathroom and bathed her, but by the time he had got around to drying her he had lost control again, then he had given up counting. He had never known a woman like her in his life; she was all Eve, a temptress, and a siren with a body to drive a man out of his mind.

As he had expected from the first time he laid eyes on Emily, she was a sexy, passionate woman. She had gone up in flames as soon as he touched her. She had wreathed in his arms, and cried his name, cried out her love as he possessed her exquisite body, convulsing in orgasmic pleasure time after time.

What was even more amazing, with remarkable aptitude in no time at all she learnt just what buttons to press to make him equally helpless in the power of their passion. She was a naturally born sensualist...

The only thing he had not expected was that she would still be a virgin. The man she had been engaged to before must have been a eunuch or an absolute saint.

He found it incredible that he was her first lover. He had never made love to a virgin before. Innocence had never appealed to him, he preferred experienced women who knew the score, and yet he was stunned by the uniquely erotic experience. And if he was honest, in a totally chauvinistic way he felt an overwhelming masculine satisfaction and pride that she had given her virginity to him. She was his…only his…

He didn't believe in love, but there was something extremely beguiling in having a wildly sexy wife who did. He had intended revealing the true reason he had married her after spending one passionate night with her. But he had already virtually dismissed the idea on the plane over here, and now, having discovered how innocent she was, he would have to be the biggest fool in Christendom to disillusion her. Anton was no fool and he thanked his lucky stars he had kept his mouth shut about her father.

His body hardened just looking at her and his mouth tightened as he fought the temptation to join her in bed, captivated by her every movement as she reached for the cup he had left for her on the bedside table.

'Good idea, drink your coffee,' he finally answered, 'and join me in the salon when you are dressed.' He didn't trust himself to keep his hands off her, and she needed time to recover. 'The chef has prepared lunch and then I will give you a tour of the yacht and introduce you to the captain and crew.' Turning on his heel, he walked rather stiffly out of the cabin.

Emily drank the coffee and, sliding off the bed, headed for the shower. Washed and wearing only a towel, she glanced around the cabin and saw her suitcase standing by a wall of cupboards. She had never thought of unpacking it the night before. In a matter of minutes she unpacked her trousseau so carefully bought over the last few weeks. One exquisite evening gown, and a host of smart summer clothes, some stylish if slightly risqué lingerie and bikinis courtesy of Helen.

As she closed the lingerie drawer a secret smile curved her

lips at the thought of wearing them for Anton. She slipped on lace briefs and a matching bra, and a pair of white cotton shorts and a blue cotton top she had chosen to wear. She brushed her hair back off her face and fastened it with a slide. She didn't bother with make-up, just a sun screen; she was in a hurry to get back to her husband.

After lunch, Anton spent the next three hours giving Emily a tour of the yacht and introducing her to the captain and crew. The chief steward and the chef, he explained, arranged all the catering and the domestic running of the yacht. She wowed them all with her natural ease and grace, and her obvious interest in the mechanics of the yacht. Surprisingly for a woman she was quite knowledgeable about the workings of a ship.

While he appreciated her interest, after half an hour all he wanted to do was get her back into bed. Her fantastically long legs were displayed in all their glory by the shorts she was wearing and he could not keep his eyes off her. It hadn't escaped his notice neither could any other man around.

'So what do you think, Emily?' he asked as he leant against the ship's rail, and clasped his hands loosely around her waist, and drew her between his splayed legs.

'I think it is the ultimate boys' toy.' She looked up at him with such love and laughter in her eyes, inexplicably his heart tightened and his body followed suit. 'I have seen cruise liners smaller than this.' She shook her head in amazement. 'I am not surprised we are anchored offshore—there is probably not a berth big enough even in Monte Carlo.' She laughed. 'I knew you were wealthy, but I had no idea how rich.' She grinned up at him. 'A helipad, a swimming pool and a wicked-looking motor launch to take us ashore. It is unbelievable, I love it, and I love you.' And he felt the touch of her lips against his chin.

'Then that is all right,' Anton answered gruffly, swallowing a peculiar lump in his throat.

'But what I want to know is when are we sailing and where to? The captain, when I asked him, did not seem to know. Is our honeymoon going to be a mystery tour?' she demanded with a chuckle, and moved seductively between his thighs increasing the ever-present sensual awareness between them.

Her bare legs brushing his sent his temperature soaring and Anton hardened still further; he could not help himself. But her question reminded him of where they were and why, and he felt a bit selfish, not a feeling he was comfortable with. He tightened his hands on her waist and lightly urged her back, then dropped his hands from her far-too-tempting body.

He let his gaze rest on her lovely face; her luminous eyes revealed her every thought. She was so open, so affectionate and this was her honeymoon.

His black brows pleated in a frown as belatedly he realized his decision to use the long-standing arrangement he had made for his annual trip to the Formula One Monaco Grand Prix to double as a honeymoon no longer seemed quite so reasonable. Emily had probably been expecting a romantic out-of-the-way place and just the two of them. Whereas he, without a second thought given the reason he had married her, had decided to do what he always did at this time of year, confident that Emily would fit in with his plans.

His frown deepened. He had never had to consider a woman's feelings before. Every woman he had known in the past had been quite happy to pander to his every whim, and why not? He was an extremely wealthy man and a generous lover for as long as an affair lasted. He had made it clear from the outset he never had any intention of marrying them, all he had wanted was good sex. He didn't do romance, and he wasn't about to start now simply because he was married.

Married to the daughter of the man who destroyed his sister, he reminded himself. He had been in danger of forgetting that fact in the throes of what was basically nothing more than great sex, he reasoned. Straightening his broad shoulders, he told her the truth.

'There is no mystery; I stay here at the end of May every year for the motor racing. The Monaco Grand Prix is on Sunday. As a sponsor for one of the teams, I usually watch the race from the pits. Then there is an after-race party,' he explained, studying her reaction through narrowed eyes.

'Oh, I see.' Her blue eyes shaded and Anton knew she did not see at all. 'I never realized you were a racing-car enthusiast, though I suppose I should have guessed. Boys' toys again, hmm? Well, it will be another new experience, I suppose.' And her sensuous lips curled in a bewitching smile. 'At least I will have you to myself until Sunday.'

Frustration and the fact she was so damn reasonable angered Anton. That and the unfamiliar feeling of guilt that assailed him because he had not told her the half of it yet. For a brief moment he wondered if he could just order the captain to set sail immediately, but dismissed the notion.

Emily was his wife, his extraordinarily beautiful, incredible, sexy wife, but he changed his plans for no one, and he wasn't about to start now. He had his life organized exactly as he liked it, and although Emily had a career it was pretty flexible—she would quickly adjust and go where he led.

'Not exactly…' He paused. 'I don't use the yacht solely for my own pleasure; sometimes it is chartered out. It would not be financially viable otherwise. But also as a single man up until now,' he swiftly added, 'it has been a convenient way to repay hospitality rather than the more conventional house party.' He was prevaricating…not like him at all, and bluntly he told her, 'Anyway, it has become a bit of a tradition of mine to invite a few like-minded guests whose hospitality I have enjoyed in the past to join me on board for the Grand Prix weekend, and they usually stay until Monday.'

For a long moment Emily simply stared at her very new husband. He was standing, his long body taut, apparently unconcerned. But she caught a glimmer of uncertainty in the depths of his dark eyes, probably a first for him, and she hid a smile. Anton had it all. Wealth, power, and as a one-hundred-per-cent-virile male he was accustomed to doing exactly what he wanted to do without ever having to consider anyone else. Women had been falling over themselves to please him all his adult life, if rumours were to be believed. But he obviously had a lot to learn about marriage—they both did.

'Let me get this straight—you have invited guests on our honeymoon to watch motor racing. Yes?'

'Yes,' he said with a negligent shrug of his broad shoulder.

'A novel honeymoon.' Emily placed a slender hand on his chest. 'But, hey, I am all for tradition, and if this is a tradition of yours, why not? In fact it will be nice to meet some of your friends. So far I have only met business acquaintances—and Max, of course. He made a very good best man, and where is he, by the way?' she asked. 'He came on board with us last night.'

'He has gone ashore in the launch,' he said, avoiding her eyes. 'The guests are arriving this evening.'

Anton was obviously embarrassed, Emily thought, and, while she wasn't delighted at the idea of spending the weekend with strangers, she allowed her smile to break free.

'Don't look so serious, Anton. It's okay. We have only known each other a couple of months, but we have a lifetime together to get on the same wavelength.' Standing on tiptoe, she kissed his cheek.

'My mum told me she and my dad fell in love at first sight. They got engaged after four months and married two months after that. They had only ever lived with their parents until they married and it took time to adjust, especially as they were both virgins when they met. At least I have started off with a great lover even if you are dumb when it comes to arranging a honeymoon.'

Anton's eyes narrowed incredulously on her smiling face and he was not in the least amused, the mention of her father hitting a raw nerve.

'Dumb,' he repeated. She had the cheek to call him dumb. Was she for real?

He scowled down at her and noted the shimmering sensuality in her sparkling eyes, and he did not know if he wanted to shake her or kiss her... For a man who prided himself on his control, he did not like the ambivalent way she made him feel. She looked about seventeen dressed in white shorts and a blue tee shirt the colour of her eyes, and her hair pulled back in a slide, and her youthful appearance simply increased his unwelcome sense of guilt and anger.

'For God's sake, Emily, you are the only dumb one around here. You can't possibly believe that rubbish you are spouting. Your mother might have been a virgin, but your father certainly wasn't. Trust me, I know,' he declared with biting cynicism.

Emily's euphoric mood took a huge knock. She stumbled back a step, her blue eyes widening at the icy expression on his brutally handsome face. The lover of a few hours ago had gone and in his place was the man with the cold, remote eyes that she had seen on the night they first met.

'You knew my father?' she asked, feeling her way through

an atmosphere that was suddenly fraught with tension. 'You met him?'

'No, I never met him, but I didn't need to to know what a womanizer he was.'

Emily could not let his slur on her father pass.

'As you never met my father you can't possibly know that. But I do know that my mother never lied,' she argued in defence of her parents. She loved Anton, she had married him, but she was not going to let him walk all over her. It was bad enough she was going to share the first few days of her honeymoon with a group of strangers. 'You're not infallible, you know, and in this case you are wrong.'

Anton heard the belligerence in her voice, saw the defiance in her glittering blue eyes and was outraged that she was daring to argue with him. Very few people argued with him and nobody doubted his word. He could not quite believe his very new wife had the nerve to say he was wrong.

'Your mother must have been as naive as you,' he opined scathingly, 'if she believed Charles Fairfax was anything other than a womanizing swine and a snob to boot.' He was seething with anger and it made him say more than he intended. 'He probably only married her for her aristocratic connection.'

Without her giving it a second thought Emily's hand scythed through the air, but Anton's strong hand caught her wrist before she could make contact with his arrogant face.

'You little hellcat.' He twisted her hand behind her back and hauled her hard against his long body. 'You dare to lash out at me, because I have told you a few home truths about your sainted family.'

'At least I have one,' Emily spat, and was immediately disgusted with herself for what was a low blow. But somehow the passion Anton aroused in her sexually seemed to just as easily arouse her anger. She who was normally the most placid of women, and it shocked her.

She glanced up at him. He was looking at her with eyes as cold as the Arctic waste. Then abruptly he let go of her wrist and moved back as though he could not bear to touch her.

'And do you know why I have not, Emily?' he said with a sardonic arch of one black brow, and, not waiting for her to answer, he added, 'Because of your lech of a father.'

'You never knew my father, and yet you seem to dislike him,' she murmured. She knew it from the animosity in his tone, the tension in his body, and suddenly she was afraid.

His handsome face hardened. 'Dislike is too tame a word. I hate and despise the man, and I have every right to.'

Emily shook her head, trying to make sense of what was happening. She was too shocked to speak. How had they gone from a simmering sensual awareness to a senseless argument in minutes?

'Once I had an older sister, Suki, a beautiful gentle girl. She was eighteen, barely more than a child herself, when she met Charles Fairfax. He seduced her and left her pregnant with his child. Five months later, after learning Fairfax had married your mother, she committed suicide. Obviously he was seeing both of them at the same time.'

All the colour leached from Emily's face. This was no senseless argument, but deadly serious. She had never even known Anton had a sister. But there was no mistaking the absolute conviction in Anton's voice, and for him to have apparently held a grudge against her father for over a quarter of a century she found totally appalling. She could not believe what she was hearing, didn't want to.

'No, that cannot be true.' She murmured a denial. 'My father would never have betrayed my mother.'

'Believe me, it is,' he said harshly. 'Women who foolishly imagine they are in love are dangerous to themselves as well as to others. My mother never fully recovered from the loss of her daughter and I was kept in ignorance of the full facts for decades. As a boy of eleven I was told Suki had died in a tragic car accident. It was only when my mother was dying I discovered the real truth.'

Her blue eyes widened in horror as she recognized the latent anger in his black eyes, the brooding expression on his face, and knew he totally believed what he had just told her. And with the knowledge came pain, a pain that built and built as the full import of his words sank into her brain.

'When did your mother die?'

He frowned down at her. 'Does it matter? Last December.'

Oh, my God! Only six months ago. No wonder Anton was so angry, with the death of his mother, the pain of losing his sister must have hit him all over again. From that thought came another, deeply disturbing. Shortly after his mother's death Anton had made the acquaintance of her brother and uncle, and taken an interest in the Fairfax family and then in her. Coincidence—or something much worse, and a cold dread enveloped her.

Her eyes swept helplessly over him, the bold attractive face, the strong tanned throat revealed by the open neck of his polo shirt, the khaki shorts that hugged his lean hips ending midthigh and his long legs. Her heart squeezed as vivid images of his naked body flashed in her mind, the body she had worshipped last night. Anton, the man she loved, and had been certain loved her. But not any more…

CHAPTER FIVE

ANTON had shaken her world on its axis and Emily was no longer certain of anything. She could not bear to look at him.

Her mind spinning, she let her gaze roam over the view of the tiny principality. The sea as smooth as glass, the spectacular marina, the gleaming buildings were picture-postcard perfect, but wasted on her. She needed to think…

The sun was still shining but the warmth no longer seemed to touch her. Yesterday she had been a blushing bride confident in the love of her husband, but now… She let her mind wander back over the first time they had met, the sequence of events, the conversations, his proposal of marriage that had led to this moment, and belatedly she realized he had never actually said he loved her…

Not even last night in the heat of passion had the word love passed his lips.

Emily shivered as cold fingers seemed to grip her heart, the icy tendrils spreading slowly through every part of her. She was an intelligent woman, and suddenly her whirlwind courtship and fairy-tale marriage were falling apart before her eyes. Slowly she turned her head and allowed her gaze to rest on her husband's hard, expressionless face.

'Why did you marry me, Anton?'

'I decided it was time I took a wife and produced an heir. I chose you because I thought you were a beautiful, sensuous woman who would fit me perfectly.' He reached out a hand to her. 'And I was right,' he stated.

Emily batted his hand away. 'And the rest.' She stared up at him ashen-faced, horrified at the cynical practicality of his reasoning, but instinctively knowing there was more he was not telling her.

'I might be dumb. But I am not that dumb. You only came into contact with my family after the death of your mother, and I don't believe in coincidences. You might as well tell me the whole truth.' And, though her heart was shattering into a million pieces, bravely she added, 'Because it is becoming increasingly obvious you did not marry me for love.' She prayed he would contradict her, declare he loved her and it was all a horrible mistake.

'Why not?' Anton said with a shrug of his broad shoulders. 'You are now my wife—Mrs Emily Diaz, a name your father refused to acknowledge or be associated with, and it satisfies my sense of justice to know you have my name for the rest of your life.'

His dark eyes, a gleam of mocking triumph in their inky depths, clashed with her pained blue. 'As for love, I don't believe in it myself. Though women seem to have a desperate need to. What we shared last night and will continue to share is great sexual chemistry, not love.'

Tears blurred Emily's vision and fiercely she blinked them away. So this was what it felt like to crash and burn. All her hopes and dreams ground to dust in a few short minutes. For a short while, a very brief two months, Anton had been the man she loved. For an even briefer twenty-four hours she had been his wife. He had made love to her, and it had been the most amazing experience of her life and she had thought she was the luckiest woman in the world to be loved by him.

But it had not been love… He freely admitted it was simply sex, nothing more.

For Anton yesterday had been about sex and some misguided notion of retribution, not love, never love…

How could she have been such a blind idiot? She had known the first time she set eyes on him, he was dangerous. She had avoided going out with him for a week. She should have trusted her gut instinct about the man.

Her shimmering blue eyes swept over him, noted the arrogant certainty in his gaze. The Anton he had been when they had first got together, the man she had thought had refrained from making love to her because he respected her, bore no relationship to the Anton before her now. Cold and cynical, he was not the man she had fallen in love with.

She shook her head in disgust, nausea clawing at her stomach as she was forced to accept the man she thought she loved did not exist… 'I need the bathroom.'

'Wait.' He grasped her upper arm, halting her retreat. 'This does not change anything, Emily.'

'It does for me.' She looked at him. 'Let me go.' And she meant it in every sense of the word. 'I really do need the bathroom.'

Anton's mouth twisted. 'Of course.' He removed his hand from her arm, wondering why the hell he had told Emily about her father when not long ago he had been thanking his lucky stars he had kept his mouth shut.

But then from the minute he had watched her walk down the aisle he had not been his rational self. The woman had that effect on him. Last night he had lost control in bed, a first for him, and this afternoon he had lost his temper at the mention of her father. He was going weak in the head and it had to stop.

Honesty was supposed to be good for a marriage; he'd been honest, he reasoned arrogantly. It was Emily who was unreasonable.

'Arguing on the deck is not a great idea. We can talk later. After all, neither of us is going anywhere,' he said dismissively.

He would catch up on some work—he had let things slide a little in his pursuit of Emily and it would give her time to cool down. She said she loved him, and she certainly wanted him. Given his experience of her sex, she'd soon get over the shock of realizing her father had feet of clay after a few days in his bed.

Emily heard the threat in his words and glanced at him in disgust and walked away. Was he really so cold, so insensitive to believe for a second they could carry on as husband and wife now she knew why he had really married her?

Emily walked into the cabin and locked the door behind her. Blindly she headed for the bathroom, and was violently sick. She began to shake uncontrollably and, ripping off her clothes, she stepped into the shower. She turned the water on full, and only then did she give way to the tears. She cried until she could cry no more. Then slowly she straightened and, picking up the shampoo provided, she washed her hair, and then scrubbed every inch of her body, trying to scrub away the scent, the memory of Anton's touch from every pore of her skin. Trying to scrub away the pain, she had a hollow feeling that would be with her for the rest of her life...

She did not know the man she had married, had never known him. It was Nigel all over again, but worse, because she had been foolish enough to marry Anton. Nigel had wanted her for her supposed fortune and connections, and Anton—he had married her simply because her name was Fairfax. He had seduced her into marriage because he believed her father had seduced his sister. To fulfil a primitive need for revenge...no more or less...and she could not pretend otherwise.

The pain, the sense of betrayal were excruciating, but slowly as she finished washing, turned off the shower and wrapped a large towel around her naked body the pain was overtaken by a cold, numbing anger.

She thought of her parents, and, no matter what the arrogant Anton Diaz thought, she knew her father was incapable of doing what he had said. Her parents had loved each other, they had married in their twenties, and when her mother had died it had broken her father's heart. She firmly believed it was the stress of losing his wife that had helped cause the heart attack that had killed him far too young.

It was her mother who, when she was terminally ill, had constantly told Emily to embrace life to the full, and not to waste time dwelling on past failures or grudges—life was much too short. A theory her uncle Clive had first taught her when as a child of twelve she had had to accept she was never going to be a ballet dancer.

A trait that Emily had inherited from the Deveral side of her family.

So why was she even giving Anton's tragic tale a second thought? Where he had got it from she had no idea, and she cared even less. As for her marriage, as far as she was concerned it was over...

Five minutes later, dressed in casual drawstring linen trousers and a matching sleeveless top, Emily lifted her suitcase onto the bed and began to methodically pack the clothes she had unpacked only hours before.

She heard a knock on the door but ignored it.

She was immune to everything except the need to leave. She snapped the suitcase shut, and straightened up. Now all she needed was her travel bag and she was out of here.

'Just what the hell do you think you are doing?' a deep voice roared. And Emily spun round to see Anton striding towards her. 'How dare you lock me out?' he demanded. His black eyes leaping with fury, he grasped her shoulder. 'What the hell do you think you are playing at, woman?'

'I am not playing. I am leaving… The game is over,' she said, standing tall and proud. 'Your game,' she said bitterly.

Emily felt nothing for him. She was cocooned in a block of ice. The hands on her shoulders, the close proximity of his big body had no effect on her. Except to reinforce her determination to leave. It was bad enough she had made the mistake of marrying him. She was certainly not going to allow him to manhandle her.

Anton was furious. He had got no work done, he couldn't seem to concentrate, and finally he had given up and decided to smooth things over with Emily, only to find she had locked him out of their cabin. Not that it mattered—he had a master-key. But his temper was at breaking-point.

'Over my dead body.'

'That would be my preference,' Emily tossed back.

She felt his great body tense and his hands fell from her shoulders. She watched his handsome face darken and for a second she thought she saw a flash of pain in his eyes, and for a moment she was ashamed of her hateful comment. She would not wish anybody dead. But Anton had the knack of making her say and feel things she did not want to.

'Well, I think I can safely say, barring accidents, you will not get your wish any time soon. Though for the foreseeable future it appears I must watch my back where you are concerned, my sweet loving wife, because I have no intention of letting you leave. Not now. Not ever.'

'You have no choice.' She tilted up her chin and drew on

every ounce of her pride to face him. 'As far as I am concerned the marriage is finished.'

Anton's dark eyes studied her.

He was furious at her defiance but he did not let it show. Because in a way he could understand her distress, her desire to lash back at him, though he had not appreciated her wishing him dead.

He didn't do emotions, other than over death and birth maybe. But Emily was an emotional, passionate woman, as she had proved spectacularly last night. She had been brought up on love and happy ever after. Hell, he could still hear her cries of love ringing in his ears when he had taken possession of her exquisite body. And he would again, he thought confidently. She just needed time to adjust to the reality of life as his wife.

'We always have a choice, Emily,' he murmured silkily, and, snaking an arm around her waist, he pulled her into the strength of his powerful body. 'Your choice is quite simple. You stay with me, your *husband*,' he emphasized, grasping her chin between his fingers and tilting her face up to his. 'You behave civilly as my wife and the perfect hostess I know you to be with our guests and you can continue to dabble at your career until you're pregnant with my child. Something that was implicit in the promise you made yesterday, I seem to recall.'

She stared at him. 'That was before I knew the truth. Now let me go.'

Her usual luminous blue eyes were impenetrable, her body rigid in his hold, and it made Anton want to pierce her icy control… Something he would never have imagined she was capable of.

'You have two choices. One, you stay with me. The other is you return to your brother's home, and his pregnant wife, and inform them you have left me.' He let his hand stroke down her throat, a finger resting on the pulse that beat wildly in her neck. Not such icy control as he had thought...

'Then you can explain that naturally, as I am deeply upset, I am severing all ties with your family,' he drawled with mocking sarcasm. 'Which unfortunately for Fairfax Engineering will mean an immediate repayment of the loans I forwarded some months ago for the expansion of the company.'

Then, like all good predators, he watched and waited for his victim to recognize her fate.

He saw the puzzled expression on her face, could almost see her mind assimilating what he had said, and knew the moment she realized. Anger flared in her wide blue eyes and flags of colour stained her cheeks. She twisted out of his hold and he let her, smiling inwardly. He knew she was not going anywhere...

Emily took a few steps back on legs that trembled. The numbness that had protected her since his shocking revelation about her father was fading fast and the effort to remain un-affected by his closeness had taken every bit of control she possessed. She was horribly conscious that just being held against him had made her traitorous body achingly aware of him and was furious at herself and him... She drew in a few deep steadying breaths and wrapped her arms defensively around her midriff, grittily determined to control her anger and the rest...

The silence lengthened.

She could feel Anton watching, waiting, and finally, when she was confident she could speak to him without tearing the lying rat's eyes out, she glanced across at him.

'And what exactly does that mean for Fairfax?' she asked in a cool little voice.

'An educated guess. The expansion will have to stop and they will be in deep financial trouble, and probably ripe for a hostile takeover.' He gave her a humourless smile. 'As I said before, the choice is yours, Emily.'

He didn't need to add a takeover by him. Emily figured that out for herself. 'You would do that…' she prompted, and saw his proud head incline slightly, the glimmer of triumph in his dark eyes, and she knew the answer.

'If I have to. I will do anything to keep you.'

A hysterical laugh rose in her throat and she choked it back. *He would do anything to keep her.* A few hours ago she would have been flattered by his words, now she was just sickened.

Suddenly her legs threatened to collapse beneath her, and abruptly she sat down on the bed, her hands clasped tightly in her lap, and stared up at him in sheer disbelief…

She shook her head and looked down at her hands, her gaze lingering on the gold band on her finger. What a travesty…

Slowly she reran the scenario of the future of their marriage Anton had painted in her head. It did not take a genius to work out he must have planned this all along. She also realized there was one glaring flaw in the choice he had given her as far as she was concerned.

'If what you say is true you can take the company any time, whether we are together or not,' she said slowly. 'And you freely admit you don't love me, or anyone else for that matter. We both know you can have any woman you want without much effort, and frequently do by all accounts.' Though picturing him in another woman's arms doing what he had done to her was like a knife to her heart. She paused for a moment, drawing on every bit of will-power she could before lifting her head and asking, 'So why on earth, Anton, would I stay with you?'

He stood towering over her, his expression unreadable. He was so close she imagined she felt the warmth of his body reaching out to her, and she trembled and despised herself for it.

Then he smiled—he actually smiled, all confident macho male, and she wanted to thump him. He sat down beside her, his great body angled towards her, and hastily she moved away, but banged against her damn suitcase and sent it tumbling to the floor.

'Steady, Emily.' He reached across her to put a restraining hand on her arm and she flinched at the contact. 'And though I am flattered you think I can have any woman I want, I want only you.'

Anton knew he had her. He had noted her tremble. His original assessment was right—in a few days she would forget this nonsense about leaving him. But he had to tread warily. Naturally she was upset and angry because he had forced her to face reality and accept he was not quite the Prince Charming she had imagined...but as human as the next man.

He had not got where he was today without being ruthless when it came to what he wanted. He never took an insult to his integrity without seeking retribution. Anything less was a sign of weakness, and no one could accuse him of that.

But he could do charming...

She was as skittish as the newborn foals he bred on his ranch in Peru and needed gentle handling. She would stay with him anyway, of that he was determined. But he would prefer her to stay with him willingly and what he wanted he always got.

'I regret arguing with you, but you have a knack of inflaming all my passions.' He grimaced. 'I never meant to tell you the truth about your father, but your rosy view of him spiked my temper and for that I apologize. So now can we put this argument behind us, and get on with our marriage? It is up to you, Emily, but I promise if you stay I will never harm your family firm in any way.' He reached for her hand, and he found he was grasping air as she shot off the bed at the speed of light, and spun around to stare down at him.

Surprise didn't cut it; he had been at his caring best, what more did she want? His mouth grim, Anton studied her. God, she was magnificent. Statuesque, her blue eyes blazing, her perfect breasts rising and falling in her agitation, her hands placed defiantly on her slender hips. He was aroused simply looking at her, and then she spoke, and his softly-softly approach flew out of the window.

'Are you mad? After today I would not believe a word you said if you swore it on a stack of bibles,' she yelled.

'Then trust this,' Anton snarled, his temper and frustration finally boiling over, and, catching her around the waist, he tumbled her onto the bed.

The breath left Emily's body and before she knew it she was flat on her back with Anton's long body pinning her to the bed.

For a moment she was too shocked to move, and then his mouth was crashing down on hers, and instantly her pulse rate surged and she was wildly, passionately angry. She fought like a woman possessed, she kicked out and he retaliated by pinning her legs between his heavy thighs. She bit his tongue, her hands tangled in his hair and pulled. He did the same.

'Hell—Emily—'

His voice was ragged and then his mouth slammed back down on hers. Still she tried to resist, but his big body pressed against her, his hand in her hair holding her firm, his other hand cupping her breast, kneading, igniting a different kind of passion.

His hand left her hair, and he shoved her top and bra up over her breasts, his mouth covering her already-straining nipples. Wild excitement ripped through her and all thought of resistance was blown away in the storm of passion engulfing her.

'You want me,' he rasped.

'Yes,' she groaned, her arms involuntarily wrapping around him. She didn't notice when he removed her trousers. She wanted him; he was right—she could not help herself.

His lips brushed her breast, her throat, her mouth, and her mouth twined with his in a desperate greedy kiss. Involuntarily her slender body arched up beneath him, and she gloried in the pressure of his surging masculine arousal. He moved sensually against her, and she moaned as his teeth and tongue found her aching nipples, teasing and tasting until she was wild with wanting. Anton's hands curved around her buttocks and her body jerked violently as he plunged to the hilt into the sleek, tight centre of her, the sensation so intense, she could barely breathe.

Hard and fast, he thrust repeatedly, and her body convulsed in an explosion of pleasure so exquisite she could only gasp as he plunged on to his own shuddering release.

She lay there, her eyes closed, exhausted and fighting for breath, the shuddering aftermath still pulsing inside her. She felt Anton roll off her and say her name. But she kept her eyes closed. She could not face him, a deep sense of shame and humiliation consuming her.

Knowing he did not love her and had an ulterior motive for marrying her... Nothing had stopped her melting like ice in the sun as soon as he had kissed her. In one passionate encounter he had turned her lifelong belief in love on its head. She felt his hand smoothing back her hair from her face, his fingers trace the curve of her mouth.

'Emily, look at me.'

Reluctantly she opened her eyes. He was leaning over her, determination in every angle of his brutally handsome face.

'No more pretence, Emily. You want me and I want you. You may already be carrying my child, so no more arguments. We are married and that is the way it is going to stay.'

She almost told him then...

Emily was a practical woman and she had started taking the pill a week after their first date as a precaution for the affair she had hoped would follow, marriage not on her mind at the time. Now she kept her secret. Why feed his colossal ego by letting him know how ridiculously eager she had been to go to bed with him?

'And I have no say in the matter.'

'No.' Anton's dark eyes swept over her, his lips curving in a brief satisfied smile as he straightened up, flexing his shoulders. 'Your body said it for you.'

He was so damned arrogant, Emily thought bitterly. He was standing at the foot of the bed, his shirt in place and zipping his shorts, and suddenly a fiery tide of red washed over her as she realized he had not even removed his clothing. Whereas she... She looked down... Oh, God... Hastily she tugged her bra and top down over her breasts. She was mortified and glanced wildly around for her trousers.

'Yours, I believe,' Anton drawled, a hint of amusement in his black eyes as he dropped her white trousers and briefs on her legs. 'Though you might like to change for dinner—our guests will be arriving soon.' And he strolled out of the cabin without a backward glance, while Emily fumed.

She leapt off the bed, and headed straight for the shower for the third time that day. She wasted no time, knowing Anton would be back to change.

Washed and wearing only bra and briefs, she unpacked her case yet again. She would allow Anton to think she agreed with him, until she could figure out a way to leave without harming her family.

She chose a short, black, thankfully crease-proof slip dress, and put it on. She slapped some moisturizer on her face, covered her lips in pink gloss and brushed her hair. She saw no reason in dressing up to the nines for Anton and his friends. They were not hers and never would be now. He had had the nerve to say earlier she could dabble with her career until the children arrived. The word 'dabble' said it all. So much for his promise to support her given on the night he proposed. He obviously had no respect for who or what she was. As for children... She hardened her heart against the image of a dark-haired beautiful baby, a replica of Anton, in her arms... Like all her foolish dreams of love, that was never going to happen now.

She slid her feet into black sandals, and exited the cabin. She needed some fresh air.

Emily walked to the seaward side of the yacht and, half hidden by a lifeboat, she leant against the rail to watch the thin crescent of the sun sink beneath the horizon in a last red blaze of glory. She stood for a long time, her mind swirling, trying to find a way out. She looked at the darkening night sky and felt as though the same darkness were wrapping its way around her heart and soul.

She would never do anything that might harm her brother and family. After today, her trust in Anton was totally shattered. How could she love a man she didn't trust? It wasn't possible. Yet when he had tumbled her on the bed her anger had been fierce but fleeting, she had welcomed his possession, and with bitter self-loathing she knew she would again. She was helpless to resist. She also knew she had no alternative but to go along with what he wanted. She was trapped...

CHAPTER SIX

EMILY heard the sound of raised voices and realized the launch must have arrived with the guests, but she didn't move, reluctant to go and face strangers with her emotions so raw.

A deep painful sigh escaped her. Short of discovering she had married a homicidal maniac, she must have had the worst first day of marriage in history. Still, it couldn't possibly get any worse, she told herself, and, taking a deep breath, she turned.

'Emily.' Anton was moving towards her. He was dressed in a lightweight beige suit, his shirt open at the neck, and his black hair slicked severely back from his brow, and she realized with a sick sense of shame he looked more gorgeous than ever to her tortured mind.

'I wondered where you were hiding,' he drawled sardonically. 'Our guests have arrived.' He took her arm and led her into the salon.

Emily was wrong: the day could get worse...

Seated on Anton's left, Emily glanced around the table. The dinner party from hell was a pretty fair assessment, she mused.

They were seven couples in all, a single young man and, with the inclusion of Max, sixteen around the dinner table in the sumptuous dining area of the yacht.

Anton at his eloquent best had introduced her as his wife, and she would have to have been an idiot not to notice the surprise and outright disbelief at his pronouncement. While in an aside to her he had warned her to behave impeccably in front of his guests…or else…

Else what? Emily wondered. He could not hurt her any more than he already had. The congratulations were gushing, but the looks she got from the six other women on board varied from genuine pleasure to curiosity to almost pitying and, from one, simply venomous.

She smiled and Anton kept the conversation going with very little help from her through five courses that she barely remembered eating. She was in shock.

Wouldn't you just know it? she mused. The first person she had seen was Eloise. Anton had introduced her to Eloise's Italian husband, Carlo Alviano, and his twenty-two-year-old son from a previous marriage, Gianni.

She raised her glass and took another sip of wine, and glanced around the table. Sally and Tim Harding she recognized from a business dinner she had attended in London with Anton. As for the other four couples, they seemed pleasant enough. One couple was Swiss, another French, and a rather nice middle-aged American couple, and the last pair were Greek. It was a truly international gathering of the seriously rich, and, from the designer dresses and jewellery on show, she wouldn't like to estimate how much their combined worth came to. Billions no doubt…

She glanced at the young man, Gianni, seated on her right. There was something familiar about him but she could not quite place him. She took another sip of wine, and let her gaze roam over him. He was classically handsome with perfect features and thick black curly hair. Maybe he was a model; perhaps she had seen a picture of him in a magazine.

'More wine?' the steward offered and Emily nodded. She knew she was probably drinking too much, but she was past caring and let her eyes stray to rest on Eloise, with a kind of morbid fascination.

Eloise was obviously Anton's type of woman.

She was wearing a red minidress, that barely covered her voluptuous breasts or her bum. She was seated on the right of Anton and had spent most of the meal trying to hold his attention, gossiping away to him about old times with much touching of his arm and anywhere else she could reach. As for her husband, Carlo, who was seated next to her, she virtually ignored him.

Why Carlo put up with her Emily could not fathom. A sophisticated, handsome man in his fifties, he was quite charming and owned a merchant bank. Maybe that was why Eloise had married him, she thought cynically.

She took another sip of her wine. And maybe Carlo didn't care so long as the sex was good... Maybe he was the same type of man as Anton—look at the reality of her marriage after one day—and she giggled, seeing the black humour in the situation.

'Oh, please, you must share the joke,' Eloise trilled, all fake smiles.

Emily glanced across at her, saw the spite in the other woman's eyes and said, 'It was nothing. Just a humorous thought.'

'Let us be the judge of that,' Eloise prompted. And for one moment Emily was tempted to tell her exactly what she had been thinking. But although she had consumed a little too much wine, it was far from enough for her to make a fool of herself.

'No,' she said and froze into immobility as Anton lifted a hand to her cheek and trailed his fingers down and around the nape of her neck, urging her head towards him.

'Some coffee or water maybe.' His gaze locked with hers and something moved in the dark depths of his eyes. 'You have had a couple of very full days, my darling, as I know,' he drawled, his finger pressing on the pulse that beat strongly in her throat.

Her eyes widened, and she barely controlled an involuntary shiver until he added, 'Any more wine and you will fall asleep.' And she realized that his show of affection was purely for the guests and to add insult to injury he had implied she was drunk...the swine.

She drew in a deep steadying breath. 'You're right as always, darling,' she mocked, and reached up to remove his hand from her neck, digging her nails into his wrist in the process. 'Coffee, thanks.'

Anton's eyes narrowed, promising retaliation, then he turned to beckon the steward and coffee was provided.

Hot and angry, Emily silently seethed. The atmosphere stank, there was no other word for it, and she wished she could go out on deck for some clean air. Better still dive overboard and swim to shore—it couldn't be more than half a mile...

'That's it,' she cried and slapped her hand on the table, making the glass and cutlery rattle.

'Gianni, I thought I knew you.' She turned to the young man at her side, the first genuine smile of the evening lighting her face. It had come to her out of the blue when she had thought of swimming.

'You were in the under-twenty-ones swimming team for Rome University at the European Universities' sports challenge held in Holland four years ago.'

'Yes, señora, I recognized you immediately, but I thought you did not remember me.'

'Oh, please call me Emily—you did before,' she reminded him. 'I watched you win in an amazing split-second finish in the fifteen hundred metres—you were fantastic, and we met at the party afterwards.'

'That's right, and I saw you win the two hundred metres with two seconds to spare. You were brilliant.'

'Thank you. That was one of my finer moments.' She preened and laughed and so did Gianni.

His father intervened. 'You two know each other.' And his handsome face was wreathed in smiles. 'What a happy coincidence.'

'Yes. And you must be very proud of your son. Did you see him win that race? It was such a close finish after such a long race. He was incredible,' Emily enthused.

'Regrettably, no. I was in South America at the time,' and Emily noticed his eyes stray to Eloise.

'Enough about swimming,' Eloise cut in. 'That is all the boy ever talks about, that and the bank, just like Carlo,' she said petulantly. 'It is so boring.'

'I found it rather enlightening,' Anton said. 'I never knew you were a champion swimmer, Emily.'

Emily caught the faintly sarcastic tone and a hint of anger in the dark eyes that met hers. 'Why should you?' She shrugged. 'You have only known me a couple of months, and anyway I am not any more.'

Suddenly she felt bone-tired. Only an idiot could be unaware of the undercurrent of tension beneath the surface of the supposedly friendly conversation all evening, and it had given her a horrendous headache. That and the appalling realization that all she had to look forward to were countless more such encounters with Anton and his friends had stretched her nerves to breaking-point.

Pushing back her chair, she stood up. 'Well, it has been a delightful evening meeting you all.' She cast a social smile around the table. 'But I am afraid I will have to call it a night. Please excuse me.' The men made to rise. 'No, please, Anton will keep you entertained.'

Anton placed an arm along the back of Emily's waist and she stiffened in shock—she had not realized he had risen with her.

'I will escort you to the cabin, Emily.' His tone was as smooth as silk, and then, raising his voice, he added for his guests' benefit. 'If you need anything ask the steward. I'll be back soon.'

'A champion swimmer. I'm impressed,' Anton declared as he stopped and opened their cabin door, and ushered her inside. 'You are full of surprises, Emily, but if there are any more on the horizon pass them by me first,' he drawled sardonically. 'I do not appreciate being made to look a fool in front of our guests, while you flirt and reminisce with another man.'

'You made to look a fool?' She shook her head and twisted out of his arm to cast him a look of utter disgust. 'I am the only fool around here, for being stupid enough to think I could ever love a man like you. A man who invites his mistress Eloise on his honeymoon.'

'Eloise is not—'

'Oh, please, you have had sex with her; it is in her eyes every time she looks at you. So don't bother denying it.'

'Once, a decade ago,' he snapped. 'Carlo is an old and valued friend of mine and I introduced them. I was best man at their wedding four years ago. Eloise is an old friend, nothing more.'

'You don't need to explain. I couldn't care less, though I am amazed her husband puts up with it—he seems like a really nice man. Whereas you have to be the most devious, arrogant snake of a man it has ever been my misfortune to meet. And if you imagine for one second making me stay with you will change how I think of you…it won't. Now go back to your guests, Anton. I have a headache and I am going to bed. Alone.'

Anton fought down the furious impulse to shut her smart

mouth with his own. 'Not alone, Emily,' he said with implacable softness and took her arm.

She struggled to break free, but he tightened his grip. 'You are my wife and sharing my bed—that is not negotiable.'

His dark brooding eyes held hers. He saw the anger, the pain she tried to hide in the blue depths, and surely not fear?

Shocked, he let go of her arm. He was a huge success at everything he did; women looked at him admiringly, hungrily, with adoration, wanting to please him, but never with fear. So how the hell had he managed to make his bride of one day actually look afraid of him?

'You look worn out. I'll get you some painkillers, and you can get some sleep.'

Hmm. Emily sighed her pleasure as a strong hand slowly massaged her breast. She settled back against a hard male body and arched her neck as firm lips caressed the slender length of her throat, a warm tongue lingering on the steadily beating pulse there. Her eyes half opened and fluttered closed as she gave herself up to the wondrous world of sensations engulfing her. Long fingers caressing, arousing her eager flesh, she was lost in a sensual dream, her heart beating with ever-increasing speed. She turned, restless heat spreading through every cell in her body, her hands curving over strong shoulders. His mouth was on hers, his muscular legs parting hers.

Her eyes flew open. It was no dream—it was Anton lying over her, the morning sun highlighting his blue-black hair, his dark molten eyes scorching through to her soul promising paradise and it was way too late to resist. She didn't want to resist. She wanted him, burned for him. She felt the velvet tip of him against her and raised her pelvis, pressing up to him.

'You want me?' Anton husked throatily.

'Yes, oh, yes,' she moaned.

His hands curved around her thighs, lifting her, and in a single powerful thrust he filled her. He thrust again harder and faster as her body caught his rhythm and they rode a tidal wave of sheer sensation. Emily climaxed in seconds with a convulsive pleasure so intense it blew her mind, and Anton followed, his great body jerking in explosive release.

Later when the tremors stopped Emily felt a wave of shame at her easy capitulation. She opened her eyes and lifted her hands to push at his chest; instead she found them gathered in one of his. He lifted his other hand and she felt him brush a few tendrils of hair from her forehead.

'You okay, Emily?'

'As okay as I will ever be as long as I am stuck with you.'

'Hell and damnation.' He swore. 'We had a fight yesterday. It is over, done with. The two people we were fighting over are dead—that is the reality. Now we move on.'

'The only place I want to move is out of here.' She couldn't help herself. He had cold-bloodedly deceived her, and he rubbed her up the wrong way with his blasted superior tone and his flaming arrogance.

'Your trouble is you can't admit that you want a man like me, can you?' he grated, bending his head and crushing her mouth under his. Then he pulled back to look into her eyes.

'You can't face reality, that is your problem; you want love and sweet nothings, a fairy tale, when anyone with any sense knows the love you imagine does not exist.'

He ran a hand through his rumpled hair, and swung his legs off the bed to sit looking down at her, totally unconscious of his nudity.

'Sexual chemistry brings a couple together, they marry and

after a year or two the lust is burned out, but usually there is a child to cement the union. For a man it is a natural instinct to protect the mother and child, and in most cases a moral duty that ensures a marriage lasts.'

Emily listened in growing amazement. 'Do you actually believe that?'

'Yes.' He stood up, stretching like a big, sated jungle beast, and turned to glance down at her. 'Mind you, from where I am standing I can't imagine ever not lusting after your naked body.' And he had the nerve to grin.

Emily grabbed the sheet and pulled it up over herself, blushing furiously. 'You are impossible.'

'Nothing is impossible if you try, Emily.' The amusement faded from his eyes. 'That is what marriage is all about,' he stated. 'Having realistic expectations.'

He was completely sure of himself, his powerful, virile body magnificently naked, and she could feel her insides melting just looking at him, and in that moment she realized she still loved him…always would…and it saddened and infuriated the hell out of her.

'And you're the expert? Don't make me laugh,' she snapped.

'I will certainly make you cry if you keep up this ridiculous fight. We can be civil to each other, the sex is great and we can have a good marriage, or you can turn it into a battlefield—it is up to you. I need a shower; you can join me, or make your mind up before I come back.'

There was only one answer, Emily realized.

Being civil and having sex… That was Anton's idea of a perfect marriage. She could do civil and sex, and a lot more. He had said he had not intended telling her what he thought of her father, but his temper had got the better of him. Well, maybe she could convince him he was wrong about her father.

Not now, not with a boatload of guests, but when they were finally alone.

He had said he would do anything to keep her. Maybe there was hope for their marriage, maybe he cared about her a lot more than he was prepared to admit…and pigs might fly…

The bottom line was, even if she proved her father had nothing to do with his sister, she could not escape the fact that was the main reason why Anton had married her.

Anton emerged from the bathroom and Emily hastily sat up in bed, dragging the cover up to her chin.

His only covering was a white towel slung precariously around his lean hips. And as she watched he moved to open one of the large wardrobes that covered one wall, withdrew something and turned.

'So what is it to be, Emily?' he asked, and discarded the towel, giving her a full-frontal view of his toned bronzed body, and stepped into a pair of Grigio Perla aqua shorts.

Emily recognized the brand because she had seen the James Bond movie that made them famous. On Anton they looked even better than the star of the movie. Fascinated by the sheer masculine perfection of his physique, she simply stared.

'I asked you a question.'

'What? Oh! Yes.' She was so mesmerized by the sight of him, she replied without thinking.

'Good,' was all he said as he pulled a polo shirt over his head. 'Make yourself decent. I'll send the chief steward in with your breakfast, and you can have a chat with him. He knows how the weekend works. It is a pretty casual affair, but if there is anything you want to change just tell him.'

Who was it said fascination is the very absence of thought, the denial of reasonable brain function? Emily wondered. She was so mesmerized by Anton she could not think rationally.

'I will see you on the pool deck when you are ready. Friday everyone tends to laze around until lunch. Then go ashore, the men to check out the cars and the women to shop. Later we all meet here to eat and then sail along to St Tropez for those who want to hit the Caves du Roy nightclub, a favourite among a few of our guests.'

He strolled over to the bed, and held out a credit card. 'Take this—you will need it later.'

She took the card and turned it over in her hand. Mrs Emily Diaz was the name inscribed.

She looked up. 'How did you get this so quickly?' she asked, no longer mesmerized but mad. Anton was so confident in his ability to get exactly what he wanted in life, including her, she realized bitterly.

'I arranged for the card to be forwarded here the day we married, as I did your passport,' Anton said, a hint of a satisfied smile quirking his wide mouth.

She affected a casual shrug. 'You're nothing if not thorough,' she said coolly. But inside she was seething with a mixture of emotions, from hate to love and, yes, lust, she admitted. But her overriding desire was to knock the smug look off his face.

'Thank you. But I don't need your money; I have enough of my own.'

'You won't for much longer if you insist on this confrontational attitude,' he drawled with a sardonic arch of one brow. 'Give it up, Emily. You're my wife—act like one. I'll expect you on deck in an hour to take care of our guests.'

The timely reminder of his hold over Fairfax Engineering knocked all the defiance out of her. 'Okay.'

She watched him walk out. He really was quite ruthless, and she had better not forget that. But if he thought she was going to be a meek little wife he was in for a rude awakening.

* * *

The number of gorgeous women lining the pit lane came as a shock to Emily. She would not have thought that so many women were keen on motor racing to bother coming for the time trials. She said as much to Max, and he gave her a grin.

'It is not the cars they are interested in, but the men—they are motor-racing groupies.' He chuckled. 'Pit Ponies.'

'Oh.' It had never occurred to her, but now she saw exactly what he meant. No wonder Anton was such a passionate fan of motor racing. Fast cars and fast women lined for his delectation, she thought scathingly.

Personally she hated the scene. The noise was horrendous, the choking smell of oil took her breath away, and she cast a baleful glance at Anton. He was standing by a low-slung racing car having an animated discussion about the engine with the chief mechanic. He looked almost boyish in his enthusiasm and at that moment, as if sensing her scrutiny, he turned, his dark eyes clashing with hers. He smiled and in a couple of lithe strides was beside her. 'So what do you think? Isn't this great?'

'Put it this way,' she said dryly, 'I can see now why they call it the pit. The place is full of men, noise, and stinks of oil and super-charged testosterone, and if it is all the same to you I think I'll go back to the yacht.'

He grimaced. 'You're right—it is probably not the place for a lady. Max will take you back, and I'll see you later.'

Back on the yacht, she heaved a sigh of relief when she learnt most of the guests had gone ashore. 'I'm going to change and have a swim,' she told Max and headed for the cabin.

She had spent yesterday being polite to their guests, and playing the perfect hostess. The nightclub in St Tropez had been a real eye-opener, all the beautiful people—she had recognized a famous American film star and a chart-topping singer to name just two. She had drunk champagne and smiled until her face ached and had hated every minute.

Then later when they had returned to the yacht she had vowed she would not respond to Anton. But when he had slid into bed naked and reached for her, her resolve had been strained to the limit. His kiss had been hungry, possessive, and passionate. She had tried to resist, her hands curling into fists at her side. But when he had lifted his head, and caught the strap of her flimsy nightgown and moved it down to palm her breast, a groan had escaped her.

'Give it up, Emily,' he said harshly. 'You know you want to.'

He was right, shaming but true...

Now with Anton on shore she felt not exactly relaxed, but at least in control for the first time in two days. Slipping into a shockingly brief black bikini, courtesy of Helen, she headed for the swimming pool. She lathered her body with sun lotion, and was wondering how to do her back when Gianni appeared, and did it for her.

Anton stepped out of the helicopter, and took the stairs two at a time to the lower deck. He was feeling great, fired up... His passion for motor racing had been fulfilled with a day in the pit watching the time trials for tomorrow's big race. The team he supported had pole position. He flexed his shoulders...and soon his other passion would be fulfilled with Emily.

She had appeared to accept his take on marriage without further argument, and yesterday she had proved to be a hit with their guests.

Last night had been incredible; his body stirred thinking about it. He had climbed into bed, taken her in his arms and kissed her. At first she had tried to play it cool, but within minutes she had gone up in flames just as she had every time before.

Yes, life was just about perfect... He needed a shower. Maybe Emily would be in the cabin. She wasn't and, ten minutes later, dressed in shorts and shirt, he walked out on deck looking for her. Carlo was leaning over the guard rail with Tim Harding and Max beside him, but there was no sign of Emily.

Anton strolled over. 'Hi, guys.' He leant against the railing next to him. 'Have you seen Emily around?'

Max pointed to a small yacht anchored about two hundred metres away. 'She is over there with Gianni. Apparently the boat belongs to friends of his and the pair of them decided to race each other across and back. They arrived there twenty minutes ago.'

The feel-good factor vanished. He felt as if he had been punched in the stomach and realized it was gut-wrenching fear. His impulse was to dive off after them, but he realized it was pointless, and then blind rage engulfed him and he turned on Max.

'You let my wife dive thirty feet off the bloody yacht,' he swore. 'Are you mad? You are supposed to be a bodyguard.'

He stilled, his chest tightening as he recognized the source of his rage. He felt an overwhelming need to protect Emily, something he had never felt for any other woman except his mother and sister.

'Sorry, boss, I couldn't stop them. They were balancing on the rail when I came out on deck. But you have nothing to worry about. Emily swims like a fish. In fact the three of us still can't decide which one won.'

'That is why we are waiting here to see them come back,' Carlo said. 'We have a little bet on the result.'

Anton could not believe his ears. 'Forget your damn bet. Nobody is swimming back. I am getting the launch.'

Carlo lifted a pair of binoculars to his eyes. 'Too late.'

Anton looked across just in time to see two figures dive into the sea.

He'd kill her; he'd shake her till her teeth rattled. He'd chain her to him… But first he needed her back safely. A boat could cut across her path, she might get cramp—the opportunity for disaster loomed huge in his mind and with bated breath he watched with Carlo and Max as the swimmers drew closer.

Reluctantly he had to admit Emily was superb. She glided through the water with barely a ripple, her long pale arms rising and falling in a perfect crawl, keeping a punishing speed. He watched as they approached the stern and saw Emily grab the ladder first.

'I won,' Emily cried, hanging onto the ladder with one hand and brushing the hair from her eyes. Gianni's arm came up and grasped her waist.

'OK—so it is one all.'

Breathless and grinning, they scrambled up onto the deck.

Anton stood transfixed. Emily, wearing the briefest of bikinis, stood glowing with life and vitality laughing with Gianni. Jealousy ripped through him and he had to battle the urge to rush across and shove the younger man overboard.

'Best of three. I'll race you tomorrow,' he heard Gianni say and his wife was totally oblivious of him as she responded.

'Right, you're on.'

Anton moved to grab Emily, but Carlo's hand on his arm stopped him. He looked up at him and said softly, 'So, my friend, now you know how it feels?'

'What do you mean?' Anton demanded.

'You know Emily and Gianni are just friends, as I know you and Eloise are just friends. But when you love a woman it doesn't always follow that you can easily accept her male friendships. Take my advice—don't make an issue out of their harmless fun.'

Carlo's words gave him pause for thought. Of course he did not love Emily. But he knew Carlo imagined he loved Eloise, and it had never occurred to him his friendship with Eloise might hurt Carlo.

Then again he wasn't Carlo, and Emily wasn't having fun with anyone but him...

'You will not be racing tomorrow, Emily.' He strode across and took her arm. 'And you, Gianni, will not encourage my wife to risk her life in such a damn-fool way.'

'Oh, don't be such an old fuddy-duddy,' Emily said, lifting her eyes to his. 'You have your motor racing. I prefer a more natural race.'

He felt every one of his thirty-seven years and he did not appreciate the reminder. His dark eyes narrowed on her beautiful face. 'Have you forgotten tomorrow we are all attending the Grand Prix? And Gianni is leaving on Monday so it is never going to happen,' he said bluntly.

'Oh, yes.' She turned away from him. 'Excuse me all, I need to shower and get ready for the party.' And he had to let her go, as Tim Harding asked him a question about the time trials.

Coloured lights strung from prow to stern lit up the great yacht. Dinner was a buffet as the original guests had been increased by about another thirty from shore. Apparently another tradition of her indomitable husband. She glanced across to where he stood surrounded by friends, mostly of the female variety. He was wearing a white shirt open at the neck and dark trousers, and looked devastatingly attractive. The dress code for the men appeared to be smart casual, actually designer casual, Emily amended, glancing around, but her eyes were helplessly drawn back to her husband.

As she watched he laughed down at the woman hanging on his arm, and Emily looked away. Anton was always going to be the centre of attention, the outstanding Alpha male, in what she quietly conceded was quite a gathering of such men. But then why not? Monaco was the playground of the rich and famous and never more so than this weekend.

'Hi, Emily.' She glanced at Gianni as he stopped beside her. 'May I say you look wicked,' he said with undisguised appreciation in his golden eyes. 'Mind you, I think you are wasted on this crowd. What say we do a bunk to my friend's yacht?'

But before she could respond Carlo appeared in front of them. 'Damn Eloise. That woman could shop for Peru,' he declared, exasperation in his tone. 'You do know she only arrived back ten minutes ago—the helicopter had to go and pick her up, hopelessly late as usual.' He snorted. 'She said it wouldn't take a minute to change.' And grasping a glass of champagne as a waiter walked by, he added, 'I will believe that when I see it.'

Gianni responded with, 'Here she comes now, Dad.'

Emily's mouth fell open in shock. The woman was wearing a white off-the-shoulder dress that revealed her breasts almost to the nipples—not that it mattered as the fabric was see-through, a silver belt was slung around her hips, and the rest of the garment barely covered her behind. Emily glanced up at Gianni and saw the slight tinge of embarrassment on his handsome young face and she felt for him.

'New dress?' Carlo demanded and Emily's attention returned to him. His eyes were popping out on stalks. He had obviously not seen it before, she surmised, and her lips twitched in the briefest of smiles. Not that there was much to see other than the fact the woman was also wearing a thong. Outrageous didn't even begin to describe it.

'No, darling.' Eloise pouted. 'You told me to hurry so I just flung this old thing on.' She preened, doing a twirl.

'She obviously missed,' Emily said under her breath to

Gianni. His golden eyes widened and he cracked up with laughter, as did Emily.

'Oh, Emily.' He flung an arm around her shoulder. 'You are priceless.' He offered between guffaws, 'And so right.'

Anton broke off mid-sentence in a rather serious discussion he was having with the Swiss banker, his attention diverted at the sound of Emily's uninhibited laughter. Her head was thrown back, revealing the long line of her throat and the upper curves of her breast; her blonde hair fell in a silken curtain almost to her waist. The dress she was wearing was red and strapless and faithfully followed every curve of her body to flare out at thigh level and end just above her knees. She looked drop-dead gorgeous and as he watched Gianni's arm went around her.

In a few lithe strides Anton was at her side. 'I am all for you enjoying yourself, Gianni,' he drawled, 'but not with my wife.'

He reached down and caught her hand as Gianni's arm fell from her shoulders.

Surprised, Emily raised laughing eyes to her husband's face and was struck by the deadly warning in the black depths of his, and looked away.

Gianni said nothing, but moved back a step; the look in Anton's eyes had said it all.

'I said be civil.' Anton slid a hand around the nape of her neck and tilted back her head so she had no choice but to look up at him. 'Not flirt with the guests and make a spectacle of yourself. What was so funny anyway?' He was jealous—not an emotion he had ever suffered from before—and he was fed up as he saw all expression drain from her face.

'You had to be there at the time to appreciate it,' she said, 'but I take your point and I am sorry. I will endeavour to be civil at all times.' And she smiled.

A perfect social smile that didn't reach her eyes.

He kept her by his side for the rest of the evening, and later in bed he utilized every bit of control and skill he possessed to drain every drop of response from her incredible body. Only when she lay exhausted and sated in his arms was he satisfied.

He gazed down at her. She had been helpless in the throes of passion as he had brought her to the knife-edge of pleasure time after time, and had held her there shuddering and writhing until finally he had possessed her completely and she had convulsed in wave after wave of excruciating delight.

Then he had started again.

She was his… He had exactly what he wanted. He frowned slightly. So what was niggling at the back of his mind? Surely not conscience… No—something else. It would come to him later, he assured himself before sleep overcame him.

The following night Emily stood in front of the floor-to-ceiling mirror in their cabin and studied her reflection. She was wearing the one floor-length gown she had packed and she grimaced. Blue shot through with silver, the halter neck left her shoulders and back bare down to her waist, and the plunging neck revealed more than a glimpse of cleavage. The rest clung to her body like a second skin. A side slit enabled her to move. When she had bought the dress it had been with her honeymoon in mind. For Anton's eyes only. Because she had loved him, even after their argument she had still harboured a lingering hope of convincing him he was wrong about her father, and making him care for her. Not any more. Once trust was destroyed there was no going back.

She had no illusions left regarding her arrogant husband. Last night he had taught her what an avid sensualist she was, and she had relished the lesson. He had driven her to the erotic height of pleasure and beyond until it had almost been pain. He was a magnificent lover.

Today she had had her relatively inexperienced opinion verified...

They had all gone to watch the Grand Prix at the home of a friend of Anton's. Settled on a long terrace overlooking the race with their guests and some more friends of the owner, Anton had asked if she minded if he went to the pits. She had bit her tongue on the caustic comment *he was the pits*. Deciding she still loved him had not lessened her feeling of betrayal. But deep inside she had still held a faint hope that their marriage might work and instead she said, 'Not at all.'

Bored out of her skull watching cars roar past at intervals, she drank a couple of glasses of champagne. And then went inside to stretch her legs. She was standing behind a huge column admiring a sculpture set in an alcove when she heard the click of heels on the marble floor and a cut-glass English voice mention her name.

'Emily Diaz has my sympathy. He is incredibly wealthy, a handsome devil, and great in the sack, as I know from personal experience. But, let's face it, the man is not marriage material. I mean, bringing her here for her honeymoon, with over a dozen guests for company—how crass is that? I couldn't believe it when we arrived. But then we never knew he had married. Heaven help the poor girl, is what I say. She seems a really nice woman, well bred by all accounts and far too good for him. I bet she has no idea that he has had affairs with at least two of us on board and probably more.'

Staying out of sight, Emily recognized the voice as the footsteps faded away. It was Sally, the wife of Tim Harding, and Emily's humiliation was complete. She had known about Eloise, but to discover another of his ex-lovers was on board was beyond belief.

That any man could be so incredibly insensitive as to invite one ex-lover on his honeymoon was the stuff of nightmares, but two... She had more or less accepted Anton's version of why Carlo and Eloise were guests...but not any more. This latest revelation was the last straw.

At that moment something finally died in Emily.

Thinking about the conversation now, Emily briskly turned away from the mirror, slipped her feet into silver stiletto sandals, and straightened up.

CHAPTER SEVEN

'You look incredible.'

Emily hadn't heard Anton enter, and turned slowly to face him. 'Thank you.' He was still wearing the same chinos and a polo shirt he had worn all day, and he was still grinning. The team he had sponsored had won, and the driver was now leading the world championship race and Anton had been in a celebratory mood ever since.

But then he won at everything, Emily thought sourly, but at least while he was celebrating on deck, with the other men on board, it had given her the chance to slip away.

'But a bit premature.' His hooded gaze raked over her with blatant masculine appreciation, and the eyes he lifted to hers were gleaming with a hot sensuality she could not fail to recognize as he stepped closer. 'I was hoping we could share a shower.'

'Too late.' She forced a smile, and cursed the curl of heat in her stomach his suggestion had ignited. 'I thought as this is your guests' last night, I should make an appearance at the cocktail hour, before we go ashore to the party, so if you will excuse me.' She moved to walk past him, but he caught her arm.

His lips curved in a wry smile. 'You're right, of course—the perfect hostess. I can wait, and I won't spoil your lip gloss.'

His head dipped and he brushed his lips against her brow. 'But I have something for you.'

She watched as he crossed to a small safe set in the wood-panelled wall of the cabin and withdrew a velvet-covered box.

'I meant to give you this on our wedding night,' he declared, moving to her side. 'But I was distracted.' And he opened the box to withdraw a sparkling diamond necklace. 'You might like to wear it tonight.'

Emily glanced at the necklace, and reached out to stop his hand as he would have slipped it around her neck, and took it from him.

'Thank you. It is beautiful.' She let the waterfall of diamonds run through her fingers, and slowly raised her eyes to his. 'But unfortunately it is not right for this gown.' She handed it back to him. 'I'll wear it some other time.'

It was a first for Anton, a woman rejecting his gift, not just any woman but his wife... How dared she? Grim-faced, he scanned Emily's exquisite features and slowly it dawned on him while he thought they had had a great day, his wife did not share his enthusiasm. He had given her a fortune in diamonds and yet she looked singularly unimpressed. No woman of his acquaintance would have dreamt of doing that—usually they fell over themselves in gratitude. But Emily had actually handed them back to him.

'If you say so.' He placed the necklace back in the box and returned it to the safe, and when he turned back Emily had fastened something around her neck, and was slipping a bracelet on her wrist.

Anton moved towards her and stopped. Her long blonde hair was swept back in a smooth knot on top of her head, the severity of the style emphasizing the perfect symmetry of her delicate features. The shimmering blue dress caressed her superb body like a lover's hand. The simple tie at the back of her neck left the shoulders bare and revealed the silken-smooth skin of her straight back almost to her waist. But it was the platinum chain with a heart-shaped diamond and sapphire-encrusted locket suspended between the creamy soft curves of her breasts that captured all his attention.

'Nice pendant.' He reached out and fingered the locket and wondered who had bought it for her. Maybe her ex-fiancé? Not that it mattered, he wasn't jealous…he was never jealous…he was just curious, he told himself.

'Yes, I like it,' she said and, stepping back, she added, 'and I have the bracelet to match.'

She held out her wrist for his approval. The heart motif was followed in a string of diamonds with smaller sapphire centres around her slender wrist.

'I have never seen you wear them before.' He wasn't going to ask her… But he did. 'Who gave them to you?'

Emily glanced up at him. So far Anton had got all his own way in this farce of a marriage, but not any more, and she took great delight in telling him.

'The locket was a present from my parents for my eighteenth birthday. And the bracelet was a present from my father on my twenty-first birthday. Beautiful, aren't they? And surprisingly they match the ring you bought me. Isn't that fortuitous?'

Anton frowned at the mention of her father, though, if he was honest, in a way he was relieved. 'Yes, very,' he agreed. Better a father than the ex-fiancé he had imagined.

She turned to leave, and he caught her wrist. 'Wait.'

'Was there something else?' Her eyes flicked over him.

'No, not really.' It was not like him to be so indecisive. But there was something… She was as exquisite as ever, as polite, but the blue eyes that met his no longer revealed her every thought. Instead, he realized, they looked cold, almost cynical…

He let go of her hand and she left.

Was he responsible for the change in Emily, her cynicism? he wondered for a moment. He shrugged his shoulders. No... In his experience all women were notoriously volatile; wrong time of the month, wrong clothes—anything could upset them. Problem resolved, he headed for the shower.

Emily looked around her. Not only did it make it easier for her to ignore Anton's hand resting lightly on her waist, it enabled her to study the glittering throng, or, if she was honest, the women.

Anton was at home in this crowd. He had introduced her to the winning owner of the team, and a host of other people whose names she didn't even try to remember. But all the time in the back of her mind was the nagging question if he could invite two of his ex-girlfriends to stay with them for the weekend, how many more of the women here had he slept with?

By Anton's own admission he had been attending the Monaco Grand Prix for years, and she had not forgotten what Max had told her about the 'Pit Ponies'. What a degrading nickname for female groupies, and what did it say about the men who used them? Her husband probably one.

'So, Emily, have you had enough?' Anton said softly. 'Want to go back to the yacht?' She felt the warmth of his breath against her ear and tensed.

His hand tightened on her waist and the warmth of his long body against hers was a temptation, a temptation she was determined to resist.

'No.' She looked up at his brutally handsome face. His dark eyes held a wealth of sensual knowledge that excited and shamed her.

'Actually, I would like to go to the casino,' she said sweetly. 'Carlo told me you usually all go after the party—it is another tradition of yours, apparently.' Along with bedding any beautiful female he fancied, she almost added...

Anton cursed Carlo under his breath, and, much as he ached to get Emily back in bed, he could not deny her the trip. He had already taken all the eye-rolling and ribbing he could stand from his motor-sport acquaintances when he had introduced her as his wife, when Emily had quite blithely told them this was his idea of a honeymoon. 'Yes, okay.'

Anton gritted his teeth as the roulette wheel spun again.

'Oh, my God!' Emily exclaimed as the white ball landed on her age, number twenty-four, on the roulette wheel. 'I've won again.'

The croupier gave her a broad smile and shoved a huge stack of chips towards her, and Anton wanted to shove him in the face.

'Yes, Emily,' he said, stopping her hand as she went to place another bet. 'But we have been here over three hours. The others left ages ago. You have won at least ten thousand, so don't push your luck.'

The euphoria of his team's win, his earlier good mood had totally evaporated and slowly he had begun to realize that Emily was delaying going back to the yacht. Trying to avoid going to bed with him. Well, not any more; she enjoyed sex with an appetite that matched his own, and he had waited long enough.

She cast him a look. 'Have I really? That rather proves the maxim—lucky at cards, unlucky in love.' And she gave him a brittle smile.

'Cut out the sarcasm. Collect your chips—we are leaving.'

He was angry. She had with very little persuasion been a willing bed partner after their original argument. She had agreed to continue their marriage in a civilized manner. He could not fault her—she had been perfectly polite to their

guests, if a bit sarcastic to him at times, which he could understand given her upset over her father and the honeymoon, he
silently conceded. But he wasn't a fool. Now there was definitely something else bugging her...

He was sure of it when they finally got back to their cabin
and he drew her into his arms.

She tried to pull away from him, but he merely tightened his
hold on her and looked down at her with smouldering eyes.

'I have waited all night for this,' he said, and bent his head
to take her mouth. But she averted her face and his lips
brushed her cheek.

'Do you mind, Anton, but it is four in the morning and after
the last few hectic days I am exhausted.' Her eyes avoided his,
and her body stiffened in his arms. 'Plus I need to be up in a
few hours—a couple of your guests are leaving early.'

'One kiss.' He grasped the nape of her neck and tipped back
her head; she closed her eyes, and parted her lips, and he
kissed her.

He kept on kissing her until she was melting in his arms.
Then he lifted his head, and stared down into her flushed face.
No woman manipulated him with sex, never had, never would.

'Are you sure you are too tired?' he drawled mockingly.

She looked at him for a long moment, and he could actually
see her withdrawal, the sensuality fading from her eyes,
freezing him out.

'Yes, sorry,' she apologized, and slipped out of his arms. 'But
don't let me stop you. I have it on good authority there are at
least two other women you have slept with on board. I'm sure
one will oblige. If not you could always nip ashore and pick up
a motor-racing groupie with no trouble at all.'

Anton stiffened in outrage, and for a moment he said nothing
as he fought to control the fury that surged through him at her

insult to his moral integrity, his dark eyes narrowing to slits as he took in her cool face.

'That is some opinion you have of me, Emily, and in the future I might take up your generous offer,' he drawled. 'But first I'd like to know who fed you such lies?'

'Well, I knew about Eloise, of course, but while you were doing your man thing with cars I overheard Sally Harding describing your incredible sexual skill in the bedroom, and pitying me because what man would be so crass as to invite, I believe her exact words were *at least* two of his ex-lovers on his honeymoon.'

Her explanation was delivered in such a cool, disinterested voice that Anton simply glared at her. He did not trust himself to speak—disgust and anger washing over him.

'And you believed her?' he finally demanded through gritted teeth.

She gave him a derisory glance. 'The number of women you have bedded is legendary according to the press and I don't hear you denying it.'

His reputation in the business world was first class, and he would defend it to the hilt. But he had never concerned himself with the vastly exaggerated claims the press made about the women in his life.

'I don't have to,' he snapped. 'As for Sally Harding, she is a married woman who came on to me. A woman scorned and all that.'

'If you say so.' She shrugged her shoulders and Anton saw the patent disbelief in her face as she turned and disappeared into the bathroom, slamming the door behind her.

He stepped forward, his knee-jerk reaction to go after her, convince her of the truth. Then he stopped, masculine pride coming to the fore. He had never seen the need to justify himself to a woman in his life and he was not going to start now. It smacked too much of begging...

It was another new experience for Anton. No woman had ever rejected him and *apologized*. Then insulted him so thoroughly that he was still having difficulty believing Emily...his wife of mere days...had casually suggested he seek out another woman for sex.

The anger he had held in check for so long engulfed him. A string of Spanish expletives rolled off his tongue, and in a mood as black as thunder he stalked out of the cabin and up on deck. He did not trust himself to be around Emily right now without losing control, and that was unthinkable...

When he had cooled down and returned Emily was curled up in bed fast asleep.

She was so innocent and so gullible, the Harding woman had probably known Emily was listening and had fed her a pack of lies. She was no match for some of the female sharks that moved in the circle of the super-rich, or for the news hounds that preyed on a man in his position.

Given his family background, he had learnt long ago that it was pointless issuing denials—it only added fuel to the flames of gossip. Any woman he was seen with was automatically labelled his latest mistress. Yet he had never actually kept a mistress in the true sense of the word. The knowledge of his mother's not particularly happy life spent waiting for a man to visit, a second-class lover, and for her son a virtually non-existent father, was a salutary lesson.

Sure, as a single, healthy, sexually active male, of course there had been women in his life, women he had had relationships with lasting from a few months to over a year, though he had never lived with a woman. He preferred his own space. But they were women he respected and when the inevitable parting had come, they had for the most part remained friends. In fact he could count them on his fingers, and he had only once had a one-night stand and that had been with Eloise, and a disaster. Whether Emily would believe him was questionable. But whatever her father had done to his sister, he realized, revenge and pride aside, it was up to him to reassure her. She deserved that much.

Quietly he stripped and showered, then slid into bed beside her. He looped an arm around her waist and drew her into his body. She didn't stir and for a long time he lay with Emily enfolded in his arms. She was his…and he could set her straight in the morning, was his last arrogant thought as he drifted off to sleep.

Emily stood at Anton's side as they waved farewell to the last of their guests, the picture of marital bliss, she thought, when nothing could be further from the truth.

She flinched as Anton's hands cupped her shoulders and he turned her to face him. 'So, Emily, where would you like to go? I have to be in New York next Monday, but we have a week to do what you want. We can cruise anywhere in the Mediterranean or we can go to my Greek island villa, whichever you prefer.'

She glanced up at him; his dark eyes held hers and she knew what he was thinking. She had awakened this morning wrapped in his arms, and their early morning love-making was a potent sensual memory simmering between them. No, sex session, she amended with a now familiar dull ache in the region of her heart.

Afterwards he had explained why Sally Harding had lied— apparently she had come on to him a couple of years ago and Anton had knocked her back. Her husband was a friend of his. He also told her that naturally there had been a few other women in his life. But if he had slept with the number the press accredited him with he would never have made a fortune and would have been dead from exhaustion by now. Emily had said she believed him, because lying sated beneath him she couldn't have done much else, but she noted he never said how many! He had given her a very masculine satisfied smile and a tender, but in Emily's opinion vaguely condescending, kiss.

It was amazing to her how a brilliantly clever, highly successful man in the business world could so completely separate the physical from the emotional when it came to his sex life.

She could not do it... But she was trapped, and not just by worry over her family. She was trapped by her helpless desire for him. It was like a fever in her blood. She had thought after what she had discovered yesterday that she was cured of her helpless response to him. But this morning he had proved her wrong.

He had awakened her with a kiss, she had tried to resist, she had hit out at him, and tried to wriggle from beneath him, but he had simply pinned her down with his great body and had the audacity to laugh at her feeble attempt to dislodge him. 'So you want to play rough, hmm?' he had drawled, and kissed her again, his strong hands roaming over her body, finding erogenous zones she never knew she had, until the fire in her blood overwhelmed her, and she was reaching for him...kissing him...

She knew every day she spent with him she would just fall deeper under his sensual spell. She could not resist him, and he knew it. Before she had had no idea sex could become so addictive, but she did now. She craved his touch and it filled her with shame and seriously dented her self-esteem.

Max had left earlier with the guests and, alone now apart from the crew, paradoxically the yacht seemed smaller. Spending a week with no escape from the vessel filled her with alarm. At least on land there was the possibility of walking away from Anton for a while, escaping the overwhelming physical attraction he held for her. On the yacht there was nowhere to hide...

'I suppose home is out of the question,' she said with an edge of sarcasm.

'Your home is with me. Decide or I will decide for you.'

His hands tightened on her shoulders and she saw the ruthless implacability in his dark eyes. 'In that case your villa sounds nice.'

'Good. I will inform the captain. Unfortunately I have some work that can't wait. Amuse yourself for a while, and try the pool.' He drew her to him and kissed her with a possessive passion that made her senses swim and, lifting his head, he added, 'I'll catch you later, and that is a promise.'

By the gleam of masculine anticipation in the dark eyes that met hers she knew that was one promise he would keep.

'Okay,' she murmured, and watched him stride away. Probably the only promise he ever kept where women were concerned, Emily thought sadly.

Leaning over the rail, she recalled the promise he had made in church. It seemed like a lifetime ago now. She had meant every word of her vows, but she realized they had meant nothing to him—they had simply been a means to an end. As for his excuse about his ex-lovers...if they were ex, she amended, she didn't believe him for a moment.

Anton was a man with a very high sex-drive—even she in her innocence had gathered that in the last few days. She doubted he had even noticed the difference from their wedding night, when she had loved him freely and told him so frequently, to the silent lover she had forced herself to become. If it wasn't her he was having sex with it would be some other woman.

The thought caused her pain, and with the pain came a hint of an idea, maybe a way out...

Anton was an incredibly wealthy man, and yet by some oversight he had never suggested she sign a pre-nup. Or, more likely in his conceit, his supreme confidence in his ability to keep her sexually satisfied, and with the lavish lifestyle he offered, he probably didn't think he needed one.

But the likelihood of him staying faithful to her or any woman wasn't very great. Suddenly it occurred to her all she had to do was wait. He had said she could carry on with her career, and his took him all over the world. Inevitably they would spend a lot of time apart; she could make sure of it. Once, only once, would she need to discover he had been with another woman, and she could divorce him. Then take rather a lot of his money, at least enough to make sure he could never threaten her family ever again.

It was a horrible cynical idea and not like her at all, but then living with a cynic like Anton it was hardly surprising she was learning to think like him.

In fact she could take a leaf out of his book, and spend the time on his island indulging the sexual side of her nature, a side she had never known she had before. He had said it was just lust that brought a couple together, and eventually it burnt out. Well, by the end of the week, her body sated, she might finally be rid of her helpless longing for him, or at least better able to control herself.

Yes, she decided. She would do it—make the rest of her honeymoon a sensual feast even though the marriage was a fiasco.

Washed and dressed in shorts and a tee shirt, Emily walked downstairs and out onto the veranda where breakfast was laid out. Anton had already eaten, by the look of it. He had left their bed to take an urgent call an hour or so ago. Where he was now, she didn't know.

She crossed to the balustrade and stood admiring the view. The villa was set on the top of a hill that overlooked a beautiful bay; the gardens ran down in a riot of colour almost to the beach, the white sand reaching out to the deep green sea. Around the headland she knew was a small harbour and fishing village, because that was where they had docked yesterday afternoon. But here it felt as if she were the only person in the world.

A hand wrapped around her waist and settled on her stomach, urging her back into the warmth of a large male body.

'So do you like my home?' Anton's deep voice rumbled against her ear.

'Like is too tame a word—this place is like paradise.' Or it could be under different circumstances, she silently amended.

The villa was beautiful with five bedrooms, three reception rooms, a study and a circular, elegant hall with a marble staircase. Not excessively large, but with a basement gym and games room, and fabulous terraced gardens including an infinity swimming pool. A staff of four ensured the house ran like clockwork, and a team of gardeners kept the grounds in perfect condition. The place had everything; much like the man who owned it, she thought, and inwardly sighed.

'Good. So what do you want to do today?'

'Explore, swim in the sea,' she said, wriggling around in his arms, and placing her hands firmly on his chest. 'So far I have only seen the harbour when we arrived, the house and the bedroom suite.'

'Your wish is my command.' He grinned, and half an hour later they were driving along a narrow road in an open-topped Jeep, Anton wearing the most disreputable pair of cut-off jeans that bordered on the indecent and nothing else, Emily with a baseball cap on her head at Anton's insistence, her arms and legs liberally covered in sunblock.

The Jeep screeched to an abrupt halt at the harbour, Anton leapt out and before Emily could move he had reached over and lifted her to the ground.

'First I'll take you for the best cup of coffee in the world, but don't tell my housekeeper I said that.' He chuckled, and pulled out a chair for her by a rickety table outside a small café.

Immediately the owner came out, and Emily's eyes widened in surprise as the man greeted Anton with a bear hug, and hearing Anton speaking in Greek, so obviously at home, she felt her heart squeeze a little. She was introduced to the owner, coffee was served, with small sweet-tasting cakes, and as they sat there the entire population of the village must have walked by and she was introduced to them all, old and young alike.

This was an Anton she had never seen before, laughing, chatting and totally relaxed.

'Come.' He reached down a hand to her. 'Time to explore.'

They spent the day driving around the island, which actually did not take long. They lunched on bread and cheese, high up in the centre of the island as guests of a goat-herder that Anton knew, and then spent the afternoon down on a secluded beach.

Anton stepped out of his disreputable shorts, and, totally naked, persuaded her to do the same. They swam and laughed and Emily discovered it was possible to have sex in the sea. Finally they returned to the villa as the sun was setting, Emily slightly sunburnt and covered in sand, Anton looking more bronzed and fit than ever. They shared a shower, dined on the veranda and had an early night.

It was the honeymoon she had hoped for, and, even though she knew it was a sham, Emily shed all her inhibitions and enjoyed every second. She knew she would never love another man the way she had loved Anton, and with that in mind she blocked every negative thought from her brain. One week of sensual bliss was what she had promised herself, and amazingly it was.

CHAPTER EIGHT

'So WHAT would you like to do for your last day?' Anton asked, letting his eyes rest on Emily. She had pushed her chair back from the table, and was sitting with her long legs stretched out before her, cradling a cup of coffee in her hands, her gaze fixed on the garden and sea below.

She turned her head slightly. 'I thought I might have a swim in the pool, and then pack.'

God! But she was stunning. She positively glowed, a golden girl in every respect. The whole population of the island adored her; she was fun and friendly to everyone. She had obviously got over their argument about her father and that stupid Harding woman. But then he had always known she would after a week in his bed, he thought complacently.

Actually, he had never spent a better week in his life. She was his perfect match, in bed and out, and more than he could ever have wished for. She was wearing a flesh-coloured bikini with a fine sarong loosely draped around her and fastened with a knot between her breasts, and he felt his body stirring even though it wasn't long since they had indulged in the shower. Actually, for an innocent she had surprisingly seductive taste in lingerie, he realized, but then she was naturally sensuous, and so long as it was for his eyes only not a problem.

'Then I suppose I better make arrangements for a flight.'

Lost in contemplation of her body and what he wanted to do with it, Anton almost missed the rest of her reply. Regrouping his thoughts, he corrected her. 'No need, that is all taken care of. The helicopter will pick us up tomorrow morning and take us to Athens where my jet is waiting.'

She looked at him quizzically. 'Oh, but I thought you were going to work in New York.'

'Yes, I am.'

'Well, I have to be back in London for Tuesday. I have arranged to see some special, very fragile documents at the maritime museum to help in my research, and you did say I could carry on with my career.'

Anton's face darkened momentarily. Yes…he had said that, but that was before… Before what? Before he had developed an insatiable desire for her…

Maybe it was best he went to New York alone. He had meetings lined up all day every day and Emily was too much of a distraction. No…his nights were free and Emily could amuse herself during the day. He had never known a woman who did not love shopping and New York was a shopper's paradise.

'Yes, I did. But you have never been to my penthouse in London before. I need to accompany you the first time, clear you with Security, and introduce you to the staff,' he explained airily. 'It will be much more convenient if you reschedule your research for a later date, when we can go to London together. You will like New York, and while I work you can shop to your heart's content.'

Convenient for whom? Emily wondered dryly. He was so arrogant, so confident she would fall in with his plans like a meek little wife, and she had no intention of playing along.

She had enjoyed the week living in a fool's paradise. The

long days in the sun and the equally long steamy nights of sex—
she had indulged the sensual side of her nature to the nth degree.
It had not been difficult—Anton relaxed and among plain-
living island people was a different person.

They had laughed and talked about anything and everything.
He had told her how his Spanish Peruvian grandmother had
ended up a madam in a voice filled with affection, and no re-
crimination. Apparently when her lover had disappeared a few
months after his mother was born, a bitter enemy of her es-
tranged father had proposed an arrangement beneficial to both
of them. He had needed someone to front a high-class brothel
he owned, which his family had naturally known nothing about.
No sex was involved, he had assured her. It had been enough
for him that her father's name via his unmarried daughter was
very publicly discredited twice over... She had had nothing
more to lose and accepted.

To Emily, Anton's past went some way to explaining why
he had been so determined she should share his name, Diaz.
Polite society was hard on what was seen as immoral, most
would say rightly so. Anton was a fiercely proud man and,
though she knew he would never admit the past history of his
family affected him in any way, deep down as a young boy in
Peru he must have suffered for it. He was half Greek and yet
she realized he was probably more Peruvian than anything
else. He had freely admitted his work was his life and his only
other great interest was breeding horses at his ranch in Peru.

They had swum naked in the sea and made love whenever
the mood arose, which was pretty much constantly. But now it
had to end, because underneath, in her few solitary moments,
and even understanding a little better why he behaved as he did,
she still could not forgive or forget the main reason he had
married her, and, based on a lie, it had nothing to do with love.

'I am not keen on shopping and I can easily stay with Tom and Helen,' she finally answered.

She saw him stiffen, his darkly handsome face suddenly grim. No, he didn't like that... In his masculine conceit he thought he knew everything about her, but actually all he knew was her name and body.

'I'll be fine, and you don't need to worry,' she continued conversationally. 'I will not tell Tom and Helen the real reason you married me. There is no point in upsetting them by repeating your lies about Dad.' She rose to her feet. 'But I think I will go and book my flight before my swim.'

'No.' Anton shot up, and caught her wrist. 'I did not lie about your father, damn you, and I have a letter to prove it,' he snapped. That she could once again try to defy him after the perfect week they had shared puzzled and enraged him.

'I'll believe that when I see it,' she said with the delicate arch of one brow.

'You will—believe me,' he opined hardly.

'If you say so.' She shrugged her shoulders. 'But for all I know your sister could have lied.' She was being deliberately insulting and it pained her to do it, but she needed to make the break. She lifted wide blue eyes to his. 'After all, she was certainly no Mother Teresa, if as you say she was single and got pregnant at eighteen, a trait that seems to run in your family.' His dark eyes blazed and for a second she thought he was going to hit her.

Instead he twisted her wrist behind her back and hauled her hard against him. His mouth crashed down on hers in a deeply savage kiss that was more punishment than passion. She shuddered and he lifted his head, his dark eyes blazing down into hers.

'Hell, what's got into you? I thought...'

'What did you think?' She gasped. 'That your expertise in

the bedroom would make me forget why you married me? Well, sorry, it hasn't and it never will.' It took every shred of self-control she possessed to continue. 'You said civil and sex. And civil and sex is what you get. I need to be in London by Tuesday to continue with my career as agreed,' she reminded him emphatically.

She felt his hands tighten and then she was free. He stepped back and looked at her for a long moment with narrowed eyes, and then he gave her a dry smile.

'You're right, of course. But we will have to spend some time in the next few hours comparing schedules. I have no intention of being a celibate husband,' he drawled sardonically.

He reached out and she flinched, but all he did was tuck a stray tendril of hair behind her ear. 'And as for booking a flight, Emily—forget it.' His hand lingered for a moment on her nape. 'Go have your swim; one of the maids can pack for you. We will leave after lunch. I will see you safely settled in the London apartment and fly on to America tomorrow morning from England—it makes no difference to me.'

She looked at him quizzically. Such an about-face was unlikely from what she knew of him. But his expression was unreadable; he looked curiously detached.

'Do you really mean that?' she asked.

'Of course. Obviously the honeymoon, such as it was, is over. There is not much point in spending another night here.'

'Well, thank you.'

'You can thank me properly later. I need to call my pilot.' And, turning, he walked away.

Lunch was set out on the veranda overlooking the gardens, but there was no sign of Anton. Emily picked desultorily at a few bits of cold meat. She wasn't hungry. The maid appeared with a message from Anton. He was too busy to join her and had requested a tray in his study. He had also told her to inform Emily to be ready to leave in an hour.

Emily walked down the stairs exactly an hour later; she had changed her casual clothes for the blue suit she had worn on her wedding day. A day that seemed a lifetime ago now. Anton was standing in the hall, a laptop in one hand and a cell phone in his other pressed to his ear.

She paused halfway down. He was wearing a light business suit, immaculately tailored to his long, lithe body. He looked stunning, but she could almost feel the tension in him, could hear it in the clipped, impatient tone of his voice, and she pitied the person on the other end. He was no longer the laughing companion of the past week in disreputable shorts, but the cold, remote tycoon. Well, it was what she wanted...wasn't it?

Anton turned at the sound of heels on the marble floor, his dark eyes narrowing on his wife descending the stairs. The memory of her descending the grand old staircase of Deveral Hall on their wedding day flashed in his mind. She had been wearing the same suit, her blue eyes shining with happiness and the smile on her face enough to light up the huge hall, and it had been solely focused on him.

Suddenly he recognized the difference in her that had been niggling at the back of his mind since the arrival of the guests in Monte Carlo. The sex was great, but he had never seen the same unbridled happiness in her eyes, or heard the soft cries of love and delight she had showered him with on their wedding night. This past week on his island he had thought perfect, Emily had been enthusiastic, a truly amazing lover, but apart from a few sighs and groans a very quiet one.

Not that it mattered. She was his wife, and he had got what he wanted.

So why was he not satisfied?

'Good, you're ready.' He crossed to the foot of the stairs, and at that moment a startling idea formed in his mind, the hint of a wicked smile curving his lips... 'The helicopter is waiting.'

Emily saw his smile but did not reciprocate. She simply allowed him to lead her to the waiting helicopter. The flight to Athens was smooth and they boarded Anton's private plane for England with the minimum of communication between them.

As soon as they were airborne Anton removed himself from the seat next to her and crossed to the other side of the cabin, and, seated at a table, he opened his laptop and worked.

John the steward served coffee, and, having provided her with a handful of magazines, asked if there was anything else she wanted. He was a friendly young man and chatting to him she discovered his ambition was to travel the world and this job was one way of doing so.

As for Anton, he barely glanced at her.

She flicked through a magazine, and found an article on the discovery of a new tomb in Egypt that contained the mummy of a female pharaoh that predated all the others. She read it with interest, then, closing her eyes, she allowed her mind to drift.

Was she doing the right thing insisting on returning to England? she wondered. She wasn't ready to face Tom and Helen—they knew her too well, and would quickly realize there was something wrong with her marriage. Still, she would be staying in Anton's apartment—she could quite easily keep out of their way and a few days of her own company was exactly what she needed, she concluded, and drifted off to sleep.

When she opened her eyes, some time later, she glanced out of the window...

John appeared, quietly offering her a drink, tea or alcohol, before asking if she would like to order dinner.

It was the dinner that got her attention. 'But surely we must be landing soon.' She glanced at her wrist-watch. It was a four-hour flight, and they had been in the air almost that now.

'No, we are only about halfway.'

'Halfway!' she exclaimed. 'Halfway to where?'

'New York,' John began. 'We—'

'Shut up, John, I can take it from here.' Anton appeared and, catching her arm, he lifted her to her feet, his dark eyes gleaming with devilment. 'Time to show you around, darling.'

Flushed and almost choking with anger, she stared up at him. The filthy rotten swine had told her he would take her to London and she had actually thanked him... He had lied... The barefaced audacity of the man was unbelievable. Rotting in hell was too good for him.

'Why, you arrogant lying bast—' was as far as she got before his mouth descended on her in a kiss so deep, so passionate, she could hardly breathe, and when he finally let her come up for air she was slumped weakly against him, only his strong arms wrapped around her preventing her collapsing at his feet.

'You didn't really think I would allow you to dictate to me,' he murmured with a sardonic arch of one black brow. 'No woman ever has or ever shall.'

Speechless with rage, she gazed wildly around. Of John there was no sign. And she was stuck thirty thousand feet up over the Atlantic...

'You can't do this,' she hissed. 'It is little better than kidnap-ping.' His hand slipped around the nape of her neck, and he tipped her head back.

'I already have,' he drawled mockingly. 'Accept it, Emily.' Curving his arm firmly around her waist, he almost frog-marched her to the cabin at the rear that housed a double bed and a shower room.

As soon as he closed the door behind them Emily tore out of his hold and spun around. 'You rotten, lying toad,' she spat, boiling with rage. 'You said…'

He snaked an arm around her waist and hauled her back against him and she lashed out wildly with hands and feet. His other hand slipped between the lapels of her jacket and cupped her breast, and he laughed, he actually laughed as he tumbled her back on the bed.

Emily tensed, her moment of rebellion over, suddenly fiercely aware of his big body sprawled on top of her, his long fingers edging beneath the lace of her bra to pluck at her hardening nipple. She groaned almost in despair, appalled by the ease with which her body, even in anger, was incapable of resisting his slightest touch.

'Anticipation can be hell, my sweet,' he said, his sensuous lips curving in a knowing smile, and she wanted to strangle him. 'But also heaven.' He brushed his mouth against hers, and inserted a long leg between her thighs.

'We have plenty of time. How do you feel about joining the mile high club?' he asked teasingly as his fingers teased her breast.

He thought this was a huge joke…and from somewhere she got the strength to grasp his wrist and tug his hand from her breast and say, 'No.' Wriggling from beneath him, she sat up, her back to him, and adjusted her clothes with trembling hands.

She wanted to scream, rant and rave in frustration at the conniving devil that was her husband. But what was the point? It would only draw the attention of the crew, and make her look a bigger idiot than she already was.

After all, what woman in her right mind would fight with a filthy-rich handsome man who had actually done her the honour of marrying her?

She flashed a furious look back at Anton; he was sprawled

on his back, his hands behind his head. He had shed his jacket and unfastened the top three buttons of his shirt. He looked relaxed, completely unaffected by their passionate encounter, while she was still trembling.

'Feel free to change your mind any time. Long flights can be so boring.' He grinned and closed his eyes. 'Wake me when you want me.'

When hell freezes over, Emily thought, furious and frustrated.

On arrival in New York they were met by Max with a limousine and driven silently to Anton's apartment overlooking Central Park. She still had trouble believing he had actually brought her to the city against her will. But then she had very little will around him, she silently conceded.

Anton ushered her out of the car into an apartment building and straight into the elevator. He pressed the button, then leant negligently against the wall, his laptop in one hand, looking at her, a brooding expression in his dark eyes.

In the close confines of the elevator she felt the tension mounting as the silence lengthened and finally she said, 'I thought Max was coming with us?'

'No, he is parking the car, and then he will deliver your luggage and leave. He has his own place here, but he will be back tomorrow afternoon.'

'He seems to spend a lot of time with you.' She'd never really thought what Max's actual job was; she supposed he was a sort of PA. 'What exactly does he do?

'Max is the head of my security and a friend I can trust.'

'You mean a bodyguard? But that's ridiculous.'

'Not ridiculous. Inconvenient at times, but a necessity in my world. I run a highly successful business and there is always some crook wanting to make easy money or a business rival wanting to cut in on a deal. Max watches and listens out for me, ready to inform me of any danger. In fact, from the day we got engaged you have also had a bodyguard.'

'You mean I have been watched all the time?' Emily declared, appalled and furious at the thought. She felt as though her privacy had been invaded along with her body and everything else in her life since she had met Anton. 'Well, I won't have it. I will not be followed around by anyone.'

He shrugged negligently. 'Max's operatives are first class and incredibly discreet. I can guarantee you won't even notice. I am an extremely wealthy man and as my wife you could be a target for kidnappers.'

'And you would certainly know all about kidnapping,' she fumed.

'Forget it, Emily. You are here and the security is not negotiable… Understood?'

She understood just fine…but she had no intention of going along with the restriction on her privacy and she had no doubt she could slip the surveillance when she wanted to. Letting none of her feelings show, she glanced coolly up at him. 'Perfectly.'

'Good. I knew you would see reason.'

Emily almost lost it then. He had to be the most confident, arrogant, egotistical man on the planet. Instead she bit her lip and said not a word…

The elevator stopped, and Anton ushered her out with a hand at her back. Involuntarily she stiffened. His hand fell away and he cast her a sardonic smile.

'The entrance is this way.' He indicated the double doors at the end of a thickly carpeted hall and walked on, leaving her trailing in his wake.

He opened the door and stepped back. 'Your new home.' He gestured for her to enter.

He followed her and introduced her to his Spanish house-keeper, Maria, and her husband, Philip, who looked after the place for him.

'I will leave Maria to show you around. I have work to catch up on.'

'Wait…may I use your telephone?' Emily asked. 'I want to ring Helen, tell her where I am.'

Anton turned back. 'You didn't bring your cell phone with you?'

He knew she had one—he had called her frequently before they were married—and she saw the surprise in his eyes. 'Oddly enough, I did not think I needed it on my honeymoon,' she sniped.

His dark eyes shadowed. 'Okay, there is no need to labour the point, Emily. I get the message. My mistake, the honeymoon was not what you expected, but then life is rarely what we expect,' he said enigmatically. 'This is your home now; feel free to use the telephone and anything else you please. But a word of advice: there is a four-hour time difference. It will be eleven in the evening in London. I doubt Helen will appreciate the call.'

'I forgot, but I would, however, like to check my e-mails. Could I borrow a computer?'

'No need. I will have one provided for you tomorrow. As for now, Maria has prepared a meal. It is better to stay awake to avoid jet lag, though I can think of better things to do than eat, but by the look on your face I doubt if you would agree,' he drawled sardonically. 'I will see you at dinner.' And with that he left.

He had the last word as usual, Emily thought bitterly.

Maria showed her around the apartment. A huge lounge and formal dining room, a day room and study. Plus three *en suite* bedrooms and an incredible master bedroom with huge *en suite* bathroom including a wet room. The floors were polished timber, the décor traditional rather than modern, and the view over New York through a wall of glass enough to take her breath away.

She returned to the master bedroom to discover Maria had unpacked her clothes, and thoughtfully brought her a cup of coffee. 'To keep you awake after big flight,' she said in her broken English.

Showered, Emily dressed in skimpy white lace bra and briefs, white harem pants and a fitted white silk top embroidered in silver. She grimaced at her reflection; she did not have a lot to choose from. Her honeymoon wardrobe was limited, and much more revealing than the clothes she usually wore.

In her day-to-day life she preferred casual clothes, but she also kept a core wardrobe of designer clothes to suit any occasion. But taking Helen's advice she had bought her trousseau with a romantic honeymoon in mind, to please her husband. More fool her, she thought, disgusted with herself for being so stupidly trusting.

Then and now—why else was she in New York instead of London?

Dinner was a tense affair. Anton asked if the apartment was to her liking, and told her if she wanted to change anything to ask Maria. He had tomorrow morning free, and he would show her something of the city.

She looked at him across the dining table. 'There is no need. I'm sure Max will be more than enough to assure I don't get lost,' she said, still fuming at being hauled here and stuck with a bodyguard.

'Give it up, Emily,' he said, exasperation in his tone. 'Tomorrow morning I am taking you out. We are going to be here a while—you will have plenty of time to explore later.'

'Why would I want to? Especially as I did not expect to be here,' she said bluntly.

'I spend a lot of time here and as my wife so will you,' he responded curtly. 'At present I am in the process of a big takeover, and in the last stages of negotiation. I have great faith in my staff but any slip-up can cost a fortune so my personal involvement is a necessity,' he explained.

'I see. A lot more important than my research, which earns you nothing,' she said sarcastically.

'Be honest, Emily.' His dark eyes hardened on her pale face. 'Your career, though interesting, is not the major part of your life. You freelance as a marine archaeologist. I know you have been on three expeditions in the Mediterranean. But basically by far the vast majority of your time has been spent in London, researching at various libraries and museums.'

Emily sat up straighter in her chair, his disparaging but clearly informed awareness of her career enough to stiffen her spine. 'And how would you know that?' she demanded.

'I had you investigated.' He shrugged.

'Of course, silly me—what else is a prospective groom to do?' She lowered her long lashes over her eyes, and stabbed at a prawn on her plate. She was hurt that he had such a dim view of what she had worked so hard to achieve over the years. Well, what was one more hurt on all the others he had heaped on her? she thought philosophically and, picking up her wineglass, she drained it.

'Emily, ignoring reality is dangerous. You are in New York now, whether you like it or not. A place you are not familiar with and you will have protection,' Anton stated, looking directly at her. 'Especially as I do spend a good deal of time here.'

'I could not live here,' Emily said firmly. 'It is too...' She paused. She had only seen the traffic on the way from the airport and the streets teeming with people. 'Fast.'

'You won't have to all the time. My head office is here. But my home in Peru I consider my main residence,' he said smoothly. 'I think you will like it there.' And he had the gall to smile.

Not if she could help it, she thought. And she did not trust his sudden change of tone or his sensuous smile, and she recognized the darkening gleam in his eyes. Abruptly she got to her feet. 'With you there I doubt that, and I have had enough to eat,' she said curtly. 'I am going to bed...alone,' she added and turned to walk out of the room.

She had almost made it when a strong arm grabbed her around the waist.

She tried to move but his arm was like a steel band around her, and she was suddenly terribly conscious of his hard thighs against her own, and she laid a restraining hand on his broad chest.

'You are angry I brought you to New York. I understand that, Emily. But be aware my patience is not limitless.' His other hand reached up and tangled in her hair and his dark head descended, claiming her mouth with his own.

'Remember that later,' he husked when she was breathless in his arms.

She looked up into his dark, smouldering eyes, her heart racing, and she swayed slightly, then stiffened.

For heaven's sake, woman, she derided herself. The man kidnapped you, stuck you in New York—what kind of weak-willed idiot are you? And she pushed out of his arms.

CHAPTER NINE

SHE woke up alone in the big bed, only the indentation on the pillow reminding her Anton had shared it with her for the second night running without touching her. Emily told herself she was glad. She had been asleep when he had joined her the first night and she had turned her back on him when he had slid into bed last night and his mocking comment still echoed in her head.

'I often wondered what the cold shoulder meant, and now I know.' And two minutes later the even sound of his breathing had told her he was asleep.

But then yesterday morning with Anton had been a disaster, and the rest of the day not a lot better...

Like a general leading his troops, he whisked her around Manhattan. Bought her a cell phone and programmed it for her with all the numbers he thought she needed. Then he bought her a mountain of clothes, overriding all her objections. As his wife she had a position to uphold and the few clothes she had with her were not enough. Which was hardly her fault.

By the time the limousine stopped outside his office at one in the afternoon, they were barely speaking. She refused his offer to accompany him inside. Instead she had the chauffeur drive her around the main attractions. On returning to the apartment she was surprised when Maria told her her computer had arrived, and been set up in one of the spare bedrooms for her exclusive use.

She stared in disbelief at the bedroom. A computer was on an obviously new desk, a black leather chair positioned in front and the walls were lined with bookshelves—a perfect study, in fact.

She spun around on the new chair a few times, then started to work. She quickly began answering a backlog of e-mails.

One lifted her spirits no end. A confirmation that the expedition she had been researching for the last few months was definitely going ahead. All the licences and permissions had been obtained from the Venezuelan government. The expedition was to find a pirate ship sunk off the Las Rocas archipelago. She was to join the research ship in Caracas on the twentieth of September, as the onboard marine archaeologist to map out in detailed scale drawings any finds they might make on the seabed. Hopefully they would find signs of the ship and the cargo, which was reliably reported in ancient documents to include gold and treasure from all over Europe.

Hunched over the computer, she laughed out loud as she read the reply to her acceptance. Jake Hardington was a world-renowned highly successful treasure hunter and a great flirt, though Emily knew he was an extremely happy married man—his wife, Delia, was a friend of hers.

'Something has made you happy.'

She jerked her head up in surprise at the sound of Anton's voice. 'Where did you come from?'

Six feet four of arrogant male was standing looking down at her, dressed in an immaculately tailored business suit, but to her dismay the instant picture in her mind's eye was of the same body naked. His dark gaze met hers, and she fought back a blush at the thought.

'Work,' he drawled sardonically. 'And I guess I am not the cause of your good humour.'

'No. Yes...' she garbled her response. Because half the reason for the embarrassing colour tingeing her cheeks was guilt. She had no intention of telling Anton her news. His derogatory statements about her career, and the very fact she was here instead of in London, were enough to keep her lips sealed.

'I mean I was delighted.' She retrieved the moment. 'You bought me a computer and everything. Thank you.'

He bent over her and brushed a strand of hair from her brow, and ran his fingers down her cheek and around her throat to tip her head back. Nervously she licked her lips as his hooded eyes ran slowly over her, and inwardly she trembled.

'Anything you want you can have, you do know that,' he said huskily.

His mouth came down to cover hers, and as his tongue stroked against hers a familiar heat ignited deep inside her.

'Is now pay-back time?' she muttered resentfully as she remembered where she was and why, and abruptly Anton straightened.

'You disappoint me, Emily. I have never paid for a woman and you demean yourself by trying to play the whore, when we both know you are the opposite,' he said, his cold hard eyes looking down at her—in more ways than one. 'Why let resentment cloud your judgement?' He shook his dark head. 'Why deprive your body of what you so obviously want?' His dark gaze lowered to where her nipples pressed taut against the soft cotton of her top. 'You're a stubborn woman, Emily, but no match for me,' he warned and, turning on his heel, he left the room.

Inexplicably Emily had felt about two inches tall...

* * *

Thinking about it now made her grimace. Still, this morning was a new day, she told herself, a free day, and leapt out of bed. Quickly she showered and dressed in navy linen trousers and a brief self-supporting white top; she popped her cell phone in her trousers pocket for easy access in case she saw something she wanted to photograph, slung her bag over her shoulder and ventured out again into the city, a gleam of mischief in her blue eyes.

Anton was not going to have it all his own way. She dismissed the chauffeured limousine, insisting she was only going for a walk, and sauntered along the street.

At the first subway station she dashed down the stairs and squeezed on board a train that was just leaving the platform. She watched as the doors shut, and saw a look of shock on the face of a young man as he lifted a cell phone to his ear. She leapt off at the next station and dashed across the platform and jumped onto another one. She stayed for two stops, then exited the train and walked back up to the street.

She had no idea where she was and she did not care. She was free…

The street was crowded, someone bumped into her and she laughed. It was great to be one of the masses again.

Anton surveyed the six men around the boardroom table. It had taken months to get this meeting arranged and if they all agreed it was going to be one of the biggest deals Wall Street had ever seen. He was sure they would. Sitting back in his chair, he let the Texan hold the floor—the man had been his guest on his yacht and they had already worked out how to present the deal.

He felt a vibration on his chest. Damn his cell phone. He pulled it from his pocket and glanced at the screen. Then leapt to his feet.

'Sorry, I am going to have to postpone this meeting.' Angry—he was furious by the time they had all left.

He lifted his cell phone to his ear. 'What the hell happened, Max? How could you possibly lose her?' He listened, then responded with a few choice words and strict instructions to find her immediately.

Emily glanced around. The skyscrapers she had thought so great after six hours of jumping on and off underground trains and walking around now seemed threatening. She had realized when she had sat down in a restaurant for lunch, whoever had bumped into her had stolen her cell phone. But it had not bothered her because she had still had her purse and money. Except now she wanted to flag a taxi home, she had suddenly realized she had no idea of her address...except overlooking Central Park...

She did anyway, but the taxi driver didn't appear to speak very good English. She got the impression Central Park was huge and she thought he asked if she was east or west. But looking at his swarthy features half hidden by a beard and the speculative gleam in his eyes he could have said *easy* and *western*. Not wanting to risk it, she looked for a public telephone. The only one she found had been vandalized and as a last resort she walked into a nearby police station.

The policeman on the desk looked at her as if she was crazy when she explained that her cell phone had been stolen with all her contact numbers in it, and she did not know her address, and the trouble she had with trying to get a taxi. Then she finally asked if she could use their telephone to call her husband and reluctantly gave him Anton's name as she did not know his number.

He made a call and then was perfectly charming, offering her a seat and coffee. Gratefully she took the cup and gave him a brilliant smile. American policemen were really great, she thought, sipping her coffee and leaning back in the surprisingly comfortable chair he had found for her. But inside her stomach was churning. Anton would be furious. He would probably send Max for her and Max certainly would not be very happy either, she realized rather belatedly.

The door opened and the hairs on the back of her neck prickled. Slowly she looked up, her gaze riveted on the man who stood silhouetted against the opening. With the light behind him she was not able to see his face clearly, which was maybe just as well. It was Anton and her heart missed a beat; the waves of rage coming off his big tense body were intimidating enough.

He strode past her and up to the desk. 'Thank you, officer, that is indeed my wife. I will take her off your hands now. Sorry for the inconvenience.'

Emily rose to her feet. 'Hello, Anton, I didn't...' She looked at him and the words froze in her throat. His black eyes returned her look with a glittering remorseless intensity that sent a shiver down her spine. Her legs threatened to cave in beneath her, and when he wrapped his big hand around her upper arm, rather than protest, she needed the support.

'Thank you, Grant,' she threw over her shoulder at the policeman as Anton marched her out of the door.

'"Thank you, Grant."' He mimicked derisively as he shoved her into the seat of a big black Ferrari parked in a no-parking zone, and slid in beside her.

He gunned the engine and never spoke a word until they were back in the apartment.

She turned to glance warily up at him. 'I'm sorry I got lost.'

Anton stood towering over her, his eyes scathingly raking her feminine form with a blatant sexual thoroughness that brought a blush to her cheeks.

Emily could feel the unwanted flush of awareness flooding through her body at his insulting scrutiny. He looked dynamic and supremely masculine in his light grey suit jacket taut over his broad shoulders, his white shirt open at the neck, his tie hanging loose, and helplessness engulfed her as she stared at him.

Anton's grim voice broke the lengthening silence. 'You are lucky you only got lost. The desk sergeant told me about the taxi driver.' He cast her a hard, contemptuous look. 'Rather than wasting your time and talent trying to dodge Security and almost getting raped... Why don't you grow up? When are you going to get it in your damn-fool head you are no longer a foot-loose girl? Diving thirty feet off yachts and heaven knows what else. You are my wife, you are under my protection and yet you deliberately put yourself and those around you at risk. Two men lost their jobs today because of your actions, and I have probably lost the biggest deal ever as I had to walk out halfway through a meeting to find you. I hope you are proud of yourself.'

If Anton had shouted and raged at her as she had expected she could have handled it, but his contemptuous condemnation of her behaviour brought home to her how stupidly reckless she had been.

'No,' she said simply. 'I never meant anybody to lose their job. Please don't fire them.'

One dark brow arched sardonically. 'I won't...if I have your word you will stop this rebellious behaviour and start behaving as a wife should.'

'You mean bow and scrape to you,' she flared.

'Cut out the dramatics, Emily,' Anton responded and finally touched her, his hands closing over her shoulders. 'You know what I mean,' he grated, his hand sliding down her back to cup her buttocks and pull her hard against his thighs, and she trembled as the evidence of his masculine arousal pressed against her stomach.

'But, so help me God, Emily—' his black eyes burned down into hers '—if you ever put me through that again, I will lock you up and throw away the key.' She gasped, and his mouth crashed down on hers, his tongue thrusting desperately between her parted lips, passionately demanding.

She should fight, she knew she should because there was no love involved and for a million other reasons. But two long days of frustration were having a debilitating effect on her ability to resist him. Then why should she? The impish question slid into her brain.

Anton was satisfied with lust, he wanted nothing more, and, if she was honest, she finally admitted she no longer had the will or the conviction to fight the sexual attraction she felt for him. There was no point in pretending it was love even to herself...

She looped her arms around his neck, and felt his great body shudder and realized he really had been worried about her. It gave her a fuzzy feeling inside, and, though she was loath to admit, hope for the future. She ran her fingers through his thick black hair, and held him closer, responding with a hunger that matched his own. Later in bed two nights of abstinence took a long time to satisfy.

The next morning when she walked in the kitchen Max was seated at the table, waiting for her. 'Max, I might have guessed. Anton told you.' And pulling out a chair, she sat down opposite him, and poured herself a cup of coffee. Of Maria there was no sign.

'He didn't have to tell me. My operative informed me the minute you got on the subway yesterday. You do realize, Emily, it was not skill, but blind luck you caught that train and lost him. And sheer bloody luck—' he swore '—that you were not mugged, raped or worse...'

'You are forgetting kidnapped,' she said facetiously and

smiled. She had not forgotten the reason she was here instead of London.

'You think that is funny?' he snapped. 'Well, let me tell you, Emily, I have had to tell a couple in the past that their child was found dead after having been buried alive for three days in a hole in the ground, and it is not funny.'

'Sorry.' Emily instantly sobered. Max probably did not know Anton had tricked her into coming to New York.

'So you should be. What the hell are you trying to do to Anton?' She had never seen Max so coldly angry. 'I thought when he met and married you, it was the best thing that ever happened to him. At last he had love in his life, something he has never had before, but now I am not so sure. What on earth were you playing at?' He eyed her contemptuously. 'I have never in all the years I have known him seen him so distraught. He is a wealthy, powerful man and as such has enemies, and you are his wife, and should be aware of the danger. He damn near had a heart attack yesterday when you disappeared. He is by nature a loner, a very private man, not to mention a workaholic. But yesterday he dropped everything to call out the police, anyone and everyone, even the press to try and find you. The man worships the ground you walk on, and you repay him with a childish trick. Well, not any more. One of my top operatives will be arriving any minute now, and I want your word you will not try to give her the slip…understood? The alternative is I stick to you as well.'

Reeling under the verbal tongue-bashing, and amazed Max actually thought Anton adored her and was distraught she had gone missing, Emily meekly agreed.

Mercedes arrived moments later. She was a little older than Emily, and after half an hour of conversation over coffee Emily liked her. She had a wealth of experience of life in New York and a great sense of humour. From that day on she arrived every morning and accompanied Emily on visits to museums, art galleries. She showed her the best places to shop—not that Emily found herself actually enjoying her time in New York.

On a Friday night two weeks later Emily stood in front of the mirror and hardly recognized herself. Her blonde hair was swept up in an intricate twist. The black dress was strapless and clung to her every curve, one of Anton's purchases, as was the diamond necklace she fastened around her throat. He had arrived back from the office ten minutes ago and dropped the necklace he had first given her on the yacht on the dresser as he headed for the bathroom shedding his clothes, with instructions that she wear it tonight.

Their relationship had developed since Emily had got lost. She had quit sniping at him, and begun to accept his perception of marriage, and it seemed to work. The sex was great and, if sometimes she wished for the love she had dreamt of, she told herself no one could have everything. But what she had with Anton came close.

She had spent the last two weeks exploring New York with Mercedes when she was not sitting at her computer working. Which was just as well, because apart from a few social dinner engagements Anton said they were obliged to attend, she did not see a lot of him.

Max was right about him; he was a workaholic. He left for the office at six in the morning and rarely returned before eight, they dined and went to bed and the passion between them flared as white-hot as ever.

Civil and sex was easy under the circumstances and she could understand why it appealed to Anton. He had no time for anything else…

The only reason he had returned by seven tonight was because they were attending the opening of an exhibition of Peruvian art, as guests of the Peruvian ambassador to the USA, and they had thirty minutes to get there.

She heard the shower switch off, and, with one last look at her reflection, walked out of the bedroom and into the lounge. She stood looking out of the huge window, wondering how her life had come to this, waiting for Anton…

'The necklace looks good.' She turned. Anton, wearing a dark evening suit and snowy white pleated shirt, was standing a few feet away.

'How did—?'

'The reflection in the glass.' He read her mind.

He looked strikingly attractive and it wasn't just the suit. Tall and brutally handsome, he exuded an aura of strength and power and tightly leashed sexuality that took her breath away.

'We should leave; we are going to be late,' Emily said coolly. And he nodded his dark head in agreement and took her arm.

Slowly it had dawned on Emily that outside the bedroom Anton had an air of detachment about him that rather confirmed Max's comment that he was a loner. And the longer they stayed in New York, the more she began to accept that this was the real Anton. Not the deceitful seducer or the fun-loving companion he had been on the island. But the one hundred per cent seriously focused international tycoon. His work was his life; everything else was peripheral.

In a way it made life easier, she thought as they entered the Prestige's art gallery half an hour later.

Anton was a man with little or no emotion; even his revenge had lost its flavour for him, after he had revealed it to her. She remembered his dismissal of it with why spoil their marriage as the two people concerned were dead. She should have realized then… The death of his mother was probably the only event that had touched his heart in any way. Everything else was business.

'Emily. You seem miles away.'

She cast him a sidelong glance and a smile. 'No, I'm fine.' She glanced around the vast room. The walls were hung with paintings, sculptures stood on podiums, and a grand staircase led to another level and more paintings. All New York's élite seemed to be present. Waiters with loaded trays of champagne moved smoothly through the crowd, others with loaded trays of canapés circled non-stop. 'This looks very nice.'

'Damned with faint praise,' Anton murmured against her ear. And then she was being introduced to the Peruvian ambassador and his wife, and his beautiful daughter Lucita.

She was small and voluptuous with huge sultry eyes. She gave Emily a saccharine smile before turning to gush all over Anton.

Not another one… Emily thought, and found herself standing alone as Lucita wrapped her arms around Anton's neck and made to kiss him. He subtly averted his head so she caught his cheek instead of his mouth. But Emily knew… She saw it in the spiteful glance Lucita gave her, when Anton caught her shoulders and put her back at arm's length.

'So you are his wife. We were all surprised when we heard Anton had married. Have you known each other long?'

Emily opened her mouth to reply, but Anton's arm slipped around her waist and he pulled her lightly against him and answered for her.

'Long enough to know Emily was the only woman for me.'

Congratulations were offered, but Emily could sense the underlining hostility. She glanced up at Anton and caught the savage satisfaction in his expression as he smiled and they moved on.

'What was that all about?' she demanded. 'I thought the ambassador was a friend of yours.'

Something moved in the dark depths of his eyes. 'Not really. I have very few friends—plenty of business acquaintances, though,' he said, leading her slowly towards a wall to view the artwork. 'As for the ambassador, he has to appear to be my friend or lose his job, and that is what gets his goat,' he drawled mockingly.

'Are you really that powerful?' she asked.

'Yes.' One word and he took two glasses of champagne from a passing waiter and handed her one and slipped his arm around her again.

For a moment Emily looked at him. 'Is that all?'

'I sponsored the exhibition, and I also sponsor the artists.' He gestured with his glass to a huge abstract painting, all red, green and black. 'What do you think of that?'

'I'm amazed.'

'You like it?' His dark brows rose quizzically.

'No, I hate it,' she answered honestly. 'But I'm amazed you sponsored the event and the artists. I wouldn't have thought you had time.'

Anton chuckled, a low husky sound, his arm tightening around her. 'Your honest opinion is charming, though I doubt the artist would appreciate it. As for my sponsoring the event, it does not take time, just rather a lot of money.'

'I'm impressed all the same,' Emily declared as he propelled her further around the room. 'I am also hungry,' she murmured and took a canapé from a passing waiter and popped it in her mouth.

At just that moment someone spoke to Anton, she swallowed the food, and was introduced to an eminent banker and his wife.

For the next hour they circled the gallery. Anton was greeted by a host of people, and Emily shook hands and smiled in between sipping champagne and popping canapés in her mouth.

As for the paintings, two she really liked. A somewhat abstract landscape of the Andes with mist swirling that looked almost mystical, and a small painting of a little Indian boy squatting on the ground and laughing, with what was obviously his father's big black hat on his head.

Anton bought both.

'You didn't have to do that.'

'I wanted to.' He pulled her close and led her through the crowd towards the exit. 'And if I had given you the choice we would never get out of here—women take a notoriously long time to make a decision, and we are going to dinner. I am hungry.'

Emily gave him a dazzling smile. 'Anton, that is a terrible chauvinistic comment, even for you.'

'So? I want you...out of here.' His dark eyes held hers and she was captivated by the amusement, the sensual warmth in the inky depths. For a second she was back on his Greek island, and her pulse began to race, and anticipation shivered through her. Was he aware of it?

'We're leaving,' he rasped and she knew he was as they made for the exit.

'Going?' Lucita with three friends stopped them as they reached the foyer.

'Why don't you join us, Anton? We are going on to a supper club.' She spoke solely to Anton, ignoring Emily.

'No, Lucita,' he said in a voice that held an edge of steel. 'I have better things to do,' and with that parting shot he urged Emily outside.

But the moment was broken for Emily. 'That was a bit brutal—you obviously know the lady very well,' she said, moving out of his protective arm. 'And I saw the look on your face when you spoke to the ambassador, and it wasn't very edifying.'

'Edifying?' He raised an eyebrow. 'You are *so* English, Emily.'

He ushered her into the back seat of the limousine without saying another word, and slid in beside her. He closed the glass partition, and then turned to look at her.

'Yes, I know Lucita well, but not as well as you imagine. I knew her brother a lot better.' His face, shadowed in the dim light, was hard. 'Do you want to know the truth, or do you want to mark her down as another woman I have slept with? You seem to be under the impression I have slept with hundreds, which I have not. I would not even make double figures, but my reputation goes against me. Something you could not begin to understand, given the charmed life you have led.'

'I wouldn't say—'

'Say nothing and listen for a change. I was twelve when my mother brought me back to Peru to live with my grandmother. At first I went to the local school, but at fourteen I was sent to the best boarding school in the country, and that is where I met Lucita's brother. We became friends, because he was bullied unmercifully by the other boys and I stood up for him. Unfortunately for Pedro, he took after his mother, who, you might have noticed, is a small, quiet lady who I have great respect and sympathy for, but she is and always has been completely under her husband's thumb.

'Pedro and I studied together; we visited each other's home in the holidays, and played football, badly.' He grimaced. 'He had an artistic soul, and for two years we were friends, Lucita as well, until his father discovered my parentage. They were forbidden to see me again. And the man did his damnedest to get me thrown out of school.'

'Oh, Anton….' She couldn't imagine how he must have felt. He had made light of his parentage, but now she realized for a young boy it must have been hard.

'Don't worry. He was a minor government official at the time and he did not succeed. But he ruined his son's life, he sent him to another school, where apparently he was bullied again, and twelve months later Pedro committed suicide. I stood in the background at his funeral, the only teenage friend there.'

No wonder Anton had been distraught discovering his sister had committed suicide; his childhood friend had done the same.

'So you see why it gives me great satisfaction to watch the man having to be polite to me now, and I am not going to apologize for that. As for his daughter, she is just like him— the only difference is she would have me in a heartbeat simply because I am wealthy.'

'I'm sorry. I had no idea.'

He sat back in the seat. 'I told you the first time we met. I just knew you would feel sorry for me, and your sympathy is misplaced. You're too naive for your own good, Emily.' But the indulgent smile he gave her took the sting out of his words.

'I might be naive...' she looked at him curiously, a sudden thought occurring to her '...but answer me this. Why didn't you marry Lucita to get back at her father? Rather than waiting to marry me to get back at mine?'

He stilled. 'The idea never entered my head.' He shook his head, his dark eyes widening on her, and then he burst out laughing. 'Oh, Emily, I might have a vengeful streak, but I am not a masochist. You are delightful and drop-dead gorgeous and Lucita is an evil witch in comparison.'

Emily stared at him in shock. Was that a compliment? She did not know what to think...and, taking full advantage, Anton leant forward and kissed her.

The limousine stopped and Anton helped her out. 'I thought we were going to eat out,' she said as he led her into their apartment.

He smiled a soft, slow curl of his firm lips, and moved his hand from her arm to snake around her shoulders, staring into her eyes from mere inches away. 'I am still hungry, *niña*,' he said softly, his slight accent more pronounced than usual, 'but the food can wait till later.' His dark eyes smouldered as he held her and he bent closer and she felt the hard warmth of his mouth brush against her parted lips.

Far into the night Emily made love with Anton with a long, slow tenderness, a passion that brought tears to her eyes because she knew to Anton it was still just sex…

CHAPTER TEN

ANTON snapped shut his laptop, and fastened his seat belt.

They would be landing in ten minutes, and it could not be too soon. He had clinched a major deal and cleared his work schedule for the next month.

He had not seen Emily in weeks, it was becoming ridiculous and he was determined to do something about the situation. A frown crossed his broad brow. They had been married three months, the sex was great and he should be satisfied. Yet the amount of time they had spent with each other was limited.

After three weeks in New York they had returned to London. Emily had caught up with her research. But he had been obliged to travel to the Middle East. In July they had returned to Greece, but he had taken frequent trips to Athens and Moscow.

The beginning of August Emily was supposed to have accompanied him to Australia. But Helen had given birth to a baby boy and Emily had gone back to England to help look after the mother and Anton could hardly object.

But after almost two weeks on his own he had called her last night and told her to be packed—they were going to Peru tomorrow. Which gave him time to kiss the baby's head and leave. It was time they had a baby of their own; in fact Emily might already be pregnant. Not that she had said anything during their telephone calls, but then she never said much anyway...

A frustrating hour later, after discovering she was not at their apartment, he stopped the Bentley outside the Fairfax home in Kensington.

Mindy, the housekeeper, showed him into the drawing room.

Emily was sitting on a low chair, the rays of the afternoon sun shining through the window casting a golden halo around her head, and in her arms she held a baby.

She was totally oblivious of his arrival, her whole attention on the tiny infant, her beautiful face wreathed in smiles. 'You are a beautiful little boy.' She chuckled. 'Yes—yes, you are, and your aunty Emily loves you.' And as he watched she kissed the baby's cheek.

He choked...and felt an unfamiliar stab of something like emotion in the region of his heart. 'Emily.' She turned her head to look at him.

'Anton, I never heard you arrive.' Slowly rising to her feet, cradling the baby, she walked across to him. 'Look, isn't he gorgeous?'

She was gorgeous. Her hair was parted in the middle and tucked behind her delicate ears to fall in a silken mass down her back. She was wearing blue jeans that clung to her slim hips and long legs, and a soft white sweater.

He looked at the child. The baby was snuggled against her breast, and he wished it were him...

'Yes, wonderful.' He reached a finger to touch the baby's cheek.

'Helen and Tom have decided to call him Charles after our father.'

Anton looked down into her blue eyes and saw the flash of defiance she made no attempt to hide, and his mouth tightened. She was an exquisitely beautiful but wilful woman and she was never going to accept the truth about her father. As for him, he didn't care any more…

'A solid name. I like it,' he said smoothly.

'Charles Thomas.' Helen, coming in, moved to take the child from Emily's arms. 'Anton, good to see you—now, would you mind taking your wife back home, before she takes over my baby completely, and try making one of your own?' She laughed.

They all laughed but he noticed Emily avoided his gaze.

'I intend to do just that.' Anton reached for Emily and drew her into his arms, his dark eyes searching her guarded blue. 'This is a brief visit, Helen,' he said without taking his eyes off his wife. 'We are flying out to my place in Peru tomorrow.'

Just seeing Anton walk in the door had made Emily's heart lurch. It had taken all her self-control to walk slowly towards him and show him the baby, and now, held in his arms, she felt a bittersweet longing shudder through her. When he kissed her the warmth of his lips, the scent of him, aroused her in a second.

'We are leaving.' Anton lifted his head and she looked up into his dark eyes, and saw the promise of passion, and knew hers showed the same.

'Get out of here, you two,' Helen said with a chuckle. 'You're embarrassing the baby.'

As soon as they entered the penthouse Anton slid an arm around Emily's waist and pulled her towards him.

'I have waited two long weeks for this,' he husked.

'Why? Were there no willing women in Australia?' And Emily was only half teasing. She knew in her heart of hearts she loved him, yet she could not let herself trust him, and the green-eyed monster haunted her thoughts when he was gone. Not something she was proud of.

'Plenty willing but none that looked like you.' His brilliant eyes gleamed as he bent his head and covered her mouth with his.

So he had been looking, was Emily's last thought as, help-lessly, her eyelids fluttered down and she raised her slender arms to wrap around his broad shoulders, her body arching into his.

His kiss possessive, his tongue traced the roof of her mouth and curled with hers, and her blood flowed like liquid heat through her veins. His hand slipped up beneath her sweater and trailed up her spine, making her shudder as he opened her bra. Then his hand stroked around to slip up beneath the front of her sweater to find the thrusting swell of her breasts.

'You are wearing far too many clothes,' he rasped, and suddenly she was swept up into his arms, his mouth desperately claiming hers again as, with more haste than finesse, he carried her to the bedroom and dropped her on the bed. 'Get them off.'

Her eyes opened and her gaze fixed on Anton ripping off his clothes like a man possessed. Naked, he was masculine perfec-tion. Tall and broad, his muscular chest rising not quite steadily and his lean hips and thighs cradling the virile power of his fully aroused sex.

'You want me to do it for you.' He chuckled, a deep sexy sound that vibrated across her nerve endings, and, leaning over her, he stripped her jeans and briefs from her legs, before just as efficiently dispensing with her sweater and bra.

His hands cupped her naked breasts and her nipples hardened beneath his skilful touch.

'Missed me…?' He looked deep into her eyes, and she could not lie.

'Yes,' she sighed and reached for him. But inside her heart cried for what might have been. She could have been the happiest woman alive, a loving wife, but Anton had destroyed that dream with his revelation about his real motivation for marrying her.

The really soul-destroying part was that Anton didn't even see it. He was perfectly content so long as the sex was good.

Angry with herself for loving him, she reared up and, pushing him down, straddled his thighs, determined to drive him mad with desire. Why should she be the only one?

'You are eager—maybe I should stay away more often,' he said with a husky amusement in his tone, his great body stretched hard beneath her.

'Maybe you should.' She stared down into his brutally handsome face. He was watching her, a sensual gleam in his night-black eyes. He reached out a hand and captured her breast, his long fingers tweaking a pouting nipple. She jerked back, heat flooding from her breast to her thighs, but she would not be deterred from her mission to make him squirm for a change. She wrapped her fingers around his aroused manhood and lowered her head, her long hair brushing the length of his torso, and tasted him.

His great body bucked and she heard him groan, she felt his tension, and she shook with the effort it took to control her own heightened desire for him. She continued until he was straining for release, then stopped.

She raised her head. His eyes were smouldering like the depths of hell, his face taut, and she closed her fingers gently around him.

'Not yet,' she murmured. Running her tongue around her full lips, she saw the fiery passion burn brighter in his eyes. Deliberately she leant forward and trailed a row of kisses from his belly up the centre of his chest, straying once to tongue a small male nipple before moving on to finally cover his mouth with her own, her hand stroking lower to cup the essence of the man. Suddenly he was lifting her, impaling her on his fiercely erect manhood.

Wild and wanton, she rode him, his body arching up as he filled her to the hilt with increasingly powerful thrusts. His hands gripped her waist, making her move, twisting, turning her where he desired, as they duelled for sexual supremacy. She cried out at the tug of his mouth on her rigid nipples, and arched back, fighting for control.

Emily succumbed first, convulsing around him. She was mindless in her ecstasy, clenching him with every spasm in a ferociously prolonged orgasm. She heard him cry her name and his body shuddered as he joined her in a climax that finally stopped her breath. The little death.

Some time later she opened her eyes to find Anton staring down at her. 'That was some welcome home, Emily,' he said, curving her into the side of his body. She brushed a few tendrils of damp hair from her face, smoothing the long length over one shoulder and down to her breast, where his hand lingered.

'Yes, well...' It was what he expected, she thought, suddenly feeling cold inside. 'Two weeks without sex is not good for anyone,' she threw out. And saw a flicker of some emotion she could not put a name to in the depths of his dark eyes.

'Tell me about it,' he said dryly, and then added, 'It must be tough for Helen—no sex for a few weeks after the birth, I believe.'

'I doubt if Helen minds. She has a beautiful little boy to love.'

'And would you mind, if you were pregnant? You could be.'

The question blind-sided her. No, she couldn't be, but, seeing Helen with her baby for the last two weeks, it had brought home to her how much she would have loved to have Anton's child if only he had loved her... But there was no future in thinking like that. Anton did not believe in love and was therefore incapable of loving anyone; he had told her so quite emphatically.

Whereas she had been a trusting soul all her life and Anton had destroyed that part of her nature with a few words, and if he ever found out she loved him it would destroy her completely; all she had left was her pride.

'I have never thought about it, and I am not in any hurry to find out,' she lied and moved along the bed, away from the warmth of his big body.

He caught her chin between his finger and thumb and turned her head back so she had no choice but to look at him. 'Seeing you with the baby today I realized you are a natural, Emily. You will make a wonderful mother.'

A tender, caring Anton was the last thing she needed. She felt guilty enough as it was, though she had no need to be. He had deceived her into marrying him; her deceit was nothing in comparison.

'Maybe.' She shook her head, dislodging his hand, and tried a smile but suddenly a thought hit her… And, jumping off the bed in a show of bravado, she stood up totally naked and stared down at him. 'But we have only been married a few months, and, let's face it, we hardly have a marriage made in heaven. A bit of time to adjust to each other before having to adjust to a baby is no bad thing,' she offered and, turning, she walked quickly into the bathroom. She had just remembered she hadn't taken her pill the last two nights, because she had spent the weekend with Tom and Helen…

She snagged a large towel from the rail and tucked it around her body sarong-style. Then found the packet in the back of the bathroom cabinet where she had carelessly left it while Anton was away.

She took two out… Was it dangerous to take two? She had a feeling it was. She scanned the packet, but it didn't say. She placed the packet on the back of the vanity unit and popped one pill in her mouth and dropped one in the basin. Then, filling a glass with water, she swallowed it down, and let the water run to wash away the other.

'Headache?' She heard his voice and spun around to see Anton naked and leaning against the bathroom door. 'So soon?'

'Kind of,' she murmured.

Something predatory and ruthless glinted in his dark eyes as he strolled towards her and reached over the basin to where the packet lay and picked it up. 'A contraceptive pill that doubles as a headache cure. How convenient.' She saw the banked-down anger in his black eyes and was afraid.

A naked man should not be able to look threatening, she thought distractedly, but Anton did. As though sensing her thoughts, he grabbed a towel and wrapped it around his hips.

'What—no response, Emily?' he drawled, closing in on her, and she took a few steps back until she met the wall. 'No excuse, you devious little bitch?'

She sucked in a furious breath. 'That is rich coming from you,' she threw at him, her eyes flashing. He was not going to intimidate her, and she would not allow it. 'As for an excuse, I don't need one. Yes, I am on the pill—so what?' she challenged him, her anger laced with scorn. 'My body is my own—you borrow it for sex. Nothing more and, may I point out—' and she poked him in the chest with her finger '—it was your own idea; love does not come into the equation.'

Emily was on a roll and could not stop. She didn't notice the sudden narrowing of his eyes or the tension in his great body. She was too overcome with emotion—something he knew nothing about. 'Do you honestly think I would bring a baby into the world without love, just to fulfil some dynastic craving of yours? You must be joking.'

For over three months she had fought to keep control of her

emotions around Anton, but now her composure was beginning to shatter.

'Nothing to say?' she demanded into the lengthening silence, and dragged an angry if slightly unsteady breath into her suddenly oxygen-starved lungs. 'Why am I not surprised? You are so damned sure of yourself, with your limitless wealth and arrogance, it is probably the first time in years you have found something you can't buy…a baby.'

She shook her head despairingly. Was it possible to love and hate someone at the same time? she wondered. Because right at this moment, with Anton standing half naked, bristling with rage, her stupid heart still ached for him, and yet her head hated him. She tried to walk past him. What was the point in arguing?

Anton had kept control on his temper by a thread and now it broke. Ice-cold fury glittered in his eyes as he looked at her. 'That's right. I bought you,' he stated coldly. 'And nobody does me out of a deal. Certainly not you, my wilful little wife.'

He wanted to tear her limb from limb as she stood there, her long hair falling around her shoulders in golden disarray, the expression on her beautiful face one of contempt. Yet she had been deceiving him for weeks, possibly months.

'How long—how long have you been taking the pill?' he demanded, and, grasping a handful of her hair, he twisted it around his wrist and pulled her head back, the better to look into her deceitful eyes.

'Since the week after we met,' Emily shot back and told him the truth. 'When I was foolish enough to think you and I might have an affair. After all, that is what you are renowned for and that was all I expected.' She trembled at the rage in the depths of his eyes, but refused to back down. 'Imagine my surprise when you proposed marriage. And, idiot that I was, I accepted, labouring in the misguided notion that I loved you. But you soon put me right on that score, Anton. Lucky for me I already had the pills.'

Anton stared down into her blazing blue eyes fiercely battling the urge to cover her mouth with his and drive her hate-filled words down her throat. Emily had quite confidently expected to be his mistress, going so far as taking the pill in preparation. But he had surprised her with offering marriage. There was only one conclusion he could draw—she thought she was too good to have his child.

'Did you ever intend to tell me?' he demanded. 'Or was I to remain in ignorance for years?'

'Oh, I doubt it would be for more than two at the very most,' she drawled scathingly. 'You said yourself lust burns out and, for a man with your sexual appetite, I know I will not have to wait long before you are unfaithful, and then I can divorce you and you can't do a damn thing about it. Except pay up... But I'm not greedy, just enough to make sure Fairfax Engineering is totally free from you. Your one mistake was not asking me to sign a pre-nup. I would have done—I would have done anything you wanted until you revealed your real reason for marrying me. Well, you should be proud, Anton. You taught me well.' As Emily watched a shuttered expression came over his face, and his hand fell from her hair and he moved back from her.

'Too well, it would seem.' Reaching, he tugged the towel from her slender form. His rapier-like glance raked her from head to toe as though he had never seen her before, and she trembled.

'You are beautiful, but you have just proved you are a Fairfax just like your father, and now I find I would not have you as the mother of my child if you paid me,' he drawled derisively, and with a shrug he turned and strode out of the bathroom.

She watched him warily for a moment; there was a defeated look to the curve of his broad shoulders as he walked towards the bed. He ran a hand distractedly through his black hair, and then he straightened. Emily picked up the towel and wrapped it around her shivering body and took a hesitant step towards the open door, concerned. She must have made some sound because Anton spun around.

'No need to be wary. I am not going to jump you.' He smiled a bitter twist of his sensuous lips. 'The bedroom is yours, but be aware a divorce is not, unless I choose.'

She must have rocks in her head, worrying about him, Emily thought, advancing into the room.

A hand on her shoulder woke her from a restless sleep; she blinked and opened her eyes. And found Anton standing over her, dressed in a black shirt, black trousers and a black leather jacket, a mug of coffee in his hand. 'Drink this and hurry up and dress. You can have breakfast on board—we are leaving in less than an hour.'

She pulled the sheet over her breasts. 'Leaving...going where?' She was confused. 'I don't understand...I thought after last night...'

'That I would leave you? No, Emily, not yet. You are coming to Peru with me. I promised to prove to you what a stuck-up degenerate your father was. Unlike you, I keep my promises.'

She looked at him. His face was hard, his eyes cold and dead. He caught her shoulders and hauled her into a sitting position. 'After that you can go where the hell you like,' he said with icy finality in his tone.

For Emily the flight to Peru was horrendous. Twelve hours of Anton being scrupulously polite when the steward was around, and ignoring her the rest of the time. Unfortunately the atmosphere gave her plenty of time to think, and she didn't like her thoughts. She was in love with Anton, always was and always would be, and there was absolutely no future in it. Their marriage had ended the day after the wedding…

Even now Anton was still sticking to his ridiculous story about her father. Yet at one time he had told her to forget it as the people concerned were dead. Memories of the past few months flooded her mind. Their battles at the beginning, and then, after her disappearance in New York, the passionate way they made up and Max's certainty that Anton cared for her. The art gallery where she got a better understanding of why he was as he was… After that night, if she was honest, they had got along rather well. Anton had come back to London with her while she did her research. The next time in New York they had had a weekend in the Hamptons with a stockbroker and his wife and, apart from discussing business with their host one night, they had had a wonderful relaxing weekend.

She glanced at him. He was seated at the opposite side of the plane as far away from her as he could get, his dark head bent as he concentrated on the article he was reading in a financial magazine. He had shed his jacket and the dark sweater he wore stretched across his wide shoulders. As she watched he flicked a hand through his black hair, sweeping it from his broad brow. Something she had seen him do a hundred times when he was concentrating, which she found oddly endearing.

No, not endearing—she must not think like that. Their marriage was ending, and this was the last act. Only the formalities of a divorce lay ahead. She had no illusions left, and maybe that was no bad thing.

Anton had told her once to grow up…well, now she had.

Emily stared down fascinated as the helicopter transported them from the Lima airport to Anton's ranch high up into the Andes.

The fertile plains on the coast gave way to a rocky terrain and ever larger majestic hills and mountains, but with miles of jungle-like vegetation, and amazing half-hidden valleys.

The whirring blades slowed as the helicopter descended into one such huge valley. Her eyes widened at the sight of an enormous sprawling house with castellated turrets that seemed to cover half an acre, with smaller buildings, and a road surrounding it. The place was a village all on its own. Lush green paddocks and cultivated fields gave way to the natural rolling hills rising ever higher in the far distance.

'Is this it?' she asked, glancing at Anton as he removed his headphones.

'Welcome to Casa Diaz,' he said and, leaping out of the helicopter, he came around and took her hand and helped her down. He kept a hold of it as they ducked beneath the whirling blades and dropped it when they straightened up. A battered Jeep was waiting for them.

The driver, wearing a big sombrero and an even bigger smile, leapt out. 'Welcome, boss and Señora Diaz.' Sweeping off his sombrero, he bowed and ushered them into the Jeep. A moment later her suitcase was dropped in the back, and they were off.

The next half-hour was a blur to Emily. All the staff were lined up in the hall to meet her and Anton made the introductions, then requested the housekeeper serve them coffee.

Emily was intensely conscious of his hand on her bare arm, and the tension in his long body, as he led her through wide double doors set to one side of the massive marble staircase that dominated the huge hall and into a room that had to be at least forty feet long. She pulled her arm free and glanced around.

Her eyes widened in awe and for a while she forgot his icy, intimidating presence. A vaulted ceiling, heavy dark timbers, white walls, almost completely obliterated by paintings and artifacts. The place was like a museum, and she was fascinated. Spanish and Indian art and sculptures were displayed together, some really ancient, and very probably original.

She walked slowly around the room, lost to everything as she examined paintings, pictures and sepia snapshots of family with avid interest.

CHAPTER ELEVEN

THE HOUSEKEEPER arrived with a tray bearing coffee and delicate little cakes. 'Your favourite, señor.' She smiled and placed the tray on a beautifully carved antique occasional table, set between three large sofas.

'I had no idea your home was so old,' Emily finally said, turning to Anton as the housekeeper left.

He quirked an eyebrow as much as to say *So what*? but actually said, 'Sit down and pour the coffee.'

She bristled at the brisk command, but did as he said. Automatically she spooned sugar into his, black and sweet just how he liked it, and grimaced. She knew the little things about him, but not the big, she realized sadly, and never would now. She added milk to hers, and held his out to him as he sat down on the sofa adjacent to her.

'To answer your question—' he drained his coffee-cup, placed it back on the table '—the Diaz family has lived on this land since the first Sebastian Emanuel Diaz arrived in South America with the conquistadores,' he said flatly. Rising to his feet, he walked across the room to the fireplace.

'But you told me your grandmother was disowned,' she said, her eyes following him as he leant negligently against the ornate wood-carved mantelpiece. 'How did you get it back?' she asked, tearing her gaze from his impressive form. Then she realized the stupidity of her question. 'Stupid question—you probably made the owner an offer they could not refuse.' She raised her eyes to his and answered for him, sarcasm tingeing her tone. He was a ruthless devil. What Anton wanted Anton got, and it would suit his sense of justice to retrieve the family home.

'No, I did not.' His firm lips quirked in the ghost of a smile, a reminiscent gleam in the dark eyes that met hers. 'My grandmother did, thirty years after being thrown out by her father, and a few years after he died. By then her older brother had managed to bankrupt the family. My grandmother stepped in, bought the place, and spent many happy years here with her own mother. A beautiful but weak woman, and of the old school who obeyed her husband in everything, but she died happy with her daughter at her bedside. Then for the last ten years of my grandmother's life my mother and I lived here.'

'Your grandmother must have been an amazing woman,' Emily exclaimed. To go from the disowned daughter and owner of a brothel to a landowner again was an enormous leap.

'She was a true descendant of the original Diaz with all the courage that entailed,' Anton responded, one dark brow arching sardonically. 'Unfortunately my mother and sister, though kind, loving women, did not inherit her strength of character.'

'I never realized—' Emily began.

'You never realized that my family was a lot older than yours, even though it is the illegitimate side that flourished,' he drawled mockingly. 'But then life is full of little surprises.' Straightening up, he moved towards her.

She glanced up. He was towering over her, his face hard, his eyes as black as jet. In that moment she could see him as a conquistador, ruthless and cruel as they swept through South America centuries ago, and a shiver of fear snaked up her spine.

'Now is the time for your surprise. Come. What I wish to show you is in my study.

'Sit down.' He gestured to a deep buttoned leather Chesterfield, placed a few feet away from a massive leather-topped desk in the wood-panelled room. He then walked behind the desk, and, taking a key from his pocket, he opened one of the drawers and withdrew an envelope. He looked at it for a moment, and she felt the tension in the room, the tension in Anton as he walked back towards her.

'Read this.' He held out the battered envelope, a gleam of mocking triumph in his dark eyes. 'Then call me a liar if you dare.'

Reluctantly she took the envelope by one corner, avoiding touching his hand. The postmark was English. Slowly, with a hand that trembled, she withdrew the folded notepaper, and opened it. A gasp of surprise escaped her. The return address was their family home in Kensington. No, it could not be... Then she began to read.

Two minutes later Emily carefully folded the letter and placed it back in the envelope and rose gracefully to her feet. 'Very interesting,' she said and forced a smile to her stiff lips. 'But would you mind if I studied this in my room?' she asked. 'I am exhausted after all the travelling. We can discuss this at dinner.'

'Still in denial,' he mocked, but rang a bell fitted in the wall. 'It never ceases to amaze me the lengths that the female of the species will go to, to avoid facing an unpleasant truth,' he drawled cynically. 'But as you wish—dinner will be early, at seven, to accommodate your exhaustion!'

A maid arrived at his call to show Emily out of the room.

Anton watched them leave, a frown creasing his broad brow. Emily had surprised him. He had thought she would be devastated seeing the proof of her father's deceit, but instead she had smiled coolly and asked for time to study the letter. But then why was he surprised? Once he had regretted telling her about her father, but not any more. Once he had thought that was the only stumbling block to a long and successful marriage, but that was before last night when he had realized she never had any intention of being his wife or having his children. She would have been quite happy to be his mistress, but when it came to anything else she was just as big a snob as her father.

He had dealt with slurs on his upbringing all his life, and they did not bother him. But the least one expected from a wife was respect. He would be well rid of her. A wayward thought slid into his cool mind...

Why not keep her as a mistress until he tired of her luscious body? Let her earn the divorce she wanted on her back.

No, he immediately dismissed the notion because his pride would not let him. Bottom line, for all her innocence she had used him as nothing more than a stud. Nobody ever used Anton Diaz.

He left to check his horses—at least they were honest.

Emily followed the maid up the grand staircase along a wide corridor and into a lovely bedroom. Definitely feminine in white and with the occasional touch of pink. A lace coverlet with a pink satin trim running through it graced a four-poster bed delicately draped in white muslin, the tie-backs pink satin to match. Definitely not the master suite, Emily concluded, and, casually dropping the letter onto a frill-trimmed dressing table, she looked for her suitcase. A shower and change and dinner.

The last supper, she thought, and opened a wardrobe door to find her clothes had already been unpacked. Walking into the *en suite*, she glanced at the free-standing bath, but opted for a shower. She really was tired after a sleepless night, followed a long-haul flight almost halfway around the globe, followed by the helicopter flight and, although because of the time zone it was late afternoon, she had been awake for over thirty-six hours.

Stripping off the trousers and blouse she had travelled in plus her underwear, she stepped into the shower.

Emily looked at her reflection in the mirror. She had left her hair loose, simply tucked it behind her ears, but she had taken care with her make-up, subtly shading her eyelids to emphasize the blue of her eyes, with a light coating of mascara on her long lashes. Her full lips she coated in a rose gloss. And the slightest trace of blusher accentuated her cheekbones.

She needed all the help she could get. She was no actress, but she was not about to let Anton see how much leaving him was going to hurt her. She loved him, but she had too much character to live life on his terms, knowing it would eventually destroy her.

The dress she wore was a pale blue crêpe sheath with small sleeves and a square-cut neck that just revealed the upper curves of her breasts and ended a few inches above her knees. She slipped silver sandals on her feet, and fastened the diamond and sapphire locket around her neck and the matching bracelet on her wrist, but left off her engagement ring. Let Anton make of that what he will, she thought bitterly. He would anyway—but he was in for a rude awakening…

She walked down the staircase at five to seven, and stood at the bottom of the stairs looking around. She had no idea where the dining room was.

'Señora, this way—the master, he wait.' The housekeeper appeared and beckoned her to follow. Taking a deep breath, Emily entered the room. Anton was standing at the head of a long table set with the finest linen, china and crystal.

He was wearing a dark evening suit and looked every inch the Spanish grandee: arrogant, remote but devastatingly attractive. The breath caught in her throat. His dark head lifted, his black eyes roaming over her. She saw the moment he recognized her jewellery and watched him stiffen.

They were like two strangers staring at each other across a room.

Then for one tense moment their eyes fused. Emily imagined she saw a flicker of some emotion in his before his hooded lids lowered slightly, masking his expression, and he spoke.

'Emily, you look lovely as always. Please be seated,' he offered, and pulled out a chair.

She smoothed suddenly damp palms down her thighs as she walked towards him and sat down. She picked up a napkin and folded it on her lap—anything rather than look at him again, until she got her breathing under control.

The hour that followed was surreal.

The housekeeper served the food course after course, and Anton ate everything with obvious enjoyment. His conversation was icily polite, restricted to each dish and the ingredients involved, and the relative merits of the red and white wine that was served.

While Emily had a problem swallowing anything, and her replies were verging on the monosyllabic.

'Excellent meal,' he complimented the housekeeper as she served the coffee, smiled and left.

'You did not seem to eat much, Emily.' He straightened back in his chair and fixed her with black gimlet eyes. 'Something not to your liking or has something given you indigestion—or someone…like your father?'

The gloves were off with a vengeance, and actually Emily felt relieved. But before she could respond he continued.

'Not very pleasant, is it, when you find out someone you love deceived you, as I discovered last night. And you have discovered tonight.' It was then she saw the tightly leashed anger in his black eyes.

And what did he mean…someone he loved deceived him…? He had never loved her, and the only reason his nose was out of joint was because she was not the brood mare he had been hoping for.

'Not at all,' she said smoothly. She was not going to respond to his taunts. Cool, calm and collected—that was her strategy. 'In fact I am greatly relieved. I have read the letter you gave me, and, true, it is disgraceful, the sentiments expressed disgusting and totally unacceptable. Please accept I deeply regret what happened to your sister.' She was painstakingly polite. 'The poor girl must have been heartbroken.'

'Deeply regret?' he snarled. 'Is that all you have to say?'

'No.' Emily had given a lot of thought to the people and circumstances surrounding the letter after reading it and she was curious, and wanted to delve a little deeper. 'Tell me, Anton, did you see much of your father?'

'Not a lot, but what the hell has that got to do with anything?'

'Humour me. Did he treat your half-sister like his own child? Was he older than your mother?'

'No…and thirty years older.' He rattled off the answers.

'Then that might explain it.'

'Explain what—that your father seduced my sister? Don't even try to make excuses.'

'Okay, I won't.' She sat up straighter in her chair. 'My father never wrote that letter. You were wrong.' His face went dark with rage, the veins at his temples standing out so prominently she thought he was going to burst a blood vessel. 'But you were also right,' she got in quickly. 'The writing is that of my grandfather, Charles Fairfax, who had to be over fifty when he had an affair with your sister, which I suppose, in a way, makes it worse.'

Anton's black eyes flared in shocked disbelief. 'Your grandfather.'

She had been wrong, Emily thought, seeing the horror in his eyes. Anton was capable of emotion, but not one she envied him. 'Yes. My grandfather,' she said bluntly. 'An easy mistake to make,' she offered to soften the blow. 'Charles is a family name—the eldest son is always called Charles until my brother Thomas. Because my father was never on good terms with his own father so was never going to name his own son after him.'

'I cannot believe Suki…' Anton began and stopped.

He looked shell-shocked—a first for her arrogant husband, Emily was sure. 'It is true,' she continued. 'My father and aunt Lisa were horrified by the behaviour of their father when they were old enough to realize what he was really like. He was an out-and-out womanizer, a complete waster, the black sheep of the family. My grandfather and grandmother led completely separate lives but divorce was never an option. They shared the same house—you have seen my family home, it is more than big enough,' she said dryly. 'After he died when I was about seven, his name was never mentioned again. He was a horrible man and the whole family was disgusted by him,' she said flatly. 'Did you never wonder why Uncle James, an in-law, is Chairman of the Board?'

Anton listened in growing horror as Emily continued.

'Aunt Lisa worked in the offices of Fairfax as a girl. She met and married James, who was employed as the manager at the time and was actually responsible for keeping the firm viable. Grandfather Fairfax had no head for business and spent a fortune on his women. When my father was old enough to join the firm it was James who taught him the ropes and he was twenty-eight when he took over. As a result when my father died it was James he named as Chairman until Tom reaches the age of twenty-eight.'

Emily really was exhausted and, pushing back her chair, she rose to her feet, still holding her napkin. 'So now you know the truth. I am no psychiatrist, but what I was trying to say before was maybe your mother and sister were looking for a father-figure—maybe that's why they behaved the way they did. Who knows?' She shrugged. 'It is amazing how some things affect people. Look at my uncle Clive. You know why he dresses so outrageously and encourages me to?' She smiled. 'Remember the silver lamé?' Then wished she had not said it as she saw Anton grimace in disgust and, nervously twisting the napkin in her hands, she finished. 'Well, Uncle Clive is of the opinion my father and Tom have gone too far the other way. Too conservative, too strait-laced, too frightened of turning out like Grandfather Fairfax, so need shocking once in a while. Maybe he is right. I don't know.'

'Emily.' Anton rose to his feet, and reached out to her, but she took a few hasty steps back.

She didn't want him to touch her; she just wanted the whole sorry mess over with. 'But what I do know is Grandfather Fairfax instead of my father changes nothing. Though I am surprised. You're usually so thorough with your security, your investigators and everything. Why, you never noticed the letter read "*even if I were free which I am not*". That should have given you a clue—when it was written my parents were not even engaged at the time.'

'Emily. I don't know what to say.' Anton reached for her again but she shook off his hand.

'There is nothing to say.' She tilted back her head and looked straight up into his brutally handsome face. 'The truth is out; you were wrong, but right in a way. As usual for you, Anton, you always end up the winner.'

'No, Emily.' He grabbed her by the shoulders. 'I can't tell

you how sorry I am I mixed up your father with your grandfather. I would never have upset you that day on the yacht if I had known. Let me make it up to you somehow. Tell me what you want and it is yours.'

She wanted his love, but he did not have it to give. Sadly she shook her head. 'You don't get it, Anton. Whether it was my father or grandfather does not matter a damn. Nothing has changed—you married me to get back at a Fairfax. And then you wondered why I kept taking the pill. You broke my trust. Can you give that back? I don't think so. Now, if you don't mind I am going to bed and I would like to leave in the morning.' And, turning on her heel, she walked out.

Anton was waiting for her the next morning when she walked downstairs, and simply said, 'The helicopter is here, and my jet is on standby at Lima to take you anywhere you want to go. The apartment in London is yours. I will not be using it again and you have nothing to fear in regard to Fairfax Engineering—I am no longer interested.'

'That is very generous of you,' Emily said, looking up at his expressionless face. Willing him to show the slightest weakness, a gesture he cared. But the black eyes that met hers were cold and hard.

'No doubt we will have to meet again some day, but if you are hoping for a quick divorce, forget it. As far as I am concerned it will not be any time soon. Now, if you will excuse me I have my horses to attend to. I expect you to be gone when I return.'

'Be assured of it,' Emily said coolly. 'As for the divorce, I don't much care when. After this I am not likely to get married again in a hurry. But to ease your mind I don't want a penny of your money. I don't want anything from you, except you keep your promise via a written guarantee you will not interfere in any detrimental way whatsoever with Fairfax Engineering.'

'You will have it,' he snapped, and she watched as he swung on his heel and walked out. She told herself it was for the best, it was what she wanted, and kept telling herself, all the long flight back to London. Then cried herself to sleep in the bed they had shared.

CHAPTER TWELVE

EMILY leant on the rail of the ship, her friend Delia by her side, watching the dinghy taking the divers closer into one of the tiny rocky islands that formed the Las Rocas archipelago off the coast of Venezuela.

'Do you think we will strike lucky this time?' Emily asked.

Delia, older and wiser, grimaced. 'I hope so. It is over a week since we left Caracas, and this is the fourth set of coordinates we have tried, and I don't think we have much more time. I have been checking the weather forecast on the radio and there is a report of a hurricane heading for Florida and on down over the Caribbean islands. It is expected to hit Jamaica, which is not far from us, in three days.'

Emily managed a grin. 'Thanks for the positive report, pal. I think I'll go and check out the computer. It looks like they are ready to dive.' And she went below.

Jake, the head of the expedition, was one of the divers on the dive boat, wanting to explore at close hand the seabed for himself, but his second in command, Marco, was hovering over the bank of computers.

'Anything yet?' she asked.

'No. They have only just reached the site.'

Emily slid into a chair and watched the divers exploring the seabed on the computer screen. Looking for maybe a shape of the prow of a sailing ship or just wood. Or better still the shape of a cannon. After three hundred years anything down there would be buried under sand and encrusted with sea life. Vague silhouettes in the ocean bed could give up the secret of a shipwreck.

It was Emily's job to map the position on the seabed and discern what any find was from the film sent back to the computer by the diver's cameras. She loved her job, and this was the most exciting expedition she had been on so far. Yet somehow, in the five weeks since she had left Peru, she had difficulty getting excited about anything.

She tried not to think of Anton. But he haunted her thoughts day and night. Especially at night as she lay in the bed they had shared. She had yet to tell Helen and Tom that Anton and she had parted. But she knew she was going to have to after this trip. Helen had already started asking pointed questions regarding Anton's whereabouts before Emily left.

Straightening up, Emily fixed her attention on the computer screen. Her marriage was over, done with, and she had to move on. This expedition was the beginning of the rest of her life, she vowed. No more regrets…

Anton steadied the horse between his thighs as the sound of a helicopter disturbed the morning air. Max again…

Two weeks ago Max had found him drunk, and they had had a furious row. Max had told him he was heading for disaster. He had let his wife walk out, a wonderful woman who, if he had any guts, he would be fighting to win back. He was letting his business slide, and ignoring the few friends he had.

Anton had told him to get lost, he knew nothing. But after Max left he had stopped drinking. He had made a few calls consolidating his business interests and delegated the work that could not be avoided to his senior managers. He had no desire to go back to his old life flying around the world. In fact he had no desire for anything with one exception: Emily.

He rode back to the stables and dismounted and handed the reins to the groom. 'Give him a rubdown.' With a pat of the stallion's neck, he walked up to the hacienda.

Max was waiting, a deep frown on his craggy face. 'Why the hell haven't you answered your phone or e-mails?' he demanded. 'I have been trying to get in touch with you since yesterday morning.'

'Hello to you too, Max.'

'At least you look better than the last time I saw you.'

'Yes, well, fresh air and no booze help,' Anton admitted wryly.

'And help is why I am here,' Max said, following Anton into the large hall. 'It's Emily.'

Anton spun around. 'What about her?' he demanded.

'We kept a watch on her, as you said. She stayed in your apartment until ten days ago, when she flew to Caracas.'

'What? Caracas...in Venezuela...?'

'Yes,' Max said with a grimace. 'I know—not the safest place in the world.'

'Was she alone?'

'Yes.' Max nodded.

'Now I need a drink.' Anton strode through into the living room and poured a stiff whisky into a crystal glass and offered one to Max. He shook his head. The thought of a woman like Emily wandering around Venezuela on her own didn't bear thinking about. 'Why, for God's sake?'

'She has joined an expedition led by Jake Hardington and his wife, Delia, friends of Emily's from her university days, apparently. You might have heard of him—the treasure seeker. They hope to find a pirate ship supposedly sunk off the Las

Rocas archipelago by the French navy three hundred years ago. Emily is the marine archaeologist on board.'

Anton stared at his old friend as if he had taken leave of his senses. 'You are telling me that Emily has seriously gone looking for a pirate ship with a bunch of treasure hunters.'

'I know, boss. Strange, but true.'

'Actually, it is not strange.' Anton drained his glass and slammed it down on the counter. 'It is just the damn-fool sort of thing she would do. Why the hell didn't you stop her?'

'You told me to keep a watching brief, nothing more, and get in touch with you if I thought it necessary. I tried to telephone when she left London but you were not answering. I figured, well, it is her line of work, and had my man in Venezuela keep tabs on her. She joined the ship and they set sail on the twentieth, eight days ago. They are at present anchored off a reef. I might add it is not very easy to keep track of them. Treasure seekers are notoriously secretive—they up anchor and move without warning.'

'So why are you here now?'

'Because yesterday there was a hurricane warning. It is heading across the Caribbean and the treasure seekers are not that far from its predicted path. I thought you needed to know. I have hired a high-speed—'

Anton cut him off. 'Five minutes and we leave.'

Emily stood at the rail and watched anxiously as the divers' dinghy ploughed through the heavy waves and finally came alongside. The weather was getting worse by the minute. The wind had risen and the torrential rain had soaked her to the skin. The ship was rolling from side to side making her feel sick. Which was worrying enough in itself, as she had never suffered from seasickness before, but then she had never experienced gale-force winds at sea before.

Everything on board was done at high speed as the threat of drifting onto the reef was imminent. The anchor was lifted, the engines roared and the ship turned to head further out to sea.

Only to see two high-speed Venezuelan navy frigates heading towards them. A loud hailer was utilized demanding they stop, and to everyone's stunned amazement a group of gun-toting sailors boarded them. The ship was seized and ordered back to port and they were all under arrest. Jake tried to ask why but was met by a wall of silence.

Darkness was falling when the ship berthed, not at a commercial port but at a naval base.

Wearing only a cotton tee shirt and shorts, and with her hair and clothes plastered to her body, Emily was beginning to feel afraid as she was led with the others at gunpoint off the vessel.

In the fading light she saw a towering figure approaching. The naval guards parted and her mouth fell open in shock as Anton, ignoring everyone else, strode up to her.

His black eyes were sunken deep and burned like coals of fire in a face that was thinner than she remembered. She had never seen him so angry. Livid...

'That is it, Emily,' he raged, grasping her by the shoulders, his fingers digging into her flesh through the damp cotton. 'What are you trying to do—drive me out of my mind?'

Held close to him, the heat of his body reaching out to her, she shuddered in the old familiar way, though she guessed the heat he generated was more rage than anything else.

'You go off looking for some damn-fool pirate ship in the middle of a hurricane. Well, no more...I have had as much as I am going to take from you. You are coming home with me and that is final. You are not safe to be let out on your own. And I will not be responsible for your death. Hell, even Max can't keep tabs on you.'

'Emily, is this man bothering you?' Jake Hardington asked, moving to face Anton even as recognition of whom he was challenging hit him.

'Bothering her?' Anton snarled. 'I should have talked some sense into her months ago. As for you—how dare you take my wife on your idiotic expedition? I shouldn't have just had you arrested, I should have had you shot.'

'Anton!' Emily exclaimed, finally finding her voice.

'You're his wife?' Jake asked, turning to Emily. 'Anton Diaz's wife?'

'Yes,' she confessed.

Jake looked at Emily and at the man holding her, and whatever he saw made him smile and shake his head. 'You're on your own, Emily.' And stepped back to watch.

'So now you remember you are my wife,' Anton snarled. 'Why the hell could you not have remembered that before you went on this mad adventure? What is it with you? Is it your mission in life to scare me half to death?'

In a state of shock Emily simply let Anton rant on—not that she could have stopped him. He was like a man possessed.

'Why can't you be happy like other women with diamonds and designer clothes and living in the lap of luxury? But no...I had to call out the police force in New York to find you and drop the biggest deal of my life. I had to negotiate with the Venezuelan government to call out the navy to rescue you. Have you the slightest idea what you do to me? You terrify me, Emily, *madre Dios*! Loving you is liable to kill me if you do not bankrupt me first.'

Loving—had Anton said he loved her? And deep down inside a tiny flicker of something very like hope unfurled. Then she stopped thinking as his arms wrapped fiercely around her, moulding her to his hard body, and his mouth crashed down on hers.

The rain poured down on them but Emily was oblivious to everything but Anton. His mouth ravaged hers with a passion that bordered on violence and she clung to him, her hands linking behind his neck, and returned his kiss with a hunger, a desperate need she could not deny.

She moved restlessly against him, her wet clothing and his accentuating the hard pressure of his arousal against her belly.

'Hell, Emily, you could have died.' He groaned and buried his head in her throat, sucking on the pulse that beat madly there, his hands feverishly roaming up and down her body. 'Are you sure you are all right?' He groaned again and lifted his head, his hair plastered like a black skullcap to his scalp, and to Emily he had never looked better.

'Did you say you loved me?' was the only question in her mind.

'Love you…' He paused, and glanced away to the people surrounding them. His dark eyes returned to her upraised face, and, in a curiously reverent gesture, he pressed a kiss to her brow, each soft cheek. 'Yes, I love you, Emily Diaz.' And his lips curved in a wry smile. 'Why else would I be standing here making a complete and utter fool of myself in front of all these people?'

Emily had spent too long mistrusting him and thinking he was not capable of loving anyone to immediately believe him. Her blue eyes, wide and wary, searched his haggard features, looking for some sign that would convince her.

'Damn it, Emily,' Jake Hardington cut in. 'The man loves you, tell him you love him, and let us get out of here. In case you have not noticed, the rest of us are still standing here with guns pointed at us and Diaz is the only one who can set us free.'

Startled, Emily looked at Jake and back at Anton. 'Is that right?'

'Right that I love you, and right I can set them free. The other is up to you.' And she saw a hint of vulnerability in his eyes and her own softened as the hope inside her burst into flame.

They had a lot to sort out, she knew, but she had to take the risk and tell him she loved him if they were to have a future together. But she never got the chance to speak.

'But either way I am not setting you free,' Anton added, his arms tightening around her.

Emily burst out laughing. That was *so* Anton—vulnerable for seconds but quickly as arrogant and indomitable as ever. 'Oh, Anton, I do love you.' And, reaching up, she kissed him as a round of applause broke out.

'At last, Emily, and now you have got your husband in a good mood, get him to sponsor my next expedition,' Jake Hardington called out. 'Because he wrecked this one.'

Anton looked at Jake. 'Hardington, you are pushing your luck.' But he smiled, taking the sting out of his words, and, sweeping Emily up in his arms with a few instructions to the officer in charge, he carried her away.

The hotel was luxurious and Anton paced the sitting room of the two-bedroomed suite listening to the sound of the bath running. Emily was in there, and he ached to join her. But, instead, on arriving he had told her to go ahead and have a bath and he would order dinner from room service. He had done it though he had never felt less like eating in his life. He had quickly showered in the *en suite* of the other bedroom and was now wearing a white towelling robe courtesy of the hotel, pacing the floor like an idiot.

For some bizarre reason he was ridiculously nervous. This love thing was a whole lot harder than he had ever imagined— not that he ever had imagined, he admitted self-derisively. With damp palms, a pounding heart and a churning stomach, he had a whole new respect for love.

Emily had said she loved him, but it had been with an audience urging her on. She had said she loved him on their wedding night, but the next day, when he had made the catastrophic mistake about her father, she had changed her mind. How could he know she was certain she loved him now?

It was his own fault and he had spent what seemed like ages running over and over in his head what he would say to her. How he would apologize to her for his past mistakes. Straightening his shoulders, he walked into the bedroom. He had it all planned in his head. All he needed was Emily.

Emily slipped on the hotel's towelling robe and, barefoot, exited the bathroom happier than she had ever been. Anton was standing in the middle of the room, a serious expression on his handsome face. 'Anton,' she said rather shyly, 'did you order dinner?'

His dark head lifted. 'Yes.' And in two lithe strides he was beside her. '*Dio*! Emily, how can you ever forgive me?' Anton groaned. 'When I think what I have said and done since we met I cringe.' And placing an arm around her, he pulled her close. 'That first day on the boat you called me dumb and I was...' He curved a strong hand around the nape of her neck and tilted her head up to his. 'My only excuse is I didn't know if I was on my head or my heels.'

'It does not matter now, Anton,' Emily said softly. 'The past is behind us. People say the first six months of marriage are the worst, so we have two more to go,' she tried to joke.

'I could not stand another two minutes, never mind months, at odds with you.' He lifted her and laid her gently on the bed and stretched his long length out next to her. 'I need to tell you this, Emily. To confess, if you like,' he said, his dark eyes serious as, propped on one arm, he looked down at her.

'Couldn't it wait?' She smiled impishly up at him. His robe had fallen open and she rested her hand lightly on his broad chest.

'No.' He caught her hand in his and linked their fingers. His dark gaze lingered on the gold band on her finger for a moment. 'I have done a lot of soul-searching over the last few weeks, and I want you to hear me out and make you understand why I behaved as I did.'

'Do I have to? I can think of better things to do.' She grinned.

'Yes,' Anton said sternly, if a little regretfully. 'After my mother died, naturally I was upset, and finding out about Suki only made me worse. I am not good with emotions and my grief turned to anger and I vented my fury on the Fairfax family. But if you believe nothing else, believe this—from the minute I saw you I fell in love with you. I know that now, but at the time I would not admit it even to myself.'

He paused for a moment, looking deep into her eyes, willing her to believe in him, and then continued at breakneck speed. 'I did not believe in love because I had seen what it did to my mother and sister. But with hindsight, much as I loved them they were basically weak, not like my grandmother. The day I proposed to you I was mad with jealousy because I thought you had dressed so strikingly for another man. The day you walked down the aisle in church I knew the image of you would be etched on my brain for ever. Watching you sleep on the jet, I decided I was not going to tell you about your father.

'Our wedding night was the most amazing night of my life. You were everything and more than I could ever have imagined, your husky words of love much more than I deserved, which in my arrogance I took as my due.' He gave her a rueful grin. 'But you know what happened the next day—I lost my temper when you mentioned your parents and told you anyway about your father. But the truth was I was feeling as guilty as hell. I couldn't believe I had been dumb enough to think for a minute my yearly trip to Monte Carlo was suitable as a honeymoon. At one point I considered just telling the captain to set sail and leave everyone behind, but it was too late.

'Then the whole weekend went from bad to worse. I behaved like an arrogant swine. You nearly gave me a heart attack diving off the yacht and that damn Harding woman filled your head with lies about me.'

'It really does not matter,' Emily said, lifting a hand to stroke his lean cheek. Though his revelations filled her heart to overflowing with love.

'Yes, it does to me. When you told me to find another woman for the night, it gutted me. I spent hours pacing the deck before returning to bed, and realizing it wasn't your fault. You were angry and had every right to be.

'Then in Greece in my conceit I thought everything was wonderful. It wasn't until we were due to leave when I saw you walking down the stairs in the suit you had worn after our wedding that I recognized what was missing. You had looked at me with such joy, such love, when you walked towards me when we were about to leave Deveral Hall that day, but not any more. And I saw the difference. We made love but you never said the word. You never said much at all. I told myself it didn't matter. But on the spur of the moment I crazily decided to take you to New York instead of London. I could not leave you without trying to change things, though I had no idea how.'

'You were actually going to take me to London and instead you kidnapped me.' Emily chuckled. 'All because of a blue suit.'

'Yes. But then you got lost and as I stormed out of a meeting without a second thought I knew I was in serious trouble, but I was still in denial about my true feelings.'

'You were angry, and did seem a little upset when we got back to the apartment. I actually wondered if you cared.'

'Cared.' He grimaced. 'Oh, I cared. But the real clincher, the moment it hit me right between the eyes, was in the limousine on the way back from the exhibition of Peruvian art, when you asked me why had I not married Lucita to get back at her father. I realized it had never occurred to me, and it wouldn't have done in a million years, and yet the two cases were in a way similar. Then I had to ask myself why you?

'It was a completely outlandish idea. I had been a bachelor for thirty-seven years and no woman had even tempted me to get married before. So why was I so determined to marry you? I am not proud of the fact, but I could have ruined your family business, but I think it was grief that fuelled my vengeance more than anything else. I needed someone to blame. But by the time I met Tom and James I was already losing enthusiasm for the project, because there was nothing to dislike about them. Quite the reverse—I had a grudging respect for them, and then I met you, Emily…

'To be totally frank, I took one look at you and could not stop myself flirting with you rather crudely.' He grimaced again. 'Then I saw you dancing with Max, and that was it.'

Anton dropped her hand and lifted a finger to her lips and gently outlined the contours of her mouth. 'All I could think of was your lithesome body under mine. You were the most sensuous woman I had ever seen. But at the time I thought anyone who danced like you must have had a few lovers and I was going to be one of them.'

'What exactly did you intend to do?' Emily asked. 'Make me your mistress?'

'No. I decided before the music ended, I was going to marry you. Your effect on me was that instant. In my arrogance I decided you would make a wonderful wife and mother.' His expression darkened. 'It was you who thought I wanted a mistress, as I found out just before we parted.' His dark eyes held hers, intent and oddly resigned. 'I know I had no right, but I was outraged to discover you were taking the pill without telling me. I felt used like some stud to perform in bed and nothing more. Not good enough to be the father of your children.'

'Oh, Anton.' Emily looped her arms around his neck and looked deep into his eyes. 'I never thought that for a second. I loved you even when I didn't want to. But you told me you did not believe in love, civil and sex you said, and I did not think our marriage could possibly last. I did not think you could stay faithful; I was green with jealousy thinking about all your other women, and knowing you did not love me made it worse.'

'I am sorry, Emily, so sorry.' He groaned. 'I never intended to hurt you. I love you, and if you don't want children that is okay by me, but I cannot let you go. I love you so much it hurts,' he declared, and she was stunned by the flicker of pain in the dark depth of his eyes that he could not hide.

Emily was shocked that he really thought she did not want his baby. Shocked that such a strong, wonderful man, a man she had thought without emotion, could be so emotionally vulnerable. She was suddenly conscious of the heavy pounding of her heart and his, the lengthening silence and his stillness... He was afraid... Surely not.

She slipped her hands up and around his neck, and smiled brilliantly up at him. 'How about you stop talking and show me some of this love you talk about?'

'You mean that—you really do love me?' Anton asked, his dark eyes gleaming down into hers, and she urged him closer.

'Yes,' she breathed. 'But as for a baby...' She felt him

stiffen. 'I think you might be too late—I am already almost four weeks late.'

Anton's brutally handsome features clenched in a frown. 'What…? How…? When…?' He loved Emily, but she had an amazing ability to confuse his normally needle-sharp brain without even trying.

'The how you know.' She laughed up at him. 'The when and where are the last time we were in London. I had forgotten to take my pills for the two days I stayed at Helen's—when you found me I was trying to catch up…'

'Do you mind?' he asked, tension in every line of his great body.

'No—if I am right, I am delighted. I would love to have your baby, but right now I would love to have you,' she said boldly, her sparkling blue eyes lit with amusement and something more fixed on his, one long leg wrapping over his as she turned into him.

Anton's arms wrapped around her convulsively as the import of her words sank in. He almost yelled what the hell was she doing on the damn-fool expedition then? But stopped in time. She was Emily. Beautiful, wonderful, wilful, but his Emily and he would not have her any other way.

'Thank the Lord.' He groaned, his heart in his eyes as he bent his head and kissed her with all the tender passion and love in his soul.

Dinner was delivered; the waiter called out, and was met with a particularly appropriate Spanish expletive. He smiled. He was a man and he had been in service long enough to recognize it was a different appetite on the occupant's mind, and left the trolley in the sitting room and tiptoed out.

MILLS & BOON®

Why shop at millsandboon.co.uk?

Each year, thousands of romance readers find their perfect read at millsandboon.co.uk. That's because we're passionate about bringing you the very best romantic fiction. Here are some of the advantages of shopping at www.millsandboon.co.uk:

* **Get new books first**—you'll be able to buy your favourite books one month before they hit the shops

* **Get exclusive discounts**—you'll also be able to buy our specially created monthly collections, with up to 50% off the RRP

* **Find your favourite authors**—latest news, interviews and new releases for all your favourite authors and series on our website, plus ideas for what to try next

* **Join in**—once you've bought your favourite books, don't forget to register with us to rate, review and join in the discussions

Visit **www.millsandboon.co.uk** for all this and more today!